George W Bird

Wanderings in Burma

I0592426

George W Bird

Wanderings in Burma

ISBN/EAN: 9783742854650

Manufactured in Europe, USA, Canada, Australia, Japa

Cover: Foto ©Andreas Hilbeck / pixelio.de

Manufactured and distributed by brebook publishing software
(www.brebook.com)

George W Bird

Wanderings in Burma

WANDERINGS IN BURMA.

All Rights Reserved.

SHWÈ DAGÒN PAGODA, RANGOON.

(Photo by Signor Beato, Mandalay.)

Wanderings in Burma

BY

GEORGE W. BIRD

(EDUCATIONAL DEPARTMENT, BURMA.)

With Illustrations and Maps

FIRST EDITION.

Bournemouth :
F. J. BRIGHT & SON, THE ARCADE.
London :
SIMPKIN, MARSHALL, HAMILTON, KENT & Co., LTD.,
STATIONERS' HALL COURT, E.C.
1897.

To The

Most Noble The Marquess of Dufferin and Ava,

Earl of Ava, Viscount Clandeboye,

K.P., G.C.B., G.C.S.I., G.C.M.G., G.C.I.E., D.C.L., LL.D., F.R.S.,

ETC., ETC., ETC.,

Who during a long life, has, with such conspicuous
and brilliant ability and success, filled so many of
the most important offices under the Crown, and
to whose sagacity and foresight is due the addition
to the dominions of the Queen Empress, of the
ancient Kingdom of Ava,

This work is most respectfully dedicated by

His very obedient servant,

THE AUTHOR.

PREFACE.

I N placing this work before the Public, my endeavour has been to give, in an interesting form, all available information concerning the country of Burma, and the histories of its old Cities and celebrated Shrines.

The book has been compiled from the best available sources, aided by a personal experience of twenty years' residence in the country.

I therefore trust that it will prove useful, not only to English residents in Burma, but also to those who, either in the pursuit of business or pleasure, may have occasion to visit the country. Extracts have been taken from the following works:—"The Census Report on Burma" for 1891; "The Administration Reports of the Province" for 1892-93 and 1894-95; "The British Burma Gazetteer," compiled by Colonel Spearman, I.S.C.; Sangermano's "Burmese Empire," edited by Mr. Justice Jardine; Colonel Yule's "Mission to the Court of Ava"; the late Sir Arthur Phayre's "History of Burma"; "The Maha-Razawin, or Royal Chronicles of the Kings of Burma"; as well as various Monographs and Pamphlets issued, from time to time, by the Government of Burma.

The Maps have been reproduced from those of the Survey of India.

I take this opportunity of tendering my best thanks to F. C. Oertel, Esq., P.W.D., of the North-West Provinces of India, and to Signor Beato, of Mandalay, for the original photographs from which the illustrations have been reproduced.

CONTENTS.

INTRODUCTION.

ROUTES.

CONTENTS—*Continued.*

LIST OF MAPS AND PLANS.

LIST OF ILLUSTRATIONS.

LIST OF ILLUSTRATIONS—*Continued.*

GEOGRAPHICAL SUMMARY.

(The following is extracted from the Administration Report of Burma for 1893-94.)

AREA AND BOUNDARIES.

The province of Burma lies to the east of the Bay of Bengal, and covers a range of country stretching from the 10th, to, roughly speaking, the 27th, parallel of latitude. It is bounded on the north and the north-east by China, and on the east by the Shan States and the kingdom of Siam. The sea line of the Bay of Bengal forms its western boundary and its north-western frontier marches with the confines of the Munipur State, and portions of the Chittagong and Assam borders. The sea-board extends from the Naaf in the Akyab district in the north to Maliwun in the Mergui district in the south, a distance of approximately 1,200 miles, and its greatest length from Maliwun in the south to the extreme north of the Bhamo district in Upper Burma is not far short of the same distance.

The estimated area of the province is, exclusive of the Shan States, 171,430 square miles.

NATURAL DIVISIONS OF LOWER BURMA.

Of the natural divisions of Lower Burma, Arakan is a strip of country stretching from the Naaf estuary on the north to Cape Negrais on the south, and lying between the range of hills known as the Arakan Yomas and the sea. The northern part of

B

this tract is a comparatively barren hill country, but in the west
and south are rich alluvial plains, containing some of the most
fertile lands in the province. In this tract are included the
districts of Northern Arakan, Akyab, Kyaukpyu and Sandoway.
To the east of the Arakan division, and separated from it by the
range of hills before mentioned, lies the country watered by the
Irrawaddy river, and extending from the old Upper Burma
frontier to the sea. The districts of Thayetmyo, Prome,
Henzada, Tharrawaddy, Bassein, Thongwa, Myaungmya, Hanthawaddy, Pegu, and Rangoon are contained in this tract. The
Thayetmyo district and the northern part of Pegu are hilly.
The remainder of this tract consists of a level plain extending to
and including the delta of the Irrawaddy, and joining in the
neighbourhood of Rangoon with the valley of Sittang. To the
east of this lie the valleys of the Sittang and Salween rivers,
which together form a compact extent of country, stretching
from the Pegu Yoma on the west to the Salween river and
adjacent hill country on the east. The northern portions of this
tract and the country on the right bank of the Salween river are
hilly, the remainder consists of large plains. The whole is
comprised in two districts, Toungoo and Shwegyin, and forms
the northern portion of the Tenasserim division. The rest of the
Tenasserim division is what was formerly known as the province
of Tenasserim, which lies between the Bay of Bengal and a high
range of hills separating it from Siam. It comprises the districts
of Tavoy and Mergui and a portion of Amherst, and includes the
Mergui Archipelago. The surface of this part of the country is
mountainous and much intersected by streams.

UPPER BURMA.

Upper Burma is portioned out into natural divisions by its
more important rivers. The Irrawaddy rises beyond its confines
in the unexplored regions where India, Thibet, and China meet,
and runs down the length of Upper Burma, dividing it roughly
into two equal portions, east and west. After completing about

two-thirds of its course through the upper province it is joined from the west by the Chindwin, the largest and the most important of its tributaries which flows into it a few miles above the town of Pakokku, and which may be said to divide Upper Burma west of the Irrawaddy into two halves. South of the fork the country, which is for the most part dry and sandy, stretches away from the western bank of the Irrawaddy to the eastern slopes of the Arakan Yomas and the Southern Chin Hills. This tract comprises the districts of Minbu and Pakokku. From the junction of the Irrawaddy and Chindwin northwards the nature of the country to the west of the latter river alters completely. From the right bank of the Chindwin the Chin Hills rise abruptly to merge themselves with the Lushai and the Naga Hills in the vast tract of mountainous country which forms the whole of the north-western frontier of the province. On the left bank of the Chindwin the land is comparatively level and stretches for the most part over low ranges of hills to the plains of the Irrawaddy valley, but further north these low ranges increase in height until the whole tract between the two rivers becomes a mass of hill country intersected by mountain streams and inhabited by semi-barbarious communities, whose country extends across the main stream of the Irrawaddy to the eastern border of the Bhamo district, and as far down on the eastern side of the river as the State of Mongmit (Momeik) where it joins the northern extremity of the Shan Hills. The country to the east of the Irrawaddy, immediately above the old Burmese frontier, is in its nature similar to that on the west of the river at the same latitude. It comprises the districts of the Eastern division, and the Myingyan and Magwe districts of the Southern division. It is comparatively dry and arid, is intersected by forest-clad ridges, and is bounded on the east by the rampart of the Shan Hills, which run almost parallel with the Irrawaddy till almost on a level with the town of Mandalay. Here the bend of the river brings it close to what is known as the Shan plateau, and from thence northward the space between the stream and the hills which form the north-

B 2

eastern boundary of the province is for the most part narrower
and more confined.

MOUNTAINS.

In Lower Burma there are four important mountain ranges :
the Arakan and the Pegu Yomas, running nearly due north and
south, and enclosing between them the valley of the Irrawaddy ;
a range running north-west and south-east between the Sittang
and Salween rivers and extending from beyond the old Burmese
frontier almost to the sea at Martaban, and a range to the east of
the Salween running southward from the Shan Hills, and in its
lower part forming the boundary between Tenasserim and Siam.
Upper Burma is encircled on three sides by a wall of mountain
ranges. The Shan and Karen Hills, which run in parallel ridges,
for the most part almost due north and south, form the eastern
boundary. In the Mandalay district the Shan Hills approach the
Irrawaddy. The hilly parts of this district, which is mountainous
throughout the greater portion of its area, may be divided into
two tracts, the northern and the eastern. The northern consists
of parallel ridges descending from the Ruby Mines district, with
peaks from 2,000 to 3,600 feet ; the eastern is comprised in the
Pyinulwin subdivision and forms a plateau of 3,500 feet above
mean sea level, which is part of the high lands known as the
great Shan plateau. The whole of the Ruby Mines district, with
the exception of the riverine portion, is intersected by high ranges
of mountains, with points here and there of over 7,000 feet in
height. In the west of this district the hill ranges run north and
south, but in the interior their course is approximately east and
west. In the Bhamo district there are four main ranges of hills,
the Eastern Kachin Hills, running northwards from the state of
Mongmit (Momeit), to join the high range dividing the basins of
the Irrawaddy and the Salween ; the Kumôn range extending
from the Khampti country east of Assam, to a point north of
Mogaung ; the Kaukhwè hills, which start from Mogaung and
run in a southerly direction to the plains in the west of the

Irrawaddy valley, and the Jade Mines tract lying to the west of the Upper Mogaung stream, and extending across the water shed of the Uyu river, as far as the Hukong valley. The Chin Hills form the western boundary of the upper province.

RIVERS.

Of the rivers, by far the most important is the Irrawaddy, which is navigable to steamers throughout the year for over 900 miles, and for purposes of communication forms the natural artery of the province. It enters Burma in the extreme north of the Bhamo district, and its three most important tributaries in that district are the Mogaung river, the Molè and the Taiping, of which the first, with its affluent the Indain river, is navigable for steamers at certain seasons of the year for some distance from its mouth. Further south the Irrawaddy is joined by the Shwèli and the Mèza, and some distance below Mandalay by the Myitngè, a tortuous stream which rises in the Northern Shan Hills. Another of its affluents is the Mû which enters the main stream near Myinmù. Its main tributary, the Chindwin, with its affluents the Uyû, the Yû, and the Myittha, flows into it some little distance above the town of Pakokkû, and the Môn joins it further south, about twelve miles above the station of Minbu. The tributaries of the Irrawaddy after it enters Lower Burma are few and unimportant. The principal are, on the right bank the Mindôn, the Madi, the Kyaukbu, and the Patashin, and on the left the Kyini, the Butlè, and the Nawin.

Of these, none are navigable at all seasons of the year except the Mindôn, which can be ascended by boats as far as the village of the same name. The Bassein or Ngawûn river is really the western mouth of the Irrawaddy. Sea-going ships ascend it as far as Bassein, which is some 90 miles from the mouth, and river steamers navigate the whole extent of it, from Bassein to its junction with the main stream. The Hlaing river rises near Prome, and flows southwards till it is joined by the Pegu and

Pazûndaung rivers, and enters the sea as the Rangoon river.
The Sittang river rises in the eastern division of Upper Burma;
at Toungoo it is narrow and navigable with difficulty, but below
Shwegyin it widens, and at Sittang is half a mile broad. It flows
into the Gulf of Martaban. The Salween river, at the mouth of
which is the town Moulmein, is a large river, but on account of
its rapids is not navigable. The greater part of its course lies in
the Shan States. Its principal affluents in Burma proper are the
Taungyin, the Gyaing, and the Attaran from the east, and the
Yônzalin and the Binlaing from the west. In the remaining
portion of the Tenasserim division, the only rivers of importance
are the Tavoy, the Tenasserim, and the Pakchan. Arakan has no
rivers of any considerable size. The coast is pierced by a number
of estuaries, of which the most important are the Naaf, which
separates Arakan from Chittagong, and the Mayû, about 40 miles
south of the Naaf. The only other rivers of any size are the
Kaladan on which is situated Akyab, the chief town of the
division, and the Sandoway river, on the banks of which stands
the town of the same name.

LAKES.

In Lower Burma there are few lakes of any note, though
part of the country abounds in ponds and marshes, most of
which dry up during the hot season. The principal lakes are
the Inma in the Prome district, the In and the Duya in
Henzada, and the Shagègyi and Inyègyi in Bassein. The
largest lake in Upper Burma is the Indawgyi, a piece of water
16 miles by 6. Situated in the west of the Bhamo district it is
bordered on the south-east and west by two low ranges of hills,
and has one out-let in the north-east corner which forms the
Indaw river. Other lakes of importance are the Indaw in the
Katha district with an area of 60 square miles, and the Meiktila
lake at Meiktila. In the highlands of the Shan Hills are the
Inlè Lakes near Yawnghwe (Nyaungywe).

SOIL.

The physical characteristics of the country exhibit many varieties. In the Arakan division the soil is mainly alluvial, in many places mixed with sand, and the rocks are composed of a dark brown sand-stone, black gneiss, and brown grey clay slate. Towards the south basalt is plentiful. Iron and limestone are found in small quantities, and petroleum is extracted in both Akyab and Kyaukpyu. The islands off the Arakan coast are of volcanic formation. The Irrawaddy delta consists entirely of rich alluvial deposit of a very high degree of fertility. The soil of the upper portion of the Sittang Valley is clayey with a considerable admixture of sand which disappears towards the south. The smaller hills are chiefly composed of laterite, and on the east of the river are found large masses of limestone rock. The soil of the northern portion of the sea-coast of Tenasserim is alluvial. In this part the prevailing rock is sandstone intersected with veins of quartz. Laterite is prevalent and bituminous shale is also found. At Amherst granite is found, and towards the south granite with white felspar becomes the sole formation, clay slate and micaceous iron ore being found on the eastern slope of the hills. Coal has been discovered in this division, so too have copper and gold in small quantities, and tin has been worked for many years in the Mergui district. Lead is found in small quantities in Toungoo and in portions of the Mergui district. Along the valley of the Irrawaddy, where that river traverses the northern portions of Lower and southern portions of Upper Burma, the soil is for the most part sandy. Granite, limestone, and sandstone are found, and certain tracts are rich in petroleum. The hills on the east of this portion of the Irrawaddy are composed mostly of brown or grey slate and clay, with beds of argillaceous sandstone, and occasional traces of basalt. Overlying the slate clay is a bed of laterite. The hills on the west of the river abound in limestone. Granite, greenstone, and hornblende are also found. In the Shwèbo district and northwards black cotton soils

predominate. Coal is found in considerable quantities in the
Shwèbo and Upper Chindwin districts. In the former district
the deposits are being worked, but in the latter the difficulties
of extraction and carriage would probably frustrate any attempt
at exploitation. In the Katha district gold is found.

The formation of the hills that encircle nearly the whole of
Upper Burma varies considerably from place to place. To
the east of the Eastern division the prevailing minerals are
granite, limestone, and sandstone, and the same features
characterise the ranges adjoining the town of Mandalay.
Further north on the borders of the Ruby Mines district the
soil on the hill-sides is stiff red clay over-lying stretches of
limestone, marble and sandstone. Besides rubies, spinels,
tourmalines, and sapphires are found in the stone-bearing
tract. The Eastern Kachin hills further north consist of
metamorphic and crystalline rocks. Limestone, sandstone, clays,
coal, and ferrugineous conglomerate are met with to the north-
west of this district. In the Jade Mines tract the hills are
composed of sandstone and clays, crystalline, limestone, and
metamorphic shales. Here jade, which is found enclosed in
an eruptive serpentine rock, is worked out by native miners.

CLIMATE.

In most parts of Lower Burma and in portions of the
Upper Provinces the abundant rainfall renders the climate moist
and depressing for nearly half the year, but in the dry zone
which extends across the country immediately above the old
Burmese frontier, from the 20th to the 22nd degree of latitude,
and comprises, roughly speaking, the whole of the Southern
and Eastern Divisions, the rainfall is less copious and the climate
less humid. North of this dry belt again the rainy season is
more marked, and though cooler than further south it is also
damper. The rainfall in the coast district varies from about
200 inches in the Arakan and Tenasserim divisions to an average
of 90 in the Rangoon and the adjoining portion of the Irrawaddy

delta. In the extreme north of Upper Burma the rainfall is
rather less than in the country adjoining Rangoon, and in the
dry zone the annual average falls as low as 20 and 30 inches.
The temperature varies almost as much as the rainfall. Except
in the dense forest tracts and the remoter portions of some of the
outlying districts of Upper Burma, where malarious fever is
prevalent, the province is by no means unhealthy either for
Europeans or for the natives of the country.

STAPLES.

The staple produce of the province is rice, which is largely
grown in every district, and for which the soil as a rule is
specially well suited. Other products of importance as articles
of commerce are teak, cutch, and india-rubber. Indian corn,
millet, peas, and sessamun are grown extensively in the dry
zone of Upper Burma. Cotton and tobacco are produced in
several parts of the province, and experiments have shown that
tea, coffee, and cinchona may be grown in the hill districts.
The native tea, *letpet*, is cultivated extensively in certain tracts
of Bhamo and the Upper Chindwin, as well as in the northern
Shan States.

SHAN STATES.

(The following exhaustive account of the Shan States is by Colonel Woodthorpe, of the Survey of India, and was read before the Indian Section of the Society of Arts. It appeared in the "Rangoon Gazette" early in 1896.)

" The Shan States under British protection form the easternmost portion of our Burmese possessions, and may be said to lie approximately between the 19th and 24th parallels of latitude and the 96th and 102nd of longitude. They do not, however, by any means cover the whole of the area included between these parallels, but presenting a broad base towards the Irrawaddy, narrow down considerably towards the east, forming a rough triangle. To the west lie the great plains of Burma proper, traversed by the Irrawaddy. To the north and east we have the province of Yûnnan, with the Chinese Shan districts of Mon Lem and Keng Hung immediately on our borders. To the south is Siam.

Dr. Cushing, a missionary and a great Shan scholar, visited these States while under the Burmese rule. He tells us that under this rule peace and quietness was seldom their lot. " Divide and govern " was the maxim which governed the policy of the Burma sovereigns towards their Shan dependencies. The sons of Sawbwas were sent to the Court of Ava, partly as hostages for their fathers' good behaviour, partly to be trained in the way that they should go, the Burmese way, when they succeeded their fathers. The Burmese government often fostered feuds which broke out between Sawbwas, and left rival princes of one family to settle their claims to the control of a principality with the tacit understanding that the victorious claimant would probably be confirmed as the Sawbwa by Royal appointment. Intestine troubles were frequently fomented by Burman intrigue when a prince seemed likely to become too prosperous for the safety of Burman authority. Bands composed of desperate characters were ever ready to avail themselves of the opportunity offered by disturbances in any principality, which invariably suffered from their visitations, the result being that the people emigrated to some neighbouring State enjoying peace. Rebellions against the royal authority were always sooner or later ruthlessly suppressed, towns and villages being burned, and the country devastated. Dr. Cushing adds that the absence of permanent peace seriously affected the wealth and prosperity of the country. The Shan States lying east of the Salween were, however, less subject to Burmese oppression than those to the west of that river.

It will be unnecessary in this brief paper to enumerate the Shan States ; suffice it to say that Keng Tung, embracing most of the country lying between the Salween and the Mekong is, from its size, population, and geographical position, as the frontier state,—the most important. Its chief is, moreover, connected by family ties with all the other important Shan States. Several years before our annexation of Upper Burma, the Cis-Salween Shan States had revolted, apparently against Thibaw individually, and his oppressive government, rather than against the principle of Burmese suzerainty ; and shortly before our operations commenced, the Burmese troops had expelled most of the Sawbwas, and driven them to seek refuge in Keng Tung, then governed by the father of the present chief, a capable ruler of great influence, who had lately executed the Burmese political officer resident at his court, with his followers, on the ground of their excessive exactions and tyranny, and was eager to form a Shan confederancy against Burma. He assisted the Sawbwas to recover their States, and the history of the next few years is one of continual struggles between the various Sawbwas to retain possession of

their own States, or to extend their borders at the expense of
their neighbours. Several pretenders also appeared on the scene
to increase the confusion and disorder, and the Siamese officials
at Chiengmai took advantage of the disturbed state of affairs to
extend their authority over some of the minor Shan States and
Trans-Salween Karenni, seizing, in the latter, elephants and
timber, and marking the inhabitants with an elephant and a
running number. As a sad instance of the ruin and depopulation
of a prosperous state, caused by this disorder, let me give you the
following powerful, but sombre picture, painted by Mr. Scott,
after his visit to Legya, in the Western Shan States, in 1888.

"The country is a wide billowy plain all of which has been
obviously, at no very remote date, under cultivation. The population must have been very numerous, for the land had evidently
been tilled even up to the *loos* of the undulations. But now it
was fast relapsing into simple prairie ; not a single traveller was
met on the road, and the eye roaming over miles and miles of
country that had once been all dry cultivation, but was now
rapidly being overgrown with coarse grass and scrub jungle, failed
to see a living creature. Even the columns of smoke, elsewhere
so universal at this time of year, where the farmer is clearing his
land for the crop of hill rice, were wanting. The face of the
land was as deserted and desolated as an American pampas or a
Russian steppe. We marched along the main north road, which
had clearly been not long since a wide thoroughfare travelled
over by many men and many cattle. Now it was narrowed to a
mere path, which encroaching bushes and rank grass threatened
at no great distance of time to obliterate altogether. Marks of
tigers were seen here and there. Small streams that formerly
had served to irrigate acres of fine paddy land now strayed
across the path, broke through the channels which once had
served to fertilise the soil, and created swamps where there
should have been wide expanses of waving grain. Village sites
had become mere tangles of impenetrable jungle, and in a
country where a few years ago there had been vast herds of

cattle, the deer barked nightly round our camp, and wild peafowl perched on the fences of the deserted cattle pens. The frontier village of On Hon was reduced to three houses ; all around stretched thousands of magnificent acres of wet bottom, now a mere noisome swamp of elephant grass. The town itself had not escaped. Fifty years ago it was one of the finest and wealthiest capitals in the Shan States ; but its fall has been gradual. Civil wars and local disturbances have ruined it slowly but surely. Twenty years ago it numbered only two hundred houses, but these have now dwindled to twenty wattled huts. The broad main road down which a couple of four-in-hand drags might have been driven abreast, has, by the encroachment of bush vegetation, dwindled to a mere tortuous footpath. South of the town there are many splendid monasteries and elaborate pagodas. These are now deserted. The roofs are falling in, and the timber is steadily disappearing to furnish firewood to those who have anything to cook. The shrines are mouldy and deserted, without a single pious offering ; the jungle comes up to their very feet, and creepers tear the bricks asunder. The Haw (palace of the Sawbwa) was at one time, next to Monè, the finest in the States. Nothing now remains of it but melancholy rows of blackened stumps. The chief lives in an ordinary bamboo hut. The brick wall which surrounded it is crumbling to a shapeless mound, and the former wooden gateways are replaced by petty bamboo wickets. The hanging gardens, which were at one time the pride of the State, are now a dismal growth of rank weeds. Nevertheless, Legya's restoration to wealth is a certainty. Round about the capital lies a stretch of land which would afford occupation and abundant crops to 10,000 farmers. One of the lakes which formerly existed near the town has dried up, but the canal which was constructed in earlier days of wealth and energy was so well built that the lapse of time and neglect in the years of fighting have not appreciably impaired it. The supply of water is abundant, and amply sufficient for the huge expanse of paddy bottom. When our column was in Legya in January, 1888, rice was more valuable than silver. Want of seed grain seemed likely to prolong the miseries of the State, but the generosity of the Sawbwa of Mong Pawn, one of the most impulsive and open-handed of men, furnished the Sawbwa with one hundred bullock loads."

For two years after our occupation of Mandalay we had our hands too full in putting down dacoity and rebellion in the plains of Burma to turn our attention to the Shan States, but gradually, and with but little bloodshed, order was restored in the Cis-Salween districts, the Sawbwas submitting to the British Government, and their submission was genuine. Trans-Salween Karenni was recovered from the Siamese, and, with the assistance of the influential and loyal Sawbwa of Mong Keng Tung was peaceably brought under our rule, and I am happy to say that the state of things described above, visible in other parts of the States, as well as in Legya, will soon be relegated to the past, and that the hopeful anticipations of Mr. Scott are in a fair way to be realised in the near future. At first, only one Superintendent was appointed to the Shan States, but as our influence was extended, this was found too large a charge for one man, and the States were divided into the Northern and Southern Shan States, and each placed under a Superintendent with several assistants, who exercised general supervision and control. Except for the peace and general security now enjoyed, things have not altered very much. As before, each state is ruled by its own hereditary chief, who has the power of life and death, and absolute authority in his own State, so long as his rule is in accordance with the principles of justice and benevolence, and free from the oppression and cruel practices of former times. Certain sources of revenue are reserved by the Government; the rest of the revenue is a lump sum levied on each State as tribute. To the devoted labours of our political officers, Messrs. Hildebrand, Scott, and Captain Daly, and their able assistants, to their resourcefulness in emergencies, and their infinite tact and skill in dealing with both rulers and people, the Shan States owe their present peaceful and happy condition, and their increasing prosperity.

These states present a remarkable variety of natural features. The country to the West of the Salween is a series of elevated plateaux, great rolling grassy downs separated by deep valleys, and intersected by lofty parallel ranges, the direction of which is north and south. These ranges, in contrast to the yellow downs, are beautifully wooded, and attain to great heights, some of the peaks rising to nearly 9,000 feet above the sea level. Along the valleys flow swift rivers, now through dark and narrow gorges, pent between mighty cliffs, now through an alluvial hollow with terraced rice fields, among which they wind with many a curve. To the east of the Salween the country is much broken up, no clearly defined range of mountains presents itself, but the eye wanders over a confused sea of forest-clad hills and narrow valleys, relieved here and there only by small plains, till Keng Tung is reached. But, perhaps, if I ask you to accompany me on a hurried march from the railway at Thazi, the station whence starts the cart road via Taunggyi, to Keng Tung, a distance of 360 miles, a better idea of the country and its general features will be obtained. From the train you will have seen the long line of hills lying parallel to the railway, and distant some 16 miles, inviting you to explore them. The road runs due east across paddy plains, past prosperous villages, with their monasteries, and clustering pagodas, to the foot of the hills, where it enters the forest and, rising gradually, crosses a low water-shed to Pinyaung, 22 miles from Thazi: here there is a village, and some good small game shooting may be obtained. Leaving Pinyaung, we pass on through a magnificent gorge, its precipitous, dark rocks giving way as we emerge from it to more inviting and gentler landscape. Tall trees rise above us, a swift, but shallow stream babbles over the stones on our left; here and there little patches of rice cultivation appear on either bank, and, occasionally the laughter of children, the crowing of cocks, and light smoke curling up to the sunlight, attract our attention to a small village, half hidden in the jungle. Then, onwards and upwards, by many turnings and zigzags, till we find ourselves at the village of Kalaw, at an elevation of 4,300 feet: this is a beautiful little sheltered spot, its smiling fields nestling among the wooded hills, crowned with white pagodas, to which long flights of bricked steps lead up. By the road-side, guarding the entrance to one of these flights, stand two huge dragons, giving us an excellent idea of their construction; for they have only been modelled in brick, and, whether from failing funds or the death of the pious builder, they still lack, and will for ever lack, that coating of plaster and cement, which should give them the appearance of finished stone work. A tinkling of bells and the shouts of drivers of recalcitrant bullocks warn us of the approach of a trading party; and, as we turn a corner, we come face to face with a long string of bullocks, bearing great loads of the leaf used in Burma for cigar wrappers, which is extensively grown in parts of the Southern Shan States. From Kalaw to Heho the road runs over open, undulating ground, stretching far away to the north. In the dips lie unpleasant swamps, which presented great difficulties to the rider, before the cart road bridged them. Low wooded hills, pagoda covered knolls, and bamboo clumps, half concealing a village or a monastery, vary the scenery. From the hills above Heho, we look over the valley of the Balu Chaung, and the view is a fine one. We stand at a height of 5,000 feet above the sea, on the edge of a plateau, whence the ground falls 2,000 feet to the broad valley below. To the north and south, wooded peaks stretch away into the distance. To the east rises a parallel wall of forest-clad slopes, ending in a broken outline of hills, the huge masses of Myn Mati and the pagoda-topped cliffs above the civil station of Taunggyi standing out most conspicuously.

The Balu Chaung rises to the North, and, flowing first through forest, loses itself in a huge swamp merging into the Inlè lake, a vast expanse of water thirteen miles long and about four miles wide at its upper end, but narrowing towards the South. It is nowhere very deep, and the bottom is overgrown with long and tangled weeds, which rise nearly to the surface. The lake dwellings of the Inthas, an amphibious tribe, said to have been originally brought as slaves from the Province of Tavoy, rise on piles out of the water, in groups near the edge, and floating gardens, on which are grown tomatoes, water melons, gourds, and the pan leaf vine, dot the surface of the lake around them. Many large villages are seen on either shore, monasteries, pagodas, built on the extremities of the spurs, running into the lake, are reflected in its placid depth, and on the eastern shore, lying back from the water on some rising ground, can be descried the houses and barracks of Fort Stedman. Far away to the South lie the blue hills of the Karenni and Brè country.

We now proceed direct by cart road to Taunggyi, or descending by a steep Shan path to the lake, cross it to Fort Stedman, whence another hill track leads to Taunggyi. The lake is worth a visit, and here we observe the novel method of rowing adopted by our Intha boatmen as they take us across. Men and women are equally expert; standing at the bow and stern of the boat, and balancing themselves on one leg, and holding the end of the paddle, they work the other leg over the upper portion of the blade, and propel it with their leg, merely guiding the paddle with the hand. They complicate matters further by frequently carrying a spear in the hand not occupied with the paddle, with which they transfix any passing fish. Their dexterity both with spear and paddle is wonderful. They supply all the bazaars in the neighbourhood with fish. At Fort Stedman you will be warmly welcomed by the regiment there, and if in the proper season, will enjoy some excellent wild fowl shooting. At Taunggyi you will be hospitably entertained by

Mr. Hildebrand, in a very nice house recently built for him by the Government. Comfortable, and well furnished with a pretty outlook, it gives one the feeling of being in a pleasant little country house in England ; and this feeling will be strengthened when Mr. Hildebrand has perfected his plans for garden and orchard, already fairly stocked and yielding a good supply of English flowers, fruit and vegetables.

Leaving Taunggyi, where the cart-road ends at the 105th mile, and threading our way among some low hills, we descend some broken ground to the town of Hopòn, 3,400 feet above the sea. The huge white pagoda, surrounded by a perfect forest of smaller spires, is visible for a long distance. Round about rise many fantastic limestone peaks.

The grassy slopes are covered with the bushes of the wild raspberry and blackberry, a gigantic honeysuckle sheds its fragrance in the air. To the east a lofty rugged range, rising to nearly 9,000 feet, presents a formidable barrier to our onward progress. Fortunately, the path finds a comparatively low point at which to cross, and a somewhat stiff ascent and descent brings us to Sa-òn, a pretty spot among the hills, where for the first time we see a curious but common feature in this country. Above the village some rice-fields are shut in by a limestone ridge. Through these fields runs a little stream, which makes straight for this barrier ; it flows under and round some fallen boulders, and then disappears in a little chasm behind. Some 200 feet below, and a quarter of a mile away it emerges from a lofty cave, and flows calmly onwards, through the terraced rice fields and the gently sloping valley. I have said this is a common feature in this country, and Lord Lamington describes a similar disappearance on a very large scale at Mong Hang. I had too much work to do while I was there to find time to visit this spot ; but Lord Lamington's account is as follows :—"The cave where the river enters on its subterranean course is in a sheer face of rock some 200 feet high. The height of the cave is about 140 feet, its width at the entrance 300 feet, broadening in the interior to nearly 500 feet; the depth is about 300 feet. At the right hand bottom corner a tunnel, at an angle of about 45° with the cave, provides a passage for the river. I followed this for some distance, but with no other result than that of getting wet. It is said of this cave that a cut teak-log floated down never reappears, whereas an entire tree, with its root and branches, makes the journey successfully." I heard a similar statement. Some of the members of Mr. Elias's Mission, in 1889, attempted to visit this cave, but were unsuccessful. From Sa-ôn another long ascent and descent brings us to the plains of Mong Pawn, a large place and the seat of the Sawbwa. The Nam Pawn, a broad but not deep stream, here winds among the fields, which it irrigates by means of large bamboo water wheels, commonly used in these States. These wheels are also used to work sugar crushing mills. Below Mong Pawn the river increases in volume, becomes confined in narrow gorges, and forms an unpleasant obstacle on the road between Taunggyi and Monè. A lofty range lies between Mong Pawn and Ban Ping, the descent to which was exceedingly steep and unpleasant for man and beast before the Sawbwa improved it. From Bang Ping to the Tein river the path lies once more over open undulating ground. The next river reached, and after crossing some elevated table-land, partly open, partly through forest, is the Ben Chaung (the Burmese name), or Nam Pong (the Shan name), a very beautiful river, which joins the Salween ten miles below Kenghkam. At Kenghkam it is a quarter of a mile broad, with lofty wooded hills on either bank; wooded islands breaking up its channels. Curious parallel ridges of rock rise to within a few feet of the surface in the cold weather; but the water is very placid here, though just above descends over a series of cascades among trees and shrubs, which grow in lines and clumps right across the river. Again, at many points in its course falls of 30ft. to 40ft. occur, and as it approaches the Salween, where the lofty green hills close in on it, it rushes down a steep descent in one long roaring rapid for several hundred yards, a mass of foaming white tumbling waters. At Kenghkam the river is crossed by boats, one of the regular ferries being here. The village itself is pretty, and a fringe of cocoanut trees curiously recalls Ceylon. The height here is 1,200ft. Ascending gradually for about twenty miles, to a height of 3,000ft., a somewhat abrupt descent brings us to the Salween at Takaw Ferry, situated 800ft. above the sea. The river here in the dry season has a width of from 150 to 200 yards, and a total width between the banks of 400 yards. The river rises some 40ft. or 50ft. in the rains. The right bank here is steep and rocky; but on the left bank is a broad stretch of sandbank and flat stones. The Salween is the Burmese name, the other name of the river being Nam Kong. From the Salween to Keng Tung the road is a constant succession of ascents and descents over hills covered with pines and other timbers of large growth. Two small oases occur in the valleys of Mong Pawn and Mong Hsen. The former is a collection of cultivation. In the monastery here I first noted an approach scattered villages in a long narrow flat valley, under rice to the style of ecclesiastical architecture obtaining in the Eastern States. An ascent of 3,000ft. brings us at 5,000ft. above the sea to the grassy wind-swept knolls of the Hpamin, a Palaung village, one of a group of six, where the poppy is extensively cultivated. Mong Hsen is situated in another sheltered cultivated valley, which in the spring time is a garden of flowers, the large white rose, discovered by, and named after, General Sir H. Collett, growing in wild profusion. The valley is closed to the south by some higher precipitous hills, into which the two streams watering Mong Hsen disappear within a quarter of a mile of each other, to find their way on the further side into the Nam Sim. At Loi Pemong the highest point of the road is reached, where it crosses the water parting between the Salween and the Mekong, at a height of 6,000ft.

Here we get our first glimpse of Keng Tung and its fine plain, lying some 3,000 feet below us. This plain is about 10 miles long and varies in width, its average breadth being about five miles. The huge spurs from the high ranges on either side break up as they descend into the plain, into gentle undulations. To the north and east the plain is perfectly flat and covered with rice fields, intersected by irrigation channels ; to the south are gently swelling downs and low grassy hills, swampy hollows lying between. The town of Keng Tung covers some undulating ground on the western side of, and overlooking, the plain. Its walls have a perimeter of some five miles ; they follow the undulations of the ground, standing highest above the plains on the north, where a pagoda, with a curious umbrella-like tree growing from its summit, forms a striking landmark. The walls, which are somewhat ruinous, are crenellated and loop-holed, and protected generally by a formidable ditch some 25ft. deep, and V-shaped, a very difficult object to negotiate at the best of times. Where the walls descend to the level of the plains the ditch disappears, but marshes cover this portion. There are several arched gate-ways, protected by brick and earth traverses ; one to the south gives egress to the road leading to a fine large tree called "Execution Tree," where, under its spreading branches, executions used to take place on the large market days. The prisoners were led through the crowds in the market, and given drink at the various liquor booths. A strong escort with bamboo ropes kept off the crowd. At the place of execution the name of the condemned man and his crime were read out by the official in charge of prisons, etc. (a court minister), and the slip of bamboo on which they had been written tossed over the man's head. He was then made to kneel down with his arms tied tightly at the elbows behind his back, and was decapitated with a long knife. The head was not held. This is evidently similar to the Chinese method of execution.

There is very little level ground within the walls of Keng Tung, and only the northern and eastern portion of the space enclosed is built over ; and even this portion is somewhat overrun with trees. There are several weedy swamps, the

largest being Nong Tung, or the lake from which the town
takes its name. The Sawbwa's palace stands close by, and is
a fine collection of teak buildings, well and solidly constructed,
and surrounded by a brick wall. There are from 1,500 to 2,000
houses inside the walls, and these are substantially built, some
with brick basements, the upper walls of planks or bamboo
matting, some with the side walls of the upper storey also of
brick. They are roofed with small well-made tiles, which afford
protection against fire. The monasteries and churches are very
numerous, and each stands in its walled enclosure.

The difference in style between these the ordinary Burmese,
and Western Shan Phongyi Kyaung, is very striking, and due,
Mr. Scott thinks, to Tartar influence. He says, "This is
particularly noticeable in the massive gateway which immediately suggests the Paifang of China. The resemblance is no
doubt due to the fact that the brickwork was run up by the
Chinese or Shan Chinese handicraftsmen. There is no similarity
whatever to the steep-roofed, parti-coloured tiled gables of the
Bangkok 'Wats.' The churches are adorned with elaborate
carvings, mosaics of coloured and silver glass and frescoes.
Each is built with a nave and two aisles, rows of lofty teak
columns, painted red and gilded, support the roof, the timbers
of which are also very ornate; the ornamentation is most
elaborate above the high altar with its huge gilded figure of
Buddha calmly meditating beneath its canopy of cut calico,
which much resembles lace at any height. Frequently there
is an ambulatory behind the altar, and then we find the altar
with a highly ornate reredos. In front of the altar is a table
for offerings of flowers, iron stands for wax tapers; a carved
and gilt stand with a crucifix is supported by a wooden elephant;
the arm of the cross carries a beautifully embroidered crimson
silk or satin banner, covering napkins used for dusting the
sacred images. Tall handsome wooden pulpits, carved, painted,
and decorated with mosaics, are conspicuous objects in the
churches. The priests' apartments in the adjoining building

are comfortable, the chief priest's being recognised by the handsome gilt and jewelled chests in which are kept the sacred records ; gay carpets and rugs cover the floor. Incidents in the life of Buddha frescoed on the walls are diversified by some advertiser's flaming idea of Her Gracious Majesty, Napoleon, or Wellington, the latest skirt dancer, or Phil May's inimitable coster cartoons, cut from illustrated papers presented by the members of our various missions, and much prized. The Dean of Keng Tung, whose church is the most elaborate, is a fine, portly, elderly man, of great presence, and unmistakeably an ecclesiastical dignitary. He has travelled to India and Ceylon. His monastery is very wealthy, and he is said to be possessed of personal wealth, contrary to the ordinances of Buddha. The clergy in the Eastern Shan States are generally less orthodox than those in the Western States and Burma, who call them "Htu," or "Imitation priests," and regard them much as the priests of the Church of Rome regard priests of the Church of England. The Eastern Phongyis travel about in great state, wear yellow caps, and carry arms. Many allow their hair to grow ; some even cultivate moustache and side whiskers, and look like the Evangelical clergy. I made many friends among the priests and their young scholars while painting in the Churches.

Outside the walls of Keng Tung are many large and populous villages. To the east of the town, lying under the wall, is a large colony of the Shan Chinese. They have been settled there for some time, and have a large and handsome church of their own. The houses are built of bamboo and their village is very dirty. They keep goats, ducks, fowls, pigs, and cows. They are good gardeners, and we obtained some very good vegetables there in the spring. They grow lettuce, cabbage, onions, radishes, pumpkins, cucumbers, beans, French beans, peas, yams, and several kinds of sweet potatoes. They do a good deal of trade, and Mr. Scott considers that they introduced the manufacture of tiles into Keng Tung, and that the pottery, plates, cups, bowls, jugs, tea-pots, spittoons, pagoda ornaments, etc., which are so varied in kind and so cheap in Keng Tung, is mainly their work. There are a few shops in Keng Tung in which cloths, tinned milk, and matches are sold. The big bazaar, or market, is held, as elsewhere, in the Shan States, every five days. On three of the other days small bazaars are held in different parts of the town. There is no bazaar anywhere on the fourth day. On the fifth day, the large market place, with its lines of booths and stalls, is thronged with enormous crowds of people from the neighbouring villages and the surrounding hills. The quantity of goods displayed, and their variety, is great. The vendors are Shan women and Chinese men. The articles on sale include English and Indian cotton goods and yarns, Manchester silks, handkerchiefs of the most startling pattern, aniline dyes, coloured paper, Japanese matches, pocket knives, needles, powder and caps, flowered rugs, etc. The butchers, who sell beef and pork, and the shoemakers, are Chinamen. Chinese merchants also sell the huge straw hats with oiled silk coverings, which are made exclusively for the Shan market, raw silk, fur coats, iron pots, Chinese pipes and padlocks, also quicksilver and rock salt. These merchants arrive in December, and having disposed of their goods, make a trip or two to Maulmain, Rangoon, or Mandalay, returning with Manchester goods, which they sell off on the way up, or in Keng Tung, and return home in May laden with cotton. Western Shans also come here to trade. They bring *dahs*, cutch and piece goods. They usually take back bullocks. There is a tendency on the part of some of these traders, principally well-to-do Taungthús, to settle down in Keng Tung, their wealth recommending them as husbands to the fair ladies of that place. Traders from Siam bring raw silk for sale, taking back opium from Mong Lem and the Wa States. The Sawbwa and principal ministers invest their money in opium, which is considered the most paying article of trade. The country women bring to market excellent cheap oranges, bananas, plums, yams, peas, onions, ground and water nuts, pressed water grass (to be eaten with curry), jaggery, cheap and fairly good tobacco, and shamshu. Silks are woven by women of the town, and considerable taste and skill are displayed in the patterns and blending of colour. Cotton cloths of good design and well woven are brought in for sale by the hill tribes. The restaurants, where cooked food is sold, are numerous, and ocular evidence supports the idea that the trade in liquor is a large one. Fish—mahseer, murrel, etc., are caught in the Nam Khun and Nam Lap, and are kept in little ponds for sale in the bazaar.

Gambling is universal in the Shan States ; and on market days respectable-looking men may be seen seated in a booth, or some other shelter, selling tickets from little books for the lottery of the " Thirty-six animals," a diagram of which hangs behind him to assist the invester in making his choice. In a central spot is a tall bamboo, from the top of which dangles a small box containing the name of the winning animal for the day. This is hauled down at a certain hour, and the winners declared. Other forms of gambling ; Odd and Even, a rough kind of Roulette, etc., are also in full swing.

Attempts are being made, with some success, in the Shan States, to reduce the excessive public gambling, but as the receipts from the licenses are very great, and in Keng Tung a portion is set apart to provide pin money for the Queen and princesses, the reform must not be effected too violently. It has been pointed out to the chiefs that, in the interests of the people, they are now exempt from the octroi and bazaar dues, monopoly on tea, and other collections exacted by Burmese kings.

The Swabwa is assisted in his government of the State by sixteen ministers. These are not paid any settled salary, but receive a certain proportion of fines, taxes, etc., and are often very poor ; the daughter of the Prime Minister keeps a vegetable stall in the market. The State is divided into districts, each under a "Hpaya," or commissioner, with four or five advisers, who are invested with certain magisterial, civil, and revenue powers. These "Hpayas" have the power of life and death with reference to the Sawbwa. Each district is subdivided into village circles, under their own head-men.

The present youthful Sawbwa, a young man of somewhat violent temper, is more feared than loved by his people. His amours are numerous, and he seems to bear a similar character to that of Henry VIII. He is, however, said to be straight-forward. He gives his ministers an audience every fifth day, when they make verbal reports of their proceedings; these he confirms, or modifies if necessary, also verbally.

I am indebted to Mr. G. C. Stirling, Assistant Commissioner, and an intelligent young Burmese official, Maung Nyo, our agent at Keng Tung, also to Munshi Abdur Rahim, one of my assistants, for much of the following information concerning the laws and customs of the Shans.

Crimes, theoretically punishable by death, are murder, dacoity, theft of valuable property; but under ancient custom every offence may be expiated by a money payment, unless in case of murder the murdered man's relations demand blood for blood. The price of an ordinary man or woman's life is Rs. 300, of a woman's body Rs. 80 (claimed in cases of adultery). A chief or high official is worth more, but in each case the death penalty is usually imposed. In cases of culprits who cannot pay, or whose relations cannot pay, death is looked upon as a fitting punishment even for petty thefts. Of course, our influence is being used *pour changer tout cela*, but, so far, success has not been conspicuous. Relatives of criminals are held responsible for the latter's misdeeds, and in case of horse or cattle theft, or of dacoity, a whole village or even small township is dropped upon, should the immediate relatives fail to pay the required compensation. Civil cases, divorce, inheritance, and the like, follow the laws of Menu, as in other Buddhist countries. Fees, in civil cases, are regulated by the rapacity of the judge, and are generally exorbitant.

If the scenery of the Shan States is varied, the tribes inhabiting them are still more diversified. It will be impossible in this paper to do more than indicate them. We may divide them into (1) The dwellers in the cultivated valleys and alluvial hollows ; (2) The various tribes living on the hills. The former are those whom we know as Shans. "Shan" is a Burmese word, and is supposed to have the same root as Siam (Sciam of old maps). British Shans generally call themselves Tai, in Siamese "Htai." The inhabitants of Keng Tung call themselves "Hkon"; of the Hsip Hsaung Panna (Keng Hing), and adjoining districts "Lu." Both, however, answer to the general name of "Htai." The alphabet of the Western Shans is founded on the Burmese ; those of the Hkon and Lu, which are identical, are very complicated, and the main features resemble the Siamese. The spoken language of all is the same, though there are great dialectic differences.

In all fair-sized villages there is at least one doctor, and the druggist's stall is conspicuous in all bazaars. The methods of the Shan medical man have not been thoroughly investigated yet ; but very many of their drugs simply appeal to the faith of the patient.

No great fuss is made over marriages. The ceremony varies from the simple arrangement of taking each other's word for it, to feasts lasting several days, with wealthy people. Even here, though, the actual ceremony is a minor feature in the proceedings. The usual form among Western Shans is for the couple to eat rice together out of the same dish in presence of their relatives and the village elders. The bridegroom then declares that he marries the lady, and will support her. Among the Lu there is more of a ceremony. The hands of the bride and bridegroom are tied together with a piece of string after they have eaten together, and an old man pronounces them duly married. The Hkons throw rice balls at each other and the couple during the ceremony. The newly-married couple then go to their house, and split betel nuts are distributed among the relatives of the bride, who give money as a return present. Divorce is readily obtainable ; but, except among young people of low rank, is comparatively rare. A man can have more than one wife if he can afford it. In case of divorce the property is divided according to the law of Menu. The applicant for the divorce (when the desire is not mutual) of the person through whose fault the divorce is applied for always loses considerably in the division. Shans bury their dead ; priests and chiefs are burnt.

Like the Burmans, Shans believe in lucky days, and sooth-sayers are consulted to fix a day for any public undertaking, for commencing a journey, etc. Their superstitions are many and various. Being Buddhists they are ashamed somewhat of worshipping " Nats " (spirits). Buddhism gets more corrupt the further east one goes, and Nat worship gains in strength. Buffaloes are openly sacrificed to the Nats east of the Salween, a thing rarely seen in the west. Certain Nats are only appeased by human sacrifice. The guardian spirit of one of the Salween ferries claims a victim every year, preferably a Chinaman. The Nat saves trouble by capsizing a boat and securing the victim. The ferry is then safe for the rest of the year. Shans still believe in the efficacy of human sacrifice to procure a good harvest. The manner nowadays is to poison someone at the State festival, held generally from March to May. The practice is discountenanced by the chiefs, Mr. Stirling says, and is probably dying out ; but he has known more than one instance of it.

Shans believe in witchcraft. Mr. Stirling has known instances of women (sometimes young women) being expelled from a State, and all the property of their relations confiscated for supposed dealings in the black art. Maung Nyo, in a letter lately received, says " Some days ago, while I was walking in the town, I heard a good deal of firing, and on inquiring the cause

was told that the house of a witch was being burned down by
order of the Court. I at once went to the scene of the fire.
The witch in question is supposed to have killed nine persons
during the last two or three years, and the people have just
discovered the fact, so the witch was driven out of her house,
which was burned. While it was in flames many guns were
fired off to drive away the witch's spirit, or familiar, which might
try to remain. The Shans believe that while a witch's house is
being burned the adjacent houses will not catch fire, however
windy it may be. In this case the adjacent houses were a little
apart, and well soaked with rain, and no wind was blowing. No
violence is said to have been committed on the witch; but her
property was looted, or confiscated."

Rice is grown everywhere in the Shan States. There are
two systems of cultivation, one on terraced and irrigated land,
the other on the hill sides. The former is that adopted by the
Shans. There are three crops, the first grown in dry weather on
land altogether artificially irrigated; the second on land wetted
by the first rise of the streams; the third and main crop during
the rains. Very pretty little fenced-in gardens are common along
the banks of the streams flowing past the villages.

The Shans never use bullocks for ploughing, only buffaloes.
Their hills were lately visited by the cattle plague, from which
they suffered severely. The Shan States are supposed to be a
great pony breeding centre. This, Mr. Stirling says, is not now
the case, and even in the palmy days of the States breeding was
more or less confined to the Northern States. The most
successful breeders were supposed to be the Palaungs.

I have neither time nor space to tell of all the various hill
tribes to be met with in this interesting country. The principal
are Kaw, Kui, Kun Loi or Tai Loi, Miso, Muhso or Lahu,
Palaung, Lauten, Taungthu, Wa, Yangsek, Yanglam, Yao Yin.
Of these the Taungthu, Yangsek, and Yanglam tribes are found
among the Western Shans. The Palaungs are found all over
the Shan States. The others live to the east of the Salween.

The men generally wear the Shan dress, and only the women's dress enables one to determine the tribe. The Yangsek are considered to be allied to the Karens; but, I believe, have a language of their own. The women wear curious long coats, like sacks, with holes for the head and arms, very short sleeves, with alternate white and red longitudinal stripes. The Palaungs are widely distributed. The approaches to their villages are always good, and the excellence of the roads in the tracts inhabited principally by them is noticeable. There is one large Palaung tract in the Keng Tung State, and in this tract lies the Samtao circle of villages, where the guns are made which are sold in Keng Tung. Till lately these were of the long gas-pipe style, with flintlocks; now Captain H. B. Walker, D.C.L.I., of the Intelligence Department, who visited the Samtao villages, tells us they manufacture muzzle-loading percussion cap guns, rough though accurate copies of the Tower musket, which finds its way into every corner of the Burmese Empire. They also manufacture pistols of a Tower musket pattern. These Palaungs are Buddhists, and in some of their villages very handsome little "wats," or churches, are to be found.

In Captain Gordon's report on his last winter's survey work in the Myèlat, that portion of the Southern Shan States lying west of Fort Stedman, he says there are over twenty different tribes, distinct in dress, customs, and often language. These tribes do not, as a rule, intermarry. They are unambitious and unenterprising, but cheerful and fond of amusements, and although constitutionally lazy, work hard enough to keep themselves in comfort. The wife does all the house-work, and a large share of the outdoor work as well. At a Taungtha village, which had suffered severely from the cattle plague, I saw a woman dragging the plough which her husband guided. So important a member of the household is she considered that in most of the States a widow is exempt from taxation. Captain Gordon also says this country is rich in minerals: lead ore is extensively mined in the Baw Saing State, where the ubiquitous Chinaman, who is always to be found where money is to be made, holds the contract for smelting lead and silver. The possession of this mineral wealth is not an unmixed benefit to the state, as the hills are so honeycombed with old mines that the people cannot keep cattle, grazing being impossible owing to these pitfalls. Coal of fair quantity is found in Pwèhla, and copper and iron were both formerly mined for in the Myèlat. Legya is now noted for its iron-work.

Crossing the Salween we meet the Muhso, a tribe rather widely scattered over the hills in the western part of Keng Tung and the northern border of Siam, where Lord Lamington came across some of them. Captain H. R. Davies, O.L.I., also of the Intelligence Department, a good linguist and Shan scholar, says the word Muhso is identical with the Shan word for "hunter," possibly because they are notoriously good shikaries. They call themselves Lahu. They are again subdivided into 16 tribes. They have come from China, and many are said to live there still. In complexion the Muhsos are fairer than the Shans. Their noses vary a good deal, some being straight, some very flat, oblique eyes are especially noticeable among the majority, and a Chinese cast of countenance decidedly prevails. They have a curious custom at their annual festival which begins on the Chinese New Year's Day, towards the end of January, and lasts five days. The village is "taboo" for that time. The paths to it are blocked by bamboo erections and symbols warning off the stranger, who, if he persists in entering the village is kept there till the feast is over ; everything he has, including his clothes, is taken away from him and he is sent naked away. The Muhso says that the spirits are displeased at the presence of a stranger. The spirits have a house in each Muhso village, which is fenced off, and surrounded with ornamental posts. These posts are renewed at the festival. During the five days the people dance, sing, play musical instruments, and fire off guns. The dance is a slow one, in a circle, each dancer being also a musician. They have too, two musical instruments, one a gourd, in which several small bamboos are fixed, the sound produced being somewhat like a harmonium. I have heard, from a hill-top, the Muhso wandering unseen in the jungle below, playing these instruments as they went : and the soft, sweet, low tunes suggested the presence of wood nymphs. The other instrument suggests a Jew's-harp, made of bamboo. Though strangers are not allowed into the village during the festival, the villagers may wander outside : and the men of a large village came to my camp one night and gave me a great entertainment, the women coming as spectators.

The Kaw tribe is very numerous throughout the whole portion of the eastern portion of Keng Tung and in Keng Cheng. The men are taller than the average Shan : their features suggest the Chinese type, and they wear pigtails up inside their puggris, and ornamented with small silver discs. They use the same musical instruments as the Muhsos, and their dance is similar. Mr. Scott graphically describes it thus : " A sort of figure which suggests the Highland fling performed by a man in the last stage of exhaustion." Of the women Mr. Scott says : " They are very small, and wear a complicated dress which exposes portions of their person in rather unexpected places. They wear cloth leggings, and the married women have an exceedingly elaborate head-dress made of bamboo, and hung round with festoons of seeds and shells."

The prettiest woman's dress we saw was that of a Miao, a Chinese tribe with whom we first came in contact on our Eastern borders. It consists of a jacket with an elaborately worked sailor collar, a full, pleated petticoat, and pretty apron, with a neat grey puggri.

The La Was are the most savage of all these tribes : they are supposed to be cannibals, but this has not been proved against them. Their villages are perched high up on the mountains, off the regular paths, and few have visited them. They are head hunters, and the accounts given of the approaches to their villages through a grisly avenue of posts, each post bearing a human skull, recall similar customs in the Naga Hills, Assam. Like some of the Naga tribes, also, the Northern Was are said to go about naked.

Time fails me to tell of others : not minutes, but hours would be required to give the information we have about them all : and even this is far from complete, and I am quite in accord with Mr. Warry, who writes : " It is a matter of marvel to me that nobody has as yet thought it worth his while to come out and study these tribes in their own country. The Abbé Huc's professor of geography, discovered a new island without going outside his library, and discoveries equally startling may perhaps be made by the stay-at-home philologist. But here are rich stores of knowledge, which can only be collected and turned to account by a qualified student willing to spend some years in the country itself. In the north and north-east parts of Shan-land are found a mixture of races and a medley of languages without parallel in any other part of the world. The tribes I have just given a slight account of are but a few of the whole number. The chance of studying these peoples to full advantage is fast slipping away. Up to now they have been almost entirely isolated, owing to the insecurity which has prevailed in the regions in which they are settled. In consequence, they have, no doubt, preserved their languages and institutions in a far purer state than members of the same races who have lived under happier and more peaceful conditions elsewhere. Now, however, an era of peace seems to have set in. These tribes are in constant contact with the outside world : their languages are undergoing modifications, or dying out, and their customs are being assimilated to those of the Shans and Chinese. Many illustrations of this have come under my observation during the past half-year. I would, therefore, recommend anyone who is interested in such enquiries

c

to come before it is too late : the inducements are surely
sufficient : a good climate, in the midst of splendid mountain
scenery, simple, friendly folks to live among "—I never required
an escort while engaged in my survey operations—" and an
occupation full of interest in itself, and sure to lead to results
of permanent value."

A few words before I close concerning the communications.
These are confined to a few well-defined tracts, and these
are not very good, even for pack animals. The path from
Taunggyi to Keng Tung was last summer widened and improved,
and made into an excellent mule track, where two laden animals
can pass each other without one of them going over the side.
This work reflects great credit on Mr. Litster, Executive Engineer
at Fort Stedman, and his assistants, who carried it out at a very
unfavourable season, and in the face of great difficulties.

I do not think that sufficient expert exploration has been
done with a view to improving the communications and
developing the resources of the country. The navigation of
the Salween might possibly be rendered easier, and the teak
trade would be largely benefited by increased facilities for
exporting it.

You are aware that work has been begun on the line of
railway from Mandalay to Kun Lon ferry on the Salween. It
is hoped that it will tap the trade of Western Yûnnan. I
should have been glad to see a line run up on to the Southern
Shan plateau at least, if not to the Salween itself. The
construction of the cart-road to Taunggyi has had most excellent
results ; but a line of rail would, in the opinion of many qualified
to judge, greatly increase the agricultural wealth of the country.
Potatoes have already been very successful, the cultivation of
wheat should be very remunerative, and a brisk trade in
vegetables and fruit might be established, while, as Mr.
Hildebrand says, there is a pasturage for sheep equal to that
of the Wiltshire Downs. This line, I venture to think, would
be most useful, both strategically and commercially.

The climate of the Shan States is generally good in the cold weather. The nights are cold till April, and the heat, though great in the valleys, is seldom so oppressive as at Mandalay or Rangoon. Frost is experienced in some parts, but snow, of course, never. The valleys, owing to the mist and damp, are generally colder than on the hills above. The rains come in the end of April, or beginning of May. Good hill stations for troops could easily be found, and the sickness we hear of at Keng Tung and elsewhere is probably due to imperfect housing and the selection of indifferent sites.

The inhabitants of the Shan States suffer from fever in the low-lying valleys, and small-pox is an ever-present scourge, as the disfigured faces of too many Shans evidence. Influenza also has, I believe, invaded even this distant and uncivilised tract.

GENERAL INFORMATION.

COMMUNICATIONS.

Burma may be reached from England by various routes. The most direct is by the Bibby line of steamers, which make the passage in from 25 to 28 days.

These vessels are provided with excellent accommodation, and have been specially built for the Burma passenger trade.

The other direct line is that known as the Patrick Henderson line, steamers leaving Glasgow and Liverpool monthly for Rangoon. The passage money by the Bibby line is £50, and by Henderson's line £30, as second-class accommodation only is provided.

Alternative routes are by the overland route to Bombay, thence to Calcutta by rail, and by B.I.S.N. steamers to Rangoon. This is the mail route.

From Bombay, train may be taken to Madras, and thence by special fast steamer of the B.I.S.N. Company to Rangoon.

Passengers by this line frequently beat the mail, which averages 23 days from London.

CUSTOM HOUSE.

No difficulty is experienced in getting luggage passed through the Custom House, the officers of which meet all vessels on arrival in port.

Firearms and ammunition are usually detained pending certain formalities, but as agents meet all passenger vessels, to whom personal baggage may be made over, the work of clearing can safely be left to them.

POSTAL, TELEGRAPHIC, AND BANKING INFORMATION.

All parts of Burma are well served by both the Postal and Telegraph departments. Offices of both are found in all District and Sub-divisional Head-quarter Stations. The English mails are delivered throughout most parts of the province within three days of their arrival in Rangoon.

Telegraph offices are, of course, met with at all Railway stations, and at most of the riverine stations at which steamers touch. The charge for a message of eight words to any part of Burma or India is eight annas if sent *deferred*, one rupee if sent *ordinary* and double that if sent *urgent*.

To all countries in Europe (except Turkey and Russia) the charge is Rs. 3 per word. To Ceylon the charge is three annas a word.

BANKS.—The following banks have agencies in Burma as below :

Bank of Bengal : Rangoon, Moulmein, and Akyab.

National Bank of India : Rangoon and Mandalay.

The Chartered Bank of India, Australia, and China : At Rangoon.

The Agra Bank : At Rangoon.

The Hong Kong and Shanghai Bank : At Rangoon.

Other firms which do banking business are :—Messrs. Thos. Cook and Sons, and Messrs. A. Scott and Co., both of Rangoon.

Currency notes of the Government of India are easily obtainable at all banks and Government treasuries, and are negotiable throughout the country.

They will be found useful to travellers who wish to avoid carrying about rupees, which in large quantities are both weighty and cumbersome.

CURRENCY, WEIGHTS, AND MEASURES.

The currency in use throughout the country is the same as in other provinces of the Indian Empire—viz., rupees, annas, and pies.

Currency notes of the value of Rs. 5/-, 10/-, 20/-, 50/-, and 100/-, are procurable at the banks and Government treasuries, and, as stated elsewhere, form a convenient mode of carrying money about. It is as well to take a good supply of small silver (2 anna, 4 anna, and 8 anna pieces), which will be found useful when small payments have to be made.

WEIGHTS AND MEASURES.—The ordinary measure of weight in use in the bazaars and throughout the country is the *Viss*. This is equal to 3·65lbs. avoirdupois. One *viss* is also equal to 100 *ticals*.

This system is used in weighing such articles as rice, flour, sugar, meat, and in calculating the weight of man or beast.

By the European firms avoirdupois weight is used.

DISTANCES are usually reckoned by the ordinary English long measure. In all parts of the country where Government roads have been constructed, mile posts, with the distances clearly marked on them, in English and Burmese, have been provided. In this way the ordinary peasant has become accustomed to the *Engaleik Daing*, or English mile.

In the more remote parts the Burmese mile is used. It is equal to a little more than two English miles.

HOTELS, &c.

Hotels under European management are to be found only at Rangoon, Mandalay, and a few of the other large towns of the province.

In Rangoon the principal hotels are "Sarkies," "Evershed's," "Barnes' Family Hotel," all situated in Merchant Street; the "British India," in Sulè Pagoda Road, and the "Great Eastern," on the Strand, facing the river.

In Mandalay the " Hotel Europe " is the only one deserving of notice. It is situated in the business quarter of the city, and is in close proximity to the walled city and palace.

There are no native hostelries such as the *yadoya* of Japan, and hence accommodation in the district and " up country " is at times difficult to obtain.

In most district head-quarter stations, however, Government has provided *Travellers Bungalows*, or *Dak Bungalows*, where furnished rooms for temporary residence are procurable, at a fixed charge of about two rupees per diem.

Attached to these Bungalows is a native *Khansamah*, or butler, who caters for the residents at rates fixed by the local Magistrate.

Residents of the country, however, whose business takes them to out-stations, generally cater for themselves, having their own cook and stores, and this plan is found to be more economical, and in every way more satisfactory.

Every village, or hamlet, is, through the benevolence of some pious Buddhist, provided with a " rest-house," or *Zayat*, as it is called by the natives of the country.

These *Zayats* are generally advantageously situated on the outskirts of the village, amidst groves of shady trees, sometimes in close proximity to the river or stream which runs past the village.

On the arrival of a European traveller, the *Ywa-thugyi* or village elder, an official appointed by Government, at once proceeds to render the place habitable by bringing mats, curtains, water-pots for the bath, fuel for cooking, and frequently articles of furniture, according to the resources of the village.

To those who, in the pursuit of sport or travel, have no objection to roughing it a little, such a lodging is not to be despised.

It was in such structures that our troops, both officers and men, were housed during the early years of the occupation of Upper Burma. No charge for such accommodation is made,

neither is the headman eager for a *douceur* for the trouble
he has been to, but merely accepts payment for any commodities
he may have been called upon to supply.

As these *Zayats* are, as noted above, to be found throughout
the land, travellers are advised not to incommode themselves by
carrying tents.

The lower, or deltaic province, is especially unsuited for the
use of tents, owing to the excessive rainfall, and the consequent
dampness of the ground for the greater part of the year.

CLIMATE, DRESS, TIME OF VISIT, &c.

As Burma is situated almost wholly within the tropics, the
climate is influenced by the regular Monsoon winds which
prevail in the Indian Ocean and countries adjacent to it.

The South-west Monsoon is ushered in about the middle
of May, sometimes accompanied by violent atmospheric
disturbances. This wind blows steadily till about the middle
of October, when its direction shifts to the North-east.

The rainy season therefore prevails from May till October,
and the dry season from October till May.

In Lower Burma, especially in districts adjacent to the
Bay of Bengal, the rainfall is excessive. The following are
the averages for the year for four stations :—

Tavoy - 173·46 inches. Moulmein 184·85 inches.
Rangoon 100 ,, Akyab - 184·46 ,,

Immediately after the cessation of the rains the weather is
close and muggy, owing to the excessive evaporation from the
soil and the drying up of swamp and surface water.

Towards November, the power of the sun is perceptibly
less daily, and the months of December, January, and February
are delightful with a cloudless sky and chilly nights, rendering
the use of warm clothes and blankets indispensable.

In the northern parts of Upper Burma, it is found necessary
to have fires in the houses at this season. March, April, and
May (up to the time the Monsoon bursts) are the hot months,

when the sun's heat is very powerful, and travelling—except in the early morning or at night—is both uncomfortable and dangerous.

The Thermometer in the sun at this period frequently rises to 160°F. especially in Upper Burma, where, owing to the dryness of the air, the climate closely resembles that of the North-West provinces of India.

In the Lower Province the heat is tempered by the sea breezes which blow with regularity at this period.

From the above remarks the traveller will doubtless gather that the best time to visit Burma will be in the cold weather. Arriving early in December, the whole country could be itinerated by the end of February and the return journey to Europe be undertaken in March, when the Indian Ocean is like a mill-pond.

As regards dress, Europeans dress in Burma very much as they do at home. For jungle travelling, flannel clothing is preferable. It is easy to carry, and easily washed, even when *dhobies* (washermen) are not procurable. *Khaki* suits will also be found serviceable for the same reasons. As ponies are easily procurable throughout the country, it is as well to be provided with riding breeches and boots. For shooting suits *Khaki* of a dark colour will be found as suitable as anything.

There are very good tailors in Rangoon who can make up material suited to the climate, at a few days' notice.

MEANS OF LOCOMOTION, LUGGAGE, &c.

The ordinary means of locomotion in Burma are the Railways, Steamers, Launches, Boats, Bullock-carts, and Ponies.

The lines of Railway in the Province at present completed, or approaching completion, are :—

Rangoon—Prome Line, 162 miles in length. Rangoon—Mandalay Line, 386 miles in length. The Mu Valley Railway, now under construction from Mandalay via Sagaing and Shwèbo, to Mogaung and Myitkyina, and the Mandalay Kunlon-Ferry, or N. Shan States Railway.

Steamers of the Irrawaddy Flotilla Company traverse all the navigable creeks and rivers of the province, and there are few places of importance which cannot be reached by these swift and well-appointed vessels.

Those intending to go off the beaten tracks, are advised to take little beyond what is absolutely necessary with them, and to compress their luggage within as narrow limits as possible. Coolies are at times difficult to procure, and the roads in the interior are bad.

A thin Cotton mattress with Pillows, and a Water-proof covering for the whole, will be found serviceable. Steel trunks of portable size will be found the most suitable receptacles for clothing. They are strong, light, and thoroughly waterproof, and can be obtained in Burma.

In Lower Burma, most of the travelling is done either by Steamer, Launch, or Boat.

Throughout the delta the country is a network of tidal creeks, running through low swampy land. Roads, of any length, do not exist.

In Upper Burma, where the rainfall is very much less, and the climate more like that of India, the country is dry and clear of tropical jungle growth, so that most of the travelling is done on horseback, the luggage being either carried on Bullock carts or by Coolies.

PROVISIONS AND STORES.

If the traveller confines his Tours to the lines of Railway, and the routes taken by the Steamers, he need not trouble himself about provisions. If however, he leaves the beaten tracks, and proceeds inland, it will be necessary for him to lay in a stock sufficient to last out the period occupied in his tours. European Stores and Shops are to be found in all large towns, at which Wines, Spirits, and Tinned Provisions are readily procurable. The European cannot exist on native food, which consists chiefly of Boiled Rice, Rank Vegetables, and Salted Fish. Fowls, Fresh Fish, Rice, Eggs, and Milk are procurable in small quantities in almost every village, and one of the chief duties of the village headman is to see that the traveller is supplied with these articles, on payment. Butcher's meat (Beef and Mutton) is to be obtained only in large towns, where a Government Bazaar is maintained.

For jungle travelling, Cooking Utensils, Plates, Cutlery, and Glasses must be purchased. All these articles can be got in Rangoon. One of the most essential articles is a Filter. Water should always be boiled and filtered before using. If this is done, it is seldom that a traveller is attacked by fever, or other disease.

Kerosine oil can be obtained in most villages, so that the traveller will find it a great comfort to provide himself with a Wind-proof Lantern. This, with a pair of spring candlesticks with shades, will be ample in the way of lights.

PLACES BEST WORTH VISITING.

Visits to particular localities, will depend very much upon the time at the disposal of the tourist, and upon the objects of his visit. If he desire scenery, he will get what he wants by sticking to the River. If he wishes to study Buddhism, he will have to visit such places as Pagan, Mandalay, Shwébo, Moulmein, Pegu, Prome, and other localities specially sacred or historically interesting.

Those in search of a cool resort in the hot season of April and May, will find Maymyo a suitable place, within easy distance of Mandalay, as also Kalaw (4,500 ft.) on the Fort Stedman Road in the Southern Shan States.

Of seaside resorts, Amherst, at the mouth of the Salween river, Momogan, on the sea coast opposite Tavoy, and Diamond Island, at the mouth of the Bassein river, will all be found enjoyable and easy of access.

Those who wish to study Burmese life, pure and simple, must, of course, avoid the large towns, where, owing to European influences, the habits and customs of the people have greatly changed.

Sportsmen must, of course, be prepared to visit any part of the country in which the game they are in search of is to be found. As most of the Big game in Burma is to be found in the most inaccessible forests of the Hills, the hunter must fix his visit when sport is procurable and climate salubrious.

In the paragraph on "Sport," special instructions will be given.

SERVANTS, GUIDES, &c.

Guides of any kind, such as are to be found in European countries, or even in such places as Malta or Colombo, do not exist in Burma. A traveller wishing to itinerate the province is advised to secure the services of a good Madras *boy*. One who has been some time in the country is to be preferred, as he will invariably be found to have a colloquial knowledge of Burmese—the language of the country—in addition to a knowledge of English and Hindustani. A knowledge of the latter is essential, as most of the Domestic servants, Messengers, Porters, Boatmen, and Cabdrivers are Natives of India, whose language is Hindustani, or a corrupt rendering of it. Burmans there are, who know English, but they are not to be relied on in observing any contract into which they may have entered, and the traveller trusting to such an one might find himself left in the lurch, and stranded in some remote part of the country without the aid of an interpreter.

Should the traveller, however, determine to visit the interior and more remote parts of the province, away from Steamer routes and Railways, he will do well to engage the services of a *boy* who understands cooking, and is accustomed to camp or jungle life. Such men can generally be picked up in all large Stations.

OBJECTS OF ART,
OR MANUFACTURES SUITABLE AS PURCHASES.

Travellers arriving from India or the far East will be disappointed in their endeavours to obtain Curiosities and Works of Art indigenous to the country.

The Art industries followed by the Burmese are chiefly Wood carving (principally in teak), Silver and Goldsmith's work, Carving in ivory, Brass work, Lacquer work, and Silk weaving.

The work of all these craftsmen is bold and impressive, but is lacking in neatness and attention to details.

A short account of each of these industries will now be given :—

WOOD CARVING.

This is carried on chiefly at Henzada, Mandalay, and Moulmein. The jails at all of these stations turn out some excellent specimens of this work.

Of larger articles of Furniture, Sideboards, Screens, Dinner Waggons, Tables, Chairs, and Writing Desks are the principal. Of smaller articles, Brackets, Gong-stands, Picture and Mirror Frames, and diminutive figures of the Races indigenous to the country are the commonest articles met with.

Very excellent work is turned out by Saya Tha Dun, of Mandalay. He was formerly the Royal Carver, and may be seen at work at any time on the Platform of the Palace at Mandalay.

As in other industries no finished specimens are kept in stock, and the article desired by the purchaser has to be "made to order."

SILVER AND GOLDSMITHS' WORK.

Goldsmiths' work consists principally in the supply of the articles of Jewellery worn by the native ladies of the country.

Unlike the natives of India, the Burmese despise Silver and Brass ornaments, and the greatest ambition of a Burmese woman, no matter how poor, is to possess a Gold Bangle, generally a plain hoop of Gold bent on to the wrist.

The principal articles of jewellery worn by the Burmese are Bangles of different sizes and thicknesses, according to the affluence or otherwise of the owner; Brooches; Necklaces of unique design; Ear-rings and Ear-plugs; the latter often two inches in circumference, the end being frequently studded with Diamonds, Rubies, or Pearls; Rings for the Finger; Ornamental Combs and Hair pins.

To give the Gold a deep red colour, which is much admired by the Burmese, the metal is exposed to the fumes of burning Sulphur, which gives the metal the desired tinge.

Of all these articles, none—except certain patterns of the Necklace—are suitable for use by European ladies. One of these: generally known by its Burmese name, *Dali-zan*, is extremely neat and pretty. It consists of a series of rows of small flowers or butterflies of Gold, the whole front of the Necklace being triangular in shape with the apex inverted, and when worn fully covers the lower part of the neck. It is much admired for its quaint design and workmanship.

Silversmiths are to be found in nearly every Town in the country. The best workmanship, however, is to be got at Thayetmyo, Moulmein, and Mandalay.

Of Burmese Silver Work the Bowl or *Palar* as it is called, is the commonest work of art. The size and weight depend of course upon the quantity of Silver used. The Bowls are first made plain the required shape and size, and the exterior is then covered with figures in *repoussé* work, and the details traced in. The scenes depicted are generally historical or mythological. The larger specimens are very bold in design, and exceedingly handsome.

Silver Cups, shaped like ordinary Tumblers, are also curiosities.

The charge for labour varies in different Towns. In Thayetmyo it is Eight Annas per Rupee weight (*tical*) of Silver used. In Mandalay it is Twelve Annas per *tical*. For more delicate work the charge is frequently One Rupee per *tical*.

IVORY CARVING.

Ivory Carving is practised chiefly in Rangoon, Moulmein, and Mandalay. Although well executed specimens are frequently to be met with, the Burmese are far behind the Chinese in the excellence of their workmanship.

The principal articles manufactured are *dah* handles, figures of Men and Animals, Chess-men, Cups, Paper-knives, and Card cases. As in other industries, the traveller will frequently be unable to procure any finished specimens, but will have to place his order, and rely upon a friend to see that it is executed. The Burman, in his happy-go-lucky way, neither advertises his wares, nor keeps a stock on view.

BRASS WORK.

This industry is carried on chiefly in Amarapura, Sagaing, and in Rangoon. The principal articles of manufacture are Bells, Gongs, Images of Gaudama, Dishes, Bowls, and other domestic utensils. Some of the Bells and Images are of vast size and weight.

The Bells—unlike those of European manufacture—have no tongues, but are suspended by a shackle to a cross beam, supported on two upright posts. They are sounded by striking the lower part of the outer rim with a deer's antler, or a piece of heavy wood.

Brass images of Gaudama—sometimes of enormous size— are to be found in nearly all Buddhist shrines. At Mandalay small specimens are to be got. These are often utilised as paper weights by Europeans and others.

Gaudama Buddha is represented in three postures :— the Sitting, as when he attained Buddha-hood ; the Sleeping, representing him as lying on his couch, prior to his entering Nevana; the Standing, the attitude he adopted when preaching. Of these, the Sitting figure is the one most frequently met with.

Very excellent Gongs are made in various localities, but the best are to be got from Indaing in the Lower Chindwin district of Upper Burma. Triangular Gongs or Brass discs are to be got in most bazaars, and are manufactured in large quantities in the neighbourhood of Mandalay.

Model figures in Brass, of Bullock-carts, Boats, Men, Crabs, Turtles, etc., can be obtained in all the stalls surrounding the Arakan, and other temples at Mandalay.

SILK WEAVING.

This industry is carried on in various parts of the province. In Lower Burma, at Bassein, Shwegyin and Prome, and in Upper Burma at Amarapura, Mandalay, Shwèbo and Paleik (in the Kyauksè district).

The common articles of manufacture are *Putsos* or Waist cloths, worn by the Burmese men, and *Ta-meins*, the Petticoats worn by the women. In addition to these articles ordinary silk cloth of different colours is produced, and is used chiefly in making jackets. In Amarapura any particular pattern or colour can be woven to order.

The most beautiful *Putsos* are made at Amarapura, near Mandalay. These are known as *A-Kyeik Putsoes* and frequently cost as much as Rs. 300/- As many as one hundred shuttles are often employed in producing the intricate patterns of the more expensive varieties.

LACQUER WORK.

Prome, Pagan, and Mandalay are the centres of this industry. Bowls, Cups, Betel-boxes, Trays, Baskets, and other domestic utensils are all manufactured of this ware.

The body of the article is shaped of very finely-plaited Bamboo work, the finer the plait the more expensive the finished article. The plaited article is then covered with

Vegetable oil (*thit-see*), and the oil is allowed to dry in. When fully dry the whole surface is smeared over again with a paste composed of fine Sawdust, Rice water, and Vegetable oil. When thoroughly dry, a second coating of a similar but finer composition is applied, and, after drying, the article is attached temporarily to a horizontal revolving wheel or lathe, and the rough surface ground down and polished. After another coat of varnish, it is ready to receive the colour and design. The usual colours are vermilion, yellow, and green. The desired colour is applied to the article, and, when dry, the pattern is scratched in with a steel style. The whole is then covered with another colour, which fills up the interstices in the surface caused by the pointed style. When dry, the box or other article is replaced in the lathe, and the surface ground down, either with Paddy husk or the skin of the Bamboo. This removes the second coating of paint from all parts except the interstices, and thus the pattern or tracing is firmly fixed in the original colour. This process is repeated until the whole design is complete. The article is then finally polished and varnished. The best Cups or Boxes are exceedingly elastic, and the edges can be pressed together till they meet, without the lacquer splitting or shelling off. The best Lacquer work is made at Pagan, on the Irrawaddi in Upper Burma. It is very interesting to watch the manufacturers at work, with their rude tools and appliances.

Very fine boxes, with trays fitting into them, and often three feet in circumference, can be purchased here for a few Rupees.

A curious sort of decorative work is carried on, chiefly in Mandalay, Prome, and Pakokkû. It consists of covering the panels of boxes, small tables, or other articles, with patterns picked out in gold. The process is similar to that employed in the decoration of Lacquer ware. Some of these articles, especially the small round tables, manufactured at Prome, are exceedingly handsome.

Very beautiful specimens of this work are to be seen in the larger monasteries at Mandalay.

Sometimes, instead of gold, a mosaic pattern in coloured glass, or looking-glass, is applied. This constitutes the chief feature in the interior decoration of the late King's Palace at Mandalay.

SHIPMENT OF CURIOSITIES.

There are several Firms in Rangoon who are Parcel Delivery Agents, the two principal being Messrs. A. Scott & Co., and Thomas Cook & Sons. The former are agents for the Globe Express.

In forwarding goods through an Agent, a complete list of contents, with value, must be supplied to the Agent by the shippers. This is done to enable the Agent to pay the Custom House Fees, should any be due. Goods are generally shipped by the Agents at Rangoon in the steamers of the " Bibby " and " Patrick Henderson " lines.

SHOOTING AND GAME.

The list appended gives the principal wild animals to be met with in the jungles of Burma.

Elephant	(*B. Tau-tsin.*)
Rhinoceros	(*B. Kyan.*)
Tapir	(*B. Ta-ra-shu.*)
Wild Hog	(*B. Tau-wet.*)
Sambur	(*B. Tsat.*)
Brown antler'd Deer	(*B. Tha-min.*)
Hog Deer	(*B. Darai.*)
Barking Deer	(*B. Gyi.*)
Wild Goat	(*B. Tau-sait.*)
Bison	(*B. Pyaung.*)
Wild Buffalo	(*B. Tau-gwæè.*)
Wild Cattle	(*B. Saing.*)
Gayal, or Mit-hun	(*B. Ain-pyaung.*)
Sun Bear	(*B. Wet-wan.*)
Otter	(*B. Hpyan.*)
Wild Dog	(*B. Tau-kwè.*)
Jackal	(*B. Myè-kwè*).
Grey Civet Cat	(*B. Kyaung-myin.*)
Common Civet Cat	(*B. Kyaung-ka-do.*)
Binturong, or Monkey Tiger	(*B. Myauk-kya.*)
Tiger	(*B. Kya.*)
Leopard	(*B. Kya-thit.*)
Leopard Cat	(*B. Thit-kyaung.*)
Jungle Cat	(*B. Tau-kyaung.*)
Gibbon	(*B. Myauk-lwè-gyaw.*)
Monkey	(*B. Myauk.*)
Hare	(*B. Yon.*)

A short description of each animal and the districts where it is found will now be given. These have been taken from Blandford's " Mammalia of India" *(Government of India series).*

ELEPHANT.

The species found in Burma is the ordinary East Indian.

It is found in all the large forests, both of Upper and Lower Burma, and vast herds roam unmolested in the Arakan Yomas, the Shan hills, and the highlands of the Tenasserim province. Good sport may be obtained in the Pegu Yomas, which form the water-shed between the Irrawaddy and Sittang rivers. It was from this region that the so-called *White Elephants* were procured for the Burmese Kings, which, after capture, were escorted with great state and ceremony to the capital.

Bo-dau-paya, who reigned from A.D. 1781 to 1819 at Amarapura, possessed one which lived in captivity for more than fifty years. In Upper Burma Elephants are numerous in the Katha, Mandalay, and Bhamo districts, and in the Shan States.

Under existing rules, Elephants must not be shot without special permission from the Commissioner of the Division.

In the Rainy season, great damage is done to the Rice crops of villagers settled near the foot of the hills, by roving herds of Elephants.

The best season for Elephant shooting will be during the months of February, March, and April. At this time they are to be found in the tree forests of the higher ranges, as the Bamboo forest of the lower ranges has generally been fired by this time. In the rainy season they frequent the thick Bamboo jungle at the foot of the hills, and it is then difficult to stalk them. Burmese hunters, or *Môk-so,* as they are called, are to be procured in all mountain villages, and are declared to be quite the equals of their Indian *confrères.* They are certainly most enthusiastic and enduring, and will track for the entire day without giving in, especially if game is plentiful.

In the King's time, an Elephant Keddah was maintained at Amarapura, within three or four miles of the present Capital, Mandalay, and a "catch" was made every year, the animals being driven into the Keddah by the valleys debouching from the Shan Hills.

RHINOCEROS.

Three varieties of this family are procurable in the forests of Burma, viz : The lesser one-horned (*B. Kyan-tsin*), The Ear-fringed two-horned, and the Sumatran variety. Dr. Mason writes as follows on the Lesser One-horned:—"The common Singled-horned Rhinoceros is very abundant. Though often seen on the uninhabited banks of large rivers, as the Tenasserim, they are fond of ranging the mountains, and I have frequently met with their wallowing places on the banks of mountain streams two or three thousand feet above the plains. They are as fond of rolling themselves in mud as a Hog or a Buffalo. The Karens have quite as much fear when travelling of a Rhinoceros as they have of a Tiger. When provoked, the Rhinoceros, they say, pursues his enemy most unrelentingly, and with indomitable perseverance. If to escape his rage the huntsman retreats to a tree, the beast, it is said, will take his stand underneath for three or four days in succession without once leaving his antagonist. There are seasons when the rhinoceros is very dangerous, and ferocious, attacking everything that comes near its haunts."

TWO-HORNED RHINOCEROS (*R. Lasiotis.*)

Blyth remarks :—" In the Rhinoceroses of this type the hide is comparatively thin, and is not tesselated or tuberculated, nor does it form a ' coat of mail,' as in the preceding variety, but there is one great groove (rather than fold or plait) behind the shoulder blades, and a less conspicuous crease on the flank, which does not extend upwards to cross the loins, and there are also slight folds on the neck and at the base of the limbs, the skin being moreover hairy throughout."

" There is also a second horn placed at some distance behind the nasal one. Until recently the existence of more than one species was unsuspected."

" I have reason to believe that this is the Two-horned species which inhabits the Arakan Hills, those of Northern Burma, and which extends rarely into Assam."

R. SUMATRANSIS (*B. Kyau.*)

This type is much smaller than the preceding species, with a harsh and rugose skin, which is black and clad with bristly black hairs, the ears less widely separated at base, and filled internally with black hairs, the muzzle anterior to the nasal horn much broader, and the tail conspicuously longer, tapering and not tufted at the end, horns attaining considerable length and curving but slightly backwards. This species is the ordinary Two-horned Rhinoceros of Tenasserim and the Malay countries, and would seem to be replaced in Arakan by *R. Lasiotis*, which perhaps also spreads into Assam and Tenasserim. According to Helfer the *R. Indicus*, in addition to the *R. Sondaicus*, inhabit the northern portion of the Tenasserim province.

TAPIR (*B. Ta-ra-shu.*)

" Has four toes in front, three behind. Snout produced into a short fleshy mobile trunk. Hair close and short.

" The Tapir has been long known to exist in the Southern province, but has never been heard of north of the valley of the Tavoy river. It is believed that none have ever been caught or killed in the provinces, except one that was procured from a Karen by a writer of the late Major Macfarquher, of Tavoy. It was a very inoffensive animal, and became as much domesticated as a cat. It followed its master round the compound like a dog, but looked as unseemly as a hog. It differs in no respects from the Malay Tapir, has the same white-blanket-like appearance on its back, and, like that, frequents the uplands. Though seen so rarely, the Tapir is by no means uncommon in the interior of the Tavoy and Mergui provinces."

" I have frequently come on its recent footmarks, but it avoids the inhabited parts of the country."

WILD HOG (*B. Tau-wet.*)

" Four toes on all feet, toes separately hoofed. Canine teeth large in the males. Molar teeth tuberculate."

Is found throughout the united provinces. Inhabits low, swampy country in the neighbourhood of creeks and swamps.

Lives principally on roots, bulbs, and ground-nuts, and also on the fruits of trees which fall to the ground. Droves of Wild Hogs frequently commit great depredations in the fields and gardens of villages surrounded by jungle. The Karens hunt it with dogs, and when the Pig falls exhausted, rush in and polish it off with spears and *dahs*.

Owing to the dense nature and vast extent of the jungles in Burma, the sport of " pig-sticking " is not indulged in, nor is it possible.

BROW-ANTLERED DEER (*B. Tha-min.*)

This species is found throughout the country from Manipur to Mergui.

Formerly vast herds roamed the plains of Pegu and Thatôn, and before the British occupation of the country the natives used to destroy large numbers every year. As many as 200 at a time would frequently be killed. The *Thamin* frequents the open bushless and comparatively treeless plains, and lives entirely upon the grass and other herbage of such areas. It is seldom seen or met with in tree jungle. "The colour of a full-grown buck is dark brown, especially about the back and neck, with underparts lighter. The females are hornless, and in colour like the female *Sambur*, but perhaps a little lighter. The female gestates nearly seven months, and brings forth its young in October or November, amidst the jungle paddy, which is then flowering or in seed, and at its greatest height. The doe will breed a second time in eighteen months, after bringing forth, so that the young of two seasons are not unfrequently seen with their parents. Females produce but one at a birth, and the young are spotted or memilled, but this disappears with age.

In the second year the males first begin to acquire horns, which are perfectly developed in March, and shed in September. After two years they get two tines, and when about seven years old are in their prime, with twelve tines, including the brow antler. The average weight of a buck is about 190lbs. In Upper Burma the *Thamin* is plentiful in the Meiktila, Shwèbo, and Chindwin districts, where it frequents the scrub jungle, with which those districts abound.

A common way of stalking the *Thamin* is to sit quietly in a bullock-cart, which is driven through the country frequented by the animals. A bell is generally placed round the bullock's neck, the tinkling of which diverts the attention of the animal. In this way it is possible to approach within thirty or forty yards of the herds before they break away.

SAMBUR (*B. Tsat.*)

This Deer is commonly diffused throughout Burma, and is found in all the great forests.

" Horns with a basal antler springing direct from the burr, and pointing forwards, upwards, and outwards, the beam bifurcating at the extremity, a snag separating posteriorly, and pointing obliquely to the rear.

Colour dark brown, in summer somewhat slatey. The chin, limbs within tail beneath, and an irregularly marked patch on the buttocks, pale yellowish or orange yellow neck and throat with long hair forming a sort of mane, tail moderately long. Female and young dusky olive-brown, lighter than the buck."

WILD GOAT (*B. Tau-scik.*)

Colour grizzled black, bay colour on the flanks. A black dorsal stripe. Fore arms and thighs anteriorly reddish-brown, the rest of the limbs hoary. Below whitish. Length 5ft. or more. Weight 200lbs.

This species (*N. Bubalina*) is found in W. Yûnnan, at elevations of 6,000, and 7,000 feet.

WILD GOAT OF BURMA. (*B. Tau-seik.*)

"This species varies much in colour, from red to black, and the black sometimes with white nape, or the hairs of the nape may be white at the base only. Those from Arakan are of a pale red-brown colour, with black dorsal list.

This species is found in the mountains of Tenasserim and Arakan, and generally frequents the rocky crags of mountain summits.

HOG DEER (*B. Darai.*)

Colour a bright rufous brown or bay, the hairs having pale tips, giving a speckled appearance. The belly and underparts white. Tail beneath and inside of ears also white. Height about twenty-four inches at the shoulder, length from muzzle to root of tail 42in. to 44in., and tail about 8in. in length. Horns not more than 10in. or 12in. This is the most common variety of deer found in Burma, and is abundant in all the alluvial plains and grass jungles. It is also very plentiful in the mangrove swamp jungle on the banks of creeks in proximity to the sea.

Hog deer are not gregarious, and it is seldom that more than three or four are seen together.

They are usually shot by employing beaters to drive them from the tree or grass jungle which they frequent. The Burmese have a way of securing them, by means of what is known as the *mi-oke*.

On a dark night a light is placed in a three-sided box, with extended sides. This is carried on the leader's head. Two or three followers accompany the leader, provided with small bells attached to bamboo clappers. As the leader advances through the clearings, the followers rattle away merrily on their clappers. The deer, on the approach of the light, is probably fascinated by it, together with the noise of the castenets, and either slowly approaches the light, or stands staring at it in an idiotic way. The sportsman (if such he can be called) then fires. Burmans, as a rule, are not allowed to carry firearms, so they generally rush in, and with their *dahs* hamstring the animal before it has time to get away.

BARKING DEER *(B. Gyi.)*

This variety is the *Cervulus Munt-jac* of naturalists. Colour, deep bay on the back, and paler under the belly; height 20in. to 22in., length of head and body about 35in.; weight 38lbs.

Found throughout the country in the wooded hills and tree forests, It only leaves the forest to graze on the outskirts in the hill clearings, generally in the early morning, or at dusk, when it may easily be stalked.

It is called the "Barking deer" from the peculiar call it utters, which resembles the single bark of a dog. This cry is frequently heard at night when the animal is alarmed, or during the rutting season.

BISON *(B. Pyaung.)*

The *Bos Gaurus* of naturalists.

This animal is thus described in Blandford's Mammalia of British India. "General form massive, body deep, limbs and hoofs small. Ears long. A high ridge along the anterior half of the back terminating abruptly about halfway between the shoulder and the tail and caused by the spinous processes of the dorsal vertebræ being long and those of the lumbar vertebræ short, the change in length taking place suddenly. Skull bearing a high ridge, convex on the vertex between the horn cores, in front of this ridge the forehead is deeply concave. Horns considerably flattened towards the base, curved throughout the tips, turned inwards and slightly backwards. Thirteen pairs of ribs. Tail just reaching the hocks. No distinct dewlap. Hair short, very thin on the back in old bulls."

"Colour brown, almost black in old males, less dark and sometimes more rufous in females and young males, especially during the cold season, and in those inhabiting drier parts of the country, where there is less shade. Lower parts rather paler. Hair about axil and groin golden brown. Legs from above the knees and hocks to the hoofs white. Head from above the eyes to the nape ashy-gray, becoming in some animals white-brown or dirty-white. Muzzle pale coloured. In calves, according to Blyth, there is a dark stripe down the back. Horns pale greenish or yellowish with black tips."

DIMENSIONS.—" This appears to be the largest of existing bovines. Large bulls are said to exceed six feet in height at the shoulder, but this is rare and exceptional, 5ft. 8in. to 5ft. 10in. being the usual height. Cows are much smaller, about 5ft. in height. A huge bull measured by Elliot was 6ft. 1½in. in height, 9ft. 6in. in length, from nose to root of tail ; tail 2ft. 10in. long : girth behind shoulders, 8ft. A cow, 4ft. 10½in. in height measured 7ft. from nose to rump over curves, and 6ft. 9in. in girth."

" Average male horns measure 20 to 24in. round the outside curve, with girth at base of 18ins."

The Bison is found throughout Burma, and is met with in the Arakan Yomas, the Pegu and Siam Yomas, the Shan Hills, and the mountains separating Upper Burma from Arakan and Assam. It inhabits the forest or high grass jungles in the hills, and ascends to 5,000 or 6,000 feet. It generally feeds in the early morning and evening, and rests all day under the shade of the thick forest trees. It is very agile and swift, and can climb the steepest hills. It is very timid, but not particularly wary. Wounded animals have been known to charge, but they are not generally aggressively savage.

Burmans affirm that the hunter, if charged suddenly, may save his life by throwing himself flat on the ground, the Bison's horns being so placed that it cannot get within 18in. of the ground.

THE GAYAL OR MITHAN *(B. Tsaing.)*

" Very similar to *B. Gaurus* but smaller, with proportionally
shorter limbs, somewhat less developed dorsal ridge, a well
marked dewlap, and very different skull and horns. The head is
shorter, with shorter nasals, the forehead quite flat, and the
transverse outline of the vertex between the horn cores straight,
not arched. The horns are much less curved, in fact, nearly
straight, spreading outwards, and directed more or less at the
tips, but not inwards. Colour very similar to that of the
B. Gaurus. Head and body dark brown in both sexes, legs
from above the knees or hocks white or yellowish. Many tame
individuals are mottled and some are white throughout. Horns
blackish throughout."

DIMENSIONS.—Considerably less than in *B. Gaurus,*
especially in height. The skull of an old bull, known to be
that of a wild animal, measured 16·2 inches in basal length,
8·5 inches in breadth across the orbits, lengths of nasals,
6·5 inches, length of horn, 14 inches, girth at base, 14 inches.
This animal is found in a more or less domesticated state among
the uncivilized tribes inhabiting the mountains separating
Manipur, Assam, and Burma. It is domesticated by the
Chins, and roams the forest at will, returning to the village
of its owner in the evening.

THE BANTING *(B. Tsaing.)*

The *Bos-Sandaicus* of naturalists, and the true *Tsaing* of
Burma.

It is thus described by Blandford. "This animal appears to
be slighter than the *Gaur,* with the legs longer in proportion, and
the dorsal ridge less developed. The tail descends below the
hocks. The dewlap is of moderate size. The head is much
more elongated, the forehead not concave, the horn smaller,
cylindrical in the young, flattened towards the base in adults, and
curving outwards and upwards at first, and towards the tips
somewhat backwards and inwards."

COLOUR.—" Cows and young bulls have the head, body, and upper portions of the limbs bright reddish brown, approaching chestnut. Old bulls are black in both sexes, the legs from above the knees and hocks, a large oval area on the buttocks, extending to the base of the tail, but not including it, a stripe on the inside of each limb, the lips and the inside of the ears are white. Calves have the outside of the limbs chestnut throughout, and a dark line down the back."

DIMENSIONS.—" A full grown bull measured 5ft. 9½in. high, at the shoulder, the length of the head and body was 8ft. 6in., and of the tail 3ft. The largest Burmese specimen recorded was 16 hands high (5ft. 4in.) "

The *Tsaing* is fairly plentiful in the Arakan and Pegu Yomas, and in the Shan States. It is also found in the hills abutting on the Chindwin river below Kindat.

It is gregarious in its habits, as many as 15 or 20 keeping together in a herd. It confines itself more to the bamboo jungle and grass downs of the lower ranges, and does not appear so adapted to mountain climbing as the *Pyaung*.

TIGER (B. Kya.)

COLOUR.—" Ground colour, above and on the sides, varying from pale rufous to brownish yellow below, white striped transversely with black throughout the head and body. The tail is marked with black rings. Ears black outside with a large white spot on each. The ground colour is much more rufous in some animals than in others, and forest tigers are probably darker and redder than those inhabiting thin jungles. Young animals, too, are born striped. Both black and albino tigers have been met with, though both are very rare."

DIMENSIONS.—" Adult males measure 5½ft. to 6½ft. from nose to insertion of tail, the tail being about 3ft. long. The head 16in., neck 12in., body 4ft., tail 3ft. 2in."

DISTRIBUTION.—The Tiger is distributed throughout the country from the confines of Manipur and Assam to the Malay peninsula. The finest specimens are to be met with in the mountain ranges which intersect and bound the province. Owing to the vast extent of jungle tracts Tigers are not as easily procurable as in India.

Man-eaters are comparatively scarce, and consequently loss of life from this cause is of infrequent occurrence.

HABITS.—The Tiger is generally found solitary or in pairs. It rests during the day in shady places, or in grass jungle near water, and roams the forests at night in search of food. It has a singular habit, in common with other beasts of prey, of frequenting particular haunts, to which it always resorts to sleep, although its nightly wanderings may circuit several miles of country. It lives chiefly in its wild state on pigs and deer, and other forest animals, and it is only when the latter become scarce, or the tiger becomes old and lazy, that he changes his habitat to the neighbourhood of villages, and takes to killing cattle, and generally ends his career by becoming a " man-eater," when he is hunted down by enterprising sportsmen, and destroyed.

The Burmese in the hill districts have an ingenious way of trapping and destroying the tiger and other feline beasts of prey. A trench is dug with inverted V shaped sides ($\triangle$) At the inner end a dog is tied. The tiger crawls in, seizes his prey, is unable to turn and effect his retreat with his quarry, and is attacked and speared by the hunters lying in wait.

LEOPARD (B. Kya-Thit.)

The *Felix Pardus* of naturalists.

COLOUR.—" Ground colour above from rufous to yellowish white or pale brownish yellow, sometimes darker, sometimes paler ; below white. The whole animal is spotted. The spots or rosettes on the back, sides, and dorsal portion of the tail are black externally, pale coloured within ; they vary much in size, colour, and form. Young Leopards are of a brownish colour, and the spots are much less clearly defined."

DIMENSIONS.—" Very variable, the total length of head, body, and tail together ranging from 5ft. to 8ft. It is more common than the tiger, and is found throughout Upper and Lower Burma. It is frequently found near villages, in the neighbourhood of which it lurks in the day-time, entering the village at night to steal off with a Goat or Dog, or to rob a Hen-roost."

It will not, if possible to avoid, face man, and is easily frightened away. When wounded though, it displays more courage than the tiger, and will charge its adversary repeatedly.

SUN BEAR (B. Wet-wun.)

The *Ursus Malayanus* of naturalists.

COLOUR.—Black, brownish in some parts. The muzzle often whitish. Has a crescentic patch of white on chest. Claws pale, horny, sometimes dusky. About 4ft. long, seldom exceeds 4½ft. Ears very short, not more than 2 inches.

It is found throughout the tree forests of the country, and lives principally on fruits. It is very fond of honey and will attack the nests of wild bees in the jungle trees, regardless of the stings of the enraged owners.

This species can easily be tamed, and when treated kindly becomes docile and amusing.

OTTER (B. Hypau.)

COLOUR.—Hair dark brown above with a rufous tinge: woolly under fur, white at base then brown, tips paler, producing the grizzled appearance generally noticeable in the Indian species.

The Otter is found in all the rivers, creeks, and " Fisheries " of Burma. Sometimes as many as twenty or thirty are seen together. They live together on the rocky eminences near the water, or, in the bases of rocks in burrows close to the water. They generally hunt in concert, and usually kill more fish than they consume. Hence they are most destructive in the large Fisheries.

Their skin, or fur, is beautifully soft, and is much prized.

Otters are easily tamed and in this state follow their owners about like dogs.

WILD DOG *(B. Taw-kwé.)*

This is the *Canis Rutilans* of the Malay peninsula. It is of a deep bay, or red, on the back, with lower parts whitish : end of tail black.

Head and body about 33 inches, tail about 12 inches. Is uncommon, but is seen occasionally on the outskirts of towns or villages. Generally hunt in pairs or in larger numbers.

JACKAL *(B. Myé-kwé.)*

The Jackal is not found east of the Arakan Yomas, but is common in Arakan and Chittagong. The species found there is identical with the common Indian Jackal.

Of lesser felines the grey Civet Cat *(B. Kyaung-myin)*, common civet (B. Kyaung-ka-do), the leopard cat *(B. Thit-kyaung)*, and the common wild cat *(B. Tau-kyaung)* abound in the jungles, and are sometimes shot for their skins, which are often beautifully marked.

Several varieties of Monkeys swarm in the forests and may be seen on the banks of the rivers and creeks, which intersect the Lower Province. They are comparatively scarce in the Upper Province.

LANGUAGES OF BURMA.

1. The following classification of the Languages in use in Burma, is taken from the Census Report for 1891.

The Languages may be divided into four groups :—

    A. Vernaculars of Burma.

    B. Vernaculars of India.

    C. Vernaculars of other countries of Asia, outside Burma.

    D. European and other Languages.

2. The principal vernaculars of Burma are :—Burmese, Talaing, and Karen. The principal dialects of Burma are :—Arakanese, Chaungtha, Tavoy, Danu, Kadu and Yaw.

ARAKANESE is spoken by the people of Arakan.

CHAUNGTHA is spoken by the tribes inhabiting the upper river valleys of the Arakan Division.

TAVOY is the language of Arakanese settlers on the lower Tenasserim coast.

DANU is the language spoken in a few scattered villages in the Southern Shan States. These people are generally supposed to be the remains of an ancient colony of Burmese immigrants.

YAW is the language spoken by a small tribe settled in the Yaw valley of the Pakôkkû district.

The next group of the vernaculars of Burma are the HILL DIALECTS. These are known to the Burmese by the generic name of CHIN.

These dialects are Southern Chin, Kun, Pallaing, Daignet, Sak or Thet, Aw or Anu, Mio, Kimi or Kwemi. The people

D

using these dialects inhabit the mountainous regions between Burma, Chittagong, Assam, and Manipur.

The next group is the Kachin, sometimes known as the Singhpo, or Chinpaw dialect, spoken chiefly in the hilly regions of the Katha and Bhamo districts.

Of the Môn-Annam dialects Talaing is the most important. This is the ancient language of Pegu and Tenasserim, and according to recent statistics, is still used by a quarter of a million of the inhabitants of Lower Burma.

The next groups are the Karen and the Taic Shan.

The principal dialects of Karen are Sgau Karen, Pwo-Karen, and Bghai-Karen (spoken in the Red Karen country, situated north-east of Taungû).

The Taic-Shan include the Shan, Lu and the Maingtha.

The Shans form scattered settlements throughout British territory, but are of course most numerous in the districts immediately abutting on the Shan States.

The last of the languages in group A. is the Selang or Salôn dialect. It is the language spoken by the islanders of the Mergui Archipelago, and is generally considered to have no connection with Burmese, but to be allied to Malay.

3. The principal vernaculars of India in use in Burma are Tamil, Telugu, Bengali, and Uriya. Of these Bengali is the most common, this being the language of the Chittagonians, a most numerous class in Burma.

Tamil and Telagu are the languages used by the cooly and domestic servants who swarm over in yearly increasing numbers from the Madras coast.

4. Of group C. Chinese, Manipuri, and Malay are the principal. Large colonies of Canton and "Straits" Chinese are to be found in nearly every town in Lower Burma, and the pick of the trade in these places is in their hands. Manipuri is spoken chiefly by the people of that race settled in Mandalay, the descendants of prisoners of war captured by the Burmese king Sinbyu-shin when he invaded and subjugated Manipur in 1764 A.D.

Malay is spoken by people of that nationality and also by Straits Chinamen who have settled in the neighbourhood of Mergui and Victoria point.

5. In group D. the languages of Europe are included. Of these English is of course the principal. German is spoken by the small colony of merchants of that nationality established in the different mercantile centres.

THE BURMESE LANGUAGE.

It would almost be impossible for a temporary visitor to the country to acquire a smattering of Burmese sufficient for his daily wants, in the short time at his disposal, while touring through the country. As however, the same, or similar situations occur again and again, and the traveller's wants are few, a short vocabulary of words likely to be of use, in connection with travelling, sport, or food is given. Those desirous of learning more will find Sloan's "Handbook for the Burmese Language," published by the Mission press in Rangoon, a practical work.

VOCABULARY.

Steamer	*Me-thin-baw.*	Railway Station	*Mi-ya-tah-yòu.*
Boat	*Hlai.*	Luggage	*Wun-za-lai.*
Boatman	*Hlai-tha-ma.*	River	*Myit.*
Carriage	*Ya-tah.*	Stream	*Chaung.*
Cart (Bullock)	*Nwa-hlè.*	Room	*A-khan.*
Road	*Lan.*	Dak Bungalow	*Bo-Dai.*
Bridge	*Ta-dah.*	House	*Ain.*
Village	*Ywa.*	Court-House	*Yòn.*
Town	*Myo.*	I	*Kyun-òk.*
Pony	*Myin.*	You	*Min : maung-min.*
Telegraph Office	*Kyi-nan-yòu*	He	*Thu.*
Telegram	*Kyi-nan-sa.*	It	*Hto-ha.*
Letter	*Sa.*	We	*Kyun-òk-do.*
Post Office	*Sa-taik.*	They	*Thu-do*
Bag	*Aik.*	Rupee	*Kyat.*
Box	*Thit-ta.*	Anna	*Hai.*
Railway	*Mi-ya-tah.*	Pice	*Pi-san.*

NUMERALS.			ORDINALS.	
1.	Tit.		1st.	Patama.
2.	Hhit.		2nd.	Du-taya.
3.	Thôn.		3rd.	Thur-daya.
4.	Lè.		4th.	Sa-do-ta.
5.	Nga.		5th.	Pyin-sa-ma.
6.	Kyauk.		6th.	Satha-ma.
7.	Kho-knit.		7th.	Thada-ma.
8.	Shit.		8th.	Attara.
9.	Kho.		9th.	Na-wa-tha.
10.	Ta-sai.		10th.	Da-tha-ma.
11.	Ta-sai-tit.			
20.	Hnit-sai.			
30.	Thon-sai.			
	etc., etc.			
100.	Ta-ya.			
1000.	Ta-taung.			

1 Rupee	Ta-kyat.	Curry	Hin.
2 Rupees	Hnit-kyat.	Chair	Kala-tyue.
1 Anna	Ta-bè.	Duck	Bai, bai-tha.
2 Annas	Ta-mu.	Egg	Û.
4 Annas	Ta-mat.	Food	A-sa-zaya.
8 Annas	Ngu-ma.	Fork	Kha-yin.
Bread	Paungmôn.	Fruit	A-thi.
Breakfast	Ma-uet-sa.	Knife	Da.
Bananas	Huet-yyau-thi.	Onions	Kyet-Thôn.
Butter	Tau-ba.	Oranges	Lè-man-thi.
Chicken	Kyet-tha.	Oil	Tsi.
Coffee	Kau-pee.	Potato	A-lu.
Pepper	Na-yôk-kaung.	Marsh deer	Da-rai.
Plate	Pa-gan-bya.	Brow-antlered deer	Thamin.
Rice	Hta-min.	Hog-deer	Gyi.
Sugar	Tha-gya.	Rhinoceros	Kyau.
Spoon	Zûn.	Tiger	Kya.
Soap	Sap-bya	Leopard	Kyit-thit.
Salt	Tsa.	Bear	Wet-wun.
Table	Sa-bwè.	Porcupine	Pyu.
Tea	La-pe-yè.	Tapir	Ta-ra-shu.
Milk	Nwa-no.	Wild Goat	Tau-seik.
Gun	Tha-nat.	Jungle-Fowl	Tau-gyet.
Cartridge	Yau-daung.	Pea-Fowl	Daung.
Cartridge Bag	Yau-daung-aik.	Partridge	Hka.

Powder	*Yau.*	Pheasant	*Yit.*
Shot	*Za-yeik.*	Quail	*Ngón.*
Bullet	*Kyi-thi.*	Teal	*Si-si-lee.*
Elephant	*Tsin.*	Brahminy Duck	*Hintha.*
Bison	*Pyaung.*	Wild Duck	*Tau-bè.*
Wild Cattle	*Tsine.*	Wild Goose	*Tau-nan.*
Sambur	*Tsat.*	Plover	*Zin-yaw.*
Paddy Bird	*Byaing.*		

USEFUL SENTENCES.

Please come here	*Thi-lar-ba.*
That will do	*Tau-bi.*
Thank you	*Kyi-zu-ktin-thi.*
How are you?	*Ma-e-la?*
What time is it?	*Be-ne-na-yee shi-thi-lai?*
Go and ask	*Thwa-mai-like-zan.*
Where is it?	*Bhai-ma-shi-thi-lai?*
I don't know	*Kyánôke ma-thi-bu.*
Wait a little	*Kha-na-nè.*
Go quickly	*Myan-myan-thwa.*
Have you got a cart?	*Hlè-ya-tha-la*
Have you got a pony?	*Myin-ya-tha-la.*
Have you got a boat?	*Hlai-ya-tha-la.*
We will start at day-break to-morrow morning	*Ma-net-mo-lin-kwa-twet-myi.*
Take away	*U-thwa.*
Bring	*U-Gai.*
Take hold	*Kaing-hta.*
Put down	*Kya-hta.*

RELIGION IN BURMA.

THE BUDDHIST RELIGION.

The following précis on the Buddhist religion, as practised in Burma, is extracted from the admirable articles on that subject in the first volume of the Report on Census Operations in 1891.

Buddhism is in reality not a religion at all, in the general acceptation of that term, but rather a system of philosophy evolved from Brahminism, owing to a religious revolt, headed by Gaudama Buddha, which took place about six centuries before Christ.

This revolt was brought about owing to the growing power of the Brahmins. It owes its rapid spread and acceptance among the Burmese to the fact that it supplanted the old Shamanism, or *nat* worship, which, in common with other uncivilised nations, was till then the accepted and practical creed of these races.

Much attention has been given of late years by Western scholars to the study of Buddhism, as it is revealed in the sacred writings, but it must be understood that the system of philosophy taught therein, is not the religion as practised by the people of Burma of the present day.

Burmans shew great reverence for their religion, but yet, "it plays a small part in their inner life."

Priests or *Hpongyis*, are much venerated, and the aphorism, "I worship the three most excellent things : Buddha (*Pa-ya*) ; The Law (*Ta-ya*) ; and the Priesthood (*Thinga*)," is continually on the lips of devotees. Yet in spite of these outward evidences of a purer faith, there is an older system underlying Buddhism which is known to Burmans as *nat* worship, and is nothing more or less than Shamanism.

Sir William Hunter in Chapter 1 of Volume VI. of his "Imperial Gazetteer" writes :—" Buddhism readily coalesced with the pre-existing religions of primitive races. Thus among the hill tribes of Eastern Bengal we see *Kyaungthas*, or 'children of the river,' passing into Buddhism without giving up their aboriginal rites.

They will offer rice, and fruits, and flowers to the spirits of the hill and stream, and the Buddhist priests, although condemning the practice as unorthodox, do not very violently oppose it."

These remarks will apply with equal force to the Burman himself.

A Burman, on being questioned, denies absolutely that he is a *nat* or spirit worshipper, and yet the daily acts of his life are never performed without some propitiatory offering being made to these guardian spirits.

Nat-sin (Spirit houses) are to be found outside many villages, especially among the Talaings. Trees of extraordinary size and growth, boulders of rock on mountain summits, or isolated in the jungle, waterfalls, volcanic springs, precipitous cliffs on the sea-shore, are all supposed to be the abode of *nats*, all more or less malignant in character.

These superstitions are not acknowledged by orthodox Buddhists as forming a part of their creed, but there can be no doubt that the Buddhism of the ordinary peasant is largely impregnated with them. It is from fear of displeasing the *nats* that the Burman ordinarily does one thing, and refrains from doing another.

There are two schools of Buddhism, the Northern and the Southern. Thibet, China, and Japan follow the Northern, and Ceylon, Burma, Siam, and other Indo-Chinese States the Southern School.

The sacred books are written in Sanscrit by the Northern School, while Pali is the sacred language of the Southern School.

It is generally accepted now by those competent to judge that Buddhism was introduced into Burma from Ceylon about 241 B.C. by Cingalese missionaries, who landed at the then seaport of Tha-tôn, and established themselves there. From this centre the new faith spread rapidly among the surrounding Talaing and Burmese kingdoms, and eventually extended itself eastwards to the Shan States and Siam.

Buddha Ghosa, a celebrated Buddhist divine, according to the opinion expressed by the late Bishop Bigandet, proceeded from Tha-tôn to Ceylon about the year 400 A.D., and after copying the Buddhist scriptures in Pali, returned with them to Tha-tôn.

In A.D. 1050 Anhaurata, the Burmese king of Pagan, laid siege to Tha-tôn, captured the city, and carried off the resident priests and the sacred books to his capital, Pagan. This king is celebrated for the zeal he exhibited in the cause of Buddhism, which is shown not only in this act of aggression, but by the numerous pagodas and temples he caused to be erected at his capital.

It will thus be seen that the introduction of Buddhism into Burma is of comparatively recent date, and hence it is not surprising that it should be mixed with the older or " aboriginal " nat worship, which it replaced.

THE SACRED BOOKS.

It has already been explained in the previous Article that Buddhism was originally introduced into Burma by missionaries from Ceylon. In the early part of the fourth century of the Christian Era, a celebrated Buddhist divine named Buddha Ghosa, said to have been a Brahmin, was deputed to Ceylon by Dhammapala, king of the Talaing country of Ramannadisa, the capital of which was Suvannabhummi, or Tha-tôn as it is now called. He embarked from the port of Bassein and, after an eventful voyage, reached Ceylon. Here he spent three years in making a complete copy of the Buddhist scriptures.

Having attained the object of his journey he returned safely with the sacred volumes to Tha-tôn.

By Buddhists in Burma the sacred books collectively are called *Bedegat Thôn-bôn*, *i.e.*, "The Three Baskets of the Law." These three divisions are respectively called :— (1) Wini. (2) Sutra. (3) Abhidhama.

1. THE WINI, or code of discipline for ecclesiastics, consists of five sections, which are as follows :—

(1) Paraxikan (Pali, *Parajika*), which treats of the four unpardonable sins. These are :—Murder, theft, sexual intercourse, and the claiming of supernatural powers.

(2)—(a) Bikshu Pa-sit (Pali, *Pachiti*), contains the regulations incumbent on the Priesthood.

(b) Bikshu Pa-sitni contains the rules and duties incumbent on Nuns.

(3) Maha Wagga⎫ Containing the codes of ecclesiastical
(4) Sula Wagga ⎬ and civil law.

(5) Pari-wa-Pata is an explanatory commentary on the four preceding books in a sort of catechetical form.

The Wini complete is written on 1,367 palm leaves, each containing twelve lines of writing. The leaves are eighteen inches in length, and the writing fifteen inches.

2. SUTRA. This is the second great division of the Bedegat. The term Sutra (Burmese *Thôt*), is said by Spence Hardy to be derived from the Pali *Suttan*, a line or thread. It is like a line, "because, as the line *(suttan)* is a mark of definition to carpenters, so is this *suttan* a rule of conduct to the wise." Also, "As flowers strung upon a line or thread are neither strewn or lost, so are the precepts which are contained herein united by this *(suttan)* line." The Sutras contain five sections comprising the following books.

1. Diga Nikè. ⎧ 1. Thot-thi Lekkan   87 Leaves.
⎨ 2. Maha Wa   103 ,,
⎩ 3. Pa-te-ya   98 ,,

2. Mitzima Nikè	1.	Mula Panatha		
	2.	Mitzuma	772	Leaves.
	3.	Upari		
3. Thanyutta Nikè.	1.	Thagata-Wagga	127	,,
	2.	Nidana	139	,,
	3.	Khanda	129	,,
	4.	Thala-Yatana	193	,,
	5.	Maha	236	,,
4. Anguttara Nikè.	1.	E-kin Guttara	25	,,
	2.	Du-kin ,,	30	,,
	3.	Ti-kin ,,	126	,,
	4.	Sadu-kin ,,	158	,,
	5.	Pyinsa-kin ,,	158	,,
	6.	Setka-kin ,,	90	,,
	7.	Thatta-kin ,,	77	,,
	8.	Atta-kin ,,	132	,,
	9.	Nowa-kin ,,	60	,,
	10.	Datha-kin ,,	151	,,
	11.	Eka-datha-kin Guttara	27	,,
5. Khudaka Nikè.	1.	Kheda Kapata	5	,,
	2.	Dhammapada	21	,,
	3.	Udan	66	,,
	4.	Itthi-Wut	39	,,
	5.	Thota-nipat	64	,,
	6.	Wimana Wuttu	41	,,
	7.	Pita	35	,,
	8.	Thera Gatha	49	,,
	9.	Thiri Gatha	21	,,
	10.	Buddha Win	39	,,
	11.	Sari-ya Pitat	16	,,
	12.	Thira Apadan	221	,,
	13.	Thiri Apadan	42	,,
	14.	Pata Lat	266	,,
	15.	Maha Niddi-tha	301	,,
		Sula Niddi-tha	262	,,
	16.	Padi-Thanbida	262	,,
	17.	Noti	99	,,
	18.	Peta-kan Padeitha	110	,,
	19.	Mi-leinda Pyinya	233	,,
	20.	Thotta-thingaha	95	,,

The Sutras contain the code of laws to be observed by lay-men.

ABHIDHAMA. This, the third great division of the sacred books, consists of a series of sermons and discourses delivered by Buddha himself to the celestial world of beings (Dewas and Brahmins). It contains the essence of the Law, and without a knowledge of its truths, the path to salvation is unobtainable. An acquaintance therefore with its principles is a necessity.

The Abhidhama is divided into seven sections. These are as follows :— Dhamma-thingani, We-bin, Dattu-gatha, Puggaba-Pyin-nyat, Katha-wuttu, Ye-meik, and Pa-htan.

(1.) Dhamma-thingani contains a summary of concise truths or principles.

(2.) We-bin describes the four great principles, viz :— *Saik*, the mind ; *sai-tabeik*, active faculties of the mind ; *yók*, substances affected by temperature ; *neik-ban*, i.e., *Nirvana*, or perfect rest and cessation from existence.

(3.) Dattu-Gatha describes the organs of animal bodies and their relations to each other.

(4.) Puggaba-Pyin-nyat treats of the twelve kinds of beings with respect to their degrees of development.

(5.) Katha-Wuttu contains two parts :—

    (a) Thagawa-da, one's own religion, with reasons for it.

    (b) Parawa-da, the religion of others, with reasons against it.

(6.) Yameik treats of the powers of good and evil, and of *abya-gala*, which is neither good nor evil.

(7.) Pa-htan treats of the four principles, with full bearings, and instances.

A complete copy of the *Bedegat Thên-bên* or Buddhist scriptures, contains 768 *aingas* 9 leaves, one *ainga* being equal to 12 leaves. The Wini takes 117 aingas 2 leaves ; the Sutras 433 aingas 11 leaves ; and the Abhidhama 217 aingas 8 leaves.

The leaves used are those of the Talipot palm, and in Burma the best are obtained from Tibayin in the Shwèbo district. In

Mandalay these leaves are sold at the rate of five annas for an ainga. Each leaf has thirteen lines of writing, and the rate for copying is Rs. 25/- per 100 leaves. The writing is scratched into the fibre of the leaf with a pointed metal style, the leaf being subsequently rubbed with crude petroleum, or earth oil, which serves the double purpose of making the writing legible, and preserving the leaf from the attacks of insects and vermin. The edges of the leaves are gilded and the complete volume strung together by means of two strings passing through holes near the ends of each leaf. An outer gilded or lacquered cover of wood completes the volume.

For a complete copy of the scriptures the charges in Mandalay are as follows :—

Palm Leaves	Rs. 155/-
Copying at Rs. 25/- per 100	620/-
Correcting and reading over, at Rs. 20 per 100 aingas	124/-
Gilding and numbering	90/-
Earth-oiling leaves	11/-
Covers of wood	5/-
Grand Total	Rs. 1005/-

RELIGIOUS BUILDINGS OF THE BUDDHISTS IN BURMA.

Burma is frequently referred to as being "the land of pagodas," and the name is rightly given. Throughout the length and breadth of the country, from the rock bound coasts to the peaks of the highest mountains bordering on distant Assam and China, the pagoda is always *en evidence*.

In addition to pagodas, of various shapes and construction, there are other buildings erected and set aside for religious purposes. These, briefly enumerated, are :—

    Kyaung, or Monastery.

    Tazaung, or Shrine.

Thein, or Hall of ordination.

Zayat, or Rest house.

Ohn-Min, Ku, or Cave dwelling.

PAGODAS.—As regards construction, the Burmese recognise two classes, *Zedi* and *Pa-hto*.

A *Zedi* is a solid pagoda of brick or stone, with no interior chamber, while a Pa-hto frequently has hollowed chambers on one or more sides. The distinction however between a *Zedi* and a *Pa-hto* is now not fully recognised, and the names are frequently used promiscuously.

Four classes of pagodas are erected by Buddhists in Burma. These are :—

    1. *Datu zedi.*
    2. *Pari-bauga zedi.*
    3. *Damma zedi.*
    4. *U-deksa zedi.*

1. DATU pagodas are those erected over the relics of Buddha or of celebrated Rahandas. As *Shin Gaudama*, the last Buddha, is stated to have passed 550 different existences, prior to his attaining Buddha-hood, the *dat-daw* or sacred relics may have been remains of any of these. Hence as pointed out by the late Dr. Forchammer, teeth of oxen, and other mammalia, are frequently treasured up as sacred relics, and these are believed by the present generation to be actual relics of the body of Buddha, in which he lived out his last existence *(Mr. F. O. Oertels' notes on a tour in Burma)*.

The relic chamber is called the *Ta-pana-taik*, and is generally situated in the solid base of the pagoda. It is usually constructed of stone, and one large flag-stone covers the aperture.

In some of the old pagodas at Tagaung the walls of the *Ta-pana-taik* were adorned with inscribed terra-cotta tablets, bearing figures of Buddha, surrounded by pagodas in relief.

2. PARI-BAUGA pagodas are those erected to enshrine the eight sacred utensils of a Buddha, Rahanda, or celebrated priest. These sacred utensils are :—*Du-gök, Ko-wot, Thin-baing* (three

PLAN
OF A
K'PONGYI-KYAUNG

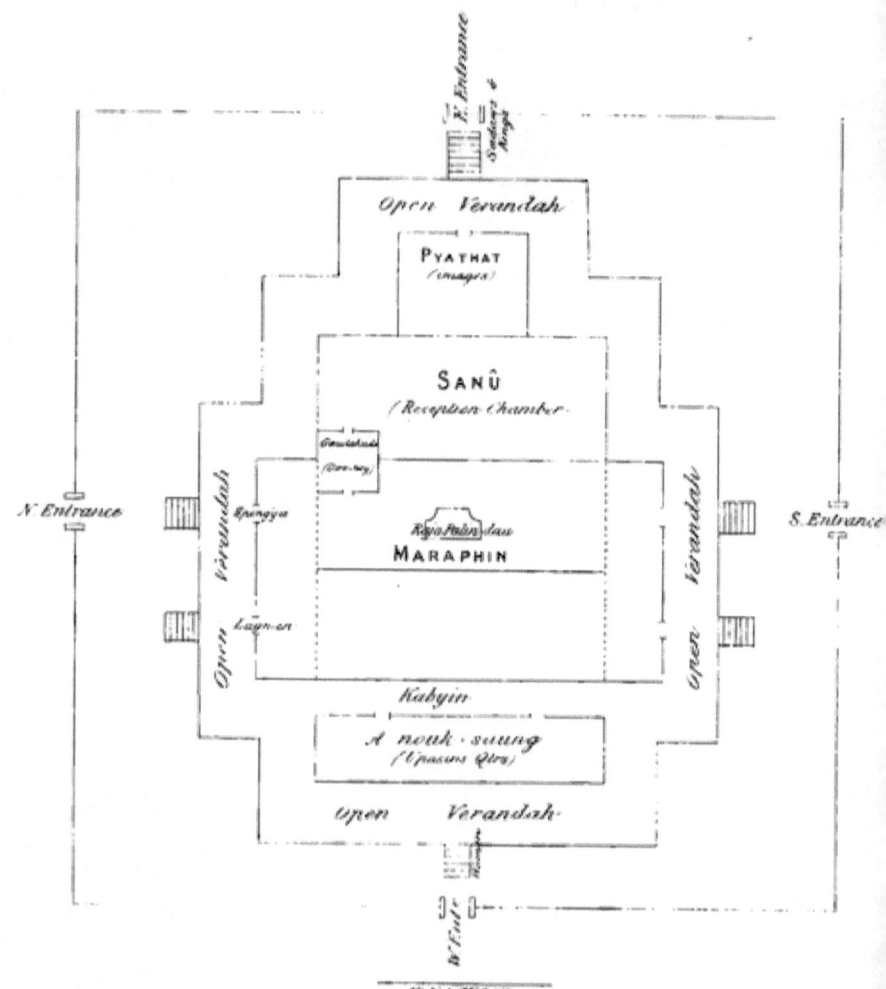

parts of the Thin-gan) or priest's robe ; *Tha-beik*, begging pot ; *Kha-ban*, belt ; *Pe-kut*, skin mat ; *At*, needle ; *Ye-zit*, filter.

3. DAMMA pagodas are those in which sacred books or writings are placed.

Mindôn Min is said to have enshrined sheets of gold and silver, on which were inscribed passages from the *Bedegat*, in the Central golden pagoda at the *Kuthodaw*, near Mandalay Hill.

4. U-DEKSA pagodas were built to enshrine images of Buddha, models in gold or silver of celebrated pagodas and other sacred articles. Nine-tenths of the pagodas in the country belong to this class.

The builder of a pagoda earns for himself the title of *Paya-taga*, by which title he is always addressed. He is also considered to have paved his way to *Neik-ban*, and to have gained great *Kutho* or merit by his pious act.

MONASTERIES.—Next to pagodas, monasteries or *Hpoungyi Kyaungs* are the most numerous of religious buildings.

As a rule they are built of teak, and many of them, especially in Rangoon and Mandalay, are highly ornamented with elaborate carving, especially on the exterior.

As the wants of the *Hpoungyis* are few, and their rule of life is fixed by the canon law of the *Wini*, the dwellings erected for them by pious founders are all more or less on one orthodox plan, any modification depending on the means at the disposal of the giver, and the wishes of the priest or priests for whom the *kyaung* is erected.

The annexed plan is that of a monastery of the usual type, and may be taken as the model on which most *kyaungs* are constructed. The arrangements of the different chambers will be seen by references to the plan. The body of the kyaung consists of the *Sanù* and the *Maraphin*.

Immediately to the east of this central chamber, or hall, is the image chamber, or shrine, surmounted by the 3, 5, or 7 roofed *pyathat*.

The Sanù is really an enclosed verandah used as a reception

chamber, and here offerings are received, and intercourse carried
on between the Priest and his supporters.

The Central hall or *Maraphin* as it is called, has its floor
slightly raised above the level of the verandah, which surrounds
the whole building. In the centre is the *Raja-palindaw* or throne,
on which is placed a large image of Gaudama. The chamber
contains the numerous offerings of the people, consisting chiefly
of lamps, chandeliers, clocks, candle-sticks, lacquered boxes in
which the sacred books are kept, mats, carpets, easy chairs, and
other articles both for use and ornament.

The *Gauda-kudi* is a small chamber used as a dormitory
by the *hpóngyi*.

To the west of the *Maraphin* is a small covered verandah
called the *Kabyin*, which is used as a refectory for the boys
located in the building. Facing this, to the west, is the *Anauk-
saung* or Western quarters, in which the Novices are housed.

As already stated, the whole *kyaung* is surrounded by a
broad verandah which is sometimes adorned with pots containing
crotons, roses, and other flowering plants. Broad flights of steps
—frequently of masonry—lead up to the verandah from different
sides of the building. That facing the Eastern entrance
is reserved for Kings and *Sadaws* (Buddhist Bishops). The
western flight is used by females. Of the others—on the North
or South sides—one is reserved for priests, and another for
lay-men.

As already stated, monasteries are generally constructed of
wood, but in the larger cities and towns brick is frequently used.
The *A-tu-ma-shi kyaung* in Mandalay, described in Route XII.,
was one of the most celebrated examples of the *ók* or *taik
kyaung*.

Another fine building is the Shwè-Yè-zaung kyaung, in close
proximity to the Arakan temple. In Moulmein the We-za-yantè
monastery, built by a wealthy Burman named Maung Hlè, at a
cost of Rs. 80,000/-, is one of the finest brick monasteries in the
country. The style of building is the same as that adopted in

the wooden structures, but the effect produced is a very coarse imitation of the graceful structures built of wood.

The builder of a *kyaung* has the honorific title of *Kyaung-taga* affixed to his name.

A *Tazaung* is generally a square shaped building surmounted by a *Pyathat* erected either as an appendage to a pagoda, or at a short distance from it. The sides are sometimes walled, and adorned with shrines and images of Buddha, and at other times left open. It is used as a resting-place for those visiting the pagoda, and the floor is either of wood, tiles, or cement.

The name is also given to the *pyathats* which adorn the gates and bastions of the city walls at Mandalay.

A *Thein* is a hall in which certain religious ceremonies are conducted, connected with the ordination of priests. They are generally erected in the compounds of monasteries. The Kalyani-sema at Pegu is one of the most celebrated buildings of this class, although now in ruins.

ZAYATS are found in every village. They are public rest-houses, erected *pro bono publico*, and are free to all.

Ohn-min, Ku or Cave dwellings are found in various parts of the country. The most celebrated are those at A-Kauk-taung on the Irrawaddi, a few miles below Prome. Others are found at Pagan, in the Sagaing Hills, in the hills opposite Mónywa, Lower Chindwin district, at Singu in the Mandalay district, and in the hills near Kyauksè. They have been excavated from the sandstone or limestone rock, and are generally provided with strong plank doors, to insure perfect isolation to the very austere hermits who inhabit them at certain seasons.

The brick temple of Pagan has been fully described in Route XVIII.

IMAGES OF BUDDHA.

Three kinds of images are found in Burma, namely :—

(1.) *Tin-bu-gwè*, or seated images. This class represents Gaudama as sitting cross-legged, his left hand open on his lap, palm upwards, the right hand resting on the right knee, palm downwards. This is the attitude supposed to have been assumed by Gaudama when meditating under the *Bhodi* tree at Gya.

(2.) *Shwè-yat-daw*, or standing images, representing Gaudama in the act of preaching, with the right hand raised.

(3.) *Shin-biu-tha-yaung*, or recumbent images, representing Gaudama in the attitude he assumed at his death when he attained *neik-ban*.

CHRISTIAN MISSIONS IN BURMA.

(From the Census Report of 1891.)

From the returns given in the last Census Report there were in 1891 a total of 120,768 Christians in the whole province, distributed as follows :—

Lower Burma...	111,982
Upper Burma...	8,786
United Province ...	120,768

The great disparity in the numbers of the two divisions of the province is due to the fact that little or no mission work was carried on in Upper Burma till after the annexation of that province in 1886.

The following table is interesting, as shewing the relative strength of each sect in ratio per 10,000 of total population :—

Denomination of Sect.	Ratio per 10,000 of total Population.
Church of England	17·053
Roman Catholics	32·268
Baptists	107·009
Methodists	·545
Wesleyans	·211
Presbyterians	·579
Lutherans	·310
Armenians	·318

Denomination of Sect.					Ratio per 10,000 of total Population.
Greeks	...	...	...	...	·019
Unitarians	...	...	...	...	·014
Plymouth Brethren		...	...	...	·004
Episcopalians	...	...	...	...	·001
Quakers	...	...	...	...	·001
Sects not returned		...	...	...	·451

By a comparison of these returns it will be seen that the Baptist, Roman Catholic, and Church of England sects are those that have met with most success, while the other sects are comparatively far behind in the race for converts. The following accounts of the foundation and progress of the different Christian missions were written specially for insertion in the last Census report, and are herewith reproduced *in extenso*.

CHURCH OF ENGLAND.

The following account of the Church of England was placed at my disposal by the Right Reverend Dr. Strachan, Lord Bishop of Rangoon.

THE CHURCH OF ENGLAND IN BURMA.

Although the English acquired a footing in Burma as early as the year 1687 by taking possession of Negrais, it was not until after the expedition of Sir Archibald Campbell in 1826, that chaplains were appointed to administer to the British troops stationed in Burma; whilst the first Church of England missionary entered upon his work in this country in 1859.

In 1855 Bishop Wilson, after visiting Akyab, landed in Rangoon on 15th November. Six days afterwards Lord Dalhousie, the Governor General, arrived, and after consultation it was agreed to build three churches to cost Rs. 35,000 each; to have one church in Rangoon, and burial grounds at all European stations. From that date the Anglican church in Burma has been under regular episcopal supervision.

Chaplains were appointed to Rangoon, Moulmein, Thayetmyo, Toungoo, and Akyab, with the primary object of ministering to the British troops stationed in those towns ; and it was not until the year 1856 that practical steps were taken for entering upon direct mission work in this country.

CHURCH OF ENGLAND MISSION IN BURMA.

Principally through the exertions of the Reverend C. S. P. Parish, Government Chaplain at Moulmein, a sum of Rs. 7,000 was collected, and the Society for the Propagation of the Gospel in Foreign Parts, on being appealed to, resolved to commence the mission with two ordained missionaries and trained school-masters with head-quarters at Moulmein.

The Reverend C. A. Shears, M.A., of St. John's College, Cambridge, reached Moulmein at the end of April, 1859. There was associated with him the Reverend T. A. Cockey, of Bishop's College, Calcutta, who spent some time in Burma. Mr. J. E. Marks arrived in 1860 and took charge of the mission school, which, under his energetic management, soon advanced both in numbers and efficiency. In 1862 Mr. Shear's health having failed, he returned to England, and the Reverend T. A. Cockey was transferred to Cawnpore. In November of the same year Mr. P. Marks joined his brother at Moulmein. During the absence of the latter in Calcutta for preparation for ordination, the Reverend R. W. Evans was placed in charge at Moulmein. The Reverend J. E. Marks returned with the Reverend H. B. Nicholls, M.A., formerly a missionary in New Brunswick, who had been appointed to the Burmese mission. His term of service was short, for being attacked with brain fever, he died on 10th December, 1864. In the beginning of 1864 Mr. Cooper arrived and took over charge of the school, the Reverend R. W. Evans having again been in temporary charge. Mr. J. Fairclough, of St. Augustine's College, joined the mission, and was ordained deacon in the month of December, 1866. At an early date in this history, girls' schools for natives were opened, both in Moulmein and Rangoon.

RANGOON.—Chiefly through the earnest representations of the Reverend H. W. Crofton, Government Chaplain, the Society resolved in 1862 to establish a mission at Rangoon. In December, 1863, a large and influential meeting was held to make known the wants of the mission ; and as a result, within a few days a sum equivalent to £570 was contributed. Early in 1864 the mission was opened under the leadership of the Reverend J. E. Marks.

ST. JOHN'S COLLEGE. The foundation stone of this, the largest S.P.G. School in the country, was laid in March, 1869, by General Fytche, and the school was opened for pupils on 26th October of the same year. Government contributed Rs. 2,000 towards the cost of building, on condition that a similar sum was provided by the Society. About Rs. 2,000 which had been expended on another site, was allowed by Government to stand as part of this sum. The rest was supplied by the Calcutta S.P.G. Committee from funds in their holding, which had been chiefly collected in Burma. Large additions have been made to the premises since they were opened.

KEMENDINE was separated from Rangoon and made a distinct mission district in 1877 under the charge of the Reverend James A. Colbeck, and Pazundaung, to the east, was made a mission district under the Reverend J. Rickard in 1883.

MANDALAY.—In 1869 the Reverend J. E. Marks, on the invitation of the king, proceeded for a second time to Mandalay. The king built a school-room, clergy house, and church for the mission, and for some time showed his favour towards it. Her Majesty Queen Victoria presented a font to the church. This was consecrated by the Bishop of Calcutta on the 31st July, 1873. The school proved highly successful, and Mr. Marks continued at Mandalay until January, 1875, when the Reverend J. Fairclough took over charge until March, 1877, being succeeded by the Reverend C. H. Chard. Towards the end of

1878 the mission was in the hands of the Reverend J. A. Colbeck, who was compelled to leave Mandalay at the close of 1879 with the British Residents and the other Europeans. By the very first passenger vessel proceeding after the annexation the Reverend J. A. Colbeck returned to Mandalay and re-opened the mission.

TOUNGOO.—Without entering into any detailed account of the causes which led up to the action of the Bishop of Calcutta and the S.P.G., it may suffice to say that a new mission was opened in Toungoo in 1873 by the appointment of the Reverend C. Warren to that sphere of labour. His arduous labours as chaplain to the English, and missionary to the Burmese and Karens, and the loss of his young wife, led to the death of this devoted clergyman in 1875, and in the following year he was succeeded by the Reverend T. W. Windley, M.A.

SHWEBO.—A desirable site being secured, a new mission was opened in this important centre by the appointment of the Reverend Francis William Sutton (M.R.C.S. Eng.) in 1887. Mr. Sutton's health failing, he had to resign his appointment in 1889 and return to England, the Reverend H. M. Stockings taking over charge of the mission.

PYINMAMA.—A new mission was opened in this town by the appointment of the Reverend J. Tsan Baw in 1890.

BISHOPS.—On St. Thomas' day, 1877, the Reverend J. H. Titcombe, D.D., was consecrated first Bishop of Rangoon. The Diocese was founded after the death of Bishop Milman, seventh Bishop of Calcutta. Grants towards the endowment were made by the Society for Promoting Christian Knowledge, by the Society for the Propagation of the Gospel in Foreign Parts, and by the Colonial Bishopric Fund. A large portion of the endowment was raised in the Winchester Diocese as the result of a meeting held at the house of Sir William Farquher, Bart., on the 7th October, 1875, when it was resolved that £10,000 should be raised for the purpose. As a perpetual memorial of this, part of the Episcopal seal of Winchester appears in that of Rangoon.

Bishop Titcombe worked indefatigably though with impaired health, and amidst much domestic affliction, when on a visitation in the Karen Hills, he slipped over a rock and received injuries from which he never recovered. He resigned the Bishopric early in 1882, and the present Bishop, the Right Reverend T. M. Strachan was appointed, having been consecrated in Lambeth Palace Chapel on 1st May, 1882. In 1887 fresh Letters Patent were issued extending the boundaries of the Diocese, so as to include all additions made to the Empire by the annexation of Upper Burma.

CHURCHES.—The first English Church built in Burma was that of St. Matthew's, at Moulmein. It was erected in 1832, and was replaced by a new and very handsome structure in 1890. St. John the Baptist's Church at Kyaukpyu, 1846; St. Mark's, Akyab 1855; Christ Church, Thayetmyo, 1860; St. John the Evangelist, St. John's College, 1869; St. John's, Port Blair, 1859; Holy Trinity, Rangoon, 1864; St. John the Baptist, Toungoo, 1870; St. John the Evangelist, Bassein, 1870; Christ Church, Mandalay, 1873; Christ Church, Port Blair, 1872; Christ Church, Insein, 1882; St. Augustine's, Moulmein, 1882; St. Michael's School Chapel, Kemendine, 1881; St. James, Tavoy, 1885; Christ Church, Tharrawaddy, 1885; St. Mark's, Prome, 1881; All Saints, Henzada, 1884; St. George's, Madaya, 1890; Meiktela, 1891; St. Luke's, Shwebo, 1887; Cantonment, 1890; St. Phillip's, Rangoon, 1887; St. Paul's, Toungoo, 1887.

THE ROMAN CATHOLICS.

The native Christians in Upper Burma who belong to this Church far out-number the native adherents of all the other denominations put together. These Christians are found in the Shwebo, Sagaing, and Yeu districts. The original of these Christian settlements and the narration of the persevering efforts of successive missions to keep alive and to further spread Christianity in Burma, form an interesting page in the history of the country.

The so-called native Christians found in the districts of Yeu, Shwebo, and lower Chindwin are the descendants of those Portuguese and natives of India, taken prisoners in 1614 when Phillippe de Britto was captured and his colony at Syriam broken up. The bulk of his followers were transported to Ava, and settled down in villages on the banks of the Mu. The tolerance of their Burman conquerors permitted them to retain their own religion.

These Christians were recruited by other captives, taken prisoners when Alaung-pya again conquered Syriam, and subsequently the capture of Yodia or Yuthia, the Siamese capital, by Sin-Byu-shin, brought a further addition, as the conquerors carried back with them the Vicar Apostolic, and part of his flock from the latter place.

As Bishop Bigandet points out, the trace of their foreign extraction is still to be seen in the faces of these Christians.

Besides these native Christians since the date of the arrival of the first Barnabite missionary, Father Calchi, the Roman Catholic Church has steadily received additions by conversion, and hence we may divide the returns of those belonging to this Church into three divisions.

  (1.) Foreign residents.
  (2.) Converts to Christianity and their descendants.
  (3.) The descendants of the old Portuguese settlers.

How the Christians fared after the transportation to Upper Burma we have but little information till in 1719 the first missionary of the Barnabite Mission arrived. He died in 1727, and was succeeded by Father Jallazia, who built a church in Syriam. In 1743 he returned to Burma, as the first consecrated Bishop of Elisma, *in partibus.*

In the troublous times that followed the Bishop was killed, and when after the capture of Syriam by the Burmans, the Christians living there were transported to Upper Burma, the missionaries still clung to their flocks, and Bishop Percoto, who succeeded, followed his people to Upper Burma, and eventually died in Ava in 1776. Among the best known of the Barnabite Fathers was Father San-Germano, who arrived in Burma in 1783, where he remained till 1806.

The mission, in spite of many vicissitudes, still continued to flourish, but the French Revolution, and the consequent war in Europe, and the heavy losses caused by death and disease in the ranks of the missionaries weakened the Order so much, that the heads of the Society were forced to give up the Burmese Mission, which was made over to the Priests of the Propaganda. One of the earliest of the missionaries of this Order was Father Domingo Carolly, who died but recently in Myaung-mya, where he had lived and laboured for more than 50 years. In 1840 the mission was made over to the Society of the Oblats of Turin. Political troubles in Italy finally caused the transfer of the mission to the Seminary of Foreign Missions in Paris in 1856. The conquest of Pegu by the British had widened the field of labour, and the usefulness of the Mission. The time had come for increasing the scope of the Mission; in 1856 the Right Reverend Bishop Bigandet was consecrated Bishop of Ramatha, and took over charge of the Pegu and Ava Missions.

PRESBYTERIANS.

The Presbyterian community in Burma is small, and is affected by any change in the garrison of the military posts in Burma.

The Presbyterian Church was first established in Rangoon in 1873, owing to the exertions of the Reverend G. Fordyce, and the present church was built in 1875. In 1884 the church was affiliated to the Presbyterian Church of England.

In 1885 new ground was broken. Hitherto the Church had not attempted any mission amongst the natives of the country, but in that year a mission to the Chinese was begun and attended with some success.

In 1884 the minister of the Kirk was recognised as Acting Chaplain to the troops.

BAPTISTS.

The following account of the American Baptist Mission is extracted from the authorised history of the Society.

The history of the Karen race for the past fifty years is so intimately connected with the foundation and success of the American Baptist Mission that any account of the Karens and Baptist Christians amongst them would be unintelligible without a brief narration of the efforts of these missionaries who have done so much for their moral and intellectual, as well as their religious welfare. The American Baptist Mission has a long record of good work. The large number of converts it can show are not the results of any spasmodic effort, which may at any time die away, but the Baptist mission has now become an integral part of the religious life of a large and yearly increasing section of the population of the country, and no excuse is necessary for entering at some length into the history of a movement that has played so important a part in the national life of Burma.

To Marsden and Chater and the Baptist Mission of Serampur belongs the credit of establishing the first Protestant Mission to Burma. In 1807 they first reached Rangoon, where they found Roman Catholic Missions already established, and were kindly received by the priests of the mission. Next year Dr. Carey's son joined the mission. In 1809 a mission house was built, and in 1803 Dr. Carey went to Ava, starting just four days before the arrival of Messrs. Judson and Rice, to whom, on his return, Dr. Carey transferred the Mission.

The American Baptist Mission was founded by Messrs. Judson and Rice, who, disappointed in their design of working in India, finally landed in Rangoon on the 14th July, 1813. From the very first the missonaries met with opposition, but nothing daunted, the mission, now recruited by several new members, set up a printing press in Rangoon in 1816. Troublous times followed, but the tact of their medical missionary, Dr. Pryce, for a time brought them into favour with the Burmese court. In

1824, war between the British and the Burmese broke out, and not altogether unreasonably, the Burmese could not distinguish the British and Americans. Messrs. Hough and Wade, who were then living in Rangoon, were seized, but were rescued on the fall of the town into the hands of the British. Messrs. Judson and Rice, who were with their wives at Ava, were imprisoned and were finally used as intermediaries when the Treaty of Yandabo was concluded in 1827.

The annexation of Tenasserim and Arakan opened new fields of labour. The mission was started in Tavoy by Mr. Boardman. He it was who first turned his attention to the Karens. Hitherto, as might have been expected, the mission was purely to the Burmese. But the conquest of the Burmese had brought into prominence the hitherto down-trodden race of Karens. The success that attended the new departure at once pointed out to the missionaries where they could most readily find converts. Mr. Boardman died in 1831, but his work was carried on by Dr. Mason. In the same year the mission at Kyaukpyu was founded by Mr. Wade. In 1834, Mr. Judson finished his translation of the Bible into Burmese, but civil war and anarchy in Ava and the dread of a new war with the British induced the missionaries in Rangoon to transfer their schools to Moulmein, Akyab, and Sandoway. Here other missions to the Karens were opened. But though their success was at the time great and Karens flocked across the passes of the Arakan Yomas to join their country-men who had already escaped from the tyranny of Burmese rule in Pegu, and readily became converts, the deadly climate of Arakan proved fatal to the missionaries, and one after the other succumbed, and in 1852 the conquest of Pegu by the British once more opened the way to re-establishing the mission in Pegu. Missions were accordingly opened in Toungoo, Rangoon, and Bassein. From the very first the Karens flocked to the missions. In Toungoo especially the labour of Dr. Mason and his coadjutors met with astonishing success; and there were in 1891 22,313 Baptist Christians in Toungoo alone, of whom

21,957 were natives. In 1872 in this district the Christians of all
denominations only amounted to 7,867. It is, however, quite
certain that many were omitted. In 1881 the number of
christians had risen to 18,191, of whom only 11,510 were
Baptists.

In Bassein in 1872, when no return of sects was made, there
were 16,078 Christians. In 1881 of Baptists alone there were
18,704, and in 1891 24,298, of whom 30 only were of European
descent. These figures speak more eloquently than words of the
fast increasing hold Christianity is acquiring amongst the Karens,
for at present in these two districts the majority of the converts
belong to that race. But, as already stated, missions to the
Burmese, though not so successful in their result, have been
steadily maintained, nor have other races been neglected. For
some years past Dr. Bunker has worked amongst the Red Karens
and Dr. Cushing amongst the Shans. The last thirty years has
consolidated the position of the mission, which is now to a great
extent self-supported by the converts.

WESLEYANS AND THE METHODISTS.

The distinction between these two sects is so slight that
it is possible there may be some confusion in the return. It
is more than probable that the few Episcopalians, of whom
only one apparently survives, have been now shewn as
Methodists, belonging to the Episcopalian Methodist Church in
Rangoon.

The following account of the Episcopalian Methodist
Church in Burma is from the pen of the Reverend Julius Smith,
the Minister of the Church in Rangoon :—

"The advent of the Methodist Episcopal Church in Burma
is comparatively recent. In June, 1879, the Reverend J. M.
Thoburn, D.D. (now Bishop Thoburn, of Calcutta), came to
Rangoon on an evangelistic tour, and preached in the old
Baptist Chapel, since pulled down. The chapel was freely
offered for the purpose. The converts growing too much for

the church, the City Hall was secured, where at the end of his
two weeks services a church was organized.

The site for a church and parsonage was immediately
secured in Fraser and Phayre Streets, and buildings immediately
erected for church and parsonage, and which are still occupied
for that purpose.

The little organization there begun entered upon a career
of great activity, which has been attended with every decided
prosperity.

The Reverend R. E. Carter was appointed the first pastor of
the church in June, 1879, and remained one year. In June,
1880, the Reverend Y. E. Robinson became pastor, and
continued till March, 1886. His pastorate was one of activity
and success. He erected a commodious building in Lewis
Street for a Girls' High School; this school and its beginning has
had a good patronage and a career of usefulness. Mr. Robinson
also started a work among the sailors, and founded the "Seamen's
Rest," which still exists and carries on the work of its founder.

Mission work has been begun in a small way among the
Tamils, Telugus, and Burmese. Our missionary force in
Burma—teachers, helpers, catechists, etc.—numbers about 25.

Of Methodists and Wesleyans the bulk are resident in
Rangoon. There is also a small Wesleyan community in
Mandalay, where the Reverend W. R. Winston, who is in
charge of the mission, has opened a home for lepers.

Flourishing missions of this community also carry on work
at Pakôkkû and Mônywa in Upper Burma; the former under
the superintendence of the Reverend A. Bestall, and the latter
under the Reverend A. Woodward. Attached to each is a
promising Anglo-vernacular school under Government inspection.

CHIEF TOWNS.

The following list gives the principal Towns in Burma, with the population :—

LOWER BURMA.

Rangoon	...	180,324
Moulmein	...	55,785
Akyab	...	37,938
Bassein	...	30,177
Henzada	...	19,762
Prome	...	30,022
Thayetmyo	...	17,101
Toungoo	...	11,232

UPPER BURMA.

Mandalay	...	188,815
Myingyan	...	19,790
Pakôkkû	...	19,972
Sagaing	...	9,934
Shwebo	...	9,934
Bhamo	...	8,048
Kyauksè	...	7,201

HISTORICAL SUMMARY.

(The following summary of the History of Burma is taken in extenso from the Administration Report for 1893-4) :—

The early History of Burma, so far as it can be gathered from the native records, show that in former days several distinct races and dynasties occupied different parts of the country. The Burman dynasties of Tagaung and Pagan, Ava, Prome, and Taungoo, the Talaing kings of Pegu and Martaban, and the Shan rulers of Ava and Sagaing exercised control over a a more or less extended sphere, at times succeeding in subduing the whole tract of Burma proper, and over-running the neighbouring kingdoms of Arakan, Siam, and the Shan States, and at times dwindling in power before the uprising of powerful kingdoms previously subjected, or the inroads of Mongols, Shans and Chinese from beyond the border.

The earliest European connection with Burma was in 1519, when the Portuguese concluded a treaty with the king of Pegu and established factories at Martaban and Syriam. Towards the close of the 16th century the Dutch obtained possession of the island of Negrais, and about the year 1612 the English East India Company had agents and factories at Syriam, Prome, Ava, and perhaps Bhamo.

About the middle of the 17th century all European merchants were expelled from the country owing to a dispute between the Burmese Governor of Pegu and the Dutch.

The Dutch never returned. In 1688, the Burmese Governor of Syriam wrote to the English Governor of Madras inviting

British merchants to settle in Syriam. A factory was built there, and others at Negrais and Bassein. The French also had a settlement at Syriam. Meanwhile the Burmese dynasty of Ava, which had obtained supremacy throughout Burma under Bayinhaung was harassed by in-roads from China and Manipur, and finally destroyed by the rebellion of the Talaing kingdom of Pegu.

After some years of Talaing supremacy, a new Burmese dynasty was established by Alaungpya, who succeeded in uniting his country-men, the Burmese, and crushing the Talaings. In 1755 Alaungpya founded Rangoon to celebrate his conquest of the Talaings, and destroyed Syriam, which resisted for some months.

The English merchants at Syriam favoured the Burmans, and the French the Talaings, but both attempted to keep on friendly terms with the other side when it appeared likely to be successful. After Alaungpya's success he found that the French had been supplying warlike stores to the Talaings, and he put all Frenchmen to death. Though the English had at times supported the Talaings they were granted the island of Negrais and a factory at Bassein, but in 1759 they were again suspected of supplying arms to the rebels and the factories were destroyed, ten Englishmen and a hundred natives of India being murdered. In the following year Alaungpya died while laying siege to Ayuthia, the capital of Siam, and the English obtained permission from his successor, Naungdawgyi, to re-establish the Bassein factory, though all compensation for the massacre was peremptorily refused. Sinbyushin, who succeeded his brother Naungdawgyi, took Manipur and Siam, and defeated two in-roads from China. He died in 1776, and was succeeded by his brother Bodawpaya, who conquered Arakan in 1784. This brought Burma into collision with the British in Chittagong. The Arakanese outlaws took refuge over the border and harassed the Burmese rulers by inroads from British territory. The Burmese demanded that they should be given up, and endeavoured to pursue them in British territory. This gave rise to friction, and in order to

assist in the adjustment of matters in dispute, an Envoy was sent
to Burma in 1795, by the Governor General of India. In 1796
a resident was deputed to Rangoon. In 1819 Bodawpaya died
and was succeeded by his grandson Bagyidaw. Matters had not
improved on the border, and in 1824 the Burmese invaded
Manipur, and Maha Bandula, the great Burmese General, started
with an army from Ava to take command in Arakan and invade
Bengal.

The British Government formally declared war against
Burma on the 5th March, 1824. The Burmese were driven out
of Assam, Kachar, and Manipur and Rangoon was occupied
by a force which was detailed from the main invasion. The
troops suffered much from sickness as soon as the rain began,
and all movements by land became impracticable. Between
August and November, Mergui, Tavoy, Martaban, and Pegu
were occupied. In December the British force occupying
Rangoon had been reduced by sickness and detached
expeditions to about 1,300 Europeans and 2,500 natives fit
for duty.

The Burmese, under Maha Bandula, made a determined
effort to drive the invaders into the sea. A Burmese army, said
to have numbered 60,000 men, surrounded the position and
advanced to the attack. The attack was repulsed with great
slaughter, and the Burmese army dwindled away, a portion of it
retiring to Danubyu, which Maha Bandula fortified with great
skill for a further effort. The British troops having been
reinforced marched up the valley of the Irrawaddy, and on the
2nd April, 1825, took Danubyu. Maha Bandula was killed in
the cannonade, and with him all serious resistance came to an
end. Prome was occupied on the 2nd April and the troops went
into Cantonments for the rains. Meanwhile a second British
army had occupied Arakan with the intention of crossing the
Yoma into Burma from the west, but owing to the difficulties of
the country and the unhealthiness of the climate, the scheme
was abandoned.

E

In September, 1825, the Burmese endeavoured to treat, but as they would not agree to the terms offered, hostilities recommenced, and in December the British advanced, and after several actions with the Burmese troops, reached Yandabo on the 16th February. Here the Envoys of the King signed a treaty ceding to the British Assam, Arakan, and the coast of Tenasserim, and agreeing to pay a million sterling towards the expenses of the war. Rangoon was retained by the British until the end of the year, when the second instalment of the indemnity was paid. The British re-built Moulmein, which became the capital of the new British province of Tenasserim. In November, 1825, a commercial treaty was signed at Ava, but it was not until 1830 that a Resident at Ava was appointed under the treaty.

In 1837 Bagyidaw was deposed by his brother Tharrawaddy, who in 1846 was succeeded by his son Pagan Min.

In 1852, owing to a succession of outrages committed on British subjects by the Burmese Governor of Rangoon, for which all reparation was refused, the British again declared war against the king of Burma, and towards the close of the same year Lord Dalhousie proclaimed that the whole of the province of Pegu, as far north as the parallel of latitude six miles north of the fort at Mye-dè was annexed to the British Empire. Almost immediately after this Pagan Min was deposed by his brother Mindòn Min, who ruled his curtailed kingdom with wisdom and success.

The pacification of Pegu and its reduction to order occupied about ten years of constant work. In 1862 Her Majesty's possessions in Burma, namely, the provinces of Arakan, Pegu, Martaban, and Tenasserim were amalgamated and formed into the province of British Burma under the administration of a Chief Commissioner. Lieutenant Colonel Phayre was appointed the first Chief Commissioner of Burma. In 1867 a treaty was concluded at Mandalay between the British and Burmese Governments providing for the mutual extradition of criminals, the free intercourse of traders, and the establishment of permanent diplomatic relations between the two countries. In October, 1878, King Mindôn died and was succeeded by his son, King Thibaw. Early in 1879 the execution of a number of the members of the Royal family at Mandalay excited much horror in Lower Burma, and matters became much strained between the two countries, owing to the indignation amongst Englishmen at the barbarities of the Burmese Court, and the resentment in the minds of the king and his courtiers at the attitude of the British resident in Mandalay, the Government of India withdrew their representative from the Burmese Court. During the reign of king Thibaw matters drifted from bad to worse. The Central Government lost control of many of the outlying districts, and the elements of disorder on the British frontier were a standing menace to the peace of the country. The court, in contravention of the express terms of the treaty of 1869, created monopolies to the detriment of the trade both of England and Burma, and while the Indian Government was unrepresented at Mandalay, representatives of Italy and France were welcomed, and two separate Embassies were sent to Europe for the purpose of contracting new, and if possible, close alliances with sundry European powers. Matters were brought to a crisis towards the close of 1885, when the Burmese Court imposed a fine of £230,000 upon the Bombay Burma Trading Corporation, and refused to comply with a suggestion of the Indian Government that the cause of complaint should be investigated by an impartial arbitration.

In view of the long series of unsatisfactory episodes in the British relations with Burma during king Thibaw's reign, the Government of India decided once for all to adjust the relations between the two countries. An ultimatum was despatched to king Thibaw requiring him to suspend action against the Corporation, to receive at Mandalay an Envoy from the Viceroy, who should be received and treated with the respect due to the Government which he represented, and to regulate the external

F. I

relations of the country, in accordance with the advice of the Government of India.

This ultimatum was despatched on the 22nd October, 1885. On the 9th November a reply was received in Rangoon amounting to an unconditional refusal of the terms laid down. On the 7th November King Thibaw issued a proclamation calling on his subjects to drive the British heretics into the sea. On the 14th November, 1885, the British expedition crossed the frontier and advanced to Mandalay without encountering any serious resistance. Ava was reached on the 26th November, and an Envoy from the King signified his submission. On the 28th November the British occupied Mandalay, and next day King Thibaw was sent down the river to Rangoon, whence he was afterwards transferred to India. Upper Burma was formally annexed on the 1st January, 1886, and the work of restoring the country to order and introducing settled Government commenced.

For some years the country was disturbed by the lawless spirits who had been multiplying under the late régime, but by the close of 1889 all the larger bands of marauders were broken up, and since 1890 the country has enjoyed more freedom from violent crime than the province formerly known as British Burma.

RELATIONS WITH CHINA.

The records of China and Burma generally speaking corroborate each other in recounting a long series of wars between the two countries previous to the accession of Alompra.

From the year 1790 complementary presents were exchanged between the Burmese and Chinese Courts with more or less regularity every ten years or thereabout. At the time of the annexation negotiations were opened with China on the subject of our relations with that country through Upper Burma. The Chinese manifested a friendly spirit in these negotiations.

A convention signed at Pekin on the 24th July, 1886, provided, amongst other matters, for the continuance of the

Decennial Missions, the recognition by China of British rule in Burma, the delimitation of the frontier and the encouragement of international trade. Negotiations are now proceeding regarding the demarcation of the boundary between the two countries.

RELATIONS WITH SIAM.

The history of the relations of this province with Siam is principally concerned with the efforts made to maintain the peace on the Siamese frontier, and to secure protection for British subjects in the Siamese province of Zimmè, which adjoins the Salween district. In 1874 a treaty, framed with a view to the repression of violent crimes on the frontier, and the protection of British subjects travelling or residing in Zimmè and the neighbouring provinces, was concluded with the king of Siam. This treaty was found to be quite ineffectual in securing the desired ends, and in 1878 Major C. W. Street, of the British Burma Commission, was deputed to visit Zimmè and Bankok with a view to ascertaining by local enquiry the real necessities of the case, and obtaining satisfactory assurances from the Siamese Government. The mission was so far successful that much valuable information was obtained, and arrangements were subsequently made for placing a British Vice-Consul at Zimmè ; the first Vice-Consul arrived at Cheingmai in May, 1884. On the 3rd September, 1883, a treaty was concluded which provided among other matters for the issue of pass-ports, the extradition of criminals, the trial in Siam of cases in which British subjects are concerned, and the working of forests in Siam by British subjects. On the 30th November, 1885, a supplementary article to the treaty of 3rd September, 1883, was signed providing for extradition of criminals between Burma and all the conterminous territories of Siam. In accordance with the treaty of 1883, pass-ports are granted by Deputy Commissioners to British subjects travelling in Siam. In 1887 an order in council prescribed the registration of all British subjects resident in Siam. This was superseded in 1889 by another order in council which regulates also the exercise of civil and criminal jurisdiction by Consular Courts in Siam. Our relations with Siam have continued friendly up to the present time.

MATERIAL PROGRESS.

This brief historical sketch may be concluded with a few statistics regarding the material condition of the people of Burma. The Census of 1891 showed that in Lower Burma the population had increased during the past decade at the rate of 2·39 % per annum, and the area under cultivation at the rate of 159,122 acres per annum. In spite of this the standard of living among the agricultural classes had in no way deteriorated, and large areas of cultivable waste land still exist, and in most districts may be had for the asking.

Upper Burma is not as fertile as the Lower province, and the rain-fall is capricious, but the soil is well able to support a much larger population than is now dependent on it. The Trade of the province has increased from Rs. 173⅔ millions in 1881-82 to Rs. 253¾ millions in 1891-92. During the same period the net demand in Lower Burma of Land Revenue, 10 % cess and Capitation Tax rose from Rs. 98,93,102, to Rs. 1,38,64,100, and the incidence of these taxes from Rs. 265 to Rs. 298 per head of the population. The wages of unskilled labour have risen from 9 annas to 10 annas 6 pies per diem. In Upper Burma wages are lower, but show a tendency to increase.

BURMESE ADMINISTRATION.

The king was a despotic ruler. He could command the unpaid services of any of his subjects, was the owner of all the land, and the receiver of all estates of persons dying intestate. No one was permitted to possess property, except by the king's favour.

A repetition of his titles will convey a clearer idea of his might and dignity. These were :—

(1.) Lord of Elephants.
(2.) Lord of many White Elephants.
(3.) Lord of Gold, Silver, Rubies, Amber, and Jade.
(4.) Sovereign of the Empires of Thunaparanta, Jambudipa, and other great empires and countries, and of all Umbrella-bearing Chiefs.
(5.) The Supporter of Religion.
(6.) Descendant of the Sun.
(7.) Arbiter of Life.
(8.) King of Righteousness.
(9.) King of Kings.
(10.) Possessor of Boundless Dominion and Supreme Wisdom.

The administration of his Dominions was carried on by ministers selected from among the most competent of his subjects. These ministers were of two classes. One class, forming what was called the *Hlutdaw* or Great Council of State, consisted of four ministers termed *Wungyis*, in whom all administrative power was vested by the King.

The term *W'ŭngyi* signifies " a big burden " or metaphorically " the bearer of the burden." Hence the term may be said to imply a Minister of State. Each of these Ministers had an assistant termed a *W'ŭn-dauk*. Besides these officers there were a number of *Sayè-dau-gyis* or Royal Scribes, who ranked as Assistant Secretaries.

The Council met in a large hall immediately to the south-east of the Palace. The King himself was President of the Council, but he seldom attended its meetings. Mindòn Min deputed one of the senior Princes to preside, but his son Thibaw, on ascending the throne, appointed himself as President.

The duties of the Hlûtdaw were to give effect to the orders of the King with regard to the government of the country, to legislate, to appoint officers to carry on the work of the Administration, to hear and decide Civil and Criminal appeals from the District Courts, to register all State documents, to direct Military operations, and to receive Ambassadors from Foreign States.

The Second class of officials were termed *Atwin-wŭns* (bearers of the burdens of the interior). They were four in number, and formed the Byè-daik or the King's Privy Council. The Council met in one of the Palace chambers, and its duties were to discuss State affairs with the King, and to communicate the King's orders to the Hlûtdaw. The officials specially deputed from the king with orders to the Hlûtdaw were called *Thandauzins* (the transmitters of the Royal Voice).

For administrative purposes the country was divided into provinces called *Myos*, which were named after the chief towns. These *Myos* were divided into *Taiks* or districts, the Taiks into town-ships, and the town-ships into *Ywas* or villages and hamlets.

The governor of a Myo or province was called a *W'ŭn*. His pay was from Rs. 200/- to Rs. 300/- per mensum, and his establishment consisted of one *Na-kan* (pay Rs. 50/-) one *Sayé* (pay Rs. 50/-) with as many more *sayé* (clerks) as he chose to appoint himself. In some districts a *Taung-hmu* was also appointed, whose duties were to arrest and detain criminals and generally assist the Wûn. For military service the Myo was also divided into *Thwè-thauks*, to each of which a *Thwè-thaukgyi* was appointed. In some districts these officers were called *Myin-gaungs*.

Immediately subordinate to the Wûn was the *Wûn-Sayè*, who was appointed by the King and worked under the orders of the Wûn or District officer. Next in rank in the descending scale was the *Taik-ôk* or Circle officer. His office was hereditary and he enjoyed the same privileges as the *Thûgyi*, only on a more extended scale. The *Thûgyis* or *Ywa-Thûgyis* formed the next and lowest grade. They received their appointments direct from the King, and the office was usually hereditary, although outsiders frequently gained the coveted post by the favour of the Hlùtdaw. The jurisdiction of a Thûgyi extended to one large village or to a group of smaller villages, and his chief duties were to collect the Revenue, to suppress Crime, and to try Petty cases, both Civil and Criminal, within his circle limits.

He had the power to appoint *Gaungs* to assist him when his circle happened to be large. These were chosen from among the Village Elders, and received for their services a small commission on the revenue collected.

The Thûgyi prepared the assessment rolls for the Thathameda Tax, and submitted them to the *Taik-ôk*, who in his turn forwarded them to the Wûn.

CIVIL AND CRIMINAL JURISDICTION.

The Table given on the following page was prepared by the Kinwûn Mingyi for Stevenson's Anglo-Burmese Dictionary, from which it is extracted. It shows at a glance the constitution and powers of the different Courts.

Name of Court.	Title of Judge.	Jurisdiction.	Value of appealable cases.	To what Court appeal lay.
Thûgyis' Court.	Thûgyi.	All suits below Rs. 500/- in value.	All suits exceeding Rs. 20/- in value.	District Wûn's Court.
District Wûns' Court.	District Wûn.	All suits below Rs. 1,000/- in value.	Ditto.	Divisional Wûn's Court.
Divisional Wûn's Court.	Divisional Wûn.	Ditto.	Ditto.	Civil Court.
Civil Court.	Civil Judge.	All suits without limit of value.	All suits over Rs. 1,000/- in value.	Judicial Commissioner's Court.
Judicial Commissioner's Court.	Judicial Commissioner.	Ditto.	All suits over Rs. 5,000/- in value.	Council of Minister's Court.
Council of Minister's Court.	Ministers in Council.	Ditto.	All suits from Rs. 5,000/- upwards.	Hlûtdaw.
Hlûtdaw.	Mingyis.	Ditto.	Ditto.	The Royal Chamber.
The Royal Chamber.	His Majesty the King.	Ditto.		.

The Thûgyi tried all petty cases both Civil and Criminal within his circle. Appeals from his court were heard by the Wûn, against whose decision appeal lay to the court of the Divisional Wûn. From this Court the appeal was carried to the Capital, the final settlement of the suit being adjusted by the King himself, in the Presence Chamber, with the assistance of the Wûngyis.

The Civil law in force was nominally that of the *Dama-thats*, but the judges knew little or nothing of these Codes, and as many of them openly received bribes, the suit was generally won by the side having the longest purse. Ten per cent. on the value of each suit was collected and paid into the Royal Treasury.

For Criminal suits justice depended more or less on the will of the officer trying the case than on points of law. The Wûn had powers of life and death, and could inflict any punishment he liked.

Nearly all crimes, except offences against the State and dacoity, were punished by fine. Dacoits were sometimes put to death, but more frequently imprisoned until ransomed by payment of a sum of money.

The principal punishments inflicted for criminal offences were Fine, Imprisonment, Whipping, Crucifixion and Transportation.

The amount of fine levied for any particular offence depended upon the caprice of the judge and the ability of the delinquent to pay the sum demanded. Imprisonment was merely nominal. The prisoners were confined at night in an enclosure under the care of a jailor.

The most desperate characters were secured by the feet between logs of wood placed parallel to one another. Sometimes these logs were hauled off the ground, and the unhappy prisoners had to spend the night suspended head down in this inhuman fashion. No arrangements were made by the officials for feeding the prisoners, who had to rely solely upon their friends for the supply of their daily food. Many were released during the day to enable them to beg their food in the city, town, or village in which the jail was situated, returning in the evening to be locked up.

Whipping was permitted as a punishment, and one of the most cruel ordeals was that known as *Maung-kyaw*. The prisoner (his hands tied behind his back) was taken to all the villages in the circle, or to the different quarters of the town, his offence proclaimed by beat of gong (hence the name given to the punishment), and at each centre was severely beaten by the Court officials appointed for the purpose. Death not unfrequently resulted from the severity of the punishment.

Crucifixion was the punishment frequently awarded for murder, dacoity, or other violent and diabolical crimes. The cross consisted of a Bamboo frame-work, to the X shaped cross-bars of which the limbs of the victim were securely fastened. The cross was then fixed in the ground, the site chosen being either on rising ground near a public road, on an island or sand-bank in the river, or on an adjacent promontory. The victim remained exposed in this state till death relieved him of his sufferings.

Transportation was the punishment for rebels. The place chosen was that most celebrated for the malarious nature of the climate. Such a place was Meza Chaung, in the Katha district,

Mogaung was also a favourite settlement in Thibaw Min's time. In most cases it amounted to a death sentence.

REVENUES.

The principal sources of Revenue in the King's time were as follows :—

(1.) Thathameda.   (2.) Kaing-gûn.   (3.) Irrigation Tax.
(4.) Fisheries.   (5.) Ferries.   (6.) Broker's Tax.
                   (7.) Monoplies.

(1.) THATHAMEDA.—This was the Householder's Property Tax, and averaged Rs. 10/- per family. The Tax was first levied in the year A.D. 1862 during the reign of Mindôn Min. The rate originally demanded was Rs. 3/- per household, but it was afterwards raised to Rs. 8/-, and subsequently to Rs. 10/-, at which rate it was levied at the time of the annexation (1886). As soon as the amount of Thathameda demanded from a particular village was fixed, the Elders of the village chose from among their number a body of assessors termed *Thamadis*, who fixed the amount to be paid by each household, due respect being paid to the paying power of its members. After the assessment had been made the amount was collected by the Thûgyi, who received as remuneration 10 per cent. on the amount collected.

Pôngyis, Kôyins (Novices), Po-thû-daus (Mendicant priests), and Mè-thi-las (Nuns) were specially exempted from the payment of the Thathameda.

Dokitas (those incapacitated from earning their livelihood) were shewn in the assessment rolls, but a reduction of 10 per cent. on the gross assessment was allowed for them.

(2.) KAING-GÛN.—This was a Tax levied on the Vegetable growers of the islands in the Irrawaddy. All such islands were considered Crown Lands, and a tax, equal to about 6 annas per 100 square feet of cultivated land was demanded from the holders.

(3.) IRRIGATION TAX.—The Burmese Government claimed from one quarter to one-third of the produce of all lands irrigated from the Royal tanks. This tax brought in large revenues in the Kyauksè, Meiktila, and Shwebo districts, where irrigation has been resorted to for several hundreds of years.

(4.) FISHERIES.—All the Fisheries were given out on lease, each lessee paying a certain fixed sum to the Wûn. The leases were not sold by auction, but were given to those favoured by the Wûn.

(5.) FERRIES.—These were leased in the same way as the Fisheries.

(6.) BROKER'S TAX.—The right to become a Broker was given by the *Hlûtdaw*, at Mandalay. Those enjoying the privilege monopolised all the brokerage in large trade centres, and received 3 per cent. on the value of all goods bought and sold under their supervision. The Revenue thus derived was paid into the Royal Treasury.

(7.) MONOPOLIES.—The sole right to purchase and sell special commodities was obtained by purchase from the King. The system of monopolies was started by Mindôn Min, and did much harm to the trade between Upper and Lower Burma. They were abolished by King Thibaw in 1885, shortly before his downfall. In times of war or political disturbance, when soldiers were required for the defence of the country, a tax termed *Le-net-kaing-kyè* was levied.

Pwè-daw-gân was a tax levied at Pagoda feasts from the bazaar sellers who frequented such assemblies for the purposes of trade. The amount realized was forwarded to the King's Treasury at Mandalay. Sometimes, by royal command, the amount collected was ordered to be spent on repairing some particular Pagoda or Shrine, or was placed at the disposal of the Wûn for religious purposes.

The total amount of Revenue realized in the King's time is not known. It is estimated that about two-thirds of the gross collections reached safely the Royal Treasury, the remaining one-third leaking out in the hands of officials, from the Thûgyis to the King's Ministers.

MILITARY FORCES.

A small standing army was maintained for the defence of the Palace and Capital. The army was quartered within the Royal city, and was supposed to receive regular pay. Under the King's rule, all men between the ages of seventeen and sixty years were bound to bear arms. In time of war orders were issued from the Hlûtdaw to the Governors of the provinces to furnish their quota of troops for the defence of the country. On some occasions the Wûngyis had to take the field in person.

The best fighting men came from Shwèbo, Yeû, and Tabayin, and were distinguished by a special tattoo mark in vermilion in the small of the back. The men of these districts who served in the army paid no taxes, and were given certain Royal lands rent free for their support.

The rank and file of the Infantry were armed with muskets and swords, and in and around the Capital some attempt was made to put the men into uniform.

The Cavalry were chiefly of Kathè or Manipuri nationality, the descendants of prisoners of war captured by Sin Byu Shin in the latter part of the last century. They were mounted on ponies, and armed with lances.

The following were the titles of military officers :—*A-Kyat*, commander of ten men. *Thue-thawk Gyi*, commander of five Akyat. *Tat-hmû*, commander of 100 men. *Bo*, commander of any number of *tats*. *Sit-bo-gyi*, commander of a division. *Sit-ba-yin*, the Commander-in-Chief of the King's Army.

In the Cavalry the officers were termed *Myin-thûgyi*, *Myin-gaung*, *Myin-sayè*, *Myin-dat*, and *Myin-Wûn*.

Although the Arsenal in the Palace at Mandalay was filled with iron and brass cannon of all sizes and calibre, the use of Field Artillery was never practised. The forts at Minhla, Ava, and

Sagaing were defended by iron guns of small calibre, which were ill-served, and comparatively useless.

In addition to the army, a strong fleet of war boats was maintained on the river, and a special officer was appointed by the king to look after this branch of the service.

All towns situated on the river bank had to keep up a certain number of these boats, fully equipped with rowers, and a complement of riflemen. Many of them carried a heavy gun or jingal in the bows, and the men were noted for their pluck and strength.

Naval encounters were frequent in the lower province during the wars waged between the Talaings and Burmese, especially during the expeditions of Alaungpya to Rangoon, Pegu, Syriam, and Mergui.

THE IRRAWADDY FLOTILLA COMPANY, LIMITED.

A work on Burma would be incomplete without a full account of the development of this prosperous Company and its connection with the mercantile trade of Burma. It was early in the Sixties that the Local Government made over a small fleet of steamers to the promoters of the Company, and from this small beginning the fleet has grown to the enormous dimensions it has now attained. In 1868 the fleet consisted of seven small vessels only, which confined itself to trading within the limits of the Province of Lower Burma. The ordinary run was between Rangoon and Thayet-myo, a distance of 350 miles only. At this time steam communication with Mandalay or the large towns on the Irrawaddy was not thought of, and the sound of the steam whistle was seldom heard in the offshoots of the main river or its delta.

The honour of extending the operations of the Company to Upper Burma was reserved for the late Mr. G. J. Swann, C.I.E., who became general manager in Rangoon in 1868. Under his skilful management and far-seeing sagacity the service of steamers was extended, not only to Mandalay and Bhamo, but to most of the navigable creeks and estuaries of the Lower Province.

The tonnage of the fleet rose to the enormous total of 75,500 tons.

Not only was a line established to Mandalay and Bhamo—a town on the confines of Western China, situated nearly a thousand miles from the sea—but an efficient service of suitable

EXPRESS AND CARGO STEAMERS OF THE I.F.C., LTD.

(From a Photograph.)

steamers was established for opening up communication between Rangoon and Bassein, the most important town and seaport on the Western mouth of the great river.

At the present time there is a most efficient service of mail and cargo steamers plying twice a week between Rangoon and Mandalay ; a weekly mail and cargo service between Mandalay and Bhamo ; a weekly mail service far up the Chindwin ; and an innumerable number of suitable ferry services on the main river, its tributaries, and the network of creeks in the delta, all giving the greatest facilities for the transit of passengers and merchandise from the interior to the great centre—Rangoon.

The steamers of the Company are of the most approved and modern type, are fitted with all the latest appliances in marine engineering and architecture, and are peculiarly adapted for the purposes to which they are put.

They have, almost without exception, been constructed in the great ship-building yards of Messrs. William Denny & Bros., of Dumbarton, on the Clyde, and the late Mr. Peter Denny, LL.D., was the Chairman of the Company in Glasgow.

An extensive and excellently managed dockyard is maintained both at Rangoon and Mandalay. At the former, not only are the general repairs to the Company's steamers and flats carried out, but vessels are constructed from materials sent out from home.

A more magnificient steamer than the *Beeloo* or the *China* is not to be found in the fleet of any other river steam navigation Company in the world. Splendid saloon accommodation is provided, and the furniture and fittings are most superb. The *Beloo* was specially fitted up for the reception of the late Prince Albert Victor of Wales during his tour in Burma in 1890.

These vessels are lighted by electricity, and several are fitted with quadruple expansion engines of enormous power, to enable them to steam against the strongest currents when the river is in flood. It is not a matter of surprise therefore, that a trip from or to Mandalay is so appreciated by all who have the good fortune to seek a change in travel.

Not only has the Company to concern itself with the upkeep of its immense fleet, but serious attention has to be paid to the river itself. In the rainy season the Irrawaddy rises from thirty to forty feet when in full flood. At this season (July to September) the difficulties of navigation are at a minimum, but towards the end of September a great fall takes place, which increases daily till the hot season of March and April, when the lowest level is attained. During this period the difficulties are very great, owing to the silting up of the old channels, and the divergence of others. The Company has spent vast sums in keeping the channels clear, and by means of sunken disused vessels and groins, insured a free passage for their steamers during this critical period. Large sums are also spent in buoying the channels during this season, and a number of pilot launches patrol the river throughout its entire length, employed in shifting the buoys as the channel alters, and supplying information to the Commanders.

On the declaration of war by Lord Dufferin, then Viceroy of India, against King Thibaw in the autumn of 1885, the Company placed the whole of its resources at the disposal of Government for the conveyance of troops and stores to the Upper Province, and the success of the expedition was in a great measure due to the skill and energy of the Company's representatives and the facilities afforded to the Government by them.

The Government of India recognized this by tendering a vote of thanks to the Company, and by creating Mr. G. J. Swann, the general manager in Glasgow, and Mr. F. C. Kennedy, the Rangoon manager, Companions of the Indian Empire.

A noteworthy feature in the history of the Company is that on no occasion between 1879, when the late Mr. St. Barbe, the British resident, was withdrawn from Mandalay, and the despatch of the expedition in 1885, did any friction arise between the Officers of the Company, and the Officials of the King's Government. This testifies in no uncertain manner to the tact

IRRAWADDY FLOTILLA CO.'S MAIL STEAMER "BEELOO."

(From a Photograph.)

displayed by the manager and his staff during this trying and anxious period.

On several occasions the Commanders of the Company's steamers shewed great tact and diplomacy in their relations with the Officers of the Burmese Government, and at times put themselves in serious bodily danger.

In December, 1884, a party of Chinese marauders came down from the hills and took possession of the town of Bhamo on the Upper Irrawaddy. At the time the Company's steamer *Kya-Byu*, under the command of Captain Turndrup, was on its voyage up, and on arrival at Sawatti some nine miles below Bhamo, the town was seen to be on fire. The next morning the steamer proceeded to its moorings at Bhamo, when it was discovered that the town was in the possession of the Chinese, that it had been sacked and fired, and the Burmese garrison driven out of the defences and forced to seek refuge on two of the King's steamers, which happened at the time to be in the river. After several interviews with the Chinese Commander, Captain Turndrup succeeded in rescuing all, or nearly all the British subjects, as well as the Americans of the Chinese Inland and Kachin Missions. For these services Captain Turndrup was awarded a gold watch valued at 500 Rupees by the Governor-General in Council, and received the thanks of the Government of India.

Another incident in which the Company's steamers and officers were concerned was the outrage at Moda, a few miles above Katha, on the Upper Irrawaddy. This occurred on the 20th of November, 1885, shortly before the capture of Mandalay by the British. The steamer concerned was the *Okpho*, under the command of Captain Redman. It left Mandalay for Bhamo on the 9th November, and arrived there on the morning of the 13th. Bhamo was found to be very excited, and on the 19th, the Burmese Governor ordered the steamer away. The first night was spent at Shwegû, and the next morning, while the steamer halted at Moda, it was rushed by about two hundred of the

King's troops, and the officers and crew were taken prisoners and conveyed to a King's steamer at anchor near by. After suffering gross indignities and cruelties, and having several times been led out to execution, they were conveyed to Mandalay, and were not released until the arrival of the British troops there.

In spite of the fact that the last trip of the *Okpho* was undertaken at the special request of Government, for the relief and withdrawal of British subjects from the towns on the Upper Irrawaddy, Captain Redman and his officers received little or no compensation, and not only suffered personal injuries and discomforts, but also the loss of valuable personal effects, which were looted by the Burmese.

The *Okpho* was eventually recaptured, and Captain Redman was reappointed to the command, but was some years ago transferred to the new mail steamer *Mogaung*, now plying between Mandalay and Bhamo.

LIST OF IMPORTANT PERSONAGES.

ALAUNGPYA.—The founder of the last dynasty that ruled in Upper Burma. Originally a petty official of Mòksobo (now called Shwèbo). He rose against the Talaings, who had conquered Upper Burma, and succeeded in driving them out of the country. He subsequently captured Pegu, Martaban, Tavoy, and Mergui, and in 1759 invaded Siam. While investing Ayuthia, the capital, he suddenly became ill, and while retreating to Martaban, died. His body was conveyed to Rangoon, and thence to his capital, Mòk-sobo, where it was burnt. A small wooden *pyathat* between the Court - house and the Public Works Department Office, marks the site where his ashes were interred. He was born in 1714, and died in 1760 A.D.

ALAUNG-TSI-THU.—A celebrated king of the Pagan dynasty. He ruled from 1085 to 1160 A.D. Builder of the Shwè-kû Temple at Pagan.

AMHERST, LORD.—Governor General of India at the time of the First war with Burma. Amherst (Bur. : Kyeik-a-mi) at the mouth of the Salween river was named after him.

ANAURHATA ZAW.—A celebrated king of Pagan, who reigned from 1010 to 1052 A.D. During his reign the Buddhist religion was firmly established in Upper Burma. He conquered Pegu and Arakan, and invaded Yûnnan.

ATHIN-KHARA.—The founder of a Shan dynasty that reigned at Sagaing from 1322 to 1364 A.D.

BA-GYI-DAU.—The seventh sovereign of the Alaungpya dynasty. He reigned at Ava from 1819 to 1837 A.D. During his reign the First Anglo-Burmese war took place (1825-26).

BANDULA, MAHA.—A celebrated Burmese General, who opposed the British in the First Anglo-Burmese war. He was killed by the bursting of a shell in the defence of the fort at Danûbyû.

BIGANDET, BISHOP.—A celebrated Roman Catholic Bishop, who worked in Burma for more than 50 years. His " Legend of Gaudama," is one of the best works published on Buddha and his teachings. He died in 1894.

BO-DAU-PYA.—Son of Alaungpya, and sixth sovereign of that dynasty. He founded Amarapura, built the Mingûn pagoda, and brought the Maha-Myat-Mûni Image from Arakan to his capital.

BUDDHA GHOSA.—A celebrated Buddhist divine, who in A.D. 400 proceeded from Thatôn to Ceylon, and during his stay of four years copied the whole of the Buddhist Scriptures, which he brought back to Burma.

BYINNYA DALA.—The last Talaing king of Pegu. He was taken prisoner and kept in honourable restraint by Alaungpya, but was subsequently tried and executed by order of Sinbyushin in 1775 A.D.

CÆSAR, FREDERICK.—A Venetian, who visited Burma in 1567 A.D. He described the Court and City of Pegu.

CAMPBELL, SIR ARCHIBALD.—The Commander-in-chief of the British troops in the First war with Burma.

CHANDA SURYA.—The ruler of Arakan, who in 162 A.D. cast the brass image of Buddha, known as Maha-Myat-Mûni.

COX, CAPTAIN.—A British officer deputed by Sir John Shore Governor-General to the Court of Bo-dau-pya. He described very fully the building of the huge pagoda.

DALHOUSIE, LORD.—Governor-General of India at the time of the Second Burmese war (A.D. 1852-53).

DHAMMACETI.—A celebrated Talaing king of Pegu, who reigned from A.D. 1461 to 1492. He did much for the spread of religion and founded the Kalyani Sema, or Hall of Ordination for Buddhist priests.

DWOT-TABAUNG.—Son of Maha Thambawa, the founder of Tharekhettara (near Prome). Said to have reigned for 70 years from B.C. 442 to 372.

FITCH, RALPH.—An English merchant who visited Pegu in A.D. 1586-87.

FYTCHE, GENERAL.—The Second Chief Commissioner of British Burma, from 1867 to 1871. During the first year of his administration he undertook a mission to Mindôn Min's Court.

GAUDAMA BUDDHA.—The last Buddha that has appeared. He was the son of Sudhodana, king of Kapilawatta, near to the modern Nepaul, and was born in the year 624 B.C. Five days after his birth he received the name of Sidhartta, but was more commonly known by the patronymics of Sakya or Gaudama.

At the age of 16 he married Yasodhara, daughter of Suprabuddha, king of Koli. Sudhodana having heard that it had been predicted his son would become a Buddha after witnessing four omens or signs, viz., Decrepitude, Sickness, Death, and a Recluse, ordered such sights to be kept from his son. His precautions, however, were in vain. One by one the forbidden sights were witnessed by him, and after encountering the recluse he returned to his Palace to find that his wife had just given birth to a son. Having decided to renounce the world, he, the same night, called for his charger, and after taking one last look at his sleeping wife and babe, left the palace. Arriving at a certain place he dismounted and sent his horse back by the groom to the palace stables. He then took off his princely robes and assumed the character and guise of a recluse, at the same time cutting off his long hair with a sickle. (In images of Buddha the head is always covered with sharp knobs. These are to represent the stumps of hair left after the tresses had been roughly cut off with the sickle.)

He remained for six years in the forest of Winvila, leading a life of strict austerity, and at the end of this time retired to the shade of a Bo-tree *(Ficus Religiosa)* in another part of the forest, where he attained the supreme wisdom and became Buddha *(the Enlightened)*.

He ministered principally in Benares, Rajagara, Wesali, and Sewet, and at the age of 80 he died at a place called Kusinara, supposed by some to be near Delhi, and by others in Assam.

GASPER BALBI.—A jeweller of Venice, who visited Pegu in 1583.

GODWIN, GENERAL.—The Commander-in-Chief of the British army in the Second Burmese war.

JUDSON, DOCTOR.—A celebrated American Baptist Missionary, who was taken prisoner by Bagyidau and confined at Aung-pinlè, near the Capital, during the continuance of the First Anglo-Burmese war. He was eventually liberated and sent as Ambassador to treat for peace at Yandabo.

He compiled an excellent Dictionary and Grammar of the Burmese language.

KULA-KYA-MIN.—The name given to Narathu, son of Alaung-tsi-thu, king of Pagan, who reigned from A.D. 1160 to 1164. The name means "*the king dethroned by foreigners*," and was given because he was assassinated by Indians disguised as Brahmins.

MANÇHA.—King of Thatôn, who was deported to Pagan by Anaurhata Zaw on his conquest of Thatôn in A.D. 1050.

MINDÔN MIN.—The father of Thibaw, the last king of Burma. He reigned from A.D. 1855 to 1879, and was one of the best of the sovereigns of the Alaungpya dynasty.

NARAPATITSITHU.—A celebrated king of Pagan. He reigned from A.D. 1167 to 1204, and was the builder of the Gauda-palin and Sula-muni temples at Pagan.

NERINI, BISHOP.—A Roman Catholic Bishop of Burma. He was murdered by order of Alaungpya for supposed duplicity.

NICOTE.—Generally known as Philip de Breto. (q.v.)

OLCOTT, COLONEL.—A Buddhist Revivalist, who occasionally visits Burma and lectures.

PAGAN MIN.—The immediate predecessor of Mindôn Min on the throne of Burma. During his reign the Second Anglo-

Burmese war took place, A.D. 1852-53. At the conclusion of peace a revolution occurred at the Capital, Pagan Min was forced to abdicate in favour of his half-brother, Mindôn Min.

PHAYRE, SIR ARTHUR.—The first Chief Commissioner of the province of British Burma. His administration lasted from 1862 to 1867.

PHILIP DE BRITO.—A Portuguese adventurer originally in the service of the King of Arakan. He established his independence at Syriam in 1604, and ruled till 1613, when his stronghold was taken by the King of Ava, de Brito being impaled alive.

PRENDERGAST, SIR HARRY.—The Commander-in-Chief of the British army in the Third Anglo-Burmese war in 1885-86.

PRICE, DOCTOR.—An American Baptist Missionary who, with Dr. Judson, was imprisoned by order of Bagyidau during the time of the First Anglo-Burmese war.

PYIN-BYA.—The founder of the city of Pagan. He reigned from A.D. 839 to 871.

SAN GERMANO.—A celebrated Roman Catholic priest, who ministered in Burma from 1782 to 1806. He wrote an excellent work called "The Burmese Empire," which was published after his death.

SIN-BYÛ-SHIN.—The second son of Alaungpya. He reigned from A.D. 1763 to 1767, making Môksobo his capital.

SHIN-SAU-BU.—A celebrated princess who became Queen of Pegu in A.D. 1446. She was succeeded by the celebrated King Dhammaceti.

SHWE-YOE.—The nom-de-plume of J. G. Scott, Esquire, whose work, "The Burman, his life and notions," is so well known.

SIN-BYU-MA-SEIN.—The mother of Supya-lat, the chief Queen of King Thibaw.

SUPYA-LAT.—The second daughter of Sin-byu-ma-sein, who became the consort of King Thibaw.

TALOK-PYÈ-MIN.—The name given to Narathihapate, King of Pagan, who reigned from A.D. 1248 to 1279, when he fled to

Bassein on the approach of the Chinese forces. Hence his name "the king who fled from the Chinese."

THAMUD-DARET.—The ruler of the Pyù tribe who wandered from Tharekhittara, and eventually settled at Pagan.

THARRAWADDI.—Younger brother of Bagyidau, who reigned from 1837 to 1846. He was cruel and tyrannical, eventually becoming mad, when he was dethroned by his son, the Prince of Pagan.

THIBAW MIN.—The last King of Burma. He became King on the death of his father, Mindôn Min, in 1879, and was deported to India in December, 1885. He is at present a State prisoner at Rutnaghuri, near Bombay.

THINGA-YAZA.—The nineteenth sovereign of the Pagan dynasty, who established the existing Burmese Era commencing in March, A.D. 639.

TITCOMBE, BISHOP.—The first Protestant Bishop of Rangoon. He held charge from 1878 to 1882 when, in consequence of an accident, he was obliged to resign and return to Europe.

WELDON, CAPTAIN.—An officer of the East India Company, who in 1687 took possession of Haingyi Island at the mouth of Bassein river.

YULE, COLONEL.—The Secretary of the Phayre Mission to Mindôn Min's Court in 1855. His work, "Mission to the Court of Ava," is one of the best works on Burma ever published.

GLOSSARY.

AHM-ÚDAN.   A subordinate official ; one of the rank and file, a policeman.

AIN-SHÈ-MIN.   The name given by the Kings of Burma to the Prince chosen to succeed the King.   Usually the eldest son of the King, or one of the King's brothers.

A-KYEIK.   The name given to the zig-zag wavy pattern seen in silk putsos, or waist cloths.

BA-HO-ZIN.   The campanile or tower near the east gate of the palace, where the hours were struck on an immense drum.

BAZAAR.   A name used in the East for a market.

BÈ-DIN.   The practice of Fortune-telling, or Sooth-saying.

BE-DIN-SAYA.   A Fortune-teller.

BELÚ.   A fabulous monster, half man, half beast ; an ogre.

BETEL-BOX.   A small round lacquer box with trays, in which betel nut (Arica Catechu) and other condiments are carried for chewing.

BÈ-YO.   The ordinary ox-cart or gharry seen in Mandalay.

COOLY.   A hired labourer.

CREEK.   A water-way subject to the rise and fall of the tides.

DACOIT.   An armed gang robber (one of five or more. *Indian Penal Code*).

DAH.   A knife or chopper.

DAING.   A Burmese mile—$2\frac{1}{4}$ English miles.

DAK BUNGALOW.   A rest-house provided by Government for the
                  use of travellers.

DALI-ZAN.   A necklace of silver or gold with pendants covering
                  part of the breast.

DAMA.   A heavy chopper.

DHET-TON.   The vade-mecum of the Fortune-teller.

DHINGY.   A covered native row boat.

GAUDAMA.   The last Buddha.

GAUNA-GÔN.   The Burmese rendering of Konagama, the second
                  Buddha previous to Gaudama.

GHARRY.   A hackney carriage.

GHARRY-WALLA.   A driver of a gharry.

GO-DOWN.   A warehouse or shed for storing goods.

HLÛT-DAU.   The Supreme Council of the Burmese Government.

JATAKAS.   The 550 birth stories of Gaudama, describing his
                  previous existences.

JINGAL.   A small bore cannon without a carriage.

JUNGLE.   The general term in the East for uncultivated
                  land ; the district as distinguished from the town.

KALPA.   A cycle, the period of a mundane revolution.

KARAWEIK.   A fabulous bird, the Garunda of Vishnu.

KATHAPPA.   The Burmese rendering of Kasyapa, the Buddha
                  who preceded Gaudama.

KAUKATHAN.   The Burmese rendering of Kakusanda, the third
                  Buddha previous to Gaudama.

KEDDAH.   An enclosure of strong beams of timber, in which
                  wild elephants are trapped.

KHAKI.   A serviceable cotton drill of a dirty brown colour.

KANSAMAH.   A butler or caterer in a dak bungalow or hotel.

KIN-WÛN-MINGYI.   The foreign minister of the King of Burma's
                  Court.

KÛLA.   Literally a foreigner. A name given by Burmans
                  generally to Natives of India.

KÛTHO.   The Burmese rendering of *Kursala*—merit.

KYAIK.   The Talaing for a pagoda or shrine.

KYAUNG.	A monastery ; a school.
KYI-DAU-YA.	The foot-print of Buddha.
KYÛN.	An island.
LATERITE.	A kind of clay which hardens on exposure, common in the delta.
LEOGRYPHS.	The huge griffins seen about pagodas.
LOUNGYI.	The waist-cloth of the Burman.
MAHA.	Great.
MAHA-BAUDI.	The sacred banyan tree at Buddha Gaya.
MAHA-YAZAWIN.	The Royal chronicles of the kings of Burma.
MAHA-GANDA.	The name of the large bell on the platform of the Shwè Dagôn Pagoda.
MAHAUTHADA.	One of the twelve *rathu* describing a previous existence of Gaudama.
MI-DAUNG.	A torch or fire-brand.
MÔKSO.	A native hunter ; a shikaree.
MONSOON.	The regular winds which blow in the Indian Ocean.
MYO.	A town.
MYOÔK.	A native magistrate.
NAGA.	A fabulous hooded snake of enormous size.
NAMI-ZAT.	One of the twelve *rathu* describing a previous existence of Gaudama.
NAN-DAU.	A palace ; the royal residence.
NAN-MYIN	The watch-tower of the palace.
NAT.	A spirit, demon or fairy.
NAT-SIN.	The house erected for the abode of the nat.
NGAPEE.	Literally pressed fish. A fish condement consumed in large quantities by the Burmese.
PALÀ.	A bowl, or cup, generally of silver.
PADDY.	Unhusked rice.
PAGODA.	A shrine usually erected over relics of Buddha.
PALI.	The language of Magadha, an off-shoot of Sanscrit.
PALIN.	An altar, a stand, a throne.
PAYA.	A word signifying either God, lord, or pagoda.
PÔN-NA.	A Brahmin, an astrologer.

Pôn-gyi.	Literally " great glory." The name given in Burma to priests of Buddha.
Pu-tso.	The long waist-cloth of the Burman.
Pyathat.	The spire of receding roofs (5 or 7 in number) seen on palace buildings and monasteries.
Rahan.	A Buddhist priest of erudition.
Rakkha.	A demon.
Sa-daw.	A Buddhist Bishop.
Sa-môk.	The name given to certain of the palace buildings in Mandalay.
Sawbwa.	A Shan prince or chieftain.
Sein-bu.	The gem cluster at the summit of the *hti*.
Shin-bin-tha-yaung.	The prostrate figure of Buddha.
Shwè.	Gold.
Swè-dau-zin.	Relic tower near the east gate of the palace.
Shwè-myo-dau.	" The royal golden city," *i.e.*, the capital.
Sikra.	The mitre-shaped spire of temples, such as are seen at Pagan.
Tabindaing.	In the King's time the name given to the princess who was reserved as the wife of the future King.
Tagundaing.	The coloured flag-staff, surmounted by the figure of a bird, seen near shrines and monasteries.
Talaing.	The *Môn* people who originally inhabited Pegu.
Talôk.	The Burmese name for the Chinese.
Talapoin.	The name given by early Portuguese settlers to the priests of Buddha, probably because they carried fans of the Talipot palm.
Tamein.	The waist-cloth or petticoat of the Burmese women.
Taya.	The Burmese rendering of *torah*—instruction ; the sacred law, or *dhamma*.
Thabeik.	A bowl or begging pot used by priests of Buddha.
Tha-kin.	Sir, or sire. A name corresponding to *Sahib* in Hindustani.
Tha-maing.	The sacred history of a shrine, generally inscribed on palm leaf.

THATHANA-BAING.   The Buddhist Archbishop.

THEIN.   A shrine ; a building in which figures of Buddha
                are placed.

THINGA.   The Burmese rendering of *Sangha* ; the priest-
                hood.

THIT-SI.   Wood-oil.

TICAL.   A weight.   The 100th part of a viss.

TIGA-NI.   The name given to the small red gate on the East
                side, through which access to the Palace was
                gained.

TIN-BIN-NGÈ.   The sitting attitude of Buddha.

VIHERA.   A monastery.

VISS.   A weight equivalent to 3·65lb. avoirdupois.

WÛN.   A governor of a province.

WÛN-DAUK.   An assistant to a Wûn.

YOMA.   Mountains, lit. the back-bone of the country.

YWA.   A village.

YWA THÛGYI.   A village headman.

ZAT.   Caste.

ZAYAT.   A caravansarai or public rest-house.

ZÉDI.   A pagoda similar in shape to the Shwè Dagôn or
                others usually seen in the lower province.

IRRAWADDY FLOTILLA CO.'S S.S. "MOGOUNG."

(From a Photograph.)

APPENDIX TO INTRODUCTION.

The following Statistical Tables are extracted from the Administration Report on the Province of Burma for 1894-1895, and are inserted for general information.

F

CIVIL DIVISIONS OF BRITISH TERRITORY.—LOWER BURMA.

Name of Commissionership	Name of executive district	Number of Judicial and revenue establishments	Area in square miles	Population	Chief towns with population	Number of villages	How many Civil and Revenue Judges of all sorts	How many Magistrates of all sorts	Maximum distance in miles from nearest Court	Average distance in miles of villages from nearest Court	Number of Police	Total cost of officials and police of all kinds	Revenue — Land	Revenue — Customs	Remarks
ARAKAN	Akyab		5,005	416,305	Akyab ... 37,938	2,020	11	11	40	25	358	Rs. 3,06,462	Rs. 99,68,173	Rs. 13,90,256	
	Northern Arakan		1,015			387	1	6	100	30	208	31,817	7,465	11,565	
	Kyaukpyu		4,319	182,852		1,595	6	9			188	1,70,912	1,78,912	8,82,028	
	Sandoway		3,843	78,425		502	4	4				45,332	61,676	1,57,929	
	Total Arakan		31,782	675,190		4,604					879	5,74,353	13,08,226	38,74,368	
PEGU	Rangoon Town			140,904	Rangoon ... 140,324	1,901	9	18		13	701	3,61,681	10,914	34,741	
	Hanthawaddy		1,958	287,689		781	12	15		21	212	1,74,616	10,43,631	15,21,764	
	Pegu		3,158	352,429	Pegu ... 10,022	1,900	8	16			516	2,34,963	17,43,662	39,06,841	
	Tharrawaddy		2,601	347,644	Shwedaung 12,454						276	2,03,842	6,61,662	11,77,305	
	Prome			380,352	Prome ... ; Thayetgale 10,228	3,447	10	13	60	30	306	2,01,608	3,64,967	7,64,798	
	Total Pegu		9,139	1,436,900		5,888					2,009	12,03,196	38,25,001	53,69,084	
IRRAWADDY	Thayetmyo		3,809	331,445	Yandoon ... ; Maubin ...	971	12	15	95	15	312	3,04,123	14,67,240	22,73,943	
	Bassein		3,406	331,562	Bassein ... ; Nga-thaing-gyaung ...	1,139	10	24	70	24	325	2,81,422	7,25,920	12,15,348	
	Henzada		2,298	424,130	Henzada ... ; Myanaung ... ; Kyangin ...	3,320	9	11	68	11	396	3,00,065	7,65,220	12,46,865	
	Myanaung		2,299	297,874	Zalun ... ; Lemyethna ... ; Pantanaw ...	453	6	8	65		367	03,536	6,21,361	11,83,988	
	Total Irrawaddy		12,619	1,386,714		4,582					1,340	9,58,906	35,42,067	58,99,937	
TENASSERIM	Amherst		13,500	417,312	Moulmein ... 53,138 ; Thaton 9,468	1,776	18	24	80	25	641	2,03,548	9,36,586	13,24,790	
	Tavoy		5,119	94,923	Tavoy ... 10,688	569	6	8	60		322	1,60,168	1,60,860	2,64,207	
	Mergui		9,748	51,754	Mergui ... 10,117	672	4	8	60		144	61,566	1,33,660	2,60,191	
	Thoungoo		6,354	182,132	Toungoo ... 14,164	932	8	18	90	12	310	61,268	1,08,626	2,63,531	
	Shwegyin		3,127	196,521	Shwegyin ... 3,541		3	9	90		255	1,03,662	3,61,032	6,47,590	
	Salween		4,446	31,438	Kyahto ...	228	2	7	60		115	72,524	14,941	30,194	
	Total Tenasserim		46,060	976,673		4,672					1,880	7,28,541	17,11,067	28,00,006	
NORTHERN	Thayetmyo ...		4,364	350,161	Thayetmyo 12,149 ; Allanmyo 9,012	959	7	12	65	85	630	2,67,591	2,35,000	3,77,868	
	Grand Total Lower Burma	47	42,563	4,659,457		18,205	129	179			10,908	33,70,491	1,05,49,140	1,67,57,263	

Include No. 1 and No. 2, Land Revenue and Rs. 1,33,94 Gross Revenue on account of that portion of the Thayetmyo district in which the Upper Burma Revenue Law is in force.

Name of Commissionership.	Name of Executive district.	Number of judicial and revenue subdivisions.	Area in square miles.	Population.	Chief town with population.	Number of villages.	How many Civil and Revenue Judges of all sorts.	How many Magistrates of all sorts.	Maximum distance in miles of villages from nearest Court.	Average distance in miles of villages from nearest Court.	Number of Police.	Total cost of officials and police of all kinds.	Revenue (in lakhs) Land (including thathameda).	Gross.	Remarks.
NORTHERN.	Mandalay				Mandalay										
	Bhamo				Bhamo										
	Katha				Katha										
	Ruby Mines				Ruby Mines										
	Myelu				Mogok										
	Total				Total										
CENTRAL.	Ye-u				Ye-u										
	Sagaing				Sagaing										
	Lower Chindwin				Monywa										
	Upper Chindwin				Kindat										
	Total				Total										
SOUTHERN.	Pakôkku				Pakôkku										
	Minbu				Minbu										
	Magwe				Magwe										
	Total				Total										
EASTERN.	Kyauksè				Kyauksè										
	Meiktila				Meiktila										
	Yamèthin				Yamèthin										
	Myingyan				Myingyan										
	Total				Total										
GRAND TOTAL.					GRAND TOTAL										

PROGRESSIVE VALUE OF TRADE IN BURMA SINCE 1866-67.

YEAR.	RANGOON.			OTHER PORTS.			TOTAL FOR THE PROVINCE.		
	Imports.	Exports.	Total.	Imports.	Exports.	Total.	Imports.	Exports.	Total.
1866-67	1,74,95,390	1,18,80,390	2,93,75,690	80,57,090	1,12,06,900	1,89,17,990	2,55,55,650	2,31,46,690	4,86,99,470
1871-72	2,28,11,500	2,29,71,559	4,57,83,110	87,08,900	1,46,90,090	2,33,98,959	3,15,79,960	3,76,02,170	6,91,82,090
1876-77	3,68,21,000	3,39,16,470	7,00,86,190	1,04,73,980	2,13,50,070	3,17,23,150	4,70,94,940	5,54,66,540	10,22,60,580
1881-82	5,03,00,500	4,73,42,340	9,78,12,900	1,33,49,980	3,32,39,070	4,65,74,550	6,36,49,840	8,05,71,410	14,44,21,250
1883-84	5,78,24,800	5,46,18,600	11,24,43,400	1,53,09,710	3,25,63,900	4,78,98,670	7,31,34,510	8,72,02,500	16,03,37,070
1886-87	6,34,26,330	5,07,65,130	12,01,91,670	1,36,36,400	3,01,32,260	4,37,87,660	7,70,62,730	8,08,10,390	16,39,70,130
1887-88	6,71,98,600	5,74,20,000	14,46,58,720	1,41,51,790	3,16,74,360	4,58,26,170	10,13,51,450	8,91,55,440	19,04,86,890
1888-89	7,98,97,950	5,84,90,120	13,83,88,770	1,33,72,640	2,89,96,860	3,73,69,000	9,32,70,590	8,21,87,440	17,52,51,770
1889-90	8,21,11,440	7,29,00,690	15,41,12,800	1,33,14,250	2,90,32,740	4,31,89,070	9,50,25,679	10,16,33,680	19,72,79,309
1890-91	8,70,24,350	8,94,66,950	17,64,91,270	1,33,96,360	3,41,99,960	4,81,96,180	10,20,10,730	12,36,66,750	22,46,77,430
1891-92	9,03,87,495	9,00,82,102	18,03,70,067	1,17,16,362	3,86,30,660	5,18,56,098	10,56,06,247	12,67,21,070	23,17,98,125
1892-93	9,31,46,505	9,33,84,742	19,01,41,397	1,65,68,651	3,91,12,824	4,90,93,142	10,97,55,149	12,57,47,070	23,54,92,519
1893-94	6,34,16,696	8,72,32,352	17,06,51,044	1,51,75,379	2,08,28,461	4,39,01,258	9,85,94,075	11,40,56,394	21,26,52,270
1894-95	6,78,57,731	9,42,16,171	16,16,64,295	1,70,11,143	4,21,61,234	5,82,72,379	8,32,68,876	13,67,07,705	21,99,76,561

N.B. 1,000,000=One Crore.   100,000=One Lakh.

RICE TRADE STATISTICS.
Exports during past 10 Years.

YEAR.	EXPORTS OF RICE FROM LOWER BURMA TO			Total.
	Europe and America.	India, China, and Straits.	Upper Burma.	
	Tons.	Tons.	Tons.	Tons.
1885	624,016	294,829	93,328	1,053,391
1886	660,711	368,223	77,044	1,084,078
1887	700,467	248,791	127,177	1,076,841
1888	643,584	102,694	180,696	927,000
1889	706,989	245,129	59,501	1,012,503
1890	740,564	430,079	62,698	1,233,681
1891	852,760	363,423	77,840	1,294,062
1892	824,151	242,367	122,804	1,229,322
1893	778,223	328,453	110,678	1,408,354
1894	728,965	504,504	30,531	1,303,000
1895 (10 months)	792,001	411,041	19,202	1,225,214

FORESTS (LOWER BURMA).
TIMBER WORKED OUT OF FORESTS.

	TEAK.	OTHER KINDS.	TOTAL.
	C. ft.	C. ft.	C. ft.
By Government Agency	1,912,290	76,847	1,989,300
By purchasers and under trade permits	738,943	13,226,078	13,965,021
Under Free permits	9,800	29,525	39,325
By lease-holders of Forests	40,151	29,218	69,394
Total for 1894-95	2,069,000	13,366,000	16,077,000
Total for 1893-94	3,390,000	11,800,000	15,190,000
Increase or decrease in 1894-95	611,400	+ 1,558,000	+ 888,000

EXPORT OF TEAK TIMBER FROM BURMA.

YEAR.	FROM MOULMEIN.		FROM RANGOON.		TOTAL.		
	Tons.	Value.	Tons.	Value.	Tons.	Value.	Average value per Ton.
		Rs.		Rs.		Rs.	Rs.
1890-91.	64,227	47,01,434	110,888	78,75,794	175,115	1,25,77,228	719
1891-92.	62,320	43,86,367	99,647	73,15,307	161,967	1,17,01,664	722
1892-93.	104,650	72,57,412	109,530	91,85,043	214,180	1,64,42,455	766
1893-94.	85,722	69,39,428	85,623	61,76,973	171,345	1,30,16,401	760
1894-95.	81,450	58,66,527	109,810	83,31,657	191,260	1,42,03,184	743

COMMERCIAL MARINE STATEMENT OF TONNAGE VISITING THE PORTS OF BURMA.

PORT.	1892-93.				1893-94.				1894-95.			
	Entered.		Cleared.		Entered.		Cleared.		Entered.		Cleared.	
	Vessels.	Tonnage.	Vessels.	Tonnage.	Vessels.	Tonnage.	Vessels.	Tonnage.	Vessels.	Tonnage.	Vessels.	Tonnage.
Rangoon	1,275	1,201,795	1,221	1,198,001	1,222	1,291,991	1,167	1,237,902	1,125	1,233,097	1,118	1,238,921
Akyab	300	170,040	298	170,630	304	150,301	300	145,741	180	229,093	183	215,810
Bassein	43	55,960	41	51,920	21	33,390	31	32,212	24	67,991	41	78,706
Moulmein	301	240,072	647	204,005	567	260,822	504	265,810	612	292,558	621	288,240
Smaller Ports	966	109,739	954	170,107	964	228,441	966	217,507	954	107,214	984	107,139
Total	3,361	1,676,949	3,361	1,657,826	3,142	1,676,434	3,188	1,918,602	3,135	1,999,214	3,140	1,943,060

TABLE SHEWING EXPORTS OF GOODS TO EUROPE
FOR FIVE YEARS.

COUNTRIES	1890-91.	1891-92.	1892-93.	1893-94.	1894-95.
	Rs.	Rs.	Rs.	Rs.	Rs.
United Kingdom	1,54,58,870	2,06,51,628	2,70,33,242	2,90,60,019	2,11,85,188
France	1,30,110	2,74,112	2,83,142	2,43,118	2,7,190s
Germany	99,000	16,90,268	12,36,698	6,79,106	8,90,239
Italy	3,290	82,511	18,465	25,000	2,80,428
Spain	1,33,280	1,71,318	2,95,048	2,19,900	3,85,631
Egypt*	2,96,43,560	3,65,30,039	3,11,37,815	2,92,26,398	3,6,02,287
Malta*	69,76,700	58,16,606	7,09,015	20,25,325	16,92,772
Other Countries of Europe	1,40,170	20,347	1,55,565	1,67,915	4,31,825
	5,93,91,170	6,74,95,130	6,12,41,362	5,57,87,155	6,19,80,253

* Rice is usually shipped to Port Said or Malta "for Orders"; hence the large shipments under this heading.

REVENUE STATEMENT FOR LOWER BURMA.
FOR THE YEARS 1893-94 AND 1894-95.

ITEM OF REVENUE.	1893-94.			1894-95.			Increase or Decrease.
	Demand.	Remission.	Net Demand.	Demand.	Remission.	Net Demand.	
1. Land Revenue	1,07,70,265	33,287	1,07,41,078	1,06,72,580	18,389	1,06,54,384	1,13,697
2. Customs	83,26,917		83,26,917	87,17,590		87,17,590	+21,90,963
3. Capitation Tax	39,66,714	16,058	39,67,726	39,91,190	29,311	39,51,612	25,147
4. Excise	33,67,702		33,67,702	30,54,163		32,74,204	2,13,144
5. Forests	34,89,758		34,89,748	32,71,296			+2,79,068
6. Stamps	21,56,900		21,56,900	24,36,480		24,36,487	
7. Fisheries	19,02,892	3,302	17,97,390	16,91,123	2964	17,98,375	1,04,212
8. Miscellaneous Land	1,56,090		1,16,090	1,61,707		1,61,707	+45,237
9. Marine	2,02,680		2,02,680	2,27,508		2,27,508	+20,828
10. Land Rate in lieu of Capitation tax	83,097	371	82,726	79,588	342	79,471	3,252
11. Salt Excise	1,93,212		1,93,212	1,87,185		1,87,185	+2,627
12. Registration	51,372		51,372	55,699		55,699	+4,327
Total	5,27,32,319	77,651	5,26,44,668	5,13,10,253	70,948	5,17,19,397	+16,74,669

REVENUE STATEMENT FOR UPPER BURMA,
FOR THE YEARS 1893-94 AND 1894-95.

ITEM OF REVENUE.	1893-94.			1894-95.			Increase or Decrease.
	Demand.	Remission.	Net Demand.	Demand.	Remission.	Net Demand.	
	Rs.	Rs.	Rs.	Rs.	Rs.	Rs.	Rs.
1. Thathameda	55,06,719	30,224	54,76,495	57,79,656	37,055	57,46,601	+2,70,106
2. State Land	10,33,924	9,198	10,16,726	14,38,314	17,756	13,98,558	+4,51,832
3. Excise	3,50,513		3,50,513	6,18,130		6,18,130	+6,61,617
4. Forests	22,95,752		22,95,752	21,62,578		21,62,578	1,83,174
5. Stamps	2,89,609		2,89,609	3,36,205		3,36,205	+38,977
6. Miscellaneous Land	7,56,171	828	7,56,343	10,73,082	17,046	10,56,006	+2,95,728
7. Salt	10,597		10,597	14,598		14,598	+4,111
8. Marine	5,513		5,513	3,603		3,603	−1,698
9. Registration	4,954		4,954	5,231		5,231	+277
10. Ferries	41,720		41,720	48,307		48,307	+6,687
Total	1,03,15,400	40,250	1,01,65,830	1,14,81,292	47,807	1,14,39,673	+12,66,487

PHYSICAL GEOGRAPHY.

1.—Climate. Lower Burma. 1894.

Division.	Place at which observations taken.	RAINFALL IN INCHES.				AVERAGE TEMPERATURE IN THE SHADE.												CLOUD PROPORTION 0 TO 10.		
		January to May.	June to September.	October to December.	Total.	May.				July.				December.				January to May.	June to September.	October to December.
						Mean of maximum readings.	Mean of minimum reading.	Highest reading.	Lowest reading.	Mean of maximum readings.	Mean of minimum readings.	Highest readings.	Lowest readings.	Mean of maximum readings.	Mean of minimum readings.	Highest reading.	Lowest reading.			
ARAKAN	Akyab																	Not recorded.		
	Northern Arakan																			
	Kyaukpyu										Not recorded.									
	Sandoway										Not recorded.				*					
PEGU	Rangoon Town																	5.0	8.5	3.5
	Henzada																			
	Tharrawaddy										Not recorded.									
	Pegu																			
	Prome																			
IRRAWADDY	Bassein																	5.1	9.3	4.0
	Henzada										Not recorded.									
	Myaungmya																			
SOUTHERN	Thayetmyo																	3	4	3
TENASSERIM	Amherst																	5	10	1
	Tavoy																			
	Mergui																			
	Toungoo																			
	Salween																	Not recorded.		3 to 1

* Thermometer out of order.

PHYSICAL GEOGRAPHY.

3.—Climate.   Upper Burma.

1894.

Division	Place at which observations taken	RAINFALL IN INCHES				AVERAGE TEMPERATURE IN THE SHADE												CLOUD PRECIPITATION 0 TO 10		
						May				July				December						
		January to May	June to September	October to December	Total	Mean of maximum readings	Mean of minimum readings	Highest readings	Lowest readings	Mean of maximum readings	Mean of minimum readings	Highest readings	Lowest readings	Mean of maximum readings	Mean of minimum readings	Highest readings	Lowest readings	January to May	June to September	October to December
NORTHERN	Mandalay																			
	Bhamo																	Not recorded	Not recorded	
	Katha																			
	Ruby Mines																			
	Mywedo																			
CENTRAL	Ye-u																			
	Sagaing									Not recorded								Not recorded	Not recorded	
	Lower Chindwin																			
	Upper Chindwin																			
SOUTHERN	Pakokku																			
	Minbu																	Not recorded	Not recorded	
	Magwe																			
EASTERN	Kyaukse																			
	Meiktila																	Not recorded	Not recorded	
	Yamethin																			
	Nyaungu																			

POPULATION — Lower Burma.

| District. | INHABITED HOUSES | | | POPULATION | | | | | | CLASSIFICATION OF POPULATION. | | | | | | | | OCCUPATION. | | | | |
	Number of Masonry dwellings	Number of all other kinds	Total	Men.	Women.	Children under 15 years (Male)	Children under 15 years (Female)	Total	Number per square mile	Christians (Europeans)	Christians (East Indians and other mixed classes)	Natives	Hindus.	Mahomedans.	Parsis.	Buddhists and Jains.	Aborigines.	Agriculturists.	Non-agriculturists.	Prevailing languages.	Emigrants.	Immigrants.	Remarks.
ARAKAN:—																							
Northern Arakan																							
Kyaukpyu																				Burmese, Hindustani and Bengali.			
Sandoway																							
Total																							
Pegu:—																							
Rangoon Town																				Burmese and Karen.			
Hanthawaddy																							
Pegu																							
Tharrawaddy																							
Prome																							
Total																							
IRRAWADDY:—																							
Bassein																				Burmese, Hindustani and Tamil.			
Henzada																							
Myanaung																							
Total																							
THARRAWADDY																							
THAYETMYO																				Burmese and Hindustani.			
TENASSERIM:—																							
Amherst																				Burmese, Hindustani, Talaing and Karen.			
Tavoy																							
Mergui																							
Toungoo																							
Shwegyin																							
Salween																							
Total																							
GRAND TOTAL, LOWER BURMA																							

a) Includes Meiktmein Town.

POPULATION.—UPPER BURMA.

*Revised figures.

(a) Includes 24,493 population of the excluded tracts, details of which are not available.

STATISTICS OF INSTRUCTION.
A.—ECCLESIASTICAL.
Return of Persons according to Religious Denominations for the year 1894-95.
LOWER BURMA.

		1	2		3	4	5	6
Denomination.			NUMBER OF PERSONS.		Number of ministers or priests.	Number of churches or buildings designed or used for worship.	Total annual income from government.	Remarks.
			A. Natives.	B. Others.				
Church of England	..	..	3,144	6,668	13	14	Rs. 24,700	
Church of Scotland	..	..	2	327	1	1	..	
Protestant Dissenters	..	..	78,349	2,145	1,405	399	..	
Roman Catholics	..	..	43,129	5,006	79	177	4,800	
Greek Church	..	..	..	13	..	..	..	
Armenians	..	..	58	138	1	1	..	
Syrians	..	..	..	..	..	..	..	
Jews	..	..	206	..	1	1	..	
Parsis	..	..	87	..	1	1	..	
Hindus	..	..	142,522	..	24	24	..	
Mahomedans	..	..	299,049	..	205	203	..	
Buddhists and Jains	..	..	4,043,501	..	..	..	..	
Sikhs	..	..	373	..	..	..	..	
Other sorts	..	..	149,320	14	..	..	..	
Total	..	..	4,643,633	14,994	1,686*	821*	33,560	

* Figures according to the census of 1891. Figures according to the census of 1891 are not available.

STATISTICS OF INSTRUCTION.
A.—ECCLESIASTICAL.
Return of Persons according to Religious Denominations for the year 1894-95.
UPPER BURMA.

	1	2		3	4	5	6
Denomination.		NUMBER OF PERSONS.		Number of ministers or priests.	Number of churches or buildings designed or used for worship.	Total annual income from Government.	Remarks.
		A. Natives.	B. Others.				
Church of England	..	349	2,812	9	14	Rs. 15,432	
Church of Scotland	..	13	99	..	..	..	
Protestant Dissenters	..	1,312	386	19	19	1,528	
Roman Catholics	..	2,630	1,084	81	30	3,296	
Greek Church	..	1	1	..	..	..	
Armenian Church	..	1	52	..	1	..	
Syrians	..	..	..	..	..	..	
Jews	..	83	..	..	1	..	
Parsis	..	9	..	..	..	..	
Hindus	..	20,655	..	73	55	..	
Mahomedans	..	42,382	..	188	111	..	
Buddhists and Jains	..	2,844,560	..	..	..	..	
Sikhs	..	2,591	..	5	4	..	
Other sorts	..	135,957	37	25,686*	12,802*	4,464*	
Total	..	3,058,675	4,471	26,063	13,037	24,620	

* Includes figures for Buddhist and Jains.

EDUCATION.

1.—*Abstract Return of Colleges, Schools, and Scholars in Burma for the official year 1894-95.*

AREA AND POPULATION				PUBLIC INSTITUTIONS.								PRIVATE INSTITUTIONS.			
				University education.		School education (School education, general. special.)									
Total area in square miles.	Number of towns and villages.	Population.	Institutions { For males. / For females. } ... Total / Scholars { Males / Females } ... Total	Arts colleges.	Professional colleges.	Secondary schools.	Primary schools.	Training schools.	All other special schools.	Total of public institutions.	Advanced.	Elementary.	Grand total.	Percentage of	Remarks.
1	2	3	4	5	6	7	8	9	10	11	12	13	14	15	16
171,430	Towns .. 80 / Villages .. 28,730 / Total .. 28,730	Males .. 3,987,356 / Females .. 3,740,412 / Total .. 7,727,568	For males	2	..	180	4,162	7	36	4,381	..	10,481	14,862	Institutions to number of towns and villages	
			For females	..	..	20	145	3	4	172	..	70	242	·52·03	
			Total	22	..	180	4,307	5	30	4,553	..	10,551	15,084		
			Males	36	..	13,002	80,387	166	601	110,963	..	100,061	219,124	Male scholars to male population of school-going age	36
			Females	3	..	3,445	18,987	83	120	22,640	..	2,980	25,600	Female scholars to female population of school-going age	·456
			Total	71	..	12,345	114,344	198	723	132,728	..	112,011	241,734		

1	2	3	4		5
District.	Name of press.	Name of proprietor.	PUBLICATIONS THEREAT:		Remarks.
			Newspapers.	Periodicals.	
Akyab	The Arakan News ...	Kaing Sun Ki ...	" The Arakan News ...	The Annual Reports of the Akyab and Kemree Municipalities.	Newspapers published bi-weekly, 150 copies reports yearly executed.
Kyaukpyu {	Victoria Press ... The Arakan Industrial Press	Maung Tha Zan Maung Saw Hla Saug Nu		" Burma Gazette," English ... " Burma Gazette," Vernacular " Police Gazette," English " Police Gazette," Vernacular " English and Vernacular.	Weekly. Circulation 1,000 copies. Ditto. Weekly. Circulation 800 copies. Weekly. Circulation 600 copies. Weekly. Circulation 500 copies.
	The Government Press The Central Jail	Government of Burma, J. F. Regan, Superintendent.		Proceedings of the Chief Commissioner in the several departments under his control. History of Services of Gazetted Officers " Quarterly Civil List " Provincial Administration Report Forms and other departmental reports. Government publications.	Monthly. Circulation 20 copies.
Rangoon Town {	The American Baptist Mission Press	American Baptist Mission ...		" The Morning Star " (Karen) " The Evening Star " (Karen) " Burmese Messenger " (Burmese) " The Sunday School Lesson Paper " (Burmese) " The Sunday School Lesson Paper " (Karen) " The News " " Kyaup " " The Life Line "	Monthly. Circulation 1,750 copies. Monthly. Circulation 600 copies. Monthly. Circulation 2,500 copies. Monthly. Circulation 1,000 copies. Monthly. Circulation 600 copies. Monthly. Circulation 2,000 copies. Monthly. Circulation 300 copies. Monthly.
	The Victoria The Rangoon Gazette Ditto British Burma Advertiser The Friend of Burma	S. Goebhs ... Stuart, F. M Curthy, and V. J. Mariano }	" Rangoon Gazette " " Rangoon Weekly Budget " " British Burma Advertiser " " Friend of Burma "	Burman Directory and Diary	Ditto. Weekly. Circulation 750 copies. Weekly. Circulation 450 copies. Weekly. Circulation 600 copies. Monthly. Circulation 300 copies.
	The D'Vasa Press The Burma Herald Press The Rangoon Times The Rangoon Commercial Advertiser	Messrs. J., Dickinson & Co. Maung Po Oh ... W. O'Brien ... Ditto	" D'Vasa Press Advertiser " " Burma Herald " " Rangoon Times " " Rangoon Weekly Summary " " The Rangoon Commercial Advertiser."		Daily. Circulation 250 copies. Daily. Circulation 1,500 copies. Daily. Circulation 1,000 copies. Daily. Circulation 800 copies. Daily. Circulation 600 copies.
	The Epi Gye Newsline The Nature The Mogul Thit The Hanthawaddy The Church	Ma Me Maung Pe Maung Kywet Ni A. Ripley Ditto			Daily. Circulation 500 copies. Daily. Circulation 150 copies. Weekly. Circulation 600 copies. Weekly. Circulation 300 copies.
Bassein {	St. Paul's Orphan The Naw-Kaws St. Peter's Seminary	Rev. Heudier Valens J. F. Kock Roman Catholic Mission	" The Burma Catholic News " " The Diocesan Quarterly Paper " " Karen Weekly News and Municipal Reports Advertiser.		Job-work executed. Monthly. Circulation 200 copies. Ditto. Quarterly. Circulation 600 copies. Ditto. Weekly. Circulation 200 copies. Ditto. Weekly. Circulation 200 copies. Municipal Reports 10 to 20 copies.

SCIENTIFIC AND LITERARY.

2.—*Press*

District.	Name of Press.	Name of proprietor.	Publications thereat.		Remarks.
			Newspapers.	Periodicals.	
Amherst (Moulmein Town).	The Moulmein Advertiser	J. O. Hughes	"The Moulmein Advertiser"	"Advertiser and Mercantile Gazette"	Tri-weekly. Private work only.
	The Eden	Edria	...	...	Jobwork only executed.
	The Bulletin	J. Copley Moyle	...	...	
	The Cassim	Cassim	...	...	
	The Ranaporn	Maung Tuk Bya	...	...	Ditto.
	The Burma Times	Maung Po Kin	"Burma Times"	...	Ditto.
	The Zina Wapni	Ko Tha Nyo	...	...	Ditto.
Tavoy	Dawnagon	Maung Kyin U	...	"Lee ba tah"	Monthly.
	The Karen Mission A B M Union	C. H. Heptonstall	...	...	Ditto.
Toungoo	The Church Mission	Rev. A. Salmon	...	"The Pole Star" (in Karen)	Monthly.
	The Roman Catholic Mission	Rev. G. Gœtz	...	be Dodona" (in Karen)	Fortnightly.
Mandalay	Mandalay Herald	Z. M. D'Silva	"Mandalay Herald"	...	Tri-weekly.
	Mandalay Times	Maung To	"Mandalay Times - Daily Advertiser"	...	Bi-weekly. In Burmese. In English.
	Star of Burma	Maung Shwe Lein	"Star of Burma"	...	Bi-weekly. In English.
	Mandalay Express	Mrs. C. Calderwood and Mrs. M. Hostace	"Public Advertiser"	...	Job-work.

Statistics of Telegraph Lines and Offices in Burma for the year 1894-95.

LINES.

MILEAGE OF LINES.				MILEAGE OF WIRES (INCLUDING CABLES)			
At end of the previous year.	Added during the year.	Deducted during the year.	Remaining at the end of the year.	At the end of previous year.	Added during the year.	Deducted during the year.	Remaining at the end of the year.
4,954	34	66*	4,922	10,081	62	120*	10,023

* Line along Myu coast dismantled.

OFFICES.

Particulars.	Number of telegraph offices open at end of previous year.	Add number opened during the year.	Deduct number closed during the year.	Number open at the end of the year.	Number of telegrams despatched during the year from Government offices.	Decrease as compared with previous year.	Indian Share of Collections.		
							Rs.	A.	P.
Government offices ..	107	4	1	110	264,680	22,627	7,48,068	3	9
Railway and Canal offices	104	..	..	104					
Offices not open for paid telegrams	129	12	1	140					
Total ..	340	16	2	354					

Names of offices opened and closed during the year.

OPENED.		CLOSED.
GOVERNMENT OFFICES.		GOVERNMENT OFFICES.
Mona. Myothet.	Namkhon. Taungayi.	Mannaung.

RANGOON TOWN & SUBURBS.

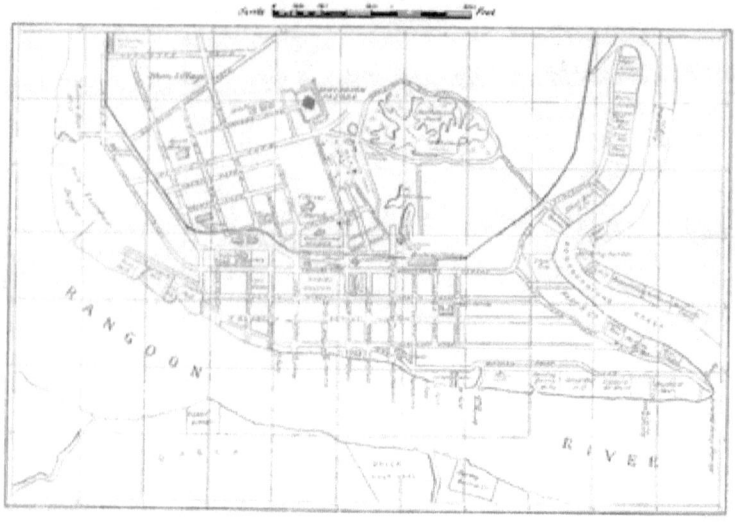

ROUTE I.

RANGOON AND NEIGHBOURHOOD.

RANGOON.—The chief seaport and capital of the province, 21 miles from the sea, situated on the right bank of the Hlaing river at its junction with the Puzoondaung and Pegu rivers.

Talaing traditions say that the first settlement was made about 585 B.C. by two brothers, who, on their return in their ships from Bengal, brought with them some hairs of Gaudama's head, given to them by Gaudama himself, who told them to enshrine them on a small hill about two miles from the river bank. This shrine is now known as the Shwè Dagón Pagoda. The neighbourhood remained a small village till the middle of the eighth century A.D., when Pona-reeka, the King of Pegu, rebuilt and beautified it, and changed its name to Aramana. It remained a place of small importance till Pegu was conquered by Alaungpya in 1755, when the new city was laid out, and its name changed to Rangoon, or, as the Burmese call it, *Yan-gôn*, signifying "the end of strife."

Gaspar Balbi, one of the first European travellers who visited the country, wrote of it in 1579-80 :—

"After we were landed we began to goe on the right hand in a large street about 50 paces broad, in which we saw wooden houses gilded, and adorned with delicate gardens after their custom wherein their Talapoins, which are their Friars, dwell and look to the Pagod or Varella of Dagon. The left side is furnished with portals or shops . . . . . and by this street they go to the Varella for a good mile straight

forward, either under paint houses or in the open street, which
is free to walk in."

The next account we have is that given by Captain
Symes, who in 1795 A.D. was sent by Sir John Shore, the
Governor-General of India, on an embassy to the court of
Ava. His description is as follows :—

"It stretches along the bank of the river about a mile,
and is not more than a third of a mile in breadth. The city
or *miou* (*myo*) is a square surrounded by a high stockade, and
on the north side it is further strengthened by an indifferent
fosse, across which a wooden bridge is thrown. In this fosse
there are two gates, in each of the others only one. Wooden
stages are erected in several places within the stockade, for
musqueteers to stand on in case of an attack. On the south
side, towards the river, which is about twenty or thirty yards
from the palisade, there are a number of huts and three
wharves, with cranes for landing goods. A battery of twelve
cannon, six and nine pounders, raised on the bank, commands
the river, but the guns and carriages are in such a wretched
condition that they could do but little execution. Close to
the wooden wharf are two commodious wooden houses, used
by the merchants as an exchange, where they usually meet in
the cool of the morning and evening to converse and transact
business. The streets of the town are narrow, and much
inferior to those of Pegu, but clean and well paved ; there
are numerous channels to carry off the rain, over which strong
planks are placed, to prevent an interruption of intercourse.
The houses are raised on posts from the ground, the smaller
supported by bamboos, the larger by strong timbers.

"All the officers of Government, the most opulent
merchants and persons of consideration live within the fort ;
the shipwrights and people of inferior rank inhabit the suburbs.

"Swine are suffered to roam about the town at large.
These animals, which are with reason held unclean, do not
belong to any particular owners ; they are servants of the

MASONRY SHRINE AT SULÈ PAGODA, RANGOON.
(Photo by F. O. Oertel, Esq., N.W.P.)

public, common scavengers ; they go under houses and devour
the filth. The Burmans are also fond of dogs, numbers of
which infest the streets ; the breed is small, and extremely noisy."

Rangoon was first occupied by the British on May 11th,
1824, at the commencement of the First Anglo-Burmese war,
and was held till the conclusion of hostilities at the end of
1826, when it was restored to the Burmese.

It was again occupied in 1852 at the outbreak of the
Second Anglo-Burmese war, since which time it has remained
in our possession.

The Rangoon of the present day is of course very
different from that of 1852. Prior to the formation of
municipal administration in 1874 the town was administered
by the Local Government, who laid it out on the block system,
and by making roads and drains, did much to improve the
sites for building.

Under local self-government vast improvements have been
effected. The water supply has been improved by the formation of the Victoria Lake at Kokaing, about five miles north of
Rangoon. From this lake the supply is carried by iron
mains to the Royal Lakes, from which smaller mains issue,
distributing an adequate supply to the different parts of the
city. As, however, the population of Rangoon is increasing
at enormous bounds, and at the census in 1891 numbered
181,000 souls, steps are now being taken to secure a supply
sufficient for the wants of a population of 300,000.

Rangoon contains over 100 miles of roads, of which about
50 miles are lighted.

Since 1892, the " Shone System " for the disposal of sewage
has been introduced, at a cost to the ratepayers of 27 lakhs of
rupees. The full advantages of this system will not be
appreciated until all houses are by law compelled to connect.

It is proposed also as soon as funds are available, to
substitute electricity as a luminant for the kerosine oil lamps at
present in use.

HOTELS.--Sarkies' Hotel, situated in Merchant Street ; Barnes' Family Hotel, also in Merchant Street ; Evershed's Hotel and the Oriental Hotel, both on the Strand Road ; and the British India Hotel in Sulè-Pagoda Road.

In Cantonments are two private hotels, viz.: "Croton Lodge" and "Allandale," where comfortable accommodation is given at reasonable rates.

CONSULATES.—The following countries have representatives : Persia, Siam, Peru, Brazil, France, Netherlands, Denmark, Austro-Hungary, U.S. of America, Greece, Germany, Norway and Sweden, Belgium and Italy.

CLUBS.—Gymkhana, in Halpin Road ; German Club, in Commissioner's Road ; Pegu Club, in Prome Road ; Burma Club, in Merchant Street ; Chinese Club, in Latter Street ; Chinese Club, in Canal Street ; Hong Kong Club, in China Street.

BANKS.—Bank of Bengal, Strand Road ; Chartered Bank of India, Australia and China, Strand Road ; National Bank of India, Phayre Street ; Hong Kong and Shanghai, Shafray Road ; Scott & Co., Merchant Street ; Burma Co-operative Society, Limited, Sulè-Pagoda Road ; Gillander Arbuthnot & Co., Strand Road ; Thomas Cook and Sons, Phayre Street.

PUBLIC GARDENS AND GROUNDS.

The Race Course, behind the Rangoon College.

Cantonment Gardens, at foot of Shwè Dagòn Pagoda.

Agri-horticultural Gardens, Pagoda Road.

Fytche Square, in centre of town.

Dalhousie Park and Royal Lakes, North East of Shwè Dagòn Pagoda.

STEAMSHIP COMMUNICATIONS.

British India Steam Navigation Company — Agents, Bulloch Bros. & Co., Limited.

SHAN UMBRELLAS, SHWÊ DAGÔN PAGODA.
(Photo by F. O. Oertel, Esq., N.W.P.)

Asiatic Steam Navigation Company—Gillander, Arbuthnot & Company.

Bibby Line : Arracan Company, Ltd., or Thomas Cook & Sons.

Patrick Henderson Line : Steel Bros. & Company, Ltd., Messrs. Bulloch Brothers & Company, or Thomas Cook & Sons.

Irrawaddy Flotilla Company, Phayre Street.

CHURCHES.

The Church of England Cathedral, Pagoda Road.
Roman Catholic Cathedral, Merchant Street.
Roman Catholic Garrison Church, Pagoda Road.
Church of England Garrison Church, Godwin Road.
Presbyterian Church, Signal Pagoda Road.
St. John's College Chapel, S.P.G., behind Central Jail.
R.C. Convent Chapel, Commissioner's Road.
Methodist Episcopal Church, Frazer Street.
American Baptist Mission, Alôn.

NEWSPAPERS.

Rangoon Times, Merchant Street.
Rangoon Gazette,   Ditto
Burma Gazette, Government Central Press.

PHOTOGRAPHERS.

P. Klier & Company, Signal Pagoda Road.
Beato & Co., Phayre Street.
Jackson & Co., Phayre Street.
Watts & Skein, Sulè Pagoda Road.
Kundan-Dass & Company, Dalhousie Street.

BOOK AND MAP SELLERS.

Miles Standish & Company, Merchant Street.
A.B. Mission Press, 35th Street.
British Burma Press, 76th Merchant Street.
Government Central Press, Strand Road.

BURMESE CURIO SHOPS.—CARVING.

Jail Sale Rooms, Commissioner's Road.
Beato and Company, Phayre Street.
Watts & Skein, Sulè Pagoda Road.
Goomanal Parasram, 20, Merchant Street.
Maung Thit, 25, Godwin Road.
Tha Maung, Godwin Road.
Maung Kyaw Yan, Godwin Road.

SILVER & GOLDSMITHS.

Beato & Company.
Goomanal Parasram.
Maung Po Thet, 19, Godwin Road.
Maung Shwè Yon, 29,   Ditto
Ngoon Hung, 54, Sulè Pagoda Road.
Eng Goon, 168, Dalhousie Street.

PLACES TO VISIT IN RANGOON.

1. SHWÈ DAGÓN PAGODA.—This is the most celebrated and ancient shrine in Burma, and indeed in Indo-China, and is visited by Buddhists from all parts of this and the surrounding Buddhist countries. Its peculiar sanctity is due to the fact that it is supposed to contain relics of all four Buddhas who have up to the present time appeared. These relics are " The Drinking Cup " of Kaukathan ; " The Robe " of Gaunagohn ; " The Staff " of Kathapa ; and " Eight Hairs " of Gaudama.

It is built on a mound which is in reality the most southern prolongation of the Pegu Yomas, situated in the angle formed by the junction of the Hlaing and Pegu rivers. This hill has been cut into two rectangular terraces one above the other, the sides facing the four cardinal points. On the upper terrace the pagoda is built. This terrace is 166 feet above the level of the surrounding country, and is 900 feet long by 680 feet wide. As in other shrines, there were originally four flights of brick steps, one on each face of the platform. Of these three remain, the

CARVED PYATHAT, SHWÈ DAGÔN PAGODA.

(Photo by Signor Beato, Mandalay.)

western one having been closed owing to the erection of fortifications and magazines since the British occupation. The principal
entrance is from the south, as the city lies in great part in that
direction. At the foot of the southern flight of steps are two
gigantic leogriphs of brick, covered with cement and painted in
gorgeous colours. The stairs are roofed the whole way up with
handsome teak carved work, and this covered way affords shelter
to the numerous beggars, lepers, and petty stall keepers who
make a living by selling candles, flags, and other offerings to the
worshippers.

The pagoda itself rises from the upper platform to a height of
370 feet with a perimeter at the base of 1,355 feet. The summit is
surmounted by a massive *hti* or umbrella, which consists of a
series of circular rings of iron, each ring gradually decreasing in
size to the top, to which the *Sein-bu* or gem crown is fixed.
These hoops of iron are all covered with beaten gold,
and from the edges are hung an innumerable number of gold
and silver bells, which fill the air with melody when the wind
blows.

This *hti* was presented in 1871 by King Mindòn Min, and
was placed in position amid the greatest excitement and religious
ceremony.

An eye witness told the writer that prior to being conveyed
up the rope incline on a car specially constructed, gold watches
and chains, necklaces, bangles, diamond and ruby rings, and
other gems were attached to it, or hung on the projecting points
by a crowd of enthusiastic devotees. This *hti* is valued at seven
lakhs of rupees.

The flagged court-yard or terrace at the foot of the pagoda is
left free for worshippers. Here and there are seen brick altars on
which offerings are placed; wrought iron umbrellas of Shan
manufacture; tagundaing or flag-staffs bearing images of the
sacred Karaweik (the Garuda of Vishnu) or other emblems.

The terrace is surrounded by shrines and image houses of
every shape and size, either of brick or wood.

Some of these contain images of Gaudama, others the
Kyi-dau-ya or sacred foot-print of Buddha. The writer has
himself seen in one of these shrines—massed promiscuously side
by side—images of Gaudama, gaudy prints of the present German
Emperor and of the Madonna. Squatting about in all kinds of
nooks and corners the sooth-sayers or astrologers are to be found
surrounded by crowds of credulous supporters.

In the north-east corner of the pagoda platform is a small
enclosure containing the graves of several officers and men who
lost their lives at the taking of the pagoda in 1852.

In a separate building on the eastern side of the platform is
an enormous bell, called in the vernacular "Maha Ganda."
With the exception of the immense bell at Mingûn near
Mandalay, which will be described later on, it is the largest bell
in the province. It was presented to the pagoda in 1840, by King
Tharrawaddi. The principal dimensions are :—

Diameter across the mouth	7ft.	7½in.
Thickness of metal	15in.	
Height	14ft.	
Weight	94,682lbs. or nearly 42 tons.	

An inscription of 12 lines in Burmese is engraved on the
side which has been translated by the late Mr. G. Hough. The
translation of the latter part is as follows :—

"For this meritorious gift, replete with the virtue of
beneficence, may he (Tharrawaddi, the King who presented the
bell) be conducted to Neikban and obtain the destined blessing
of men, Nat and Bramha by means of divine perfection. May
he obtain in his transmigrations the reigning state only among
men and Nat. May he have a pleasant voice, a voice heard at
whatsoever place desired, like the voice of Kan-tha-min,
Por-nir-ka, and A-la-wa-ka when he speaks to terrify, and like
Karaweik, King of Birds, when he speaks on the subject about
which Nat and Bramha delight to hear. Whatever may be the
desire or thought of his heart, merely let that desire be fulfilled.
Let him not in the least meet with that towards which he has no

MAHA GANDA, SHWÈ DAGÔN PAGODA.
(Photo by F. O. Oechl, Esq., N.W.P.)

mental disposition, and for which he has no desire. When
A-re-ma-de-ya shall be revealed, let him have the revelation that
he may become We-tha-dee Nat supreme of the three rational
existences. In every state of existence let him continually and
truly possess the excellence of wisdom, and according to his
desire in practices pertaining to this world and to the divine
state, so let it be accomplished. Thus in order to cause the voice
of homage during the period of 500 years, to be heard at the
monument of the divine hair in the city of Rangoon, let the
reward of the great merit of giving the great bell called Maha
Ganda, be unto the royal queen mother, the royal father,
proprietor of life, lord of the white elephant, the royal grand-father
Alaung-min, the royal uncle, the royal aunt queen, the royal sons,
the royal daughters, the royal relatives, the royal concubines, the
noblemen, the military officers and teachers. Let the Nat who
guard the religious dispensation 5,000 years, the Nat who guard
the royal city, palace and umbrella, the Nat who all around guard
the empire, the provinces and villages, the Nat who guard the
monument of the divine hair around the hill Tampa-koot-ta,
together with the Nat governing Bounma and Akatha, and all
rational beings throughout the universe utter praises and accept
the supplications."

The common report that this bell was dropped into the
Rangoon river while in transit as a prize trophy to Calcutta, at the
close of the First Burmese war is not founded on fact.

From the correspondence on the subject which appeared in
the *Rangoon Gazette* in the early part of the present year (1896),
the following extract, which describes fully the way in which the
bell was raised, is quoted. The bell here referred to was not the
Maha Ganda, which was presented by King Tharrawaddi to the
pagoda in 1840, but a smaller one which hung on the north-west
corner of the platform.

The book from which the extract is taken is the "Travels"
of Lieutenant J. E. Alexander, late H.M's 13th Light Dragoons,
which was published in 1827. Lieutenant Alexander returned

from Prome when the Treaty of 3rd January, 1826 (afterwards broken), was signed. He says :—

"Upon my arrival at Rangoon I had the satisfaction of being the first to convey the intelligence of the conclusion of peace to Brigadier Smelt, the Commandant. The news quickly spread throughout the place, and all the Europeans were dancing for joy in consequence. The Burmese were in ecstacy on another account, namely the raising of the Bell of the Great Pagoda out of the bed of the river into which it had fallen several months previous, whilst the Prize-agents were endeavouring to ship it to Bengal as a trophy. It was raised in a very simple manner, by attaching two cables to it, which at low water were made fast to a brig moored over it ; when the tide rose so did the Bell, and it was hauled on shore by thousands of enraptured natives, who testified their delight by many acts of extravagance ; they crowned it with flowers ; they performed sacrifices to it ; they danced before it and placed bands of music constantly near it. At the time I left Rangoon they were busily employed in removing it to its former position at the Shoe Dagoon."

Lieutenant Alexander left Rangoon on 9th January, 1826, in H.M.S. *Champion*, "reckoned the fastest sailing vessel in the British Navy," and reached Calcutta on 23rd January.

THE THAMAING, OR LEGEND OF THE PAGODA.

In former times a king reigned over the Talaings in the delta of the Irrawaddy, whose capital was at Ok-ka-la-ba, on the site of the modern Tûntè, about sixteen miles west of Rangoon.

Near Ok-ka-la-ba lived a wealthy merchant named Tha-ke-lè, who had received honours and gifts from the king on account of his merits in this and previous existences. This man had two sons, *Poo*, or "dove," and *Ta-pne*, or "plenty." These two, hearing that a famine existed in Bengal, collected a ship-load of rice, and set sail. After a time they arrived at the mouth of the

BASE OF TAGÛNDAING SHWÉ DAGÔN PAGODA.

(Photo by F. O. Oertel, Esq., N.W.P.)

Ganges. Landing from their ship they proceeded to the town of Bamdawa and procured 500 carts in which to convey the rice from the ship to the city. On their return to the city with the laden carts they were met by a Nat, who in a former existence had been their mother, who demanded of them : " Desire ye gold and silver merchandise, or rather desire ye treasure ? " The brothers replied " Heavenly treasure." They were accordingly guided by the Nat to the presence of Gaudama, who at the time was meditating under the Lin-lwûn tree at Gaya, near Patna.

In reply to a question from Gaudama, the brothers replied that they came from a country called Pegu. Shin Gaudama then told them that his predecessor had left behind him in Pegu a water dipper, a bathing garment, and a staff, which were buried under a wood-oil tree on the Thein-got-tara Hill. He then gave each of the brothers four hairs of his head, changed their names to *Ta-pu-sa* and *Hpa-li-ka*, and bade them deposit the sacred hairs with the other relics.

The two brothers placed the hairs in a golden casket and set out on their return journey. Stopping *en route* at Zetta and Negrais, two hairs were demanded at each place, yet on their arrival at Thein-got-tara Hill the eight hairs were found intact ! After arriving at their destination search was made for the sacred tree, and after a time it was found. On being felled it remained suspended horizontally in the air ; hence the hill on which it stood was named *Dagôn* by the Talaings.

On this site the first pagoda was raised, the relic chamber containing all the articles referred to above.

The date given for the erection of this pagoda, which was 27 feet high, is B.C. 588. In course of time a town, and the usual religious buildings sprung up around the pagoda, but after several generations both town and pagoda fell into ruins. It remained in this ruined state till A.D. 1446, when Binya-Ran ruled over Pegu. He set to work to restore the pagoda, and the works were carried on by his successor,

Queen Shin-Saw-bu, who raised its height to 130 feet, and set apart lands and slaves for its up-keep.

Successive Burmese sovereigns still further increased its height and embellished it, and in 1776 it reached its present height of 321 feet from the platform.

During the reign of Shin-byu-shin in 1774 it was re-gilt, the weight of gold used being 171 lbs. (the weight avoirdupois of the king), valued at several lakhs of rupees. In 1834 it was again re-gilded, and again by public subscription in 1870-71. On this last occasion a new "*hti*," the gift of King Mindôn Min, was placed in position. A large portion of the pagoda was again re-gilded about four years ago.

After the Second Anglo-Burmese war the platform was converted into a fortification, and at the present time is held by a guard of European troops. The powder-magazines and ordnance stores lie on the north-west face.

SULÈ PAGODA.

This pagoda lies in the heart of the city, and is visible from all sides. Unlike the ordinary pagodas, it is octagonal in shape, tapering gracefully to the *hti*. It assumed its present shape about 70 years ago, when it was renovated.

Within the last few years its has received much attention, chiefly owing to the representations of Colonel Olcott, and other Buddhist revivalists.

HISTORY.—The first pagoda was erected to commemorate the meeting of King Ok-ka-la-ba, the king of Tûn-tè, with the two brothers Pu and Ta-paw and their followers, when they landed from India in search of the Thein-got-tara hill.

BO-TA-TAUNG PAGODA.

This small but ancient pagoda is built on the bank of the river about a mile above Monkey point. It is said to have been built in A.D. 947 by Ok-ka-la-ba, king of Tûn-tè, to mark the spot where the body of his son Chin-han-da who had been drowned in

SULÈ PAGODA, RANGOON.

(Photo by F. O. Oertel, Esq., N.W.P.)

the Pegu river, was cremated. The name signifies, *Bo*—Officer, *Ta-taung*—1,000, and was given because it was erected by 1,000 of the king's officers.

THE AGRI-HORTICULTURAL SOCIETY'S GARDENS.

These Gardens are situated in Pagoda Road, immediately opposite to the General Hospital and the Rangoon College.

The gardens are merely a depôt for experimental horti-culture, and to the general public are uninteresting. Within these gardens, however, the Phayre Museum and the Zoological Gardens are situated.

In front of the museum stands the first bronze statue the city can boast of, that of Sir Arthur Phayre, who was appointed first Chief Commissioner in 1862.

The museum is poorly stocked, and contains little of interest or importance. What few antiquities it does contain are badly catalogued, and of little help to the scientist or archaeologist.

The Zoological Gardens contain the wild animals, birds, and snakes indigenous to the country, but very few from other countries are met with. These gardens are very popular with the Burmese, and the admission fee of one pice is not prohibitive.

THE ROYAL LAKES AND DALHOUSIE PARK.

These lakes are situated immediately to the east of the Shwè Dagòn Pagoda, and cover an area of 160 acres. The park, which is surrounded by the waters of the lake and its off-shoots, contains an area of 295 acres.

These lakes and the surrounding park land were set apart as a place for public recreation by Lord Dalhousie, Governor-General of India, when he visited Rangoon at the close of the Second Anglo-Burmese war.

The lakes are artificial, the land having originally been excavated for brick making for the enlargement of the Shwè Dagòn Pagoda, in the 15th and 16th centuries.

The park is now under the management of the municipality, by whom it has of late years been much improved, so that at the present time few cities in the East can boast of such a naturally beautiful and artistically arranged resort.

A drive leads round the edge of the lake to the peninsula in the centre, where band-stands and pavilions for the convenience of visitors have been erected.

Here on holidays and Sundays and on moonlight nights vast crowds of visitors of all classes and races congregate. On certain evenings in the week, when the weather permits, a military band plays here for one or two hours.

Pleasure boats are kept on the lake for the use of visitors, and the Rangoon Boat Club has its pavilion and well-selected supply of boats on its southern bank.

THE PUBLIC BUILDINGS.

This handsome block of buildings which contains the chief Government offices is situated to the east of Spark Street, in the eastern portion of the city, and has only just been erected, at a cost Rs 9,00,000. At present only the central block has been completed, but when funds are available it is intended to provide accommodation for all public offices.

THE CANTONMENT GARDENS.

These artistically arranged and well kept gardens are situated immediately to the south-west of the pagoda, and are kept in order and superintended by the Cantonment Committee. A regimental band usually plays here either one or two evenings a week. The grounds contain several orchid houses, and at certain times when the plants are in bloom the sight well repays a visit.

VIEW OF SHWÉ DAGÓN PAGODA FROM CANTONMENT GARDENS.

(*Photo by F. O. Oakley, Esq. N.B.I.*)

ROUTE II.

EXCURSIONS FROM RANGOON.

1. DALLA.—This is a suburb of Rangoon, situated on the opposite bank of the river, and is within municipal limits. It has a Government dockyard, which for a number of years has been leased to the Irrawaddy Flotilla Company. Here the steamers and flats imported from Europe are fitted together, and repairs carried out. Further down are the steam sawmills of the Bombay Burmah Trading Corporation, where the teak logs from the forests of Upper Burma are squared and prepared for export.

Dalla is reached in a few minutes from Rangoon by launch or boat.

2. KO-KAING.—This is a suburb of Rangoon, situated to the north of the Shwè Dagôn Pagoda. Up to within a few years ago it was little better than a village of market-gardeners and cattle-owners. Of late years, however, owing to the scarcity of land in Rangoon, land has been taken up by wealthy speculators for house sites, and the principal members of the mercantile community have their suburban residences there. Owing to the undulating nature of the surface and the presence of large foliage trees, better sites could not be procured. In this neighbourhood is the Victoria Lake, formed some years ago by bunding up a deep valley, for supplying Rangoon with water. From this lake the water is taken in iron mains to the Royal Lake, which acts as a distributing reservoir.

3. KYAIK-KA-LO PAGODA.—This ancient pagoda is situated on the summit of a short spur to the west of the Prome Road, and 1½ miles north of the village of San-Gyi-wa. It is 14 miles from Rangoon.

Unlike most pagodas, it is built of laterite blocks, faced with bricks. The platform is about 60 yards square. The base is octagonal in shape, each side being 14 yards long. Its total height is 90 feet.

On the north side the brick facing has fallen away, exposing the laterite blocks of the interior.

The pagoda is of no special sanctity, but is visited in the month of March by vast crowds of picnic seekers from Rangoon. For an account of this pagoda feast please see *Shwe Yoe's,* "The Burman," volume 1.

4. KYAIK-KA-SHAN PAGODA.—This shrine is situated about three miles north-east of the Shwè Dagòn Pagoda, and is about 90 feet high and 70 feet in diameter at the base.

Talaing history places its erection in the second century B.C. It covers relics of Gaudama in the shape of three hairs brought by eight Rahanda from India.

The pagoda was last repaired in 1848, when a new "*hti*" was placed on it. Like the Kyaik-ka-lo pagoda, its annual festival is held in March, when vast crowds of Buddhists assemble from all parts of the country, but particularly from the province of Pegu, the home of the Talaing race.

5. SYRIAM.—This name is the Anglicized form of the Burmese "*Than-hlyin.*" The town is situated on the left bank of the Pegu river, about three miles above its confluence with the Hlaing or Rangoon river. The present town contains about 3,000 inhabitants. The population consists of Burmese, Talaing, Karen, Mussulman, and Shan.

The Mussulman population is descended from the Indian colonists, who settled here at the time of the Portuguese occupation.

SOUTHERN ENTRANCE TO SHWÉ DAGÔN PAGODA, RANGOON.

(Photo by F. O. Oertel, Esqr., M.W.P.)

The Kan-saung quarter on the western side of the town is inhabited by Shans, who are employed in garden cultivation. The Karen-zu quarter is occupied by Talaings and Karens, who are engaged in rice cultivation.

The modern town of Than-hlyin lies partly within and partly without the old city walls, parts of which still remain.

HISTORY.—Burmese tradition places the foundation in B.C. 587 by Ze-ya-thi-na, who named it Pada, but 50 years later its name was changed to Than-hlyin, after Than-hlyin who dethroned A-nein-da-raza, son of Ze-ya-thi-na, and married his daughter. From that time till the arrival of Europeans in the country in the 17th century very little of the town is recorded.

About the commencement of the 17th century the King of Arakan, taking advantage of the quarrels between the Kings of Toungoo, Ava, and Pegu, invaded and took possession of the latter kingdom. In his service was one Philip de Brito and Nicote, a Portuguese adventurer. After the capture of Syriam, De Brito was appointed king's agent, and the collection of revenue and custom duties was entrusted to him. For this purpose he built a brick custom house, and after a time a fort, ostensibly to protect the custom house. In connivance with another Portuguese named Salvado Ribeyro, the Arakanese garrison was expelled from the town, and De Brito proclaimed himself as governor. The Arakanese twice attempted to retake the fort, but on both occasions were unsuccessful.

De Brito, during the first attempt of the Arakanese, was away at Goa, to secure the assistance of the Portuguese Viceroy. In this he was successful, and he returned to Syriam with six ships. He was then recognised as King of Pegu. He at once set to work to strengthen his capital, repaired the fortifications, built a church, and laid out the city.

The King of Arakan again sought to recover possession in 1604, but on this occasion, was forced to retire, after his son had been taken prisoner. He was subsequently released on payment to De Brito of a ransom of 50,000 crowns.

G

De Brito now reigned supreme for a time, but in consequence of his interference with the Kingdom of Toungu, which was tributary to the Kingdom of Ava, Maha-Dhama Raja, King of Ava, determined to punish De Brito for this insult. In 1612 he therefore left his capital and proceeded to invest Syriam both by land and water. After a lengthened siege, the King of Ava, having no artillery to strengthen his attack, the gates of the city were opened through the treachery of those within, and De Brito taken prisoner. He was impaled in front of his own house, and lingered for three days in the most dreadful agony. Those of the Portuguese whose lives were spared were deported with their families to distant parts of Upper Burma, where their descendants are still to be found.

It was not long before other European nations sought to obtain settlements in Syriam, which at that time was the principal port of Pegu.

The Dutch established a factory in 1631, which they held till 1677.

The date of the establishment of the first English factory is not known, but its re-establishment took place in 1698.

In 1743, the English factory was burned to the ground for duplicity on the part of the factor Mr. Smart, when he, with all the establishment, withdrew from the country.

Beyond the ruins of a Roman Catholic Church, some masonry tombs, and the foundations of a few houses, nothing now remains of the once flourishing European settlements.

6.—The Church was built on a hill or ridge just outside the old walls. It was erected in 1749-50, by Mons Nerini, the second Vicar Apostolic of Ava and Pegu, and a member of the Barnabite Mission. The following account of its erection is taken from the life of one of the missionaries, Mons Percoto, who for some years laboured in this country.

" He (Dom Nerini) was received with favour by the King of Pegu, to whom he made himself useful by his skill in astronomy, fore-telling eclipses and so forth, and he ultimately received

RUINS OF R.C. CHURCH, SYRIAM.

(Photo by J. O. Urdell, Esq., N.W.P.)

permission to erect a Church of Masonry at Syriam. The funds for building the Church were found by a good Armenian merchant, and the building was designed by Father Nerini. So well did he succeed, that the Church when finished was the admiration not only of the country, but even of the foreigners who came to the place. In plan it consisted of a single nave, ornamented with arches and columns, both inside and out. Its dimensions were as follows : — Length 81 feet, breadth 31 and height 40 French feet. It was intended to have a domed roof, but the arrival of the Coromandel workmen who were sent for to construct it, was prevented by the war which arose, and the roof was therefore completed in another style. The whole building was a marvel to the Peguans, but what they more especially admired, was the spiral staircase going up inside the tower. The following inscription was placed inside the Church :—

D. O. M.

"Ad fidem Propagandum Clerici regularis sancti Paulli Nicolaus de Aquilar nationi Armenus.

Margarita conjux.

Aedificabant.

Anno Domini.

No trace of this inscription now remains ; the roof and west wall have fallen in, as well as other parts of the building, but the place where the spiral staircase was, with the marks of the steps, the north and south walls and the eastern end are still standing." (B. B. Gazetteer.)

In addition to the Church a commodious clergy house and mission school were built, with accommodation for boarders and a convent in which abandoned children were received. Almost the whole cost of these buildings was defrayed by Nicholas de Aguilar whose name was inscribed on the stone fixed in the Church.

Bishop Nerini was in 1756 murdered by Alaungpya, who at the time was besieging Syriam, because he was suspected of having sent for a French ship, then in the harbour, to assist the Talaings.

G 2

Syriam was finally abandoned as a mission field in 1760, and new work commenced in Rangoon.

During the First Anglo-Burmese war Syriam was occupied by the British under Colonels Kelly and Elrington, and on the conclusion of peace was the head-quarters of the Talaing rebellion against the Burmese government. This rebellion was suppressed in 1827, and the leaders escaped into British territory.

During the second war the town was occupied without opposition.

7. KYAIK-KAUK PAGODA.—This ancient Talaing structure is built on the summit of the hills stretching between Syriam and Kyauk-dan, close to the village of Ka-myin-gôn, about five miles from Syriam. It is 130 feet in height and 1,200 feet in circumference at the base, and is built almost entirely of laterite blocks. The platform is flagged with stones, probably procured from Upper Burma. The upper part of the pagoda is covered with alternate bands of yellow and blue metals which from a distance somewhat resembles the more expensive gilding of the Rangoon and Pegu pagodas.

HISTORY.—According to traditional history, Shin Gaudama, after attaining Buddha-hood, visited Burma, and when resting on the Martaban Hills, gave two hairs of his head to a hermit. In 580 B.C. the hermit presented the hairs to Ze-ya-thi-na, King of Syriam, who caused the present shrine to be built over them. After a lapse of 350 years, or in 223 B.C., eight Buddhist phongyis visited the shrine and presented Bau-ga-thi-na, the King, with a bone of Gaudama's forehead and one of his teeth. These relics were subsequently enshrined. The pagoda was extensively repaired by Bo-dau-pya in 1781, and subsequently by other pious devotees.

8. PA-DA is at the present time a small village to the east of the rising ground between Syriam and Kyauk-dan, but was formerly a place of some importance and the capital of a small kingdom. The name is supposed to be derived from the Pali " pa-da "—a footstep—because the old town was built in the

KYEIK-KAUK PAGODA, SYRIAM.

(Photo by F. O. Oertel, Esq., N.W.P.)

form of a footstep, the toes pointing towards the north. The ruins of the old laterite walls of the town are still to be seen, and the original shape traced from the summit of a pagoda in the neighbourhood.

The remains of the palace and elephant enclosure are also to be seen.

The town was entirely destroyed by the troops of Anaurahta, King of Pagan, when he invaded and conquered Pegu at the beginning of the 11th century.

Two old pagodas in the neighbourhood are known locally as the Tau-ya-kyaung pagodas.

Syriam is about six miles from Rangoon. A steam ferry maintains daily communication between the two places.

bricks, and there they put all their goods of any value to save them from the often mischances which happen to houses made of such stuffs. In the new city is the palace of the King, and his abiding place with all his barons and nobles and other gentlemen, and in the time that I was there they finished the building of the new city. It is a great city, very plain and flat, and four square, walled about, and with ditches that encompass the walls round about with water, in which ditches are many crocodiles. It hath no draw-bridges, yet it hath twenty gates, five for every square. On the walls are many places made for sentinels to watch, made of wood, and covered or gilt with gold. The streets thereof are the fairest that I have seen; they are as straight as a line from one gate to another, and standing at one gate you may discover the other, and they are as broad as that ten or twelve men may ride abreast in them. And these streets that be thwart are fair and large. The streets both on the one side and on the other are planted at the doors of the houses with nut trees of India, which make a commodious shadow. The houses be made of wood, and covered with a kind of tiles in form of cups, very necessary for their use.

"The king's palace is in the middle of the city, made in form of a walled castle, with ditches full of water round about it. The lodgings within are made of wood all over gilded, with fine pinnacles and very costlie work, covered with plates of gold; truly it may be a king's house. Within the gate there is a fine large court, from the one side to the other, wherein are made places for the stoutest and strongest elephants."

When Alaungpya invaded and conquered Pegu in 1757 he utterly destroyed the city, and carried the inhabitants away into captivity. When Bo-daupaya succeeded to the throne in 1781 he endeavoured to conciliate the Talaings, and took steps to rebuild the city and make it the seat of government.

Symes, who was sent on an embassy to the court of Ava in 1795, thus describes the city as he saw it :—

"The extent of ancient Pegu may still be accurately traced by the ruins of the ditch and wall that surrounded it. From these it appears to have been a quadrangle, each side measuring nearly a mile and a half. In places the ditch has been choked up by rubbish that has been cast into it, and the falling of its own banks. Sufficient, however, still remains to show that it was no contemptible defence ; the breadth I judged to be about sixty yards, and the depth ten or twelve feet ; in some part of it there is water, but in no considerable quantity. I was informed that when the ditch was in repair the water seldom in the hottest seasons sunk below the depth of four feet. An injudicious fosse-bray thirty feet wide did not add to the security of this fortress."

"The fragments of the wall likewise evince that this was a work of magnitude and labour. It is not easy to ascertain what was its exact height, but we conjectured it at least thirty feet, and in breadth at the base not less than forty.

"It is composed of brick badly cemented with clay mortar. Small equi-distant bastions, about 300 yards asunder, are still discoverable. There had been a parapet of masonry, but the whole is in a state so ruinous, and so covered with weeds and briars, as to leave very imperfect vestages of its former strength.

"In the centre of each face of the fort there is a gateway about thirty feet wide ; these gateways were the principal entrances. The passage over the ditch is over a causeway raised on a mound of earth that serves as a bridge, and was formerly defended by an entrenchment, of which there are now no traces.

"Pegu in its renovated and contracted state seems to have been built on the plan of the former city, and occupied one half of its former area.

"It is fenced round by a stockade from ten to twelve feet high ; on the north and east sides its borders are the old wall. The plan of the town is not yet fitted with houses, but a

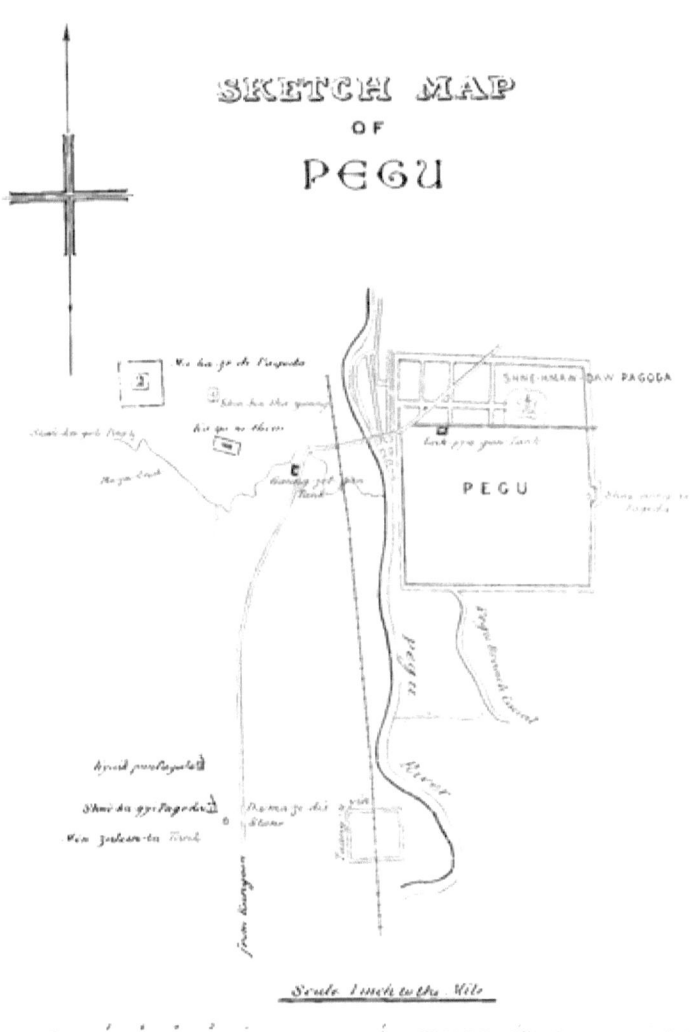

SKETCH MAP

OF

PEGU

SHWE-HMAW-DAW PAGODA

PEGU

Scale 1 inch to the Mile

number of new ones are building. There is one main street running east and west, crossed at right angles by two similar streets not yet finished. At each extremity of the principal street is a gate in the stockade, which is shut early in the evening; after that hour entrance during the night is confined to a wicket. . . . . There are two inferior gates on the north and south sides of the stockade.

"The streets of Pegu are spacious. The new town is well paved with brick, which the ruins of the old plentifully supplied. On each side of the way there is a drain to carry off the water." (*Symes' Embassy to the Court of Ava, p. 182, et siq.*)

During the First Anglo-Burmese war Pegu was occupied for a time by the British troops. They, however, found the town deserted by the inhabitants, so after a short stay retired to Rangoon.

In the second war the town was handed over to the British by the Talaings, who threw in their lot with us. A garrison was placed in the city, the citadel of which was the Shwè Hmaudau Pagoda.

The Burmese, strengthened by numerous partizans from Shwè-gyin and Martaban, advanced in force and recaptured the pagoda from the Talaings, to whom it was made over on the withdrawal of the British troops.

After the capture of Prome, General Godwin despatched a force to the relief of Pegu. This was effected, and a garrison left under the command of Major Hill.

The Burmese again invested the place, and a second force had to be despatched to its relief. After one or two sharp engagements the Burmese retired, and the city was left unmolested.

The old Pali name of the city is Hansa-watti, so called as being the supposed resting-place of the "Hansa" or Brahminy duck, when the surrounding country was beneath the sea.

The principal archæological remains in the neighbourhood of Pegu are the Shwè-hmau-dau Pagoda; the Shwè-tha-yaung, or huge recumbent figure of Gaudama ; the ruins of Zaing-ga-naing, comprising Kalayanisema, Mahaciti, Yethèmyo, Kyaikpûn, and Shwè-ku-gyi.

A short detailed description of each will now be given :—

SHWÈ-HMAU-DAU PAGODA. — This pagoda is 324 feet in height, and is built on an octagonal base, each side measuring 162 feet in length. It stands on two terraces one above the other. The lower one, which is about 10 feet from the ground, is a parallelogram in shape, with sides each 1,390 feet long. The upper terrace is about 20 feet higher than the lower, and each of its sides measures 684 feet. Both terraces are reached by flights of masonry steps. The pagoda is surrounded by two tiers of smaller ones, the lower of which, six feet from the terrace, contains 75, each 27 feet high and 40 feet in circumference at the base. The upper tier contains 53. (B. B. Gazetteer.)

The thamaing, or sacred history of the pagoda, is as follows :—

Gaudama, when staying on the Mat-hu-la Hill, near the sources of the Yun-za-lein river, gave two hairs to two brothers, Mahathala and Sulathala, who came from Zaung-du, a town near the modern Pegu. He directed them to enshrine the hairs on the Thudathana Myinthihla Hill, near the hill of Hansa-waddi. By the assistance of Nats and Brahmas the hill was discovered, and the sacred relics enshrined. The structure was then 50 cubits high and 250 cubits in circumference. The chronicle then takes a skip of many centuries, and states that during the reign of Dhammathauka, King of Pateliput, this and five other shrines in Pegu were repaired, and slaves set apart for their service. In the year A.D. 573 the city of Pegu was founded by the two brothers Thamala and Wimala. Both these kings repaired the pagoda and dedicated more slaves to its service. Successive kings repaired and enlarged it, until, in the reign of Tha-maing-dau-wot-kalè, who reigned at the beginning of the 16th century, it assumed its present proportions.

SHWÉ-HMAU-DAU PAGODA, PEGU.
(Photo by F. O. Oertel, Esq., N.W.P.)

Bo-dau-Paya carried out extensive repairs towards the end of the last century, and placed a new *hti* on it, which was 40 feet high and 46 feet in circumference.

During the Second Anglo-Burmese war the pagoda was fortified and held throughout the war by a garrison of British troops. At one time it was closely invested in force by the Burmese, and a special column had to be despatched to its relief.

Standing as it does on a natural eminence in the middle of an immense level plain, it is a striking object from a distance of many miles.

SHWÈ-THA-YAUNG.—This is the name given locally to an enormous recumbent image of Gaudama. It is a corrupted form of the word *shinbinthayaung*, the name given to the recumbent figures of Buddha, which attitude he assumed shortly before his death. The image is situated in close proximity to the Kalyanisema, and from recent measurements is 181 feet long and 50 feet high at the shoulder. This huge image, of which there is at present no known history, was found buried in the dense jungle some 15 years ago by a railway contractor, when in search of laterite to be used as ballast for the railway. So completely had Alaung-pya destroyed the place and annihilated the inhabitants, that the existence of the image was unknown to the present inhabitants of the country.

On its existence becoming known, numerous willing devotees soon cleared the site of the jungle growth and disclosed the figure of most gigantic proportions.

It is built, on a pedestal of laterite blocks, of successive layers of red bricks. Since its recovery a commencement has been made to cover the whole with stucco work, and already the head and part of the shoulders have been so disfigured. In time it is probable that the whole will be so treated, thereby destroying its interest as an object of antiquity.

Similar enormous figures are to be found on the banks of the sacred lakes at Mo-dûn, in the Amherst district.

THE MAHACITI PAGODA is now a mass of ruins; the plinth only of the pagoda remains, which measures 320 feet in width at the base, and about 170 feet in height. It was built about the middle of the 16th century by Hanthawadi Sinbyuyin.

KYAIK-PÛN.—This is an immense brick tower, about 90 feet in height, consisting of four images of Buddhas sitting cross-legged, back to back, and facing the four cardinal points. The images represent the four Buddhas who have appeared in this world cycle, namely, Kaukathan, Gauna-gôn, Kathapa, and Gaudama. In the Kalyani inscriptions this image tower is mentioned as Mahabuddha-rupa.

It is supposed to have been built by the Cambodian conquerors of Pegu, about the 10th century, A.D.

YETHÈ-MYO or the Hermit's town is close to the Kyaik-pûn pagoda. Nothing but ruins now remain, and amidst these are found large quantities of glazed terra-cotta tiles with grotesque figures in relief on them. A number of these tiles have been recovered and placed for safe custody in the Phayre Museum.

KALYANISEMA.—This is situated at Zaing-ganaing, the western part of the town of Pegu. The name was given because the "sema" was consecrated by Talaing priests who had received their ordination from the spiritual successors of Mahinda, the special Buddhist missionary to Ceylon, at the Kalyani river near the modern Colombo. The Kalyani inscriptions are recorded on ten stones, the dimensions of which, when erected, were as follows :—Height 7 feet, width 4 feet 2 inches, thickness 1 foot 3 inches. The first three stones are in Pali, both sides being inscribed, containing about 70 lines of text on each face. The inscriptions on the other seven stones are in Talaing, and contain a translation of the Pali text. A full translation into English from the Pali, has been made by Mr. Tau Sein Kho, the Government translator, from which the following digest is taken.

These inscriptions were set up in 1476, A.D., by Dhammaceti or Ramathipati, King of Pegu, or Hansa-vati, as it was then called. In emulation of Asoka and other illustrious predecessors, he was,

HUGE RECUMBENT BUDDHA, PEGU.

(Photo by F. O. Oertel, Esq., N.W.P.)

when King, much concerned on account of the heresies and
impurities that had crept into the Buddhist faith in his kingdom,
and became alarmed lest true religion should perish before the
completion of the 5,000 years assigned for the continuance of the
religion established by Gaudama Buddha, in the sixth century
before Christ. In order then to cleanse the priesthood, and to
re-establish a direct succession from the earliest Buddhist
missionaries—the succession from Sona and Uttara, the first
missionaries to Suvanna bhumi (the modern Tha-ton), having
become invalidated, owing to wars and other political
disturbances—he decided to send priests to Ceylon to be ordained
by the followers of Mahinda, the Buddhist Apostle to that island.
Twenty-two of the most learned rahans were selected and
despatched in two ships from the port of Kusimanagara (the
modern Bassein). After a voyage of some length, both vessels
arrived safely at Ceylon, and the rahans were received with great
tokens of friendship by the King, Bhuvanikabaha by name.
Valuable gifts were presented to the king by the mission from
King Dhammaceti of Pegu, and offerings made to the principal
shrines in the island. The King then issued orders for a bridge
of boats to be prepared on the Kalyani river, at the site where the
lord Buddha had on one occasion taken a bath. When all had
been arranged, the ordination of the *theras* or priests from Pegu
was carried out. On the conclusion of the ceremony, the *theras*
were interviewed by the king, and departed on their return home.
They arrived safely back to Pegu, and were received in great
state by the king himself. Dhammaceti then constructed the
Kalyanisema where the *upasatha* and *upasampada* ceremonies of
ordination to the priesthood were in future to take place. After
the consecration of the sema by the *theras* who had returned
from Ceylon, the king ordered all priests to seek re-ordination
at Kalyanisema. Those refusing to do so were disrobed and thus
did Ramadhipatiraja "purge the religion of its impurities throughout the whole of Ramannadesa, and created a single sect of the
whole body of the priesthood."

"There were at this time 15,666 priests in Ramannadesa, all of whom had received the *Upasampada* at the hands of the *theras* at the Kalyanisema."

Such is the substance of the Pali text on these stones, lying at the present time, chipped and broken, and unsheltered from the weather, amid the ruins of Zaing-ganaing.

SHWÈ HMAU DAU PAGODA, PEGU.
Photo by F. O. Oertel, Esq., N.W.P.

ROUTE IV.

RANGOON TO PROME BY RAIL.

This line, which is 161 miles in length, was the first constructed in the province, and was opened for general traffic on 1st May, 1877. The general direction throughout is north-west. The mail train leaves the Phayre Street station at 9.15 p.m., and arrives at Prome at 6.5 a.m. As the journey is accomplished by night, the traveller will have little or no opportunity of seeing the country passed through. A day train, however, leaves Rangoon at 7 a.m., reaching Prome at 5.15 p.m. the same day. Those wishing to get a view of the country passed through by the railway should therefore travel by this train.

For the first ten miles the line runs through the suburbs of Rangoon, the most important being Kemendine and Insein.

The former is the north-west quarter of Rangoon, and is inhabited principally by Burmese, who are slowly but surely being ousted from the business quarter of the city by the natives of India and the ubiquitous " John Chinaman."

A few of the rice mills are situated on the banks of the river in this neighbourhood. Both in the first and second Anglo-Burmese wars, considerable opposition was offered by the Burmese at this place, where numerous and strongly constructed stockades were held for some months by the enemy, who were with difficulty expelled from the neighbourhood of Rangoon.

Nine miles from Rangoon we arrive at Insein. This is now an important suburb, and owing to a suitable train service, is fast becoming popular as a place of residence. Air is purer, taxes lighter, and country supplies cheaper than in the city.

The construction and re-fitting shops of the Burma State Railways are situated here, and in consequence, for its size, the place has a large European population.

In close proximity to the railway station, are the Volunteer Rifle Butts, which are much frequented by the Rangoon Volunteer Rifles in the cold weather.

Hmawbe, 24½ miles from Rangoon, has grown considerably since the opening of the railway. In the neighbourhood are the remains of an old Talaing fort of brick, surrounded by a fosse. Most of the bricks were used as ballast in the construction of the railway line.

Okkan at the 56½ mile is an old Talaing village, in the vicinity of which is an old square tank, the sides of which are faced with brick. Hence the Burmese name Okkan, from *Ok*—brick, *Kan*—tank. The village is about 1½ miles to the west of the railway station, with which it is connected by a road.

The next station is Thonzè, 65½ miles from Rangoon, on the banks of the Thonzè stream, which rises in the Pegu Yomas to the east, and flows into the Hlaing or Rangoon river.

It is now part of the Tharrawaddi district formed in 1878, out of parts of the Henzada district.

The next station, Tharrawaddi, is the head-quarters of the district of the same name, and owes its rise entirely to the railway. In the uncultivated parts of the district, large forests of valuable timber exist, from which a handsome revenue is obtained by Government.

Letpadan is the half-way halting place, and has a well-managed refreshment room. The town is essentially a railway town, and is the head-quarters of many of those connected with the railway. After a halt of about half an hour, we proceed onward, passing the stations of Sitkwin, Minhla, Othègon and Okpo, the village at the latter place being at some distance from the railway station. The name is a very common one for villages, and signifies the place where bricks are burnt; from the Burmese *ok* a brick, and *po* a kiln.

ANCIENT PAGODA AT SYRIAM.

(*Photo by F. O. Oertel, Esq., N.W.P.*)

Gyo-bin-gauk, the next station, is 108½ miles from Rangoon, and has a population of 3,008.

Paungdè at the 129th mile, is the head-quarters of a sub-division of the Prome district, and had in 1891, a population of 10,233. Close to the town is the Government Reformatory to which juvenile offenders are committed.

It is the centre of a good deal of rice cultivation, and has considerable trade both with Rangoon and Prome.

From above Zigòn the country to the west gradually rises, and the line skirts along the base of these low hills, passing the stations of Padigòn, Thegòn and Sinmizwè. After leaving the latter station, the line curves round to the north-west, passing round the hills, and after a run of 6½ miles, we arrive at the terminus, Prome. A full description of this town will be found in Route V.

For Government officials a comfortable circuit house is maintained, and for the general public a dâk bungalow has been provided by Government, where both board and residence are provided at fixed rates.

ROUTE V.

PROME AND NEIGHBOURHOOD.

PROME, called in the vernacular *Pyi-Myo*, is situated in the valley of the Irrawaddi, on the left bank of that river, and is connected with Rangoon by a line of railway 161 miles in length, the journey taking about nine hours. It is one of the most picturesquely situated towns in the country, being surrounded by hills to the north and east, which here sweep down to the opposite bank of the Irrawaddi. Bi-weekly communication by express steamer is maintained with Mandalay and other riverside stations on the Upper Irrawaddi, the up journey to Mandalay being performed in three and a half days, and the down in two and a half days.

The modern town is protected from inundation by a bund, and also by the naturally high banks of the river, and on this raised ground the chief public buildings have been erected.

In ancient Burmese history the town is spoken of as of great size and strength, and as the capital of a powerful kingdom long before the commencement of the Christian era. This city, however, which was destroyed in the first century, was called *Tha-re-kettra*, and its ruins are still to be seen several miles inland from the present town. The bricks from this ruined city were utilized in large quantities as ballast in the construction of the railway, stone being difficult to obtain in the alluvial country through which the railway runs.

Situated as it was, between the rival Burmese and Talaing kingdoms of Ava and Pegu, the town was seldom independent, but remained in vassalage to the more powerful of its neighbours. After the conquest of Pegu by Alaungpya in 1757, Prome was a dependency of the kingdom of Burma till its possession passed to the British in 1853.

The town was occupied by Sir Archibald Campbell during the First Anglo-Burmese war, when little or no opposition was offered. It was garrisoned till 1826, when the treaty of peace was signed at Yandabo, and the province of Pegu was restored to the King of Ava. Prome was again occupied during the Second Anglo-Burmese war in 1852. More combined opposition on the part of the Burmese was encountered, but the heights were stormed and the defenders driven out. After the annexation, the garrison was removed to Thayetmyo, a few miles nearer the frontier, arbitrarily fixed by the British.

The only object of interest to the traveller is the golden pagoda, which rears its head above the town and surrounding country, and is a conspicuous object from the steamers plying on the river.

THE SHWÈ TSAN-DAU PAGODA is situated about half a mile from the bank of the river, and is built on the summit of a hill 138 feet high, called the Thu-dat-thana Hill.

The pagoda is built on a square base, and is 180 feet high. At the base are 83 gilded niches called Zè-di-dan, each containing an image of Buddha. These niches unite at their bases, and thus form a continuous wall round the pagoda. A small door through this wall is placed on the east side. Like other similar shrines, the platform is reached by four flights of brick steps facing the four cardinal points. The northern and western flights are covered with carved roofing, supported on massive teak posts painted vermilion, and in some cases covered with gold leaf. The platform is paved with flags throughout, and is surrounded by a number of *zayats* and *theins*, containing figures of Gaudama, of the three orthodox shapes. Advantageously placed at intervals are masts, or *ta-gûn-daing*, surmounted by the figure of the *Karawaik*, or sacred bird of Vishnu, with long pendants attached to the tops.

Several bells are also suspended from massive crossbeams, which are struck by pious worshippers with a deer's horn on the completion of devotional exercises.

HISTORY OF PAGODA.—Like the Shwè-Dagòn and Shwè-Hmau-daw pagodas, the history of this shrine is much involved in myth and uncertainty. According to the account given in the *thamaing*, Gaudama on one occasion arrived near Prome, on an island called Zin-gan, where he was met by a *naga*, or dragon, who begged the Lord Buddha to give him some sacred hairs, that he might build a pagoda over them. Gaudama, however, refused, saying that the honour of building the pagoda was reserved for two brothers, E-zi-ka and Pa-li-ka, who were then on a trading venture at Tha-tòn. The *naga* then offered an emerald box in which to place the hairs, which Gaudama accepted. Buddha then, by his supernatural power, caused the box to ascend and lodge in a clump of bamboos on the bank of the river. Here it was found by the two brothers on their return voyage up the river. The place where it was supposed to have been found is still called *Hmya-ywa*, or Emerald village. To commemorate the finding of the relics three pagodas were built, *Hmya-paya*, or the Emerald pagoda ; *U-paya*, or " Boat's-bow " pagoda ; and *Pè-paya*, or " Boat's-stern " pagoda.

Search was then made for a suitable place in which to enshrine the sacred relics. For this purpose they proceeded to the site where Prome is now built. At the place where they stopped to further discuss as to the site, the boatmen built a pagoda, which is called Tswè-ngwè Paya, or "discussion pagoda," and is now standing.

At last the Thu-dat thana Hill was fixed upon, a relic chamber of bricks of gold prepared, and the relics carefully placed in the chamber. Over this was built a pagoda seven feet high. On the departure of the brothers the pagoda subsided into the ground, but owing to the merit of Dwot-tabaung, the founder of Prome, it re-appeared, and was by him repaired and enlarged.

The *thamaing* gives no further accurate history, but tradition states that it was repaired and enlarged by successive rulers until it attained its present size. It was re-gilded by Alaungpya in 1753, and in 1841 Tharrawaddi, King of Ava, repaired it, and on it placed a new *hti*. In 1858 it was damaged by an earthquake, but was subsequently repaired at a cost of Rs. 77,000, raised by subscriptions. It has an annual festival, which takes place on the full moon of *Tabaung* (March).

Po-û-daung Pagoda.—The following account of this pagoda is taken from the memorandum issued from the Government Press by the Local Government :—

"The right bank of the Irrawaddi river near Prome is fringed by a range of hills, and Po-û-daung is the name applied to the top-most of seven hills forming part of this range.

"The Po-û-daung Hill is crowned with a massive alms-bowl-like rock called the 'Hermit's Cap.' On this rock a platform of brick is raised, and on it stands the Po-û-daung pagoda, which is about thirty feet high. Its form and architecture bespeak its being the handiwork of masons from the maritime provinces. Near the pagoda is an image-house, which bears date 1236 B.E. (1874 A.D.) In this image-house Gaudama is represented in a standing posture, with the index finger of his right hand pointing towards Prome, and Ananda, his beloved disciple, in a praying attitude, begging the sage to explain his oracle fully.

"On the eastern side of the 'Hermit's Cap'—which is surrounded on every side, except the one where it joins the next hill by sheer precipices of some thousand feet in depth—are three caves cut out of the rock ; over them are images of the two traditional moles, also cut out of the rock, representing them in an adoring attitude, and asking some boon from Gaudama Buddha. One of the caves is devoted to the custody of an inscription engraved on a piece of sandstone rock which is about four by three feet. The inscription was placed there by Sinbyuyin (1763-1776 A.D.), the second son of Alaungpaya. It

bears date 1136 B.E. (1774 A.D.), and contains a record of his
progress from Ava to Rangoon, his placing a new *hti* on the
Shwè Dagòn pagoda, and the removal of the old *hti*, which
was thrown down by an earthquake in 1769, to be enshrined in
the Po-â-daung pagoda.

"The placing of the new *hti* on the Shwè Dagòn pagoda by
Sinbyuyin was symbolical of the consolidation of the power of
the dynasty founded by his father in 1757 A.D.; of the replace-
ment of the Talaings by the Burmans in the government of united
Burma; and of the national jubilation over the successes which
attended Burmese arms in the wars with Manipur, China, and
Siam. The ceremony of placing the *hti* was witnessed by the
king in person, in order to convince the Talaings, whose abortive
attempt at insurrection in Martaban had just been suppressed,
that his rule was a personal one, and to impress on them the
splendour of his power and the resources at his command.
Moreover, to minimize the possibility of all future attempts at
rebellion, with the last of the Talaing kings as a centre of intrigue
and disaffection, and to remove all hopes of the restoration of a
Talaing monarchy, he ordered the execution of Byinnya Dala,
the ex-king of Pegu, who had surrendered to Alaungpaya."

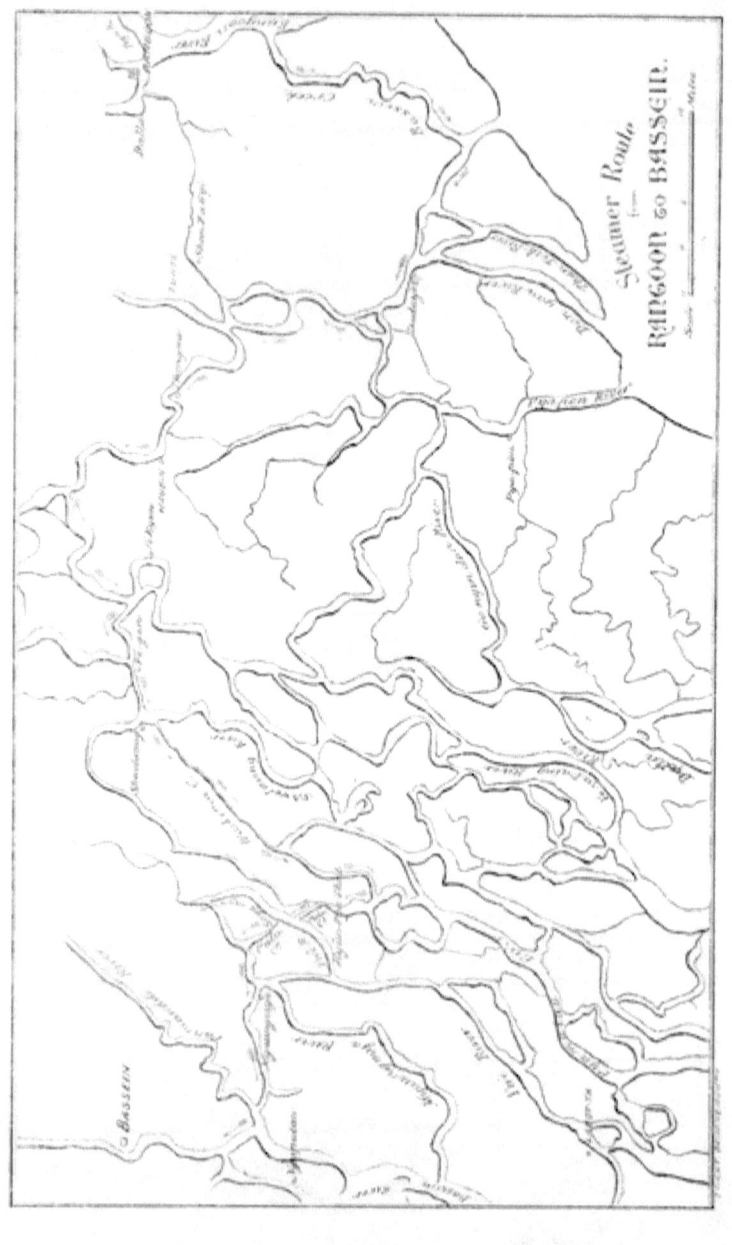

Steamer Route
from
RANGOON to BASSEIN.

ROUTE VI.

RANGOON TO BASSEIN.

This journey is made in steamers of the Irrawaddy Flotilla Company, and takes, including stoppages, from 27 to 28 hours. These steamers start from the jetty a little to the north of the foot of China Street. They are 170 feet long, 30 feet beam, with twin screws of 13 cwt. each, 450 horse power indicated, and steam from 11 to 12 knots an hour, and are well appointed and supplied with a strong electric search light to enable them to be navigated through the narrowest of tortuous tidal creeks on the darkest nights. Prior to the introduction of steam communication the journey between Rangoon and Bassein occupied from seven to eight days. The route throughout is by the net-work of tidal creeks that abound in the delta of the Irrawaddy. During the journey the steamer passes through the most productive and fertile tracts of the great delta, and it is from these parts that the largest supplies of rice are secured by the merchants of Rangoon and Bassein.

The departure of steamers from Rangoon is regulated by the state of the tide, no vessel however leaving the port after sundown. After casting off, the course is taken down the Rangoon river for about 16 miles, when the Bassein creek is entered. This creek connects the Rangoon river with the China Bakeer river. The first halting place is Dadayè, 37 miles from Rangoon, and is reached about 5½ hours after leaving Rangoon. The inhabitants of this village numbered 3,800 at the last census, and consist principally of Burmese and Talaings, who are chiefly engaged in rice cultivation, wood cutting, and fishing. Soon

after leaving Dadayè the steamer enters the Ma-û-bin river,
passing the mouth of the Tûntè Canal, and after a run of 51
miles, Ma-û-bin is reached. This town is the head-quarters of the
Thôngwa district, which was formed in 1875 out of parts of the
Hanthawaddy and Bassein districts, owing to the rapid growth of
population and cultivation in these parts. As the new district·
was formed during the administration of the late Sir Ashley Eden
as Chief Commissioner, it received the cognomen of the " Garden
of Eden." It is said by officers of the commission and police
who have been stationed there, to be the " last created place."
It is celebrated throughout the length and breadth of the land
for the size and voracity of its mosquitos. So bad are these pests
in the S.W. Monsoon, that even cattle are supplied with mosquito
curtains.

The town contains the usual District Buildings and
Government Offices, is the centre of a large area of rice
cultivation, and a place of call for all steamers *en route* from
or to Mandalay. After leaving Ma-û-bin, the Shwè-laung River
is entered. This river is one of the many mouths of the
Irrawaddi. The village of Shwè-laung is one of the stopping-
places for steamers, and is distant thirty-five miles from
Ma-û-bin.

After leaving Shwè-laung the steamer one hour later enters
the Waikèma Creek. This creek turns off sharp to the right
from the Shwè-laung River, while the river turns sharp away
to the left on its course to the sea. The Waikèma Creek is
narrow, and its windings so peculiar, and the land so flat, that
when the steamers approach they see each other over the land,
say, two miles before they meet, although they appear to be side
by side. This gives the steamer having the current against her
a chance to stop at a good place and let the other go past her.
From the entrance of Waikèma Creek to Waikèma is one hour.
After leaving Waikèma we pass Thayagôn on our right hand,
where a Mission Station of the American Baptists is maintained ;
and then Kanazogôn, where a Roman Catholic Mission is

stationed, under the superintendence of the Reverend Father Bertrand, who has laboured uninterruptedly in this field for the last thirty-eight years. One hour from Kanazogón we reach the Parmametta. The steamer from Rangoon cannot proceed further till the steamer from Bassein has come through, as it is too narrow to permit of the passage of two steamers abreast.

The passage of the Parmametta takes one hour, when the Sagamya River is entered, to be quitted after a run of twenty minutes for the Little Pulu. The passage of this small creek takes from twenty-five minutes to one hour and ten minutes, according to the state of the tide, and at the village of Pulu the Big Pulu is entered, and a run of forty-five minutes brings us to Myaungmya. The tides in the Little Pulu and Big Pulu run in opposite directions and meet at the junction.

The Little Pulu is so narrow and tortuous that it is only at certain states of the tide it can be navigated by the steamers of the Irrawaddy Flotilla Company engaged in the Rangoon Bassein service.

One of the most interesting features of the trip from or to Rangoon is the passage through this creek at night, when the electric search-light is used. The banks are densely wooded, and when the light is thrown on to the trees and jungle-growth the effect produced is most weird and effective. Troops of fisher-monkeys, startled from their sleep, set up such a chatter and stampede that their noise can be heard a long way off. Swarms of parrots are suddenly aroused and raise a dreadful din with their harsh screechings. The lamp itself is the general focus to which all insect-life flies, so now is the time for the entomologist, should one be on board. The search-light, when first applied to these steamers, was manipulated by a Lascar, who received verbal orders from the Captain as to the direction in which to throw its beams of light. On one occasion the Lascar was attacked by an indignant flight of bees, and, needless to say, beat a hasty retreat below.

Myaungmya was formerly a Royal city, and one of the thirty-two towns of which Bassein was the principal. It has lately been made the head-quarters of a separate district, and the public offices are only now in course of erection. The distance from Waikèma is thirty-eight miles. From the Myaungmya River the Panmawatti River is entered, to be shortly quitted again for the Thit-kè-Thaung Creek, generally known to Europeans as the Rangoon Creek. The navigation of this creek is exceedingly difficult, owing to its crooked course. From this creek the steamer emerges into the Bassein River, when the telegraph signals "full speed ahead," and after a run of about one and a half hours Bassein is reached, and the steamer comes to its moorings at the Iron Wharf. The distance from Myaungmya is twenty-six miles.

The fare charged for the journey is Rs. 25/- first class, Rs. 10/- second class, and Rs. 4/- deck. The first class rate includes messing. No difference is made for the return journey. Tickets can be secured on board.

BASSEIN AND NEIGHBOURHOOD.

Bassein is situated on the left bank of the Nga-wûn or Bassein River, which is the extreme western branch of the Irrawaddi, and is about 75 miles from the sea. To the natives of the country it is known as *Pu-thein*, which is stated to be a corruption of *Pu-thi*, the name given by the Burmese to the Moguls or Mahomedans of India, by whom the town was probably built. Its ancient name was Kusimanagara, from which the name *Kosmin* of the early European travellers was doubtless derived. From the earliest Talaing records it is mentioned as a port from which ships sailed to Ceylon and India.

At the present time the town contains about 28,000 inhabitants, and, next to Rangoon and Moulmein, is the most important rice port in Burma. It is situated on a bend in the river, and the approach by steamer is very picturesque. It contains the Courts of the Commissioner of the Irrawaddy Division and the Deputy Commissioner, and those subordinate to them, a Custom House, a large jail, an Anglican Church, a Roman

Catholic Church, a High School and several handsome Mission Stations and Schools of the American Baptist Mission Society.

HISTORY.—Very little of the early history of the town or neighbourhood is now procurable. No trustworthy records are now available, as the town was utterly depopulated by Alaungpya in the middle of last century.

It is first mentioned by European travellers in 1586-87, when Ralph Fitch, an English merchant visited it. It is called Kosmin by him. In 1687, Captain Weldon landed at Haingyi Island at the mouth of the Bassein river and took possession of it, in the name of the East Indian Company. In 1753, the Governor of Madras founded a settlement on Haingyi or Negrais Island.

On the accession of Alaungpya, the English had a factory at Bassein under Captain Baker, who sought and obtained the protection of the conqueror. In return they supplied the invading army with guns and other munitions of war. A treaty of friendship between the Company and Alaungpya was agreed to and signed, by which Negrais was ceded in perpetuity to the English, and a piece of land of 2,000 square yards in area at Bassein, was given for the erection there of a factory. This site is said to be immediately to the south of the pagoda on the right bank of the river below the village of Ta-kaing. It is now paddy land, and no traces of the factory remain. During the first Anglo-Burmese war, Bassein was attacked and taken by Major Sale, and held by the British till Pegu was evacuated in accordance with the terms of the treaty of Yandabo. During the second Anglo-Burmese war the town was again occupied by Commodore Lambert, and has since remained in possession of the British.

The modern town contains no objects of special interest. The Shwè-hmôk-dau pagoda is situated on a fortified hill in the centre of the town, close to the river. It was built by the Talaings, and is of no special sanctity. The thamaing states that in former times a King of Bassein had a very beautiful daughter, and her hand was sought by numerous suitors. She therefore

decided that she would marry the Prince who succeeded
in building the largest pagoda in the shortest possible
time. Three competitors entered. The builder of the
Shwè-hmòk-dau started his with brick, but finding progress slow,
he adopted the stratagem of running it up in a single night of
bamboos, covered with mats and gilt paper. He of course won
the stakes, or rather the Princess. When the ruse was detected
and he had strengthened his position by becoming the son-in-law
of the King, he built the present pagoda, which, as already stated,
is called the Shwè-hmòk-dau pagoda. The two others were
afterwards completed, and are known as the Tagaung Pagoda and
Paya-gyi. They are about three miles apart.

In the north east quarter of the town are situated the mission
schools of the American Baptist Mission Society. Two of these
are for the Karens and one (lately re-established) for the
Burmese. The Karen Schools are in a high state of efficiency,
and are well worth visiting. The missionaries in charge are
delighted to receive and conduct visitors over the buildings.
The four-part singing of glees and madrigals, and concerted
pieces from oratorios is a treat not to be missed by lovers of
music.

The station possesses a very nice Club where visitors are sure
of a warm welcome. A very good hotel, " The Shamrock," is
maintained, and accommodation also exists in the circuit house,
but this must not be occupied by visitors without special
permission from the Deputy Commissioner of the District.

HAINGYI OR NEGRAIS, is an island situated at the mouth of
the Bassein river, 83 miles from Bassein, and is important as
being the first settlement of the English in the country. It was
first occupied in 1686 by troops from Madras, on their return
from an expedition to Mergui. The first settlement was made in
1753.

By the treaty made between the Company and Alaungpya in
1757, the island was ceded in perpetuity to the English. In
1759, Negrais was partially abandoned by the Company, and

towards the close of the year those remaining were cruelly massacred by the Burmans, headed by one Antony. From this time no further settlement was made in the island. It is hilly in the north and covered with tree forest, but the southern end is a flat, sandy plain, where cultivation is carried on. In the centre of this plain are the ruins of an old fort, or factory, only the corner of two adjacent sides remaining standing. From an examination of the cement or mortar used, and also from the mode of construction, it appears to have been built by Europeans, and is probably the remains of the English factory established in 1753, or of one of older date, said to have been established by the Portuguese. The island contains few inhabitants, the majority of whom seek a living as fishermen in the estuary.

DIAMOND ISLAND is situated about 10 miles to the south of Haingyi. It is quadrilateral in shape, the corners facing the four cardinal points, and covers an area of about one square mile.

During the S.W. Monsoon landing is somewhat difficult. The island is the pilot station for ships visiting Bassein. It is also a port of call for ships "for orders," as it is connected with Bassein by a telegraph line. There are only three or four houses on the island, viz. : two pilot houses, the telegraph office, and a native house in which the turtle egg collectors live. The whole surface is covered with an almost impenetrable jungle, and cobras and other venemous snakes are commonly met with. An annual revenue to Government of about Rs. 15,000 is secured by the sale of the turtle egg licence. These creatures frequent the island for the purpose of depositing their eggs in the sand, and generally come up at night at high water. After scooping out a hole in the hard sand to the depth of about $3\frac{1}{2}$ feet, with the aid of their flappers, the eggs, to the number of nearly three hundred are laid, and the hole carefully filled in with sand.

The zig-zag tracks caused by the flappers and tail can easily be traced on the soft sand, so that no difficulty is experienced by the collectors in " spotting " the whereabouts of the nest.

The Collectors, each shouldering two baskets attached to a bamboo, are preceded by a pilot armed with a long iron rod, who finds the exact locality of the deposit of eggs by thrusting the spear into the sand. Should it, on being withdrawn, be found to have particles of yolk and sand adhering to it, the pilot places an upright bamboo at the spot. The basket carriers then dig down to the eggs which are found firmly embedded in the sand. In this way the whole island is itinerated every morning. The monthly total of eggs secured exceeds several lakhs. After being salted they are taken to Bassein in boats, from whence they are distributed all over Burma. The yolks make excellent omelettes, and have but a slight fishy taste.

It is penal to trap or kill turtles, but they are occasionally carried off on the quiet by boat's crews. The flesh is green in colour, and eats very much like coarse beef.

On the north east point of the island is a small pagoda, and at its foot a stone inscription in Burmese of no special value or antiquity. By the natives the island is generally called *Laik-kyân*, or "Turtle Island," but its proper name is "*Mein-ma-hla-kyân*," or "Pretty Girl Island," so called because it was once used as an island of refuge, to which the women were deported from the mainland, in some of the early internecine wars which devastated the country.

The island can be reached from Bassein by hired steam launch, or by the pilot or telegraph department cutters, which keep open communications. One part of the telegraph office is reserved as an inspection bungalow, permission to occupy which must previously be obtained from the Executive Engineer at Bassein.

INYÈ-GYI.—An account of the objects of interest in the Bassein district would not be complete without a description of this great fishery. It is situated about 70 miles to the north east of Bassein, and is about 3 miles from the Daga river, with which it is connected by a narrow creek. The lake is about five miles in circumference, and at its eastern end a picturesque wooded island exists on which is a village with several pagodas and kyaungs.

The annual "take" occurs at the full moon of *Nayôn* (June), soon after the first burst of the S.W. Monsoon. On the cessation of the rains, and when the waters of the lake are at their lowest level, a fixed weir is placed across the lake at its shallowest part, and another at some distance from it, shutting off between them the channel of communication between the Daga river and the lake. A huge drag net of cane, bamboo, creeper, and grass is then constructed—in length about 900 yards. This net is then slowly worked round the lake from the inside of one weir till it approaches the other. A new weir is then made to form one side of the enclosure into which the fish have now been driven. The huge drag net is then taken to pieces and reconstructed near the other weir, and the previous process repeated. By this means the fish are eventually massed together in an oblong space in front of the village. The dragging occupies nearly six months. It is not however as stated above till the full moon of June, that the " kill" takes place.

The scene on the banks of the lake is then very imposing, and a sight never to be forgotten. A temporary village with a population of several thousand men and women springs suddenly into existence, pits are dug in which the fish as caught are cleaned and pressed and salted. Sheds are also erected in which the larger varieties are salted and smoked, and the whole scene is most animated. A visit at this season well repays the curious observer. The principal varieties caught are Berco, Cyprinus, Gobio, Labeo, Cimelodus, Cirrhinus, Cyprinodon, and Silurus, some of which weigh from 60 to 80 pounds.

The larger fish, when cured, are sold to traders, and the smaller varieties are manufactured into *ugapi* or fish paste, one of the chief articles of food throughout Burma.

	Akouk-taung	Kyan-gin	Myan-aung	Kanoung	Nabût-chaung	Gyo-gyaung	Henzada	Daung-gyi	Za-lûn	Kyôn-sha	Kun-nu	Alè-myo	Danû-byu	Yandoon	Maû-bin	Dadayè	Rangoon
Prome ...	31	49	55	62	74	85	115	131	134	149	150½	154	159	175	205	258	311
Akouk-taung ...		18	24	31	43	54	84	100	103	118	119½	123	128	144	174	227	280
Kyan-gin ...			6	13	25	36	66	82	85	100	101½	105	110	126	156	209	262
Myan-aung ...				7	19	30	60	76	79	94	95½	99	104	120	150	203	256
Kanoung ...					12	23	53	69	72	87	88½	92	97	113	143	196	249
Nabût-chaung ...						11	41	57	60	75	76½	80	85	101	131	184	237
Gyo-gyaung ...							30	46	49	64	65½	69	74	90	120	173	226
Henzada ...								16	19	34	35½	39	44	60	90	143	196
Daung-gyi ...									3	18	19½	23	28	44	74	127	180
Za-lûn ...										15	16½	20	25	41	71	124	177
Kyôn-sha ...											1½	5	10	26	56	109	162
Kun-nu ...												3½	8½	24½	54½	107½	160½
Alè-myo ...													5	21	51	104	157
Danû-byu ...														16	46	99	152
Yandoon ...															30	83	136
Maû-bin ...																53	106
Dadayè ...																	53
Rangoon ...																	

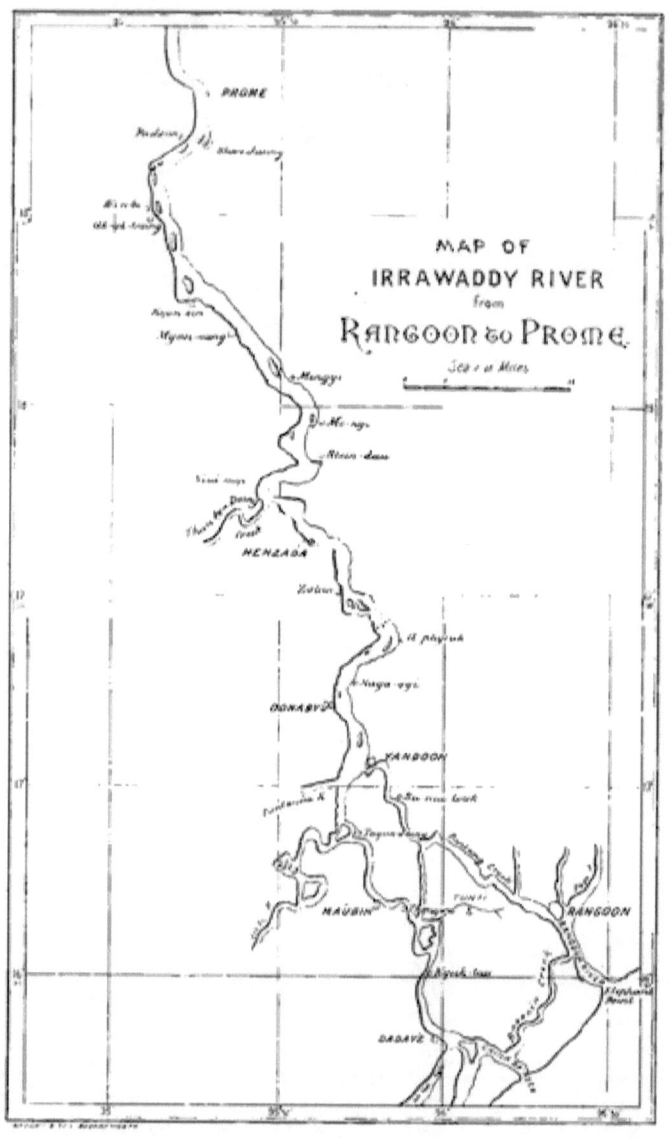

MAP OF
IRRAWADDY RIVER
from
Rangoon to Prome

Scale of Miles

ROUTE VII.

RANGOON TO PROME BY RIVER.

The express steamers of the Irrawaddy Flotilla Company leave the China Street Jetty twice a week for Mandalay. These are magnificent vessels with splendid accommodation for saloon passengers. Tickets can be secured either from the head office in Phayre Street, or on board. To prevent disappointment it is perhaps better to obtain them before starting. Wines and spirits are procurable on board at fixed rates. The journey up occupies eight days. The steamers anchor at night as soon after sunset as possible. During the rains, when the river is in full flood, the up passage necessarily takes longer than in the dry weather, when the river is low, and the velocity of the current consequently reduced.

ROUTE.—The fine weather route is the same as that taken by the Bassein steamers as far as Maûbin, viz : down the Rangoon River for about ten miles, turning to the right through the Bassein Creek, till the Dadayè Creek is reached. The Maûbin River is then entered and the steamer moors for a time at Maûbin. From this place the course is almost due north till the village of Tagûndaing is passed on the left bank. After a sharp bend to the South the northerly course is resumed, the true Irrawaddi is entered, and the town of Yandoon is reached. This is the chief centre of the the *nga-pi* industry, and passengers are warned to give the place a wide berth.

It is also a great resort for trade between the upper and lower Irrawaddi. As many as a thousand large sized boats are to be seen moored along the banks. The up-country boats here

II

exchange their cotton, peas, beans, sessamum, lacquer-ware, and other products, for rice, nga-pi, salt-fish, piece goods, and other imported articles. At this place the Panlang Creek debouches, and in the rains, when the river is in flood, this shorter route is made use of by the steamers, and a great saving of time and distance travelled is the result.

After leaving Yandoon the next place of importance reached is Danûbyu, on the right bank, about thirty-five miles south of Henzada. It is now the head-quarters of a town-ship, has a considerable local trade, but otherwise is unimportant. In the First Anglo-Burmese War, the great Burmese General, Maha Bandula, after being driven from the neighbourhood of Rangoon, entrenched himself here, with his army of 15,000 men. His main stockade was a parallelogram in shape, 1,000 yards by 700 yards, situated along the face of the river, but considerably above it. The river face was defended by fifty cannon of various calibres, and on the land side two outworks were erected.

The force originally sent against this fort was far too weak, and it was not till Sir Archibald Campbell, the Commander-in-Chief, joined his forces with the river column under General Cotton, that the stockade was captured. Heavy batteries of artillery were set up and plied shot and shell night and day, and on the morning of the tenth day, silence being observed in the fort, it was discovered that the Burmese had evacuated it during the night. It was subsequently ascertained that the great Bandula had been killed the previous day by the bursting of a shell. The fort was found to contain 140 cannon of all sizes and calibres, 260 jingals, besides large quantities of gunpowder and rice. Forty large war boats were also captured.

About seven miles above Danûbyu, on the opposite bank of the river, is the large village of Saga-gyi, from which large quantities of paddy are shipped to Rangoon. Of late years a huge sand-bank has formed in front of this village.

After leaving Saga-gyi the river bends to the north-east, passing numerous islands and groups of villages, the largest of

which is A-hpyauk. Above A-hpyauk the river takes a bend to
the north-west, threading its way through numerous sand-banks
and islands, until Zalûn is reached. This is a rising town,
having in 1891 a population of 6,006. It is the head-quarters of
a township, and contains a court-house and a police station. The
banks are here much eroded by the force of the current during
the time when the river is in flood. Close to Zalûn is a
celebrated brass Image of Guadama, which was taken away by
the British during the Second Anglo-Burmese War, but was
afterwards returned. This incident has added greatly to its
sanctity.

From Zalûn a northerly course prevails for several miles,
till just below Henzada when a sharp bend to the north-west
occurs.

HENZADA (called by the Burmese *Hin-tha-ta* :—the resting
place of the *Hintha* or Brahminy Goose) is the head-quarters of
the large and important district of the same name. It is situated
on the right bank of the river, which is here split up into several
channels, due to large sand-banks. When in full flood the
river here is one-and-a-half miles wide. Of late years,
owing to the erosion of the banks, the town has been
forced to retire considerably, in spite of the bunds built
for its protection. The town contains court-houses, police
stations, telegraph and post offices, a jail and a large market. This
latter building has some excellent carving about it, and was built
in the "good old days" when timber and labour were cheap.
The population in 1891, was 19,762, and consists chiefly of
Burmans and Talaings, with a sprinkling of natives of India.

Two mission schools are maintained here by the American
Baptists, one for the Karens, and the other for the Burmese.
Henzada is famous for the excellence of its wood carving, the best
specimens of which are produced in the local jail.

After leaving Henzada the north east direction is
maintained, through numerous islands and sand-banks, until the
mouth of the Than-bya-daing creek is passed on the right bank.

H 2

This creek is connected with the Ngawûn or Bassein river, the most western mouth of the Irrawaddi.

The channel has of late years, however, so silted up that it is only when the main river is in full flood that sufficient water is found for large boats and steamers. From Thanbyadaing the course is north-east past the large village of Nauk-myi on the right bank. No place of importance is now reached till we arrive at Mingyi on the left bank. From this village the north-west course is resumed, and after a run of about 17 miles, Myan-aung on the right bank is reached.

This was formerly the head-quarters of what is now the Henzada district, but now the head-quarters of a sub-division only. By the Talaings it was called *Ko-dût*. The name was changed to *Myanaung* by Alaungpya in 1754, A.D., to signify that his conquests so far had been expeditious. About six miles above Myanaung and on the same bank, Kyan-gin is reached. It is the head-quarters of a township, and has a population of 8,116. It is a growing place and does a large trade in paddy, which is sent down the river in large quantities. Above Kyan-gin several large islands extend, one succeeding another, till Akauk-taung and Htôn-bo are reached, both on the right bank. The alluvial or deltaic plains may be said to end here. Akauk-taung, as its name implies, was in olden times a revenue station. According to Burmese annals, the sea at one time extended up to the town of Prome, and the researches of geologists have proved that there are ample grounds for the truth of this assertion. This cliff or bluff is really a spur or offshoot of the Arakan Yomas, and is nearly 300 feet high. The face of the cliff is artificially honey-combed with caves, containing numerous carved images of Buddha of various shapes and sizes.

A pagoda has been built on the crest of the cliff, which is held in great esteem by all Buddhists. Many of the caves were in former times occupied by priests and nuns of a very austere sect, such as are found in the *Gyaungs* of the Sagaing Hills.

After leaving this place the course is taken between several large islands, passing the village of Tha-lè-dan on the right bank, at the entrance to the creek of the same name. The course thence tends to the north-east, till we arrive at Padaung, the head-quarters of a township in the Prome district. This town which contains a population of 9,000, is situated on the right bank, and is about 15 miles from Prome. It consists of one long straggling street, running parallel to the river bank. It was here that the Burman army of Bo-daw-pya assembled in 1784, when on the march *via* the Taungup Pass to Arakan. After the war of 1852-53, a Public Works Department road over this pass was constructed, and alongside of it runs the telegraph line which connects Burma by land with India. The road is now but little used, and has fallen into dis-repair. A little higher up the river, but on the opposite bank, stands Shwè-daung, the head-quarters of a sub-division of the Prome district. It is a place of considerable trade, has a population of 12,424, and is a centre of the silk industry. Eight miles above Shwè-daung Prome is reached, on the left bank. A description of this town is given in Route V. The picturesque hills opposite are covered with gardens of fruit trees, the produce of which is exported to Rangoon both by rail and steamer.

ROUTE VIII.

RANGOON TO MOULMEIN.

Four steamers of the British India Steam Navigation Company leave Rangoon every week for Moulmein and *vice versa*. The journey occupies about nine hours, the distance travelled being 147 miles. The *Rasmara* and the *Ramapoora* are built specially for this run, and leave in turn every Tuesday, Thursday, and Saturday, from the Barr Street Jetty.

The fare is Rs. 20/- saloon, Rs. 10/- second class, Rs. 4/- deck.

In the north-east monsoon the trip across is very enjoyable. Land is lost sight of for about two hours.

Leaving the jetty at 7 a.m., the steamer proceeds down the river, and at about 9 a.m. Elephant Point is passed and the open waters of the Gulf of Martaban entered. From about 11.30 to 1 or 1.30 land is lost sight of, but towards afternoon the high hills on the mainland behind Belû-kyûn come prominently into view, and to the south-west the white pagoda on Amherst Point is to be seen. The course is then shaped round the southern end of Belû-kyûn, and the Salween River entered. It is over seven miles wide at its mouth. About eight miles below Moulmein, on the point at Natmû, are seen the saw-mills of the Bombay Burma Trading Corporation. These mills have been, or are about to be, removed to a more convenient site at Mopûn.

On the river bank close to the saw-mills are the forts built for the protection of Moulmein. They contain two 68 lb. M.L.R. guns, which are worked by the Moulmein Volunteer

Artillery. After a run of five miles, passing several islands *en route*, Mopûn bight is entered. On the banks are to be seen the numerous steam-saw and rice-mills of the European merchants, and it is here that the chief trade of the port is carried on. After a run of three miles the Main Wharf is reached, and the steamer comes to her moorings.

MOULMEIN is situated on the left bank of the Salween, at its junction with the Gyne and the Attaran, and is the head-quarters of the Amherst District and the Tenasserim Division. Its classic name is *Ramapoora*. The population in 1891 was 55,785. Immediately opposite the town is the large island of Belû-kyûn, 107 square miles in area. The waters of the Salween bifurcate off Martaban, one part (the Da-rai-bauk) entering the sea north of Belû-kyûn, and the other (the Salween) flowing south past Moulmein and Amherst, and emptying itself into the Bay of Bengal. The Da-rai-bauk stream is now so silted up with sand as to be useless as a channel of communication, but was formerly the main exit of the waters of the Salween to the sea, and was used by the steamers and ships employed in the bombardment of Martaban.

A low range of hills runs north and south through the town, terminating gradually at the banks of the Gyne. These hills are covered with pagodas, temples, and monasteries in all stages of preservation or decay. Four of the five divisions of the town are on the west, between the hills and the river bank. The fifth is to the east of the range, and has the Gyne and Attaran Rivers for its frontage. This division is called Daing-wûn-kwin, and is the Burmese or Talaing quarter of the town. The other divisions are Mopûn, Maung-gan, Tavoy-zû, and Kula-dan. The total distance from Mopûn to the end of Daing-wûn-kwin is little short of nine miles. Three roads run through the town parallel to the river—the Lower Main road, close to its banks; above it the Upper Main road; and a third running along the ridge, sometimes on one side and sometimes on the other. As already stated, the European business quarter is at Mopûn, where the mills are situated. The native business quarter is Kûladan, where the big bazaar and the principal shops and stores are found. The houses of Europeans are situated either in the Upper Main road or Salween Park, or are picturesquely placed on the ridge already referred to.

To get a good view of the town and neighbourhood, the visitor should take a walk or ride along the ridge, starting from the Maung-gan side, close to the Mission and Church of the Society for the Propagation of the Gospel.

The road throughout winds along the hill-top, first on one side of it and then on the other. On the one side the Maung-gan and Mopûn quarters of the town are seen, with the broad river glistening in the sun, its course obstructed by numerous green islands, some barely above high-water mark ; while across the river the fertile plains of Belû-kyûn are seen, the wooded hills of which in the background present a scene unsurpassed by any place in the country. To enjoy this view to the full the visitor should select, if possible, a fine evening in the rains, when the gorgeous sunset adds not a little to its beauty. Proceeding onwards, the stately portals of " Salween House " are reached. This palatial building was erected by Colonel Bogle, Civil Commissioner of Moulmein, as a private residence. It was enclosed in a spacious park, which stretched from the hill-top to the Upper Main road. This estate is now the property of the Municipality. The house is at present used as the courthouse and offices of the Commissioner of the Tenasserim Division. The park has been partly leased for building sites, and the best houses in Moulmein are to be found here.

After passing Salween House the road joins another at right angles, which, coming from the town below, winds its way up the steep hill, to descend again to the cemeteries on the other side ; one branch going on to Daing-wûn-kwin. Following this for a few yards, a road, called Montgomery Road is seen on the left. Proceeding along this for some distance past several

ENTRANCE TO FARM CAVES, NEAR MOULMEIN.

(Photo by F. O Oertel, Esqr., N.W.P.)

fine *kyaungs*, the flight of steps leading up to the U-zana pagoda is reached. Although steep and formidable-looking, the view to be obtained from the terrace well repays the labour of climbing. A full description of this pagoda is given in detail further on, so we will for the time being ignore its presence and look further afield.

Looking towards the east the country, for miles in extent, lies as it were at our feet. The blue hills in the far off horizon are the Dawna chain, and to the south-east on a clear day, Mû-lè-yit, the highest summit (5,500 feet) may sometimes be seen. Beyond these hills lies the kingdom of Siam. The lower hills below the Dawna, mark the position of Kaukareit, which is situated at their base. This village is the starting point for the pass leading through Myawadi to Raheng in Siam.

Scattered throughout the plain, jagged isolated masses of rocks are seen, shooting straight up from the fields around them. These are of limestone, and were evidently upheaved by volcanic agency in remote ages, when the plains below were beneath the sea-level. Many of these masses of rock contain caves, some of which are of vast extent and adorned with stalactites and stalagmites. Those rocks to be seen immediately in a line with a small white pagoda on the summit of a low range of hills across the river, contain the Farm Caves, a description of which is given elsewhere. Those more distant to the left are the Damatha Caves, on the banks of the Gyne. The river meandering in the plain is the Attaran, which is formed by the junction of the Zami and the Win-rañ, both rising in the Siam Yomas. This river joins the Gyne about two miles above Daing-wûn-kwin. The low hills to the south-east are known as the Taung-waing Hills. In the neighbourhood are situated extensive fruit gardens. The Dorian and Mangosteen here flourish to perfection. These hills are a favourite resort for picnic seekers, and a good road connects them with the town.

Having now fairly exhausted our list of objects of interest, let us cross the pagoda platform to its western face. Taking up our station at the south-west corner a splendid view is to be obtained. Maung-gan and Tavoy-zû lie at our feet. The handsome building immediately beneath us is the General Hospital. In front of this, surrounded by a spacious compound, is the Government High School and Normal School combined. Should time permit, this institution is well worth a visit.

To the right of the school rises the stately tower of St. Mathew's Church. This handsome structure was erected about four years ago, with funds raised by public subscription, one gentleman alone giving the greater part of the necessary amount. It is of red brick, the capitals of the interior pillars being of stone, and is said to be a model of the English Church at Dresden. It contains a very good two-manual organ, which, however, is cruelly treated by the climate. (An annual rainfall of over 200 inches is hard lines on the king of instruments.)

Between St. Mathew's Church and the foot of the hills stand the Courts and Offices of the Deputy Commissioner and of the Judge of Moulmein. These are of brick, plastered, and were erected many years ago.

Descending again the steep flight of steps on the eastern face, we proceed onwards, past several old pagodas, the platform of one of which is used as a signalling station by the Port authorities.

The Jail is seen below, and to its left the Roman Catholic Convent and Church of St. Patrick. A road here descends past the Jail walls to the town, but the hill-road is continued along the crest, past the golden pagoda, and descends somewhat abruptly into Cantonments.

Mounting the steep flight of steps to the pagoda platform, the finest view of the morning (or afternoon) is to be seen. The meeting of the three rivers—the Salween from the north, the Gyne from the west, and the Attaran from the south is a sight worth remembering. Looking in the direction of the Salween; to the right will be seen the Zwa-kai-bin range of lime-stone rocks about 16 miles in length. The most prominent summit of this range is called the "Duke of York's Nose"; which particular Duke of York's Nose it is supposed to resemble has not been ascertained, certainly not the present Duke, for the name was given many years ago. On the extreme tip of the nose a small protuberance is seen, which on closer examination proves to be a pagoda!

Across the river to the north Martaban is seen; once a flourishing city, said to have been three miles square, now a miserable village. At the back of Martaban rise the Zin-gyaik Hills, the highest summit of which is Kulima-taung, 3,000 feet high.

Looking town-wards, immediately beneath lie the Madras Infantry lines, with the parade ground and race-course, the northern end of which terminates in Battery Point, where a battery of European artillery was stationed between 1825 and 1852, to overawe the Burmese garrison at Martaban. Between Battery Point and Martaban is Gaung-sè-kyûn, or "head washing island," so called because the water obtained from its wells was formerly used at "royal head washings." It is well wooded, and is adorned with several pagodas and other religious buildings, and is known as the home of all the crows in Moulmein, hence its European name, "Crow Island." The Salween here takes a sharp bend to the south, and the channel is full of rocks.

Beyond the Sepoy lines and the race-course lies the Kûladan quarter where most of the native merchants reside and carry on their business.

The growth and prosperity of Moulmein have depended entirely on its timber trade. Ever since the first occupation in 1825 this trade has steadily increased. The valley of the Salween and its tributaries, the Thaung-yin and Yûnzalin contain vast forests of teak. Most of the marketable timber, however, has been worked out, and the trade is not so flourishing now as it formerly was; hence the decline in prosperity of Moulmein. The supply is, however, still very considerable, as the table given overleaf, extracted from the Administration Report of Burma for 1893-94, shews :—

EXPORT OF TEAK FROM MOULMEIN.

Year.	Tons.	Value, Rs.	Average Value per Ton. Rs. As. P.		
1889-90	80,871	70,05,857	82	4	0
1890-91	64,227	47,01,434	71	8	0
1891-92	62,320	41,88,267	72	2	0
1892-93	160,850	72,57,412	76	0	6
1893-94	85,722	60,39,428	74	15	0

Of the total amount for 1893-94, 68,431 tons were shipped to Indian ports, and 18,859 tons to Europe.

Of late years there has been increased activity in the export of rice, and in the last ten years the number of rice mills has increased considerably. This is due to the favourable prices prevailing, and to the large increase of population and area under cultivation. Moulmein contains few objects of interest worth visiting. Of pagodas the principal are the Kyaik-than-lan and the U-zana.

Both these are situated on the range of hills behind the town, and both are comparatively modern as regards their present shape and outward decoration.

The original Kyaik-than-lan pagoda is stated to have been built by a hermit named Thi-la, who enshrined therein a hair of Gaudama. The name is said to be a corruption of Kyaik-shan-lan which means "the pagoda of the overthrow of the Siamese." This pagoda was subsequently repaired by the King of Martaban, but at the time of the British occupation was almost a ruin. In 1831 Maung-Tau-Lè, a Burman official, repaired it, the funds being raised by public subscriptions. Of late years vast sums have been spent on it by Ma-Shwè-Bwin, a wealthy widow who lives in Moulmein. It is of the usual shape, profusely gilded, and is approached by the usual four flights of brick steps, one on each face of the platform. The steps and their approaches are roofed in, as at the Shwè Dagôn pagoda in Rangoon. On one side in a special *thein* is a massive recumbent figure of Buddha. On the Eastern side is hung the large bell. It is covered with

CARVED FIGURES AT U-ZANA PAGODA MOULMEIN.

(*Photo by F. O. Oertel, Esq., N.W.P.*)

inscriptions in Pali, giving its history, and what is most curious, beneath the Pali is a further inscription in English which runs as follows :—

"This bell is made by Koo-na-lm-gala, the priest, and weight 600 viss. No one body design to destroy this bell. Moulmein, March 30th, 1855. He who destroyed to this Bell, they must be in the great Heell, and unable to coming out."

Needless to add, this inscription was worded prior to the establishment of the local High School ! As " Shwè Yoe " explains : " No doubt the priest Koona-lingana had heard of the abortive attempt to carry off the bell from the Shwè Dagôn a year or two previous, and thought it necessary to point out to the sacriligious Britisher the dire punishment in store, should a repetition of the act be attempted."

The U-ZINA pagoda is so called from the name of its restorer, who in 1838 A.D. spent several hundred rupees in improving and reconstructing it. Prior to this it was called the Kyaik pa-dhan pagoda from the *white* hill on which it stands. The people say it was one of the numerous pagodas founded during the reign of Asoka and contains a hair of Gaudama. At the present time (1895) a wealthy Burmese, by name Maung Mo, is spending large sums on its improvement. The terrace has been supported by a buttressed wall, and new steps on three sides added. The greater part of the pagoda itself has also for the first time been gilded. In a shed to the south of the platform are some curious carved figures. Those representing the four sights seen by Gaudama, when driven in state through his father's capital, prior to his renunciation, are very well portrayed. These are :—a decrepit old man leaning on his staff ; a sick man (apparently suffering from more than one of the ninety-six diseases to which Burmese doctors say mankind is a prey) ; a corpse in the last stages of decomposition ; and a hermit priest.

The " old man " formerly stood at the top of the steps on the south side, and nearly as many pious visitors have been deceived by his life-like appearance, as Londoners and others have been by the "policeman" at Madame Taussaud's in Baker Street.

The three ruined pagodas between the U-Zana and Kyaik-than-lan are called Dhat-kè, Pathada, and the Kyaik-ma-dau. The small pagoda on the point opposite to Crow Island is called Kyaik-pa-ni.

Of monasteries, some of the most beautiful and costly are to be found in Moulmein. The one in close proximity to the Town Hall is well worth a visit. Ladies, of course, must not be of the party. It is called the Wè-za-yàn-ta monastery, and was built by Maung Hlè, a wealthy timber merchant, lately deceased, at a cost of over Rs. 80,000.

MOULMEIN TO MARTABAN.

Martaban is at present a small town situated on the right bank of the Salween, immediately opposite to Moulmein, from which it is distant half a mile.

The place can be easily reached, either by Boat from Battery Point, or by taking advantage of the Thatôn Ferry Launch which proceeds daily from the jetty in the Kûladan quarter, stopping at Martaban en route. The old Talaing name of the Town is Môt-ta-ma and is said to have been founded in the sixth century A.D. In 1281 it was the capital of an independent kingdom and Warerû was its king. He had gone to the assistance of Tara-bya, the king of Pegu, to drive out the troops of the king of Pagan, who were besieging Pegu. After driving the Burmese out of the country, these two kings appear to have quarrelled ; a battle was fought and Tara-bya fled, defeated. He was subsequently taken prisoner to Martaban and put to death. Warerû was assassinated by the two sons of Tara-bya in 1306. During subsequent years Martaban was several times besieged and captured by the Peguans, Burmese, and Siamese, and was held by the power which at the time was most formidable. In 1540 it was described by Manuel-de-Faria-y-Sousa, the Portuguese

CARVED SHRINE, Ú-ZANA PAGODA, MOULMEIN.
(Photo by F. O. Oertel, Esq., N.W.P.)

historian, as the " Metropolis of a great and flourishing kingdom,"
which was besieged for seven months by Ta-bin-shwë-hti, king
of Toungû, who ultimately took the city and utterly destroyed it.
All that remains now of its former greatness are the ruins of the
old walls and ramparts.

During the First Anglo-Burmese War a force, under Colonel
Godwin, was despatched from Rangoon against the town, which,
after a short bombardment was captured. On the conclusion of
peace it was restored to the Burmese. Between 1826 and 1852
it was strongly garrisoned by the Burmese, necessitating the
maintenance of a large garrison at Moulmein. On the breaking
out of war, it was captured without much difficulty, and has since
dwindled down almost to obscurity.

The site contains few objects of interest. On the point close
to the river is a pagoda called the " Mya-thein-dan " built by
King Wareyû in 1281, A.D. It was so called because it was
supposed to have been built over an emerald (Bur : *Mya*), said
to have been worth 100,000 ticals (2½ million rupees) sent by
the King of Ceylon with an embassy in seven ships, which was
to bring back certain relics of Gaudama, buried at some spot
marked by eight masonry pillars. Search was made for twenty-
four days with the permission of King Wareyû, but no relics
were found. The eight pillars were taken away to Ceylon, and
on the site the Mya-thein-dan pagoda was erected.

On the hill-side above the Court-house, is a comfortable
bungalow, maintained by Government for the use of officials
when on circuit. Visitors are allowed, under existing rules, to
occupy spare rooms on payment of one rupee per diem, but
must cater for themselves. Near the river bank, surrounded
by jungle, are the remains of an old sugar factory erected many
years ago by a Frenchman, but long since neglected and
abandoned.

BELÛ-KYÛN.—This island is situated at the mouth of the
Salween river, and extends from Moulmein to Amherst, a total
distance of thirty miles. The name means *Belû Island*, or

the island inhabited by ogres. These Belû were supposed to be half man and half beast, who came up from the sea in search of food.

Sir Arthur Phayre considers that these traditions arose from exaggerated stories concerning the savage tribes who inhabited the country when first the Burmese race entered it. A wooded range of hills runs throughout the island, and in a dip in the middle of these, Chaung-zôn, the head-quarters, is situated. A pretty artificial lake, covered at certain seasons with lotus flowers has been formed here, by throwing a bund across the lower end of the narrow valley. A metalled road, three miles in length, runs from Chaung-zôn to Nat-mû on the river bank. The cultivated plains are exceedingly fertile, and the Belû-kyûn paddy is the best that reaches the Moulmein market. The slopes of the hills are rich in orchards and market gardens. In the Ka-hnyaû circle to the north, a hot saline spring exists, called by the Burmese Na-yè-kyûn, or "Hell Island." The whole of this neighbourhood is more or less impregnated with salt.

Near this is the *Ka-lan* pagoda, said to have been founded in the third century, B.C., by Asoka, King of Kapala-vistu, the great protector of Buddhism.

Small steam launches leave Tiger Jetty in Maung-gan several times a day for Natmû, and large dhingies are always to be obtained, to visit the northern part of the island.

THATÔN.—This ancient town is situated about 62 miles due north of Moulmein, from which it is reached by launch and rail.

These launches leave Moulmein daily (Sundays excepted) from the Kûladan Jetty, and steam for some distance up the Salween till they reach the Dôn-dami river, up which they proceed to the village of Dû-yin-zeik. A short line of railway, eight miles in length, connects this village with Thatôn.

It has lately been made the head-quarters of a new district, formed out of parts of the Shwè-gyin and Amherst districts.

It appears, from ancient records, to have been inhabited some centuries before Christ by natives from the Coromandel

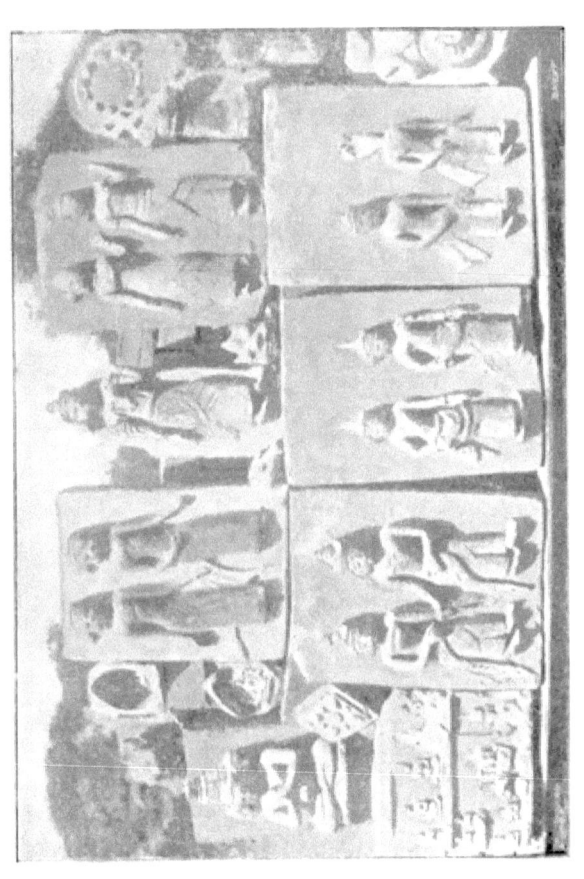

ANCIENT STONE CARVINGS AT THATÔN.

(*Photo by F. O. Oertel, Esq., M.H.F.*)

coast or Talingana, as it was then called. From this the name *Talaing* given to the inhabitants of this region by the Burmese is doubtless derived, the name being foreign to the people themselves, who style themselves *Mun*. After the great Buddhist Council held in 241, B.C., two missionaries, Thauna and Ot-tara by name, were selected as apostles to *Sûvarna-Bhû-mi*, as this part of the country was then called. After a long voyage they landed at a port called Golanagara (now called Taik-kala) to the north-east of Thatôn.

A monastery called the *Kelasavihera* was built for the mission, and one of its most celebrated inmates was Buddha-ghosa (the voice of Buddha) who in A.D. 400, sailed to Ceylon in order to copy the Buddhist Scriptures. He was away on his mission for three years, and on his return with the sacred writings, was received with great honour by the King. At that time regular communication by ship existed between Sûvarna Bhumi and the ports of Ganda and Talingana on the Carnatic Coast, and thence to Ceylon.

Thatôn declined after the foundation of Hansavati (Pegu) by the two brothers, Thamala and Wi-mala, in the 6th century, A.D.

The old city of Thatôn appears to have been built on the same plan as the more modern cities of Ava or Mandalay.

" The ground plan is a square or oblong, within which is an open space of about 153 feet, and then a second, but lower wall or rampart, and moat. The east and west inner walls are each 7,700 feet long, while those on the north and south are about 4,000 feet each, enclosing a space of about 700 acres. The angles, however, are not exact right angles. In the centre of the city is the fortified royal citadel, measuring from north to south 1,080 feet, and from east to west 1,150 feet. This was for the defence of the palace, the "throne-room" being as is now the case at the Burmese capital, nearly in the centre of the city. There are two gates or spaces for entrance in the northern and southern faces of the rampart, but it is impossible to say how many on the eastern or western. Of the citadel no remains exist, save those of a small pagoda at one corner, the shape of which is not discernable. The walls are of earth, and in some places much worn away, but some places appear to have been faced with rough stones."

From the 5th to the 10th century, Thatôn appears to have been the great centre of Buddhism, and to have had close intercourse with Ceylon. In the 11th century, Anaurhata, the King of Pagan, was much concerned at the corrupt *Naga* or dragon worship, which existed in his country. The priests of this religion were called *Ari*, and lived in monasteries like Buddhist monks. At this time a learned priest from Thatôn visited Pagan, and in the presence of the King preached the true faith. This led to the conversion of Anaurhata and the expulsion of *Ari* from their monasteries. The King then sent Ambassadors to Manûha, the King of Thatôn, asking for a copy of the "Tri-pi-taka" or Buddhist scriptures. On Manûha's refusal to comply with the request, Anaurhata invaded the kingdom, and after a siege lasting several months, the city surrendered. The King and his family were carried off as prisoners to Pagan, together with five elephant loads of the sacred books, and the most learned of the priest-hood. The city was given over to plunder, and was thoroughly destroyed. From this time Thatôn ceased to be a place of any importance, and sank into obscurity.

Of archæological remains few exist at the present day, and beyond the imperfect mounds, marking the ramparts of the old city, and a few pagodas, but little of interest is to be seen. The two principal pagodas are however still in a good state of preservation, and have no doubt retained their original shape in spite of various accessions from without.

The Thatôn or Shwè-za-yan Pagoda is of the usual shape. It is built of hewn laterite blocks, and consists of three successive platforms of diminishing size, the top-most one being surrounded by an ordinary *stupa* or bell. The lower base is 104 feet square and 16½ feet high, and the third storey 48 feet square and 12 feet high. On this the ordinary round pagoda is built, the height of the whole being about 85 feet. The second storey is reached by four flights of steps, one in the centre of each face; and contains a number of niches about four inches deep, and 2 feet 3 inches square, similar to those seen in the base of the Ananda pagoda at Pagan. These niches were originally filled with terra-cotta tablets, containing figures in relief, some most grotesque and ludicrous, others of a religious character. Many, however, of these have fallen down or been carried away by visitors. Some are to be seen in a dusty corner of the Phayre Museum in Rangoon.

The Tha-ga Pagoda is also built of laterite blocks, but in shape is similar to the dagobas of Ceylon. The successive terraces are the same, but the pagoda which crowns them is bell-shaped. Like the Shwè-za-yan, it also has a number of bas-relief terra-cotta figures, similar to those already mentioned.

It is said that this pagoda is built over the original copy of the Tripitaka brought by Buddha Ghosa from Ceylon in the 4th century; hence its special sanctity.

In a memorandum of a visit to Thatôn in 1891-92, undertaken by order of Government, Mr. Tau Sain Kho, thus writes :—

"The place where the Jubilee Fountain, erected in 1888, is now playing, is still pointed out as the site of the palace of Siharaja and Manûha, the first and last kings of Thatôn. Close by is the gold-bearing stream of Shwègyaung-San which is perennial, and issues from the Thinganeik (Singanika) hill. Gold is still worked by isolated individuals at the beginning and close of the rainy season, but the quantities obtained are not commensurate with the amount of labour involved.

"There are five Talaing inscriptions at Thatôn, four in the enclosure of the Shwè-za-yan pagoda, and the remaining one under a banyan tree at Nyaungwaing. Their paleography indicates that their age is about 400 years.

"Three brick buildings are known as the libraries whence Anawratazau, King of Pagan, is said to have removed the five

elephant loads of Buddhist scriptures in 1057 A.D. . . . . . .
There are three basso relievo sculptures on stone, representing
Vishnuic symbols, lying in the enclosure of the Assistant
Commissioner's Court-House. It has been arranged to remove
them to the Phayre Museum, at Rangoon.

"*Nat* worship is still, as in other parts of Burma, one of the
prevailing forms of belief at Thatôn. I visited the temple of the
Nat called *P'o-p'o* (grandfather). Tradition which is, in this case,
prima facie palpably false, says that when this *Nat* was a human
being he was charged by Sona and Uttara, the · Buddhist
missionaries, who visited Ramannadesa in the third century B.C.
to safeguard Thatôn against the attacks of the *Bilus* or fierce
monsters. The image of *P'o-p'o* represents an old man of about
sixty years, sitting cross-legged, with a white fillet on the head, and
a moustache and painted beard.

"The forehead is broad, and the face bears an intelligent
expression. The upper portion of the body is nude, and the
lower is dressed in a *cheik paso* or loin cloth of the zig-zag
pattern, so much prized by the people of Burma.

"The right hand rests on the right knee, and the left is in
the act of counting the beads of a rosary. The height of the
figure is about five feet. In the apartment on the left side of
P'o-p'o is an image representing a benign looking wûn or governor
in full official dress. Facing the second image in a separate
apartment is the representation of a wild fierce-looking *Bo* or
military officer in uniform. The fourth apartment on the left of
the *Bo* is dedicated to a female nat who is presumably the wife of
P'o-p'o. But there is no image representing her. It is a strange
coincidence that like in India and Ceylon, these shrines are held
in veneration by variou   tionalities professing different creeds.

The images of the Nats are in a good state of preservation,
as they are in the custody of a medium, who gains a comfortable
livelihood.

An annual festival, which is largely attended, is held in their
honour."

KYAIK-TI-YO PAGODA, THATÔN DISTRICT.

(From a Photograph.)

PAGODAS AND PLACES IN THE VICINITY OF THATÔN.

About 22 miles to the north-west of Thatôn is the modern village of Ayet-thima, which stands on the site of the ancient port of Golanagara, at which Thanna (Sona) and Uttara, the first Buddhist Missionaries to this country, landed. The site is now, however, more than 13 miles from the sea. That the sea has receded from this part is evident, from the fact that some years ago, the remains of an apparently sea-going craft were found close to this, and bits of coir rope and cable are frequently dug up. It was close to Golanagara that the Kelasa-vihera, a splendid monastery, was built for the early missionaries, and which afterwards was the home of Buddha Ghosa, and was almost as celebrated as the famous Mahavihera of Ceylon.

To the north-west of this site is the Kelasa Hill, on which is a celebrated pagoda rebuilt by King Dhammaciti, King of Pegu, who ruled from 1460 to 1491, A.D.

The hill is 2,000 feet high, and the pagoda is supposed to contain a hair of Gaudama; one of three presented to the hermit Kelasa by Gaudama himself. Near by are two stone slabs with Talaing inscriptions on them erected by Dhammaciti, describing the reconstruction of the pagoda. A fine view of the surrounding country and the distant ocean is to be obtained from this pagoda.

Kyaik-ti-yo is the name given to the northern summit of the Kelasa heights which separate the basins of the Sittaung and Salween rivers. Its height is 3,650 feet, and from the Sittaung side the hill can be ascended in two days. The ascent can be made almost the whole way by ponies. The pagoda itself is small in size, but is built on the rounded top of a huge boulder; one of many with which the summit of this hill is covered. This boulder, by a freak of nature, is poised on the extreme verge of a projecting rock, which itself is separated from the rest of the hill by a rent or chasm, across which a rough bridge is thrown. The pagoda is about 15 feet high, and is covered with gold leaf. The egg-shaped rock, surmounted by the glittering pagoda, is a prominent object from the plains below, for many miles. An annual festival to this pagoda is held in the month of Ta-bo-dwè (February), which is attended by thousands of pious worshippers, the greater number of whom are Talaings. This festival is very accurately described in the late Captain Forbes' " British Burma."

THE FARM CAVES.—These caves are situated in an isolated mass of lime-stone rock, rising abruptly from the surrounding paddy fields, about 10 miles due east of Maulmain. By the Burmese they are known as the " Ka-yòn-Caves."

They are easily accessible to visitors. Taking a gharry from the town the route lies through Cantonments, the Daing-wûn-kwin quarter of the town, and thence along the straight road through the paddy fields to the village of Naung-bin-saik on the banks of the Attaran. Leaving the gharry here, you cross the river in the ferry boat, and complete the journey on the other side in bullock-carts. A good metalled road runs right up to the entrance to the cave, the distance from the bank of the Attaran being about six miles.

These caves, owing to their accessibility from Moulmein, have long been a resort for picnic seekers of all nationalities. The Farm Cave was at one time crammed full of images of Buddha and his faithful disciples, but these alas! have now for the most part been destroyed, and the smaller ones carried away as souvenirs of the visit. The large corridor to the right of the entrance was, even 15 years ago, full of figures in various postures, exhibiting scenes from *Mahaûthada*, which describes one of the previous existences of Buddha.

This cave probably now contains more empty beer bottles and sardine tins than sacred images !!

Those that remain are for the most part headless and mutilated. A recumbent figure in the central hall forty-five feet in length is still an object of adoration to the inhabitants of the adjacent village.

FARM CAVES, MOULMEIN.

(Photo by F. A. Ratch, Rojic, N.W.P.)

It was in the Farm Cave that Lord Ripon, the Viceroy and Governor-General of India, was entertained at luncheon on the occasion of his visit to Moulmein in 1882.

About a quarter of a mile to the south of the Farm Cave is the *Sad-dan*. The entrance to it is about fifty feet above the footpath, and is reached by a somewhat rough, sloping footpath, necessitating climbing over huge boulders of rock. From the entrance the path descends abruptly over slippery, well-trodden rocks to a grand hall, or amphitheatre, abounding in most magnificent specimens of stalactites and stalagmites, some of which form noble pillars supporting the vaulted roof above. From this hall various passages and ramifications lead in all directions. To the left, a path over the rounded boulders leads up by a narrow and difficult passage to an opening half-way up the lime-stone hill. From this opening a footpath formerly led up to the pagoda which crowns the precipitous point overhanging the road. This, however, has become overgrown with jungle, and is impassable, and to strike out a path for one's-self is an impossibility, owing to the knife-like serrated edges of the rock.

Visitors to the Sad-dan Cave must provide themselves with torches and "blue-light," without which the beauties of the interior cannot be examined. Torches, made of resinous wood and oil, are to be got in the Bazaar at Moulmein. The Burmese name is *mi-daung*. Blue-light is obtained from the Port Office through the courtesy of the Port Officer, or from any ship-chandler's store.

The greatest drawback to the full exploration of the Sad-dan Cave is the innumerable number of bats with which it is infested. The floor, in some places to the depth of several feet, is covered with their droppings, and the appearance of a torch or blue-light puts millions on the wing.

A startling effect is produced by firing off a gun in this cave.

In the isolated rock about $2\frac{1}{2}$ miles to the south is another small cave, called the *Nga* Cave. It is difficult to approach, and contains nothing of curiosity.

THE DHAMMATHA CAVE.—This cave is situated in an outcrop of lime-stone rock immediately to the south of the village from which the cave takes its name. This village is peopled by Talaings, many of whom have little or no knowledge of Burmese, and is distant about eighteen miles from Moulmein.

The steam launches plying on the Gyne pass close by every day, so no difficulty need be experienced in getting here from Moulmein. The cave is situated about half a mile from the village, and consists of a comparatively straight passage about 200 feet long, running right through the rock. It contains both stalactites and stalagmites, some of them ornamented with figures of Buddha and Saints. After visiting, however, the Sad-dan Cave, this one falls very flat. The visitor is rewarded, however, by the magnificent view to be obtained from the pagoda situated on the summit of the precipitous rock, abutting the river. The ascent is made from the land side by a steep flight of laterite and brick steps. The view from the top is grand.

At the foot of the pagoda hill, and between it and the village, is a decent rest-house, where the visitor can stop till the return launch calls in for him on the following morning.

KAWGÛN CAVE.—This cave, like those already described, is of limestone formation, and is situated near the village of Pagat, about twenty-eight miles up the Salween.

In order to get to it the visitor will require to hire a launch, by means of which the trip there and back can be made in one day from Moulmein.

The mouth of the cave is about half a mile from the village, and is approached by a well-defined foot-path. At the entrance is a square tank. The cave for about 100 feet runs under an overhanging ledge of rock, and then turns sharp round and runs into the rock at right angles for the same distance. The roof of the cave, and the overhanging ledge, are covered with innumerable rows of small terra-cotta tablets, bearing on the face impressed figures of the sitting Buddha. These vary in size

KAWGÚN CAVES.
Photo by F. O. Oertel, Esq., N.W.P.)

from three to six inches in length. They are stuck to the bare surface of the rock with a very hard cement.

The most curious object is the image-tower formed from a solid stalagmite. This is situated on the left of the passage leading towards the inner part of the cave. The base of this is square, and on it rises an octagonal pillar, surmounted by an elaborately-carved *hti*, which crowns the whole. The total height is about eleven feet, and the whole is carved with rows of sitting images, each with a small canopy over it.

In the body of the cave are thousands of images of every size, shape, and material; some are evidently modern, others hundreds of years old.

From the fact that the more ancient of these images represent Buddha as wearing a crown of several tiers, and that in many cases the lobes of the ears do not reach to the shoulders, it is thought that these caves, as well as the others in the vicinity of Moulmein, were utilised by the Cambodian or Siamese conquerors of the country as shrines.

Owing doubtless to the troubled state of this part of the country for several centuries preceding the British occupation, whatever historical records there may have been, have either been lost or destroyed. Of traditional history there is none. Some are said to contain vast stores of palm-leaf records, hidden away in their innermost recesses, but casual search into remote corners has revealed little else but bats and their accompanying guano.

The Paget Cave is about two miles from the Kawgún, close to the banks of the Salween. It is so dark and infested with bats that it is better for the visitor to give it a wide berth. An official told the writer that some months ago he stood towards sundown at the mouth of the cave, watch in hand, for over twenty minutes, during the whole of which time an unceasing stream of bats emerged to seek their evening meal. It was a sight, he said, once seen never to be forgotten.

Amherst is a small town situated on the point at the mouth of the Salween River, and is thirty miles distant by river from

Moulmein, and fifty-four miles by road. At the back of the town a wooded range of hills shuts it off from the country beyond, and the Wagarû Creek enters the Salween not far from Amherst Point.

The name Amherst was given to this town in 1826 by Mr. Crawford, the first Civil Commissioner of Tenasserim, who selected it as the seat of government of the lately acquired province, in honour of Lord Amherst, during whose administration as Governor General the province had been annexed. By the natives it is called Kyaik-Ka-mi. Although the civil capital, Moulmein was selected as the chief military station, not only on account of its strategical position, but also because the supply of water at Amherst was limited, and at the same time brackish. After a few years, the civil offices were removed to Moulmein, and Amherst declined in importance.

It is chiefly used now as a pilot station, and as a seaside resort for the European residents of Moulmein and Rangoon. Several nice houses face the sea, belonging mostly to merchants of Moulmein. Government has provided a Dak bungalow for the use of occasional visitors, but the charges here are very high.

In the hot months of March, April and May, the fierce heat is tempered by cool sea breezes which blow with great regularity.

Sea bathing may be indulged in, in spite of sharks and small venomous snakes which frequent these waters. Bathers should, however, observe caution, and not venture more than a few yards out.

On the point is a small white pagoda, which acts as a beacon to passing ships. Close to the point, a small tomb marks the last resting-place of Ann, the beloved wife of Dr. Adoniram Judson, who died here, when about to proceed to America, after the cruel sufferings she had endured at Aung-pin-lè during the First Anglo-Burmese War.

The small island opposite the point is called "Green Island." It is very pleasant to look at, but should be carefully avoided, as the inhabitants are all fishermen, engaged in

ENTRANCE TO KAWGÜN CAVES.
(*Photo by F. O. Oertel, Esq., N.W.P.*)

preparing *nga-pi*, from the small prawns which abound in the adjacent waters. The beach is covered with these, in every state of decomposition, and the effluvia arising from this mass of semi-putrid animal matter is simply unbearable. About twelve miles south of Amherst Point is Double Island, on which is a stone lighthouse with an iron tower, erected in 1865, to guide ships visiting the port of Moulmein, and to prevent them running up the Sittaung River to certain destruction. A bore, twenty feet high at spring tides, rushes up the broad, but shallow mouth of this river, carrying everything before it, and woe betide the ship or steamer that is sucked into its vortex.

THE SACRED LAKES AT MÛDÛN.—These Lakes are situated near the village of Mûdûn on the Amherst Road, eighteen miles from Moulmein, and are a favourite picnic resort of the residents of Moulmein. By sending out a pony to the half-way rest house, the distance may be covered in about three hours. The road is fairly good and not particularly hilly. The lakes are called Kan-Gyi, and Kan-Glè by the Burmese. Kangyi is about three-and-a-half miles in circumference and is connected with the smaller lake by a narrow channel, and is distant from it two miles. It is said to be 300 cubits or 450 feet deep in parts. The water of these lakes is supposed by the villagers to be particularly pure. When the banks are washed by a red foam, cholera and small-pox are expected. The smaller lake has an island towards its southern end, and on its banks a massive recumbent figure of Buddha, sixty-three feet in length. The island is covered with pagodas, theins, and other religious buildings.

When Wagarù was the capital of an independent kingdom, the lakes were a favourite resort, and the people say the larger one was patronised by the King, and the smaller by the Queens.

SALWEEN RIVER TO SHWÈ-GÛN.—A steam launch, run by the Salween River Steam Navigation Co. leaves Moulmein daily for Shwè-Gûn, a village sixty miles up the Salween. The up journey occupies about eight hours, and although unprovided with cabins, European passengers are placed in the bows, away from the natives and the cargo, and with a comfortable long arm-chair, a decent breakfast provided by your "boy," and a comfortable "smoke," the journey is most enjoyable.

THE GYNE RIVER TO KYÊN-DÔ.—The Gyne River is formed by the junction of the Hlaing-bwè and Haung-tha-rau rivers, both of which issue from the Siam Yomas, and unite not far from the village of Gyne, about forty-five miles from Moulmein.

A service of steam launches keeps open daily communication with the stations on this river as far as Kyundô. European passengers are accommodated in the bows, away from the crowd of natives and the cargo.

After leaving the Kûladan Jetty, the launch proceeds up the Salween, passing between Crow Island and Battery Point. Here the waters of the Salween, Gyne, and Attaran mingle together, and the Gyne coming from the east is entered. The first halting place after leaving Daing-wûn-kwin is Zat-tha-byin on the right bank, 12 miles from Moulmein. Although this neighbourhood is very unhealthy, the village is the head-quarters of the sub-division, and on the banks are seen the Court-house and police Thana. Four miles further up, on the left bank is the village of Tarana, and two miles above this the precipitous limestone rock near the village of Dhammatha is seen, the summit crowned by a pagoda. In this rock, about a mile from the Gyne, is the celebrated cave which has been already described. After a run of about two and a half hours, the village of Gyne is passed, on the right bank, and soon after, the launch comes to her moorings at Kyûndô.

From this village a Government road runs across country and over low hills to the village of Kaukareik, which is the starting point for travellers proceeding to Siam via Myawadi to Raheng. The scenery on the Gyne between Moulmein and Kyûn-dô is not remarkable for its beauty, the only pleasing part being the neighbourhood of the Dhammatha Cave, and on the

LOOTED SHRINE, KAWGÙN CAVES.

(Photo by J. O. Wettel, Esq., N.M.P.)

return journey the view of the Moulmein Hills and Martaban Point is also worth more than a passing notice.

MOULMEIN TIMBER MILLS.—A visit to Moulmein would not be complete without a peep into one of the many steam saw-mills seen on the banks, extending from Mopûn right up to the neighbourhood of the Main or Iron Wharf. The annual export of teak exceeds 60,000 tons, and it is in these mills that the logs are squared and cut up into suitable sizes for the markets of Europe and India. In the dragging of the logs from the river bank, lifting them into position for sawing, and removing the sawn logs or scantlings, large numbers of trained elephants are employed, and to watch these huge beasts at their work is one of the most curious, and at the same time, interesting sights. When Rudyard Kipling wrote "Mandalay," he no doubt referred to Moulmein when he thought of—

> " Elephints a-pilin' teak,
> In the sludgy, squdgy creek."

The stacking is one of the most interesting sights. The huge logs, as squared are brought from the rack bench by the elephants on their tusks, being kept in position by one or two turns of the trunk. The logs are then deposited, with mathematical precision and regularity. When the stack is getting high the log is placed on end by the animal, and when in position, a sharp lift upwards with one foot sends it flying up alongside of its companions. Scantlings are carried in the same way, except that a well-trained elephant will at one time lift a cartload and carry it off.

ROUTE IX.

RANGOON OR MOULMEIN TO TAVOY AND MERGUI.

Steamers of the British Indian Steam Navigation Company leave Rangoon for the ports of Tavoy and Mergui, as below.

1. To Tavoy and Mergui *direct*—once a fortnight.
2. To Tavoy Mergui, Victoria Point, Kopah, Tongkah, and Penang—once a month.

The trip to Tavoy, Mergui, and back from Rangoon or Moulmein can be made in about a week or eight days.

TABLE OF DISTANCES.

		Miles.
Rangoon to Moulmein	...	147
Moulmein to Tavoy	...	249
Tavoy to Mergui	...	119
Rangoon to Tavoy (direct)		255

The steamers, though small, are fairly comfortable, and in the north-east monsoon the trip is really enjoyable.

By the direct route, Tavoy river is reached in one day, and Mergui in two days from Rangoon.

By the monthly steamers the voyage is longer, the time taken being as follows :—

To Moulmein	...	1 day.
To Tavoy River	...	4 days.
To Mergui	...	5 ,,
To Victoria Point	...	7 ,,
To Kopah	...	8 ,,
To Tongkah	...	11 ,,
To Penang	...	12 ,,

IMAGES OF BUDDHA, KAWGŪN CAVES.

(Photo by J. G. Nisbet, Esq., N. W. P.)

The route taken by the direct steamers after leaving the Rangoon river is south-east across the muddy waters of the Gulf of Martaban. The north, middle, and south Moscos are passed, situated from about 9 to 13 miles from the mainland, with a safe channel inside, and shortly the steamer comes to an anchor at the mouth of the Tavoy river. The town of Tavoy is situated on the left bank of the river of the same name, about 30 miles from the mouth of the river, which is here 15 miles wide. Owing to shoal water and sand-banks, the river is not navigable for sea-going vessels of any draft over 6 feet, hence they stop at the mouth, and the journey up to town is accomplished either by launch, or by country boat. Tavoy is the head-quarters of the district of the same name, which extends for about 150 miles along the coast, from the Amherst district on the north, to that of Mergui on the south. The average breadth is about 50 miles.

It is shut in from the kingdom of Siam by a lofty range of mountains of an average height of 5,000 feet, across which there are only two practicable passes. The town contains a population of 15,099, and is well laid out. The trade is principally in salt fish, ngapi, dani leaves, wood-oil and other forest products, and some of the best silk cloths are also manufactured here.

It was once the capital of an independent kingdom, but for several hundred years has been alternately subject to Burma or Siam. It was taken without any opposition by the British in 1824, and was for a number of years garrisoned by a detachment from Moulmein.

The people inhabiting this district speak a peculiar dialect of Burmese which more nearly resembles Arakanese. This is supposed to be on account of a large number of Arakanese having settled along the coast some years ago.

The pagoda on the point was erected in 1,200 A.D., by the Burman king, Nara-padi-si-thû, who also constructed the Gauda-palen, and Sûla-mûni temples at Pagan. Twenty-one miles in a N.N.E. direction from Tavoy is Nwa-lè-bo mountain, so called

because its shape is supposed to resemble the " hump " of an ox.
It is about 4,500 feet in height, and has, on several occasions,
been scaled by Europeans. From the summit a magnificent view
is obtained, extending on the land side to the range separating
the district from Siam.

From the Tavoy river the course is through the maze of
islands which constitute the Mergui Archipelago.

The first island passed is Tavoy Island, which formerly
belonged to the Tavoy district, but is now part of Mergui. It is
situated about 40 miles south of the mouth of the Tavoy river.
The large island about 30 miles south of Tavoy Island is called
Min-gyi Island by the natives, which name has been erroneously
translated as " King Island " on the charts.

The whole group of islands may be said to extend from
Tavoy Island on the north in 13° 13′ N. Lat., to St. Mathew's
Island off the mouth of the Pak-chan river in the south, in
10° 52′ N. Lat. The larger islands are covered with dense
vegetation, and contain very few inhabitants. The smaller islands
are mostly bare rocks, some of which are barely visible at
spring tides.

The scenery while passing in a small steamer amongst these
islands is exceedingly pretty, and a party of tourists once told the
writer that in their opinion it equalled, if not excelled, that of
the Inland Sea of Japan which they had visited a few months
previously. The islands have been thus described :—" A cluster
of islands and islets, with bays and caves, headlands and
highlands, capes and promontories, high bluffs and low shores,
rocks and sands, mountain streams and cascades, mountain,
plain, and precipice, unsurpassed for their wild, fantastic, and
picturesque beauty." They are the home of an innumerable
number of pythons and other snakes, and of the tiger and
the rhinoceros. The principal productions are beches-de-mer,
edible birds'-nests, and honey.

A peculiar race of people called Selung, or Se-lôn, as the
Burmese call them, are found in the neighbourhood of these

islands, on which they search for their living. They are supposed to be the remains of a distinct race, similar to the Malays, by whom they were expelled from the Malay peninsula, and for whom they have an inborn dread. Their language, customs, and manners, and mode of life are unlike those of any other races to be found in the Eastern Archipelago. They are quiet and inoffensive, and live in boats, roaming from island to island in search of sea-slugs, fish, shell-fish, sap-pan wood, turtles, shells, pearls, and bees'-wax, which they exchange with Chinese and Malay boat-men from the mainland for rice, liquor, opium, and cotton cloths. It is very seldom they can be persuaded to visit Mergui or the villages on the mainland. They are exempted by Government from the payment of taxes.

The edible birds'-nests—from the sale of the licence to collect which Government nets a considerable revenue annually—are built by the *Collocalia fuciphaga*—a species of swallow—on the sides of the rocky caverns and precipitous cliffs of the islands of the archipelago, particularly Tavoy Island.

They are much prized by Chinese epicures, and are used like the aldermanic turtle for making soup. The nests resemble in shape those of the common house-martin, though slightly more elongated, and are composed of a peculiar kind of gelatinous sea-weed mixed with a secretion peculiar to this bird.

The nests fetch as much as £7 per pound, each nest weighing about half an ounce. They are collected at Mergui for exportation to Singapore and Hong Kong.

Of late years considerable attention has been paid to the pearl-fisheries. Pearls in considerable quantities are found in the shells of an immense oyster, large beds of which exist in various parts of the archipelago. The shells themselves are of marketable value, and are exported as mother-of-pearl. These beds are sold by auction every year at the Court of the Deputy-Commissioner Mergui, and a considerable revenue is secured thereby.

I

The fisheries are mostly in the hands of a Syndicate of Singapore merchants, who employ a large number of experienced divers under European supervision.

MERGUI is situated on the north-west point of an island in the mouth of the Tenasserim River, which falls into the sea about two miles to the north and one mile to the south of the town. The view on entering the harbour is most striking. The centre is occupied by an almost perpendicular rock, which rises suddenly out of the sea, and is valuable on account of its being the nesting-place of the swallows already referred to. The station is built on elevated ground which slopes gradually down to the sea-beach. On the right are seen the islands of the archipelago, dotted about in the ocean.

The principal buildings are the Court-houses, Treasury, Police Office, Hospital, the Government School, and the Circuit-House. These are all on the hill-side, while the Bazaar is close to the beach, along which the native town is built. The population in 1891 was 10,137. Mergui was at one time the Capital of a Siamese province, and in the 17th century was an emporium of trade, and had many European residents. In consequence of an attack on the European Settlement and the massacre of seventy-six of its residents in 1695 A.D. the East India Company declared war against Siam, and Captain Weldon, with a force from Madras, was despatched to Mergui. Cæsar Frederick, the Venetian traveller, who visited the town in 1569, says of it :— "A village called Mergui, in whose harbour there lay every year some ships with veizina (sap-pan wood), nyppa, and benjamin."

In 1824, it was occupied by a British force detached from Tavoy, and after a slight resistance was captured. A small detachment of Sepoys garrisoned the town for some years, but have long since been replaced by civil police.

The principal trade of the port is in rice, salt fish and tin. This metal is procured in yearly increasing quantities from various parts of the district. In 1893, the total quantity exported was 1,308 cwts.

About forty miles above Mergui, is the ancient town of Tanasserim, founded in 1373, A.D., by the Siamese. The remains of mud walls faced with brick still exist; they enclose an area of about four square miles. All that remains of its former greatness is a village of about 200 houses, surrounded by dense jungle, and inhabited by a mixed population of Burmese, Siamese and Chinese.

In the neighbourhood of the Tenasserim river, extensive deposits of coal have been discovered. These have been carefully surveyed by Dr. Oldham, of the Geological Survey of India, who estimated in 1856, that an area of 1,920 statute acres would give an output of 174,000 tons of coal. He further estimated that the cost of placing this at the pit's mouth, should not exceed Rs. 5 per ton, and cost of exporting it to Mergui, the nearest port, Rs. 5 per ton, which would make the total cost delivered at Mergui, Rs. 10 per ton (the present cost of English or Australian coal delivered in Rangoon, exceeds Rs. 20 per ton).

At the mouth of the Pak-chan river, which separates British from Siamese territory, is the prosperous little settlement of Victoria Point.

It is inhabited principally by Chinese and Malays who are engaged in the tin-washing industry.

Across the river is the residence and capital of the Rajah of Renaung, who is nominal ruler of a small state under the King of Siam.

The old Rajah was an enlightened man who had travelled considerably, and was known for the lavish hospitality shewn by him to European visitors.

Victoria Point is about 175 miles south of Mergui.

I 2

ROUTE X.

RANGOON TO AKYAB BY COASTING STEAMER.

TABLE OF DISTANCES—RANGOON TO AKYAB.

Rangoon					
		Miles.			
Elephant Point	...	24			
Sandoway	...	499	475		
Kyauk Pyû	...	618	594	119	
Akyab	...	694	670	195	76

Steam communication with Arakan, Chittagong and Calcutta is maintained by a weekly line of steamers of the British India Steam Navigation Company. These steamers leave from the Bo-ta-taung Jetty, as below.

In the north-east monsoon (from September till May) on Tuesday mornings.

In the south-west monsoon (May till September) on Monday mornings.

As these steamers generally leave their moorings very early in the morning, intending passengers should sleep on board. Although small, they are very comfortable, and the trip round the coast is most enjoyable in the north-east monsoon.

After leaving the mouth of the Rangoon river and passing Elephant Point, a south-westerly course is taken. The low lying delta of the Irrawaddy is barely visible above the surrounding waters, and the presence of land is only known to be a reality by the clumps of palm trees which rear their straight tall stems from the surrounding plains.

ALGUADA LIGHTHOUSE.

(From a Sketch.)

Towards evening the Alguada Lighthouse is rounded, and the course is then due north. This lighthouse was erected by Government in 1861, to facilitate the navigation of ships visiting Bassein and Rangoon. It was built on a dangerous reef of rocks situated about ten miles to the south of Diamond Island.

The lighthouse is 144 feet high, built of granite masonry in alternate black and white bands, and took nearly five years to construct. It bears a first order catadioptric light, revolving once in a minute, and visible twenty miles.

Towards the afternoon of the second day, the buoy off the mouth of the Sandoway river is reached, and the steamer comes to an anchor for the night. The village on the point at the entrance to the river is called Sin-gaung, and most of the transhipment of goods and passengers is done by the villagers from this place. Sandoway is situated on the left bank of the stream of the same name, about seventeen miles from the mouth.

Surrounded as it is by hills on all sides, it is one of the most picturesque places to be met with in Lower Burma.

The old town was known in Arakanese history as "Dwa-ra-wadi"; it is supposed to have been changed to Than-dwè, the present Burmese name, from the report that it was miraculously chained to the earth. ("*Than*," iron; "*dwè*," to connect).

The inhabitants numbered 2,531 at the census taken in 1891. A small coasting trade is carried on with Gwa, Raunri and Akyab, via the tidal creeks which intersect the sea coast.

In the neighbourhood are three pagodas, called the An-dau, Nan-dau and San-dau pagodas. Each of these is situated on the summit of a hill.

Two stone inscriptions have been found in the Sandoway district. One is at Byi-wa, a village on the right bank of the Sandoway river, a few miles above Sandoway, and the other in the neighbourhood of Taungûp. Both are in Sanscrit of the 8th century, and one contains the first couplet of the Buddhist text from "Yedharma" down to the words "Maha Sramana."

Coins of ancient Kings of Arakan are also occasionally dug up, many of them of the 9th and 10th centuries A.D.

Under present contract with the Government, the steamers are not permitted to leave the offing till 7 a.m. This is to enable passengers to get on board in the early morning before the sea breezes spring up. After a run of about eight hours, Kyauk pyû harbour is entered. In the fair weather the course taken is between the islands of Cheduba and Ramri, the scenery on both sides of the straits being most pleasing.

CHEDUBA ISLAND is of volcanic formation and is about 120 miles in area. The small island to the south-east is called Flat Island.

By the natives, Cheduba is called "Man-aung" or Devil Island. It is fertile and well wooded. A level cultivated plain extends round the coast, and within this belt are low undulating hills, in height varying from 50 to 500 feet. In the north-west corner is the "volcano," which is such a terror to the inhabitants. Others are found in the centre of the island. They are geologically known as salses or mud volcanoes.

Mr. F. R. Mallet, F.G.S., who visited Cheduba and Ramri some years ago, thus explains the presence of these salses.

"The mud is not produced by chemical means, but by mere mixture of shale and clay with water. The ejecting force is evidently the pressure of gas, which is in large part at least carburetted hydrogen mixed perhaps with the vapour of the most volatile liquid petroleum hydro-carbons.

"Bubbles of gas are given off from the mud cones in their ordinary state, as well as from most of the petroleum wells. . . . . . Mud volcanoes may be caused where the other necessary conditions are present, by the pressure of gas owing merely to its continued slow generation from carbonaceous matter at the normal temperature of the strata at moderate depths."

In their quiescent state thick mud is seen bubbling up from the foot of the crater. When in active eruption, however, mud

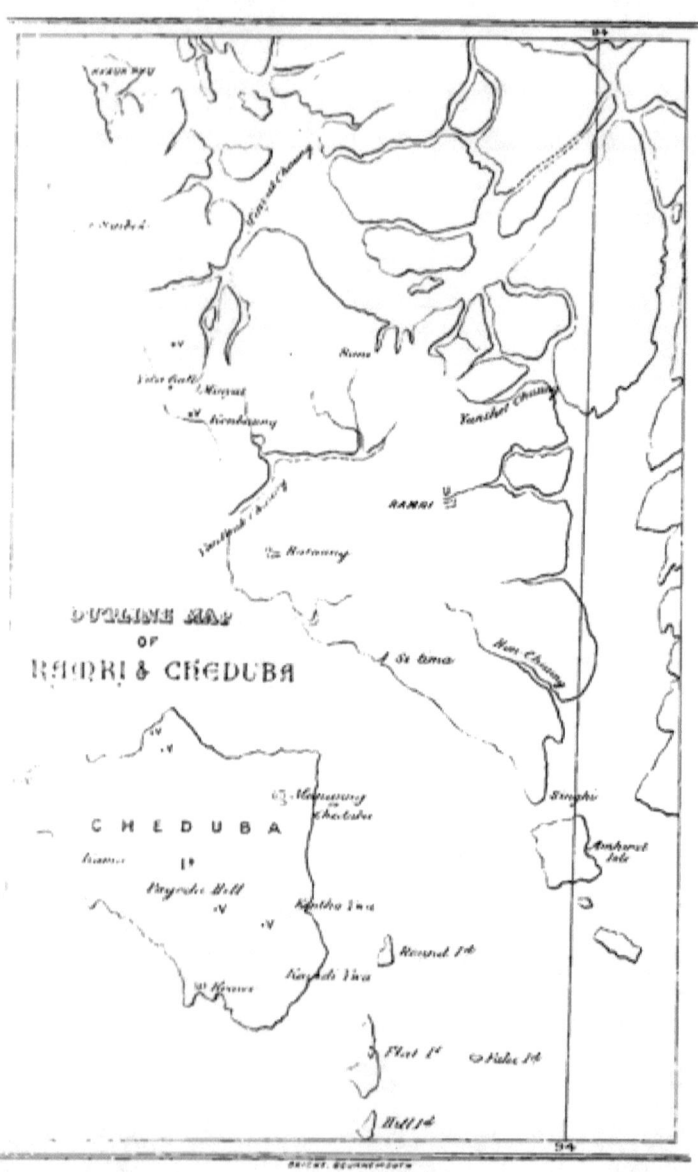

OUTLINE MAP
OF
RAMRI & CHEDUBA

CHEDUBA

and stones are shot out with great noise and force. At the same time the inflammable gas which is expelled, catches fire, and lights up the country for miles around.

This accounts for the strange phenomena often witnessed at sea by passing ships and subsequently reported at Rangoon and Calcutta. By the natives, the chief volcano in Cheduba is called *Naga-daung* or Dragon mountain, and their explanation of the phenomenon is very simple, viz.: that the *Naga* is angry, and breathes out flames of fire to notify his indignation.

Cheduba Island is celebrated for its rich pasturage, and consequently for its cattle. The chief village is Manaung, situated on the strait between the island and Ramri.

After rounding the north-west point of Ramri Island, the land-locked harbour of Kyauk-Pyû is entered. This name, which in English means "white stone," is supposed to have been given on account of the white pebbly beach which extends for some distance down the coast.

After the occupation of the Arakan province in 1825, Kyauk-Pyû was for some years the chief military station. In 1850 the garrison was withdrawn, since which time the place has decreased in size and importance. At present it is the head-quarters of the district, and contains the usual Government offices.

The climate is said to be exceedingly unhealthy for Europeans, and the abnormally large European Cemetery somewhat corroborates the report. Of late years some effort has been made to work the petroleum wells which exist throughout the island. At present, however, the supply is somewhat scanty. Salt is manufactured in large quantities along the sea coast and banks of tidal creeks.

Ramri, the former capital, is situated towards the south-east end of the island, but is now a place of small importance.

Leaving Kyauk-Pyû at daylight, Akyab is reached by about noon. It is situated at the mouth of the Kuladan river, and has a population of 37,938.

It was made the chief station of the province of Arakan soon after the close of the First Anglo-Burmese war, the old capital (Myo-haung) having been found most unhealthy for European troops and civilians. The streets were laid out, and public works carried on by convict labour, free labour at the time not being available. The principal buildings are the Court-house, Jail, Custom-house, Hospital, Bazaar, High School and Club.

There are in addition two Roman Catholic Churches, one Anglican Church, besides several Mahomedan mosques and Hindu temples.

The name *Akyab* is supposed to be a corruption of *A-kyat-dau*, the title of a pagoda in the neighbourhood, which was probably a good land-mark for ships in olden times.

By the natives it is called *Sit-twè*, because the English garrison was stationed there in 1825.

About three miles above the town is the Chirregea Creek, on the banks of which the rice-mills of the European merchants are built. About 60,000 tons of rice are annually exported from Akyab.

Immediately to the south of Akyab is situated Savage Island, on which a lighthouse was erected in 1842. The Borongo Islands further to the south, contain a considerable number of petroleum wells, which for a number of years have been worked on European methods, with indifferent results. The total out-put from Arakan in 1893, was 256,701 gallons.

MYO-HAUNG.—This was the ancient capital of the kingdom of Arakan, and only the ruins now exist to testify to its former greatness. It stands at the head of a branch of the Kuladan river about 50 miles from its mouth, on a rocky plain surrounded by hills.

The ruins of the ancient fort are still in existence, consisting of three square enclosures, one within the other, surrounded by a masonry wall of very considerable thickness, built of stone and brick set in cement; the stone having apparently been brought from the Borongo Islands 60 miles off at the mouth of the river.

The greatest works for the defence of the city, though, were the mounds of earth faced with masonry, erected to protect the approaches to the city from the hills. Some of these were of great height, and the sites from which the necessary earth was excavated, now form large tanks.

At the main gate-ways the stone walls were high and thick, but where the hills afforded natural protection, a low wall was run along their summits. These works, together with the town, now lie in ruins. In the centre the palace platform still exists, surmounted at the present day, by a Court-house and a Police Station ! !

After the conquest of Arakan by the Burmese in 1784, the city became the capital of one of the four provinces into which the kingdom was divided. By the Arakanese it was called *Myank-û*, and was founded by Min-Soan-wûn, in 1430, A.D., to commemorate his restoration to the throne. At this time Arakan was tributary to Bengal.

On the declaration of war with Burma in 1824, two expeditions were decided on. One *via* Chittagong to Arakan, and the other *via* Rangoon. The Arakan army crossed the Naaf, and after six weeks marching, arrived before the town of Arakan. After two attempts the town was captured, and the Burmese garrison driven off. In the ensuing rains, the British army went into Cantonments, during which period the loss to life was frightful. Not a single life was lost in action, but of the average strength of the two regiments, the 54th and the 44th, amounting to 1,004 men, 595 died in the country in the course of eight months, and of those who quitted it, not more than half were alive at the end of twelve months. (Report by Major Tullock, presented to Parliament in August, 1841).

About 20 miles north of old Arakan is the celebrated Maha-muni pagoda, which is still visited by large crowds of worshippers, notwithstanding that the immense brass image was removed to Amarapura by the Burmese Conqueror, Bo-dau-pava, in 1784.

To the north of the Akyab district are situated the Arakan Hill tracts. These are inhabited by semi-civilized tribes of Chins, Chaung-thas and Kwèmis.

The hills are administered by a police officer with magisterial powers, whose head-quarters are at Paletwa on the Kuladan river. A good service of steam launches is running on the Kuladan and Mro rivers, so that the district can be easily itinerated.

Akyab has no hotels worth speaking of, but there is a very good Dàk Bungalow for travellers, and also a Circuit-house, in close proximity to the courts.

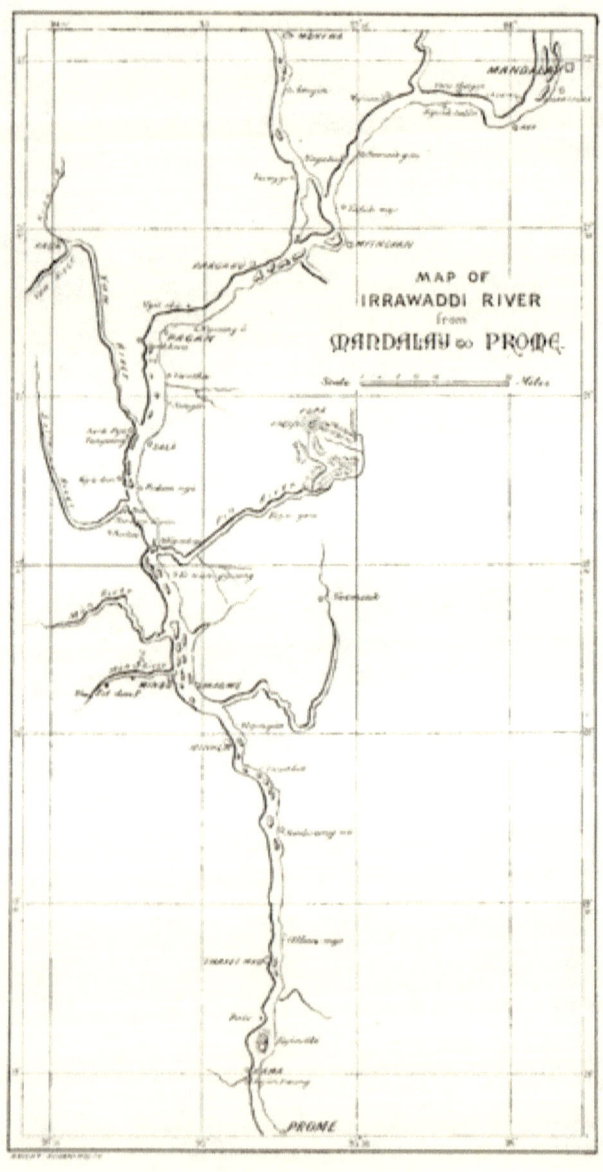

MAP OF
IRRAWADDI RIVER
from
MANDALAY to PROME.

TABLE OF DISTANCES BY RIVER FROM MANDALAY TO PROME.

	Mandalay	Sagaing	Ngazún	Myingyan	Pakôkku	Pagán	Salé	Sin-byu-gyún	Yè-nan-gyaung	Minbu	Minhla	Sin-baung-gwè	Allan-myo	Thayet-myo	Pyalo	Myaung-bin-zeik	Kama
Mandalay																	
Sagaing	15																
Ngazún	45	30															
Myingyan	90	75	45														
Pakôkku	125	110	80	35													
Pagán	145	130	100	55	20												
Salé	200	185	155	110	75	35											
Sin-bye-gyún	225	210	180	135	100	80	25										
Yè-nan-gyaung	250	235	205	160	125	105	50	25									
Minbu	285	270	240	195	160	140	85	60	35								
Minhla	305	290	260	215	180	160	105	80	55	20							
Sinbaung-gwè	323	308	278	233	198	178	123	98	73	38	18						
Allan-myo	349	334	304	259	224	204	149	124	99	64	44	26					
Thayet-myo	353	338	308	263	228	208	153	128	103	68	48	30	4				
Pyalo	364	349	319	274	239	219	164	139	114	79	59	41	15	11			
Nyaung-bin-zeik	372	357	327	283	247	227	172	147	122	87	67	49	23	19	8		
Kama	385	368	340	293	258	238	185	158	133	98	78	60	34	30	19	11	
Prome	397	382	352	307	272	252	197	172	147	112	92	74	48	44	33	25	14

ROUTE XI.

MANDALAY TO PROME BY STEAMER.

The express steamers of the Irrawaddy Flotilla Company leave Mandalay every Wednesday and Saturday morning at 8 a.m. for Rangoon, arriving at Prome on the following Friday and Tuesday, and in Rangoon on the following Sunday and Thursday afternoons respectively.

The steamers of this service are the most powerful, commodious, and comfortable of any lines maintained by the Company, and a trip by one of them to Prome or Rangoon, with a courteous and communicative commander, a well-appointed table, and a commodious cabin to which to retire at night, is a treat only to be enjoyed on the excellent service of steamers of the Irrawaddy Flotilla Company. On no other river in Asia, or for that matter, in any part of the civilized world, is such a magnificent fleet of steamers to be seen, as that of this opulent and enterprising company.

Leaving the shore at Mandalay punctually at 8 a.m., the steamer speeds on its course down the river, passing on the left bank the dockyard and repairing sheds of the company, abreast of which are moored a number of disused steamers, some still serviceable, others long since laid up, and their place taken by those of a newer and improved type. Could these old hulks speak, what tales of pre-annexation days would be revealed. On board one of them the huge cannon in front of the palace, bearing on them the mark of ownership, "Georgius Rex," were doubtless surreptitiously carried up from Rangoon.

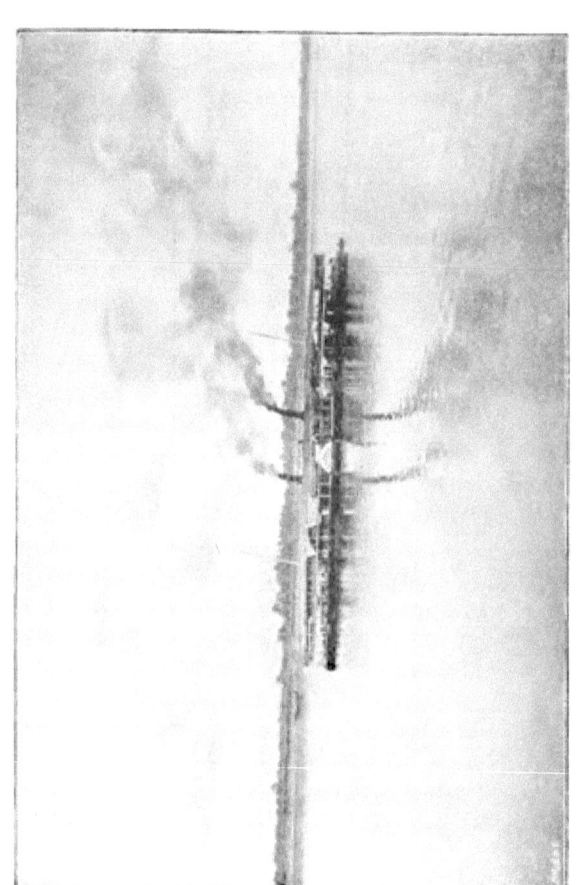

IRRAWADDY FLOTILLA CO.'S MAIL STEAMER "DUFFERIN."

(From a Photograph.)

The palmy days of the company were when these old pioneers were " chunkin' " from Rangoon to Mandalay.

The high bund on the left bank of the river was originally constructed by Mindôn Min to protect the lower part of the extra-mural city from inundation during the river floods of the rainy season.

The bund extends from the village of Obo, north of the walled city, to the neighbourhood of Amarapura. It was the bursting of the northern end of this bund in 1886, immediately after the annexation, that caused such serious damage to the lower parts of the city. The new bund subsequently constructed, was retired considerably from the neighbourhood of the river.

The channel in the dry season lies between the left bank and the large sand banks with which the river is partly blocked. On the left, amid groves of magnificent mango and tamarind trees, lies Amarapura, now a collection of villages full of busy silk weavers, but formerly a royal city, and for many years the seat of government (see Route XIV.) Below this will be seen the terminus of the Mandalay section of the Mû Valley Railway.   A steam ferry runs from the shore here to Sagaing on the right bank, from which place the railway runs almost due north to Katha, Mogaung, and eventually to Myitkyina, 140 miles north of Bhamo. (The line from Mogaung to Myitkyina has only just been sanctioned, and the extension has not yet been carried out.—1895).

After passing Amarapura ferry station, the channel contracts to about 800 yards in width, the river running between the pagoda-covered and picturesque island of Shwè-Kyet-yet on the left, and the rocky terminus of the Sagaing hills on the right bank.   Advantage of these narrows has been taken by the Telegraph Department, to throw a line across the river. This depends from two lofty iron masts, one on either bank.

After passing Sagaing on the right, the course of the river changes suddenly to the south-west, passing on the left the mouth of the Myit-ngè river, which enters the Irrawaddi

immediately above the old city of Ava. Above the mouth an
old fort, constructed by Mindôn Min is placed. A similar one
commands the river on the Sagaing side.

The navigation here was formerly very difficult, owing to
both rocks and shoals.

On the approach of the British fleet of steamers in 1885,
with the expeditionary forces, the Burmese thought to block the
channel by scuttling several steamers and flats in the fairway.
This was done, the result being that these obstructions caused
the river to scour out a new and excellent channel, which
is now fully taken advantage of by those navigating the river.
The remains of the wrecks can still be seen at low water. After
passing by Old Ava on the left bank (see Route XVI.), the river
sweeps round to the north-west, and then runs due west, passing
the large village of Ywathitgyi. Shortly before reaching this
village, the Ngazûn rocks occur. For several years the navigation
of large steamers was entirely stopped at this place, when the
river was low. Last year, however, several old steamers and flats
belonging to the Company were scuttled here, and the result has
been that a broad and navigable channel has been formed, which
admits of the passage of the largest steamers of the Company.

A little below Ywathitgyi and on the opposite bank of the
river, is the picturesque village of Kyauk-talôn ("one rock.")

It was, in the King's time, an important custom's station for
riverine traffic.

A few miles below Kyauktalôn and on the opposite side, the
Mû river enters the Irrawaddi. It rises in the high lands north of
the Shwèbo district, and is not navigable for steam vessels, even
in the rainy season.

Three miles below, on the right bank, is the large village of
Myinmû. The origin of the name is somewhat uncertain.
Village report says that a former King of Pagan stopped here on
his way up the river, and that he saw many strange and
wonderful sights (Bur : *myin-dan-mu-thi*), but this derivation
appears to be somewhat mechanical. It is a growing place, and is

SHWÈ KYET YET, SAGAING.

(*Photo by Signor Beato, Mandalay.*)

the head-quarters of the southern sub-division of the Sagaing district.

A bridged and partially metalled road runs from this village to Mônywa on the Chindwin river, and the greater part of the Chindwin-Mandalay trade is carried on by this route.

As the navigation of the Chindwin between Mônywa and Pakôkkû—during the low water season, from November to May—is exceedingly difficult owing to the yearly increasing number of sandbanks and shoals, the Irrawaddy Flotilla Company has in contemplation a scheme for running a light steam tramway from Mônywa to Myinmû, a distance of 37 miles.

If this is carried out Myinmû will be greatly benefitted. Below Myinmû the river channel broadens considerably, and in the floods is several miles in width.

Sameik-gôn, on the left bank, is a large village, and is a port for the export of cotton and jaggery from the Myôtha sub-division.

About a mile below, and on the opposite bank, is Nagabauk. This is the nearest point on the main river to Nabet, a large mission station of the Roman Catholics, peopled originally by Portuguese and French prisoners of war, carried away into captivity from Syriam, Bassein, and even from Siam, by successive Burmese conquerors. When the river is in full flood, the whole of the country between the permanent banks, which are distinguishable by the fringe of large trees and the spires of pagodas and monasteries, is inundated.

Immediately opposite Nagabauk on the left bank, and close to the water's edge, is an old Banyan tree (*Ficus Religiosa*) the base of which is surrounded by a masonry platform.

Here, on the 24th February, 1826, the Treaty of Yandabo was signed by Sir Archibald Campbell and the Burmese delegates appointed by the King. In consequence of this, the tree is usually spoken of as the " Treaty Tree." Although nominally at Yandabo, the village of that name is some two or three miles further down stream. The general direction is now due south until the neighbourhood of Myingyan is reached, ninety

miles from Mandalay. Owing to the formation of a large sand-
bank immediately opposite the town, the steamers of the
Irrawaddy Flotilla Company are unable to anchor off it, except
when the river is in flood. During the low water season they
halt at the flats moored outside the sandbank in the main stream,
and passengers have to make their own arrangements for reaching
the station some two miles distant.

For some years succeeding the annexation, Myingyan was
an important military station, as the large cantonment and
extensive range of barrack accommodation still testify. Owing
however to the complete pacification of the country around, and
to the present policy of strengthening the garrisons on the eastern
frontier, its strategical importance has decreased so that at the
present time the garrison consists of the head-quarters of one
Sepoy regiment only, with a few details of other services.

The town contained a population of 19,790 in 1891 when the
last census was taken.

The trade is principally in cotton and jaggery, the former
going chiefly to China *via* Bhamo, and the latter to Rangoon.

Immediately opposite to Myingyan, its mouth blocked by a
sandbank several miles in length, the Chindwin enters the
Irrawaddy. It is the most important of the tributaries of the
parent stream, and is navigable for steamers for several hundreds
of miles (Vide Route XXIII). From Myingyan the course is
south-west till Pakôkkñ is reached on the right bank, thirty-five
miles below Myingyan.

This is a comparatively modern town, and has quite
supplanted the older station Kûn-na-ywa, higher up the river.
Pakôkkñ is the chief port of the Chindwin, and is a place of very
considerable trade, which, as at other places, is mostly in the
hands of the Chinese. Jaggery, hides, horns, beans, and cotton
are the principal articles of export.

A timber revenue station is maintained here by the Forest
Department, at which all the timber extracted from the Chindwin
Forests by the Bombay Burmah Trading Corporation is checked

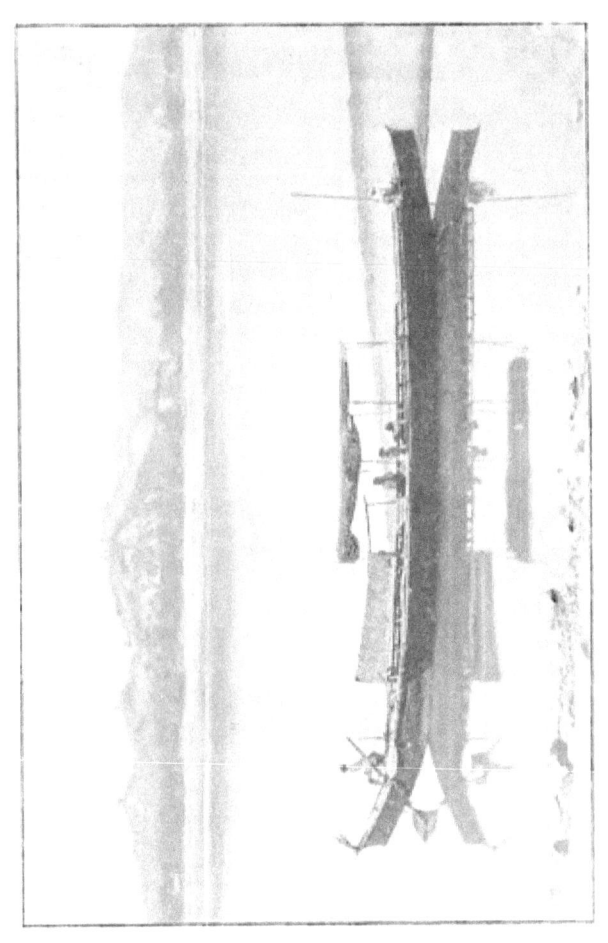

SAGAING HILLS.

(Photo by Seymour Reate, Mandalay &c.)

and passed. This Company, it will be remembered, leased these and other forests from the Burmese Government, and the failure or disinclination of the king to submit the points in dispute with the Company to arbitration, was one of the primary causes of the last war.

On the British assuming the government of the country, the leases held by the Company were allowed to hold good, and have still some time to run. During the working season of 1893-94 this Company alone extracted from the Chindwin and Yaw forests 41,983 logs of teak representing 48,257 tons of timber. It is stated that in June 1894, some 66,000 logs from the Chindwin forests were in the river and its creeks, waiting for the rise of the water to be floated out.

Pakôkkû is the first day's halting place of the express steamers *from* Mandalay, which do not as a rule proceed at night.

The south-western course is maintained below Pakôkkû till Nyaungû is reached on the left bank, twenty-five miles down. This is the nearest stopping place to the old city of Pagan, with its numerous ruined temples (Vide Route XVIII).

Nyaungû and the neighbouring village Pagan are the chief centres of the lacquer-ware industry, a description of which will be found in the introduction to this work. Vendors board all steamers on their arrival, and for a few rupees a very fair selection of cups, trays, and betel-boxes may be made.

Just above the landing place may be seen the remains of two of the king's steamers which were scuttled on the approach of the expedition in 1885.

Rounding the huge sandbank at the bend of the river, the southern course is resumed, passing on the right the Tangyi Hills, the highest summit being crowned by a white pagoda.

Tradition states that Shin Gaudama himself stood here, and looking down on the wide plains of Pauk-gan beneath him, foretold the future grandeur and glory of the capital which would afterwards arise.

The pagoda has its annual feast, and was formerly approached by a broad flight of stone steps which however are now in a very ruinous condition. On the left bank is the modern village of Pagan, and for the next four miles the eye encounters endless numbers of ruined shrines of every shape and size.

As Popa has been *en évidence* for the past twenty-four hours a short description will here be appropriate.

POPA MOUNTAIN.

This isolated and formidable peak is a conspicuous object from the river from Yènan-gyaung to some distance above Myingyan.

Although having an altitude above sea-level of 4,961 feet only, standing alone as it does, in the midst of a plain of comparatively level country, its mass and height impress the observer more forcibly than much higher summits to be seen to the west in the Yaw country, or to the east, in the mountains bordering on the Shan States.

The mountain is situated about twenty-four miles to the south-east of Pagan, from which a fairly good cart-road runs to the village of Popa, at its foot. From the river bank the country gradually ascends, so that the village of Popa is in reality 1,600 feet above Pagan, or 1,900 feet above the sea. On account of this gradual elevation, the mountain loses much of its height. The base is encircled by a flat terrace of raised ground, separated from the surrounding sandy country by precipitous cliffs nearly 500 feet in height. A steep road leads up the cliff, and after a walk of about two miles Popa village is reached.

This village was formerly a place of refuge for fugitive princes from Pagan, and here Anaurhata retired to mature his plans for seizing the kingdom and capital in the early part of the eleventh century A.D.

The village is supplied with water from an excellent perennial spring which issues from the mountain, and the inhabitants subsist principally on Indian corn, which is extensively grown in the neighbourhood. From the village the path leads through tree jungle, the size of the trees diminishing as higher ground is reached. After an ascent of about 2,000 feet above the village, the path emerges from the tree jungle, and the grass-covered slopes of the crater are reached.

The ascent to the peak on the south side is somewhat difficult. The view from the summit is exceedingly fine, stretching from the Yaw and Arakan Yomas on the west, to the mountains bordering the Shan plateau on the east. The country on all sides adjacent to the mountain, and for many miles beyond, consists of sandy plains of rocky country, covered with sparse vegetation and trees of the kutch, thorny plum, mimosa and cactus species, so common in all parts of Upper Burma.

Radiating on all sides, winding sandy beds of streams are seen, the largest being that of the Pin river, which empties itself into the Irrawaddi just above Yènangyaung.

The crater (for no doubts exist that Popa is an extinct volcano) is about a mile across, and the inner sides stretch downwards in precipitous cliffs to a depth of 2,000 feet.

The wall of the crater on the north-east side has been broken down, the gap extending from the summit to the level ground below.

Large forest trees fill the bottom of the crater and are found growing out from the sides of the precipices. On either side of the rent or chasm is a peak, separated by about half a mile of space, that to the south is about 300 feet higher than the other. The whole of the upper part of the mountain is formed of beds of volcanic ashes, and it is owing to the presence of large crystallised rocks on the peaks that they have resisted the action of rain better than the softer volcanic beds of ash immediately below them.

The most marked feature in the flora of Popa is the entire change of species that occurs at successive altitudes. At about 3,500 feet above sea-level, tree forest gives place to grass, and the common bracken ferns of many and beautiful species grow to profusion, and inside the crater the trees are covered with many varieties of orchids, the humidity prevailing being specially favourable for their growth.

Forty miles due east of Popa is the Meiktila Lake, which depends entirely on the rains at Popa for its supplies of water. This lake, which covers an area of several square miles, has been known to rise three feet in one night, owing to heavy and continuous rain on and around Popa. The water courses leading from the Popa highlands are scoured out to the depth of forty or fifty feet with almost perpendicular sides, and the noise of the rushing floods can be heard for a considerable distance.

As may be imagined, the superstitious Burmans of the surrounding country look with awe on Popa as being the dwelling place of ghosts, devils, *bilûs*, and a host of other good and bad nats.

A curious legend is connected with two celebrated *nats* called Mahaghiri and Shin-Myat-Hla, which is worth reproducing, if only to show how much the religion of the modern up-country Burman, who professes to be a Buddhist, is mixed up with the older and primitive Shamanistic belief. The legend is as follows.

In the reign of one of the kings of Tagaung there lived a blacksmith in that city whose name was Maung Tin-Dau. He had a son named Maung Tin Dè, who was celebrated throughout the country for his skill and strength. Owing to these qualifications he soon became possessed of great influence in the province.

The king, fearing his growing power, and in order to gain the favour of the blacksmith, married the latter's sister, who then became the chief queen. He then determined to rid himself of his rival, and for this purpose bade his wife call her brother to the palace, stating that it was his desire to create Maung Tin Dè a noble. On his arrival at the palace he was treacherously seized by the king's soldiers and bound with strong ropes to a *Saga-bin* growing in the palace garden. Faggots of wood were then piled around him and fired. The queen, hearing the cries, and recognizing the voice as that of her brother, rushed from the palace and threw herself into the flames to endeavour to release him. Efforts were made by the guards to recover the queen but without success, both sister and brother perishing in the flames. On searching in the ashes the heads only were recovered. These strange to say, were uninjured by the fire.

In evidence of the great affection shewn by them they became *nats* or spirits of a malignant kind, and took up their abode in the *Saga-bin* beneath which they had both perished.

From this tree they caused destruction and death to all who approached or stood within its shadow. So serious did the loss of life become, that the king ordered the tree to be rooted up and cast into the Irrawaddi. This was done, and the tree floated down the river till it became stranded at the village of Pauk-kan (Pagan) where king Thin-li-gyaung reigned.

Here the *nats* who still resided in the tree, continued to destroy all who approached it. On one occasion they appeared in the king's palace and shewed their human heads, and related to him the cruelty and treachery of the king of Tagaung.

On King Thin-li-gyaung learning who they were, he became greatly alarmed, and ordered a suitable shrine to be erected for them at Popa. This was done, and the tree was carried there and replanted in the neighbourhood of the shrine. From this time the *nats* ceased their destructive habits, and only became malignant when not properly propitiated.

The king subsequently issued a royal order that a grand feast in their honour should be held annually in the month of *Nayón* (June).

This feast has been regularly held since those times. Tharrawaddi, who reigned at Amarapura from 1837 to 1846 A.D., presented two golden heads to the shrine, placing them in charge of the chief civil officers at Popa-Myo. In consequence of the presentation of these golden heads the male *nat* has since been known as "Taung-gyi Maha Ghiri," or the "nat of the great hill," while the female is known as "Shwè-Hmyet Hna," or the "golden faced nat."

On the day appointed for the feast, the golden heads were carried to the *Nat* temple by a procession of officials and the people from the surrounding country, headed by bands of music and dancers. On arrival at the temple they were placed on an altar, when offerings were made and certain ceremonies were gone through. At the conclusion of the feast they were returned to the custody of the chief civil officer.

On the assumption of the government of the country by the British they were removed to Pagan and deposited in the treasury.

About two years ago (1893) they were offered by the Government to the trustees of the shrine. As, however, the country was still harassed by Bo Cheo and other outlaws they declined the responsibility, and the heads, I am told, have been removed to Rangoon. It would be a gracious act of the administration if the heads could be restored and the feast revived.

Twenty-four miles south of Pagan, and on the same bank, Singû is situated. Owing to the silting up of the river at this spot, the village is inaccessible to steamers except during the floods. A large trade however is carried on with Lower Burma by means of country boats. It is the principal port of supply and export for the Kyauk-pa-daung sub-division which lies around Popa.

A few miles below Singû the Yaw river enters the Irrawaddi from the west. It is not navigable, but a good deal of timber is floated down it from the forests which it taps. Zegat at the mouth of the Yaw river is a timber revenue station. About 80 miles to the west is situated "Yaw-daung"—Mount Victoria as it has been renamed. Its height is 10,400 feet, and it is the highest mountain in Burma. It has been ascended both by military officers deputed by Government, and by private individuals. Pines, oaks, and rhododendrons cover the higher slopes, and violets, primroses, and other flowers of temperate regions grow in profusion.

Owing, however, to its inaccessibility, it is highly improbable that it will ever be utilized as a hill station, although it is said to possess all the requisite qualifications—a lovely climate, a good and permanent supply of drinking water, and unlimited sites for house building. Its remoteness from the river and the mountainous nature of the intermediate country prohibit its utilization for the benefit of the " poor whites " in Burma. Ten miles below Singû, Salè-myo is passed on the left bank. This is one of the stopping-places of the express steamers, and is the head-quarters of the southern town-ship of the Myingyan district. The chief trade of the place is in lacquer ware and in cotton pillows and mattresses. Here Ŭ-Pônya, one of the most learned and celebrated Burmese authors, lived. He was the author of the *Wizaya Zat*, which is considered a work of great merit. His *kyaung* has been destroyed by fire, but his library, full of choice works, is still intact. Salè has a population of 2,500.

Pagan-ngè, or Little Pagan, is situated on the left bank, about sixteen miles south of Salè, and was originally formed by " Dragon " worshippers, who were expelled by Anaurhata from Pagan. (*Vide* Route XVIII.)

After their expulsion they halted at this place, and attempted to raise an insurrection for the purpose of establishing their corrupt religion. This place became their head-quarters, and was named Pagan-ngè. The Salin River joins the main river from the west. It rises somewhere in the neighbourhood of Mount Victoria, already described. At its mouth is the important station Sin-byû-Gyûn. It is the chief port for the trade of Salin, ten miles distant inland, a good metalled road connecting the two places. Salin contains a population of nearly 11,000, and is the chief centre of trade in the Minbû district.

The most influential section of the community in Salin are the *Thagaungs*. They are not of pure Burman descent, but have a large admixture of Chin blood in their veins. The title was first given by the King to four Chin cultivators, and from these the present *Thagaungs* are descended. They were presented with red umbrellas and *kamauks* (sun hats), as a distinctive badge, to distinguish them from the common people.

At the present time they are known for their affluence and hospitality, are strict Buddhists, and spend large sums on the erection of pagodas and monasteries, and are most charitable to those among whom they dwell. They dress very plainly, and do not allow outsiders to marry into their sect.

Kyauk-yè, a few miles below, on the left bank, has a population of about 1,000. The name is a corruption of Kyauk-Kywè, signifying "stone buffalo," a name given to a rock which formerly was seen in the river, close to the village, which somewhat resembled a buffalo in shape. The name Kyauk-Kywè has since been modified to Kyaukkyè. Three miles below this village the Pin River enters the Irrawaddi from the east. This river rises in the southern slopes of Popa. A peculiar feature of it is that at the village of *Yezôn* ("water ending") the water disappears into the sandy bed of the river, to re-appear some six miles further down at a village called Nat-Kan-û.

After passing the Pin River the channel becomes much blocked by islands and sand-banks, which are specially numerous in the neighbourhood of Yènan-gyaung. This town, as the name implies (*Yè-nan*, crude petroleum, and *Gyaung*, a ravine or chasm), is the chief centre of the oil-bearing tracts in the Magwè district. There are twenty-six demarcated square mile blocks of such land altogether. This area consists of wells, which are the property of Government, leased to the Burma Oil Company; the native reserve, assigned to native workers, or *hein-zas*, who have the privilege, subject to conditions designed to secure their rights, *inter se*, of digging wells in it; four square miles of the remaining area has been leased to the Burma Oil Company; and a similar area to the Lepel Griffin Syndicate. Several other capitalists have applied for other blocks.

The wells are situated in an irregular plateau, surrounded by ravines, about $3\frac{1}{2}$ miles from the village.

FOOT OF BUDDHA, MINBÚ.

(Photograph by Signor Beato, Mandalay.)

The workings of the Burma Oil Company are under the superintendence of experts from the United States, and the oil is conveyed in iron pipes to the oil flats moored to the bank, and there loaded in bulk and carried down the river to the Company's refining works at Rangoon.

A run of twenty-five miles brings us to Minbù, the headquarters of the district of the same name, and the residence of the Commissioner of the Southern Division.

The station has the usual Government offices, and is the nearest point on the Irrawaddi River to the Aing Pass, leading over the Yomas to Arakan.

A vast and fertile plain extends from the river bank to the foot of the hills, and measures are being taken by the Irrigation Department of Public Works to supply water to these lands by bunding up mountain streams and forming large irrigation tanks. Minbù has the notoriety of being one of the hottest places in the Indian Empire during the hot season of April and May, when the temperature is frequently 107° F. in the shade. Above Minbù two small rivers, the Môn and the Man, enter the Irrawaddi from the west.

SHWÈ-ZET-DAW PAGODA.—About twenty-five miles southwest from Minbù is situated the Shwè-Zet-Daw Pagoda. Shin Gaudama is stated to have left two impressions of his left foot, each three cubits in length by one and a half in breadth. For 2,000 years these impressions remained undiscovered, and it was not until the reign of Thalûn-Mintara-Gyi King of Amarapura that they were brought to light by Taung-pala Saya-dau, a celebrated priest of the neighbourhood.

One is situated on the top of Mikula Hill and the other at the foot, on the banks of the Man River. These are respectively called " Atet-setdau-ya " (upper footprint) and " Aùk-setdau-ya " (lower footprint).

A great feast is held here yearly from the first waning moon of *Tabodwé* (February) to the first waning moon of *Tabaung* (March), and is attended by vast crowds of pious worshippers from all parts of the province.   Both banks of the river for a long distance in the vicinity of the shrine, are covered with temporary booths, and a good deal of merchandise is disposed of.   The view from the upper foot-print, of the Man Chaung meandering through groves of shady trees, is very picturesque.

The shrine is surrounded by pagodas and other religious buildings, and the footprint is guarded by the sacred *naga* or immense dragon, with hood expanded, emblematic of the great *naga* which is said to have shielded Buddha from the attacks of demons, after his attainment to Buddha-hood.

The best route to take from Minbû, is to ride straight to Sagû on the Man River, a distance of twenty-five miles, and thence along the rocky banks of the river to the pagoda, a distance of nine miles, passing the following villages *en route* :— Thamadi, Pinlèthat, Milaing, Pigón, Mashet, Pyûgòn, Myaung-û, Kûtitha, Set-daw-gòn and Eng-wa.

In the neighbourhood of the town are the so-called "mud volcanoes" but which are in reality *salses*.   An explanation of these phenomena will be found in Route X (q.v.)

About a mile below Minbû, and on the left bank of the river, is Magwè, the head-quarters of the district of the same name. Owing to the silting-up of the channel, steamers are unable to moor off the station, so that goods and passengers for Magwè are landed generally at Minbû, and passengers have to make their own arrangements for reaching their destination.

From Minbû the general direction is to the south-east, past the mouth of the Yin-zùn River which enters from the east, until Minhla is reached, eighty miles below Minbû.   This town was, prior to the annexation of Upper Burma, the head-quarters of the governor of the frontier districts, and was defended by a fort of European construction, built of masonry and strengthened by earthworks of considerable thickness.

This fort—called the Kamyo Fort—is situated on the top of the cliffs immediately facing Minhla.   It was captured on the 17th November, 1885, by the Liverpool Regiment, scaling ladders

SALSES, OR MUD VOLCANOES, MINBÚ.

(Photo by Nizam Buttu Mandalay.)

being used to storm the heights. The assault was assisted by the gunboats from the river below.

Minhla was further protected by a redoubt which had been hastily constructed of green bamboos and earthwork. This was taken on the same day by assault, after a deal of hard fighting, in which the Burmese behaved very pluckily. The greater portion of the town was burnt down owing to the bursting of shells in its midst. After two days, the inhabitants returned, settled down to their daily avocations, and fraternized with the garrison left in charge. Minhla now forms part of the Thayet-myo district. The down express steamers generally " make " Minhla on the afternoon of the second day from Mandalay and anchor here for the night.

Below the town, the river takes a sharp bend to the southeast, past the large village of Ywa-thit on the left bank. Sinbaung-gwè, also on the left bank, eighteen miles below Minhla, is the next halting place.

At the time of the expedition it was defended by a stockade. This was captured by General Norman with a force landed from the steamers. The defenders fled precipitately to the jungles and the stockade was burnt down.

A few miles below this, the first encounter with the enemy took place. A king's steamer, called the " Tû-lû-yin-gyaw " with 600 soldiers on board was engaged and captured by the gunboats, " Irrawaddy " and " Kathleen." The soldiers jumped overboard and swam ashore and the steamer was run aground. She was towed off by the " Kathleen " and sent down to Thayetmyo with the " Jack " flying at the mast-head.

Allan-myo on the left bank, four miles above Thayetmyo, is situated close to the old Burmese fort and town of Myèdè.

It was named after Major Allan, the officer selected to fix the boundary marks of the province of Pegu, after the Second Anglo-Burmese war, in 1852-53. The large masonry pillars on either bank of the Irrawaddi were those originally erected. The spot chosen for the erection of these pillars was exactly six statute miles north of the fort of Myèdè, in latitude 19° 29' 3". An inscription in Burmese and English was placed on the original pillar erected. Following along this parallel of latitude, smaller pillars were erected at regular intervals, demarcating the northern boundary of the new province.

Thayetmyo on the right bank four miles below, is the head-quarters of the district of the same name, and was up to the time of the annexation of Upper Burma, a strong frontier garrison town. The name is derived from two Burmese words, *Thayet*, mango, and *Myo*, town. It has a population of 12,883.

In the Burmese times it was a place of little importance, and its rise is due entirely to the fact that it was selected as the site for a British cantonment after the Second Anglo-Burmese war in 1852-53. The town and cantonment are situated on high undulating ground in close proximity to the river. The climate is supposed to be very healthy for Europeans. Since the annexation of Upper Burma, the garrison has been much reduced. To the north of the cantonment, and on the bank of the river, is a small fort which contains the arsenal and commissariat stores.

HISTORY OF THE TOWN.—It was not till the downfall of the Pagan dynasty in the 13th century, A.D., that Thayetmyo rose to importance. It was founded in 1306, A.D., by Min-Shin-Saw, son of Kyaw Zwa, the last King of Pagan, who built a fort and a palace, and established his rule over the surrounding country, though nominally as a vassal to the three Shan brothers, who had overthrown his father, Kyaw-Zwa.

In 1333, A.D., the town was attacked and captured by the King of Arakan, who carried off Min-Shin-Saw, his Queen and his three sons and daughters, as prisoners to Arakan.

They were subsequently released and found their way to Panya the capital, where one of the Shan brothers was reigning. Sau-û-ma, one of the Princesses, ultimately became the wife of four successive Sovereigns, the last of whom was Tha-Dô-Min-Bya, the founder of Ava. On his death in 1367, A.D., her brother ascended the throne, and assumed the name of Min-gyi-swa-saû-kè. In 1373, A.D., the King of Arakan, who had conquered

Thayetmyo died, and the inhabitants of that country offered the throne to Min-gyi-swa-saṅ-kè, who appointed his uncle, Saṅ-mûn-gyi, to be tributary King.

To celebrate his connection with the city of his birth, he founded the Shwè-Thet-lôk Pagoda at Thayetmyo, which is still standing.

The only important station between Thayetmyo and Prome is Kama, situated on the right bank. The town is prettily situated on low hills, most of which are crowned by a pagoda or a monastery.

The Madè stream flows through the town dividing it into two portions.

The name *Kama* is said to be a corruption of the Pali *Maha-gama* (great village), so called from the large amount of revenue it paid in ancient times. Alaung-pya, finding it inferior to either Rangoon or Prome, suggested with prurient pleasantry, that in future it should be called *Kama* (sensual desire or lust).

A run of 14 miles from Kama brings us to Prome, where the steamer halts for a time to land passangers, who may desire to proceed thence by rail to Rangoon.

A full description of Prome is given in Route V.

ROUTE XII.

———

MANDALAY CITY OR FORT DUFFERIN.

The city of Mandalay was founded by Mindòn Min in 1857. It took three years to build, and the King moved to his new capital from Amarapoora in 1857, occupying a temporary palace, from which to direct the building operations.

The city is built in the form of a square, each side of which measures one-and-a-quarter miles in length. A brick wall twenty-six feet in height, and three-and-a-half feet thick, and crenellated at the top, encloses the whole. The wall is backed by an earthen rampart twenty-five feet wide, which reaches within four feet of the top of the wall, to allow of rifle fire from the apertures. At distances of 178 yards apart, buttresses are provided, which project a few feet beyond the wall alignment. At the four corners two of these meet together and form one large bastion.

The city is provided with twelve gates, three on each side, each of which on the outside is protected by a strong masonry traverse. Over each gateway rises a graceful *pyathat*, or spire of seven roofs, and smaller ones also crown the buttresses. Sixty feet from the wall, and running parallel to it right round the city is a moat, 100 feet in width, with an average depth of fourteen feet, which is kept supplied with water from the Nanda Lake behind Mandalay hill. Five bridges cross the moat, two on the west side, and one on each of the other three sides.

In the King's time the gates of the city were closed every evening, and special officers were deputed to guard them.

PLAN OF
FORT DUFFERIN

Close to the masonry traverse of each gate is a massive teak post, with an inscription in gilt, recording the name of the gate and the date of its erection. By the King's officers the gates were known by the following names :—

North Gate	*Lè-thein-taga.*
South Gate	*Kyaw-Mo-taga.*
East Gate	*Ů-Daik-taga.*
West Gate	*Sin-Shè-taga.*
South-west Gate	*Kyè-lunôn-taga.*

The small masonry house outside each gate and at the four corners are called *nat-sin*, and contain figures of *belûs*, or ogres, whose duty it is to guard the city from evil of all kinds.

The common report that human victims were interred alive at the gates and corners of the city wall is untrue. The custom is allowed, but in the case of Mandalay was not carried out. Jars containing oil were buried at each of the four corners according to custom.

The roads inside Fort Dufferin run parallel to the city walls, so that, standing at one gate the other can be seen at a distance of a mile and a quarter away. The palace of course intercepts the view from each of the four gates which are now in use. In the king's time the royal city presented a very different appearance from what it does at the present time. Then, the whole of what is now the cantonments and the civil lines was covered with the houses of ministers and their attendant followers. One of the first things done after the occupation by the British in 1885 was to remove all these to sites on the south side, beyond the city wall. Special officers were appointed to carry out these arrangements ; land was granted in lieu of that vacated, and compensation paid for loss and damage to property on removal.

At the present time the only Burmese houses inside the fort are those of Ů-Gaung, the Kin Wûn Mingyi, or Chief Minister to the late king, and the Taung-kwin Mingyi. The latter died about two years ago, but his family still occupy the house.

These houses are situated to the east of the palace, the Taung-kwin Mingyi's being to the north-east, and the Kin Wûn Mingyi's to the south-east. Both residences consist of a number of detached houses with the usual *pyathat* roof, and each is surrounded by a mat fence about 10 feet in height.

As at present arranged, to the west of the palace are the Native Infantry lines. To the east the British Infantry lines; to the north the Central Jail, the Civil lines, Officers' Quarters, and Military Hospital; and to the south, quarters for the Officers of the Native Infantry, the General's Quarters, and the Queen's parade ground.

The roads, which have been metalled and drained, have been named either after celebrated generals of the British Army, or after Chief Commissioners of the province. In the British Infantry lines they are named after the regiments that either took part in the expedition in 1885, or formed the garrison in later times. At the east gate a British Infantry guard is stationed, and at each of the others a Native Infantry or Military Police guard.

The garrison maintained at Mandalay at the present time (1895) is :—

> One Regiment British Infantry.
> Two Regiments Native Infantry.
> One Mule Battery.
> One Battery Royal Artillery.
> Two Companies Sappers and Miners.

The total population in the cantonments in 1893 was 18,744.

The cantonments extend for some distance beyond the limits of the fort, the Royal Artillery lines being to the east of Mandalay Hill, and the Transport and Commissariat lines to the east of the fort. The Sappers and Miners lines are situated to the north of the fort.

The Central Jail, situated in the extreme north-west corner, is capable of accommodating 1,112 prisoners of all classes, and the Civil Surgeon of Mandalay is the Superintendent.

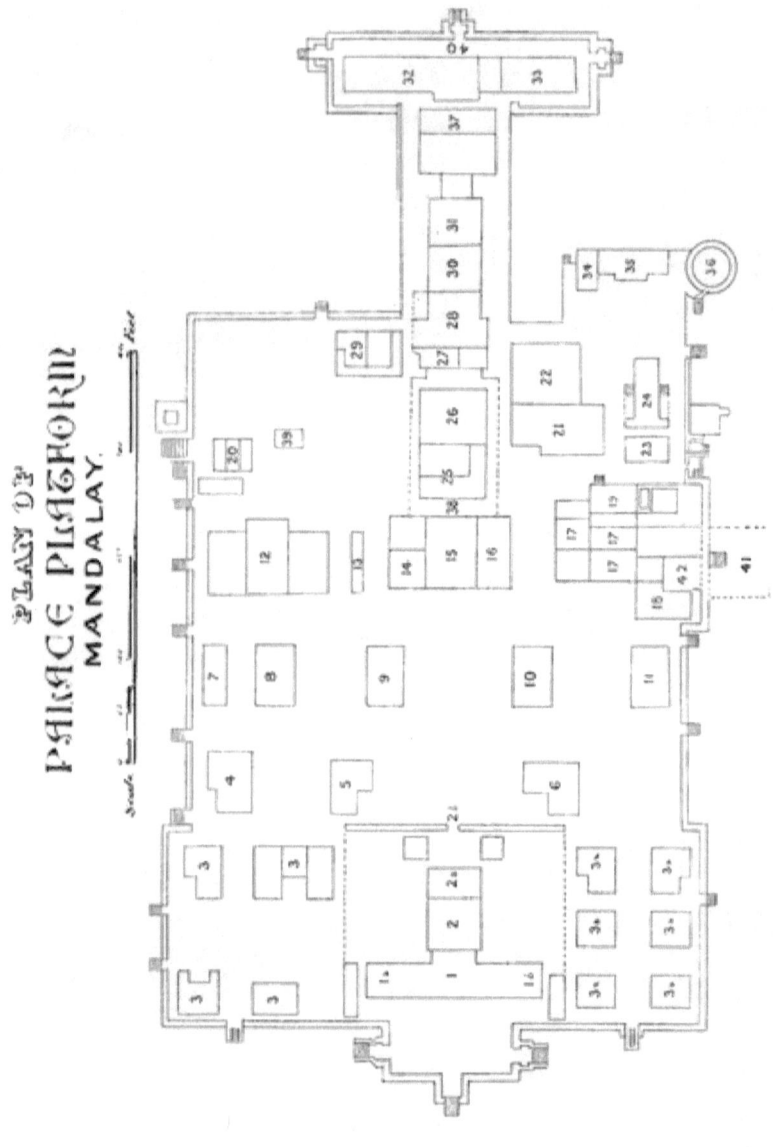

PLAN OF
PALACE PLATFORM.
MANDALAY.

Scale   Feet

Some very excellent carved work is done in the jail by the long term prisoners, and may be inspected by visitors in the jail sale room, which is situated immediately in front of the main gate. Visitors are admitted to view the jail through the courtesy of the Superintendent, to whom personal application should be made.

THE PALACE (Burmese *Nandau*).—The Palace and its environs occupy the centre of the city. In the King's time they were enclosed by a stockade of teak posts twenty feet high, in the form of a parallelogram, the north and south sides measuring 2,225 feet, and the east and west 2,125 feet. Within this stockade, and distant from it 100 feet, a brick wall fourteen feet high extended right round, parallel to the teak stockade. A second brick wall 400 feet from the outer one extended right across the eastern front of the Palace from north to south.

Skirting the ornamental water on the west side, and what are now the roads leading round the Palace north and south, another wall was placed. The space between this wall and the Palace platform, which now forms the drive round the Palace, was called the inner Palace enclosure, and the large open spaces to the east and west were used by the king for *pwès* or theatrical entertainments.

The stockade had four gates. The Northern, the Southern, the Western, and the Eastern,—the latter being the public entrance. The West gate was reserved for females, the East gate for the Crown Prince, etc. These gates, with part of the teakwood stockade, are all that remain of the outer fence. The brick walls have been cleared, but their alignment can still be distinctly traced from the brick rubble still remaining.

The Central Eastern gate in the inner defences was only opened for the King, all visitors having to enter through a smaller one called the *Tiga-ni* (or red postern) which was so low that those entering had to stoop, thereby compelling all, *nolens volens*, to render obeisance to the golden *pyathat* and the throne beneath it.

K

The eastern enclosure was the space between the outer and inner brick walls, and occupied the entire distance from the north to the south walls, with a breadth of 425 feet.

This enclosure contained to the south, the Hlûtdau or Hall of the Supreme Council, the Arsenal, the Royal Monastery and the Relic Tower, while north of the gate were the Mint, the Post Office, the Printing Press, the Campanile, King Mindôn's tomb, and two other tombs surrounded by *pyathats*.

What was called the Outer Palace enclosure was a court in front of the palace, 1,100 feet long and 330 feet wide.

This was used for the reviewing of troops, exercising the royal horses, and even for races and other sports on horse-back. Under the walls of this enclosure were the barracks for the guards and the houses of petty ministers, and Palace officials.

To the north and south of the Palace platform are the royal gardens, containing ornamental tanks and streams of water, and laid out with grottos, rockeries, winding paths, rustic bridges and arbours, sheltered by groves of tamarind, cocoa-nut, bamboo, and other flowering or fruit bearing trees. These grounds were laid out by one of the many foreigners in the King's service, and here the Court spent a good deal of its time. It was in the summer house of the Southern Garden, that the King and his Queens had taken refuge on the arrival of the British troops in 1885, and on the verandah of this house he surrendered his crown and country to General Prendergast and Colonel Sladen, the Political Officer. A brass tablet beneath the window records these facts, which took place on the 29th November, 1885.

The Palace, properly so called, was built on an oblong terrace 1,000 feet long with an average breadth of 550 feet. The terrace was supported by a brick retaining wall about ten feet high, access to the platform being gained by a number of masonry flights of steps.

We will now proceed to describe in detail the various buildings on the platform which still stand, giving the present uses of each, its Burmese name, and its history, as far as can be ascertained from reliable sources.

Mounting the steps at the western end, we enter what are now the premises of the Upper Burma Club. This 1 on Plan was called the *Anauk Samôk* and was the Palace of the chief Queen. At the end of the central hall, in what is now the Ladies' Reading room, stands the *Pa-da-ma-da-na* or Lily throne. The 1 present Dining and Reading rooms to the north, and the Bar 1a and Billiard room to the south of the entrance hall, were in 1b the King's time open on all sides as ordinary zayats or rest houses are at the present day. The unique and highly interesting Dining-room was formed from Mosaic glass panels and 1a mirrors collected from different parts of the Palace, and arranged as screens round the walls.

This Palace was used three times a year by the Chief Queen for the reception of ladies, or wives of the ministers, in their respective court dresses and ornaments, who awaited Her Majesty's arrival in the open pavilions already described, to the north and south of the Throne room.

The roof and ceiling are supported by magnificent posts of teak, the whole interior being covered with gold-leaf.

The Throne itself (called the *Raza-Palin*) is a pedestal of wood of construction similar to those seen in temples and monasteries, on which images of Buddha are displayed.

It is about eight feet high, and in shape resembles two triangles joined together at their apices. These typify fire and water, the elements mainly instrumental, according to Buddhist cosmogony, in the destruction and reproduction of a world. Hence one seated thereon represents the Lord of the Universe. This title the King of Burma arrogates to himself as the representative of the ancient Buddhist Kings of India.

(Sir A. Phayre.)

Small semi-circular pieces of mirror were let into the wood at intervals, and a number of small niches were provided, in

K 2

which were placed figures of men and animals. These of course have all long since disappeared.

The doorway behind the Throne is adorned with peculiar horn-like ornaments, similar to those seen in the earlier Pagan temples around image niches, and the sides are handsomely carved with rosettes, foliage, and figures of animals. The doors are of iron screen-work, richly gilded, and the throne is reached by a staircase from behind, in what is now the Whist Room of the Upper Burma Club.

2a on Plan

The iron rings on either side of the throne were for the reception of the white umbrellas, which were used as emblems of Royalty, and considerable numbers of which surrounded each of the thrones. The apartment to the rear of the throne was used as a guard-room, and had several gun-racks arranged on either side. Here the maids-of-honour and the personal attendants of the Queen rested, while Her Majesty gave audience to those awaiting her in the pavilions below.

2a

The block of buildings immediately to the south of the *A-naûk Samôk*, and now forming chambers of the Upper Burma Club, were in Mindôn Min's time the residences of minor Queens, and in Thibaw's time of maids-of-honour.

3a

Those to the north now occupied by regimental staff officers, were similarly occupied.

3

Having now finished the Samôk, we will proceed by the small door through the wall behind the throne-room, which leads into the next enclosure. In the King's time a broad road, called the Samôk road, ran east and west down this quadrangle.

2b

At the New Year's festivities a *Wingaba*, or maze, was constructed along this road, through which the King and his Court passed in procession. The houses north and south of this road were inhabited by minor queens in Mindôn Min's time, and in Thibaw's by princesses, sisters, or half-sisters of the King.

4, 5 and 6

That numbered 4 on the plan is now the Fort Post Office, and the next to it to the south is the Telegraph Office. No. 6 is at present unoccupied.

The next block of buildings were known as the Northern, 7 on Plan.
Western, and Southern Palaces, and were occupied in 9   10 & 11
Mindòn Min's time by inferior queens, and in Thibaw's
by maids of honour. The Northern Palace is now used as the 7
Departmental Mess.

The Western as the office of the Superintending 9
Engineer, Irrigation Circle. Next to it the office of the 10
Conservator of Forests Western Circle and the Southern
Palace, the quarters of the A.D.C. to the General Officer 11
Commanding.

The next block of buildings commences from the north with
the Sein-dòn Palace, where Sin-Byû-Ma-Sein, the mother of 12
Sûpya-lat, the chief queen of King Thibaw, lived. She was one of
Mindòn Min's queens, and it was through her machinations that
the massacres of 1878 took place, and that Thibaw came to the
throne. This building is now used as the office of the Chief
Commissary.

The open gilt-posted, triple-roofed building immediately to
the south was the residence of the *Tabindaing*. This was 13
the title given to the daughter—generally the eldest—of the King,
who was forbidden to marry till his death, being reserved as the
wife of his successor. In Mindòn Min's time the *Tabindaing*
was the Salin princess, daughter of the Limban queen, and these
quarters were occupied by her. When Thibaw ascended the
throne the *Tabindaing* refused to marry him, and, becoming a
nun, remained for about a year in the Royal garden and died.
Thibaw afterwards married her half-sister, the Sûpya-lat.

The next blocks of buildings were known as the *Hman* 14, 15 & 16
Nan, or Glass Palace, and formed the usual dwelling-
place of Thibaw and his Queen.

In the outer room, the interior of which is now covered 15
with whitewash, Sûpya-lat gave birth to her first child.

The next, or adjoining room, was used as a reception 16
chamber, and the side room for members of the Queen's 14
household.

These rooms are now used as the Court-martial Room, the Office of the Assistant-Adjutant-General, and that of the Principal Medical Officer.

38 on Plan.

The covered passage between these rooms, and those to the east was called the Sanú, and was used as a sort of private or unofficial place of reception.

25

To the east of the Sanú, are the favourite rooms of Mindòn Min, those to the south being occupied by his chief Queen. These quarters are now the offices of the Assistant Adjutant-General. The rooms are exceedingly lofty, and formed the ante room to the throne room, which comes next.

26

This is known as the "Water Feast" throne, and on it the body of Mindòn Min lay, prior to interment. It has been partly dismantled, and the room is now the office of the Superintending Engineer, Third Circle.

The Glass Palace is succeeded by a covered passage or Sanú, to the west of which is a small room used by the King for his morning levee. The large room on the east side of the passage was called the Zeta-wûn-saung, and contained figures representing the royal ancestors, and palm-leaf records, concerning the Royal Family and the Palace.

27

These rooms are now used as the office and quarters of the Executive Engineer of the Mandalay Civil Division.

28
30

The Duck Throne which is in the private quarters of the Executive Engineer, was used for the reception of foreigners, and here Mindòn Min interviewed from time to time the British resident and ambassadors from foreign countries.

31

We now come to the Lion Throne, which was the chief of all, and was used three times a year for the reception of Sawbwas (Shan Chiefs), ministers, and members of the Royal Family.

37

Over this rises the Shwè Pyathat or golden seven-roofed spire, surmounted by a massive hti or umbrella, similar to those seen on pagodas. This spire is said by Burmans to be "the centre of the universe," and can be seen from all parts of the city and extra-mural town.

CENTRE OF THE UNIVERSE, MANDALAY.

(Photo by Signor Beato, Mandalay.)

The Lion Throne is similar in shape and appearance to the Lily Throne in the *A-náuk Samók*, but the throne-room is loftier and more imposing.   2

In front of the Lion Throne a central eastern transept opens to the Great Audience Hall, which extends on either side   32 and 33 of the throne for a distance each way of 125 feet, making a total length of 250 feet, with a breadth of about forty feet. The posts are of teak, originally covered with gold leaf, which has now alas! been partly stripped off, and what is left is tarnished and weather-worn.

This "Hall of Audience" is now used as the Garrison Chapel, till such time as the Government of India sees fit to   32 sanction funds for the erection of a decent garrison Church.

It is ten years since the British occupation of Mandalay, and yet the Church of England has no representative building, other than the Church of the Society for the Propagation of the Gospel Mission, erected by Mindôn Min nearly thirty years ago.

The Roman Catholics have an imposing cathedral, built at a cost of nearly a lakh of rupees by a wealthy native convert; the Baptists, a handsome memorial Church to Dr. Judson's memory; the Wesleyans, a masonry Chapel; the Church of England, a consecrated *Hpôngyi Kyaung*, or monastery; from which the priests were evicted by the moral persuasion of British bayonets!

In front of the Hall of Audience is a promenade about twelve feet wide, at the northern end of which there formerly stood   40 a theatre, which was used for performances, and from which the King witnessed the sports held in the adjacent court-yard.

This building has long since been dismantled, as well as the *Byèdaik* or Treasury Office, immediately to the north of the Duck Throne, where the *Thein-wûns* or Privy Councillors sat for the conduct of business submitted to them by the King.

The *Myauk Samók* was used as the place for the   20 reception of offerings, and here the King went to inspect the White Elephant. This building is now used as the office of the Deputy Conservator of Forests, Mandalay Division.

The elephant shed, or palace of the Lord White Elephant, the *Sin-pyû-dau*, was situated to the north of the Duck Throne, in the quadrangle bounded on the west, south and east by the retaining wall of the palace platform. The possession of a white elephant was the symbol of universal sovereignty, and many wars were undertaken against Siam for the purpose of acquiring this sacred animal. For this purpose Bûyin-Naung invaded Siam in 1584, and captured the capital Yuthia, carrying away into captivity the King, his Queens and his younger son, and possessing himself of the three white elephants.

Sangermano, a Catholic Priest, who lived in Burma for some years during the reign of Bodau-pya, in the latter part of last century, gives a most exhaustive account of the capture of a so-called white elephant in the forests of Pegu in the year 1805, A.D.

In a foot-note to the new edition of Sangermano's work, edited by Mr. John Jardine, formerly Judicial Commissioner of British Burma, the editor states that the special reverence shewn to the white elephant was derived from Hindu mythology, which treats the elephant as one of the " signs of the Chakravarti—the great wheel-turning king or universal monarch. The dream of Queen Maya, the mother of Gaudama Buddha, about his entering her womb as a white elephant thus invests with supreme sovereignty the supreme intelligence."

" Senart and Kern trace these legends to the worship of the Sun, Vishnu, and Mahadev. The Sun, representing regularity, next becomes the Dhamaraja, who utters religious law. Yule, with his usual learning, quotes Aelian and Ibu Batuta about white elephants. Their stately caparisons are described by all the old travellers, and by our envoys. Cæsar Fredericke, as well as the native traders, had to pay a tax for the privilege of seeing them."—(*Sangermano's Burmese Empire*, page 76.)

It must not be imagined that the so-called *Sin-pyû-dau* are albinos. Far from it, they are of a mouse colour, similar in tint to the mottled spots found on the trunk and ears of an ordinary

elephant.   This mouse colour in a perfect specimen extends all
over the body, the spots on the trunk being perfectly white.

King Thibaw's elephant was a very poor specimen of a dirty
brown colour.   Strange to say it died a few days after the
occupation of the palace by British troops, pious Burmans say of
grief, but common report at the time said for want of food, its
existence having entirely escaped the notice of the authorities,
during the busy days succeeding the occupation.

Instead of a funeral befitting a king, its carcase was dragged
outside the city walls by a couple of his Commissariat brothers,
and ignominiously buried in the nearest piece of waste ground.

On the vacant piece of ground to the north of the Glass
Palace formerly stood the Golden Palace, the favourite residence
of Mindòn Min and his chief queens.

After his death—which took place on the 1st October, 1878
—and in compliance with his previously expressed wishes, the
building was pulled down and re-erected as a monastery,
immediately to the east of the A-tù-ma-shi monastery, to the east
of the city walls.   This building was destroyed by fire, together
with the A-tù-ma-shi in 1892.

We will now proceed to the south side of the platform,
where a few buildings still remain to be described.

The white portico over the carriage road on the south side
was formerly the theatre built by King Thibaw for the   41
" Parsi Victoria Theatrical Company," who, by the king's
command, proceeded to the capital in 1881 or 1882, and
were so well received and treated, that their stay extended over
several months.

The stage has been removed, and the building is now utilized
as a cab shelter during the heat of the day or in the rainy season.

The building adjacent to it was a sort of drawing room   42
where the court assembled to witness the dramatic performances
in the theatre close by.   The glass trellis work of the verandah of
this room is very unique, and the mural decorations of looking
glass mosaic work are well preserved, and give one a good idea

of Burmese ornamentation. This room is now used as the Officers' Mess of the European regiment forming part of the garrison.

17 and 18   Behind this room, the two empty rooms were formerly the Royal Nursery and the Daily Attendance Room for Queens. The brick building to the east was the special residence of King Thibaw and his queen Sûpya-lat, and its interior decoration and arrangements remain much as they originally were. It is now the office of the General Officer Commanding, but is seldom used, and is generally kept locked. The building
23   to the east of the General's office corresponding to the North Samôk, was called the South Samôk, and formerly contained the Peacock Throne, from which the king inspected the royal horses.

A strong guard was stationed here to keep watch over the steps leading up to the platform.

24   The small brick building in front of which are a number of white washed masonry pillars with a cornice running round the four sides, was built by King Thibaw as a sort of lounge or rustic retreat. The square in front was formerly a tank, with sloping brick sides, and was adorned with foliage plants and sweet smelling flowers, and here the king would take tea and listen to musicians, soothsayers, or singers. This is now set apart as quarters for the Engineer-in-Chief, P.W.D., when on circuit.

36   The *Nanmyin* is the circular tower on the south side, which was built by King Thibaw, and rises to a height of seventy-eight feet from the road, exclusive of the decorated *pyathat* with which it is crowned.

It is said to have been erected by royal command in the incredibly short space of time of twenty-three days, in order that the King might witness from the summit, the annual illuminations of the town at the Thadingyût Festival, which takes place at the conclusion of the Buddhist lent, generally occurring early in October. Fearing assassination, the king dared not, according to custom, make a royal progress through the city, so his inventive

NAN-MYIN, MANDALAY PALACE.

(Photo by Signor Beato, Mandalay.)

genius designed this eye-sore. The ascent is made by a spiral staircase which runs round the outside of the tower and was so constructed that anyone ascending or descending is not visible for more than a second or two to anyone stationed below at any particular spot, thus obviating the risks of assassination from the rifle of an unseen enemy.

King Thibaw's geography of his country was studied from this eyrie, so it is no wonder that his rule was overthrown. His exit from the palace would have been the signal for a revolt, and he knew better than to leave his nest.

From the summit Queen Sûpya-lat watched the advent of the British troops approaching from the shore, the route taken being clearly defined by the clouds of dust raised, and the martial music of the hateful "Kâlas."

A good view of the fort, the palace buildings, and the surrounding country, is to be obtained from the summit. A military guard is kept here for the purpose of watching for the out-break of fires, which are of frequent occurrence in the hot weather.

The small houses or shelters, on the ridge of the roofs of the palace buildings were for the *a-saung-tha-ma* or watchman, each " pigeon-house " being occupied day and night by a man armed with a two-stringed bow and a number of baked mud pellets. These were used to intercept the flight of vultures and birds of prey, and to prevent them from alighting on any of the Palace buildings.

The long suite of rooms north of the watch tower were used as store chambers for clothes, receptacles for offerings, etc., and in one room the Privy Council held its sittings.　34 and 35

They are now used as quarters for the Inspector General of Police and other heads of Departments when on circuit. The white-washed building to the south of, and in a line with, the levée chamber of the king, was the *Shwè-daik*, and here the　21 royal jewels and regalia were kept. The building numbered 22 was used for the Palace guard.

We have now finished the buildings on the platform, but a few still remain to be described, situated to the east of the palace.

The large building to the south of the avenue leading up to the steps on the eastern terrace, was formerly the Hlût-daw, or Supreme Court, presided over by four *Wûngyis* or Chief Ministers of State. An assistant to a wûngyi was called a *Wûndauk*. All appeals from district courts were adjudicated by this Court and leases and contracts entered into by the King with European merchants and others were here registered.

The building is now used as the office of the Executive Engineer, Garrison Division, and of the Conservator of Forests, Eastern Circle.

The high tower close to the old east gate of the palace, and on the south side of the avenue, is called the *Swè-dau-zin*, and is said to contain a tooth of Buddha. Opposite to this, on the northern side of the road is the *Ba-hó-zin* or Bell Tower, a building with a brick basement and four pillars supporting the roof. On the upper platform the clepsydra, or water clock was placed, which gave the time to the palace and city. At the end of each quarter a large gong was struck, the hour being struck on an enormous drum, the head of which was of thick buffalo hide. At the annexation this drum was removed to the Phayre Museum where it now is.

We now come to the tomb of King Mindòn Min. This is built of brick, in the form of a pagoda, with a rectangular base, surmounted by a receding roof of seven successive tiers; the summit is crowned by a *htí*, and is decorated with small pieces of glass. A neat iron railing surrounds the whole.

The wooden *pyathat* to the south of this tomb was erected over the grave of the widow of the Shwèbo Min, or Tharrawaddi, as he was more commonly called. She was the mother of Namadau-Paya-Gyi, the chief queen of Mindòn Min, and whose tomb is a little to the north-west on the opposite side of the road.

In close proximity to the last tomb is a white building on arches, covered with a *pyathat* roof. This was a favourite place of retirement of Mindôn Min's, and contained images of Guadama carved of wood from the sacred Maha-Baudi Tree of Buddha Gya. It is now used as a dwelling house.

The building with the tall chimney beyond the tombs, which is now the Government Bakery, was formerly the Royal Mint, and here the *daung dinga* or peacock rupees were manufactured. Coins of bronze, silver, and gold were issued of the following values.

Bronze :—Pice pieces.

Silver :—Pè-si, mù-si, mat-si, nga-mù-si, and kyat, their equivalents being one, two, four, eight annas and one rupee respectively.

Gold :—Shwè-pè-si, shwè-mù-si, shwè-mat-si, shwè-nga-mù-si, and shwè-dinga-gyi, equivalent to one, two, four, sixteen and thirty-two rupees.

These coins were declared legal tender for some years after the annexation, but have now been entirely withdrawn from circulation, and are yearly becoming more and more scarce. Specimens can however be procured at Signor Beato's studio and emporium for curiosities, or from the money changers in the big bazaar.

MANDALAY HILL.—This hill, situated to the north-east of the walled city, is conspicuous from a long distance both north and south of the city. Its real name is Mandayè Hill, the word meaning, " to bear a good reputation or character."

The original Mandalay hill is situated in the valley of the Mù river, and an old tradition stated that a large and flourishing city would be established near it. Mindôn Min however preferred the site near Mandayè Hill, so he caused large quantities of soil to be brought from the hill in the Mù Valley, which was deposited on the Mandayè hill and near it the capital Mandalay was built, the name of the hill being also changed. Mandalay is said to mean " bearing reputation or character."

The ascent of the hill can be made both from the south and east.

The best way will be to ascend by the bridle-path on the east side, and descend by the stone steps on the south. The bridle-path leads off from the high road which runs past the Artillery lines, about 200 yards beyond the north-east corner of the moat roads. The path is fairly good, and the ascent to the summit can be made by ponies.

On the top are two white pagodas, one on the northern spur, and the other on the southern. The northern is surrounded on three sides by a buttressed wall, which forms a temporary fort.

Starting from this pagoda, and looking to the north-east, the Nanda Lake will be seen which supplies the moat with water. The barracks on the eastern side of the hill are those of the Royal Artillery. To the south of these are the Veterinary Lines.

West of the Nanda Lake, the Madaya Canal or Shwè-Da-Chaung is seen, which was constructed by Ba-Gyi-dau, king of Burma in the early part of the present century.

The canal was dug from Madaya, sixteen miles north of Mandalay, to the Irrawaddi below Amarapura, the water being supplied by the diversion of a mountain stream called the Chaung-ma-gyi, issuing from the Shan Hills.

When, however, several years ago, Mindôn Min caused bunds to be placed to the north and west of the city, to preserve it from the inundation of the Irrawaddi during flood time, it was found necessary to block the canal at a village called Obo. Since this time the canal channel through the city of Mandalay has been more or less empty, except during heavy rain when the surface drainage finds its way into it.

The country irrigated by this canal extends on both sides of it, and is of great area. The course can be traced by the verdant banks and profuse vegetation which is seen on either side.

The hills on the opposite side of the river are the Sagaing hills, which, starting from just above the town of Sagaing, gain their greatest altitude immediately to the rear of the Mingûn pagoda which is seen to the north-west, and is recognized by its huge size and shape. (*The description of this pagoda is given in Route XV.*)

The tall chimney seen to the right of the north-west corner of the city wall is Dyer's Brewery (formerly the Royal Gun Factory) where excellent beer and stout are manufactured. Close to it are the ruins of the King's saw-mill, long since abandoned and deserted. Looking towards the extra-mural city, the principal objects seen will be the spire of the Roman Catholic Cathedral, the smaller spire beyond being that of the Judson Memorial Chapel of the American Baptist Mission.

Of pagodas, the Ein-dawya is seen beyond the bridge crossing the Shwè-da-Chaung in C. Road, while the golden pagoda near the Convent is the Shwè-Kyi-myin Pagoda.

Descending now by the flight of steps on the southern face of the hill, the Cantonment Cemetery, the Rifle Range, the Race Course, and the lines of the Queen's Own Sappers and Miners are seen to the west of the hill, and interspersed among these are numerous monasteries and other religious buildings, erected either by the King himself or some of his ministers.

Half way down you come to the platform, with the charred stumps of posts still protruding through the cement floor, on which stood the celebrated *Shwè-Yat-dau*, an immense standing wooden figure of Gaudama, thirty-five feet high, with the right hand extended, and the finger pointing to the *Shwè-pyathat* of the palace, while at the feet knelt a figure of Ananda, the beloved disciple and cousin of the Buddha. This figure was unfortunately burned down two or three years ago.

Close to the foot of the steps is the immense stone image called the Kyauk-daû-gyi Paya.

The total height of the hill is 954 feet, while that on which the Shwè-Yat-dau stood was 814 feet.

YAN-KIN-TAUNG.—This is the name given to the low hill to the east of the city, and is reached by driving straight out from the East Gate.

On one side of the hill is a cave temple in which is enshrined the *Nga-yan* or stone image of a fish.

Shin Gaudama, in one of his previous existences, appeared as a *Nga-yan* or Murrell (*Ophiocephalus Marulius*). During this time there was a drought, and the embryo Buddha recited some stanzas which caused the rain to fall.

The history of the image is as follows :—

When Alaung-Sithû reigned at Pagan, from 1085 to 1160, A.D., he was much troubled by the disobedience of his sons, his eldest, Min-Shin-Zau, was expelled the capital, and became governor of the northern part of his father's kingdom, making his capital at Tan-dôn-pû-det in the neighbourhood of Amarapura. When ruling here he commenced the excavation and embankment of the great lake Aung-pin-lè. By these means over 31,000 fields were supplied with the means of irrigation.

In consequence of the increased fertility of the soil and the extension of cultivation, the people soon became prosperous and wealthy. Owing, however, to a serious drought, which caused the waters of the lake to dry up, and brought distress on the cultivators, the Prince Min-Shin-Zau consulted his *Pôn-nas* or Brahmins, who advised him to carve the figure of the *Nga-yan* of stone, and to command the priesthood to recite the stanzas used by Gaudama in its honour. The fish image was accordingly made and set up in the palace, and the stanzas were daily recited by the priests. Very soon the rain descended in unheard of quantities, the lake overflowing its banks, flooding the surrounding country, destroying the crops and property of the inhabitants and causing the outbreak of various diseases and epidemics.

In great anxiety, Min-Shin-Zau again consulted the *Pôn-nas*, who stated that the calamities were brought on because the image had been enshrined in the palace instead of the cave in the hill pointed out by them. On its removal there, the calamities ceased, and the hill received the name *Yan-kin-taung*

KU’THODAW, MANDALAY.

(*Photo by Negeat Bards, Mandalay.*)

the derivation being *Yan*—enemy or danger; *Kin*—to be freed from; *Taung*—a hill or mountain.

The stone image of the fish at present enshrined, is several feet long, and is not the original which was about a cubit in length.

The hill is also frequently called *Nga-Yan Taung*, from the *Nga-Yan* fish image enshrined in a cave on one side of it. An annual festival is held in the month of June, when offerings are made in order to ensure a good rainy season. The festival is attended by thousands of people, the majority of whom are cultivators from the surrounding country, to whom a propitious season of rain is a necessity.

Pious old Mindòn Min, in emulation of his ancestor, Bodau-pya, at one time commenced the construction of a stone pagoda on the summit of the Yankintaung, and employed many labourers and slaves in quarrying and preparing stone for its erection. The work, however, progressed so slowly, that the King called upon one of his European Engineers to inspect the design approved by him. The Engineer estimated that at the then rate of progress, and with the same number of labourers as were then at work being maintained, the pagoda would be finished in about eighty years!

Needless to say, the project was abandoned, and the stone, instead of forming a stately shrine at Yankintaung, is now used by the Mandalay Municipality for metalling the roads.

AUNG-PIN-LÈ.—This immense sheet of water, which covers an area of nearly twenty square miles, is situated to the south-east of the city walls, from which its nearest point is about three miles distant.

As already stated in the account given of Yan-kin-taung (q.v.), the tank was commenced by Min-Shin-Zau, the eldest son of Alaungsithù, King of Pagan, in the twelfth century A.D.

It was enlarged and rebunded, and new sluices and canals were cut by Bodaupya at the beginning of the present century, as is recorded on a stone slab erected by that King on the south bund of the lake. The surface is entirely covered with lilies, so that in the rains it is perfectly green, and in the fine weather brown, owing to the dried stalks and leaves which protrude from its surface as the waters subside.

Under British rule the bunds and distributing channels have been much improved, and a vast area of land, stretching from its banks to the outskirts of Amarapura, is now irrigated by its waters. The name Aungpinlè, which was given to this tank, means the "pent-up sea "—a rather pretentious name, considering its size.

About a hundred yards to the west of the lake is the village of Aungpinlè, where during the continuance of the First Anglo-Burmese War the Christian captives were kept. The King, being unable to distinguish between Englishmen and Americans, seized the missionaries of the American Baptist Mission, together with any other Christians who, on the outbreak of the war, happened to be in the country. Among the former were Dr. and Mrs. Judson and Dr. Price.

The indignities and cruelties suffered by these saintly people are melancholy chapters in the history of the Mission.

After six months' incarceration they were released on the cessation of hostilities, and Bagyidau employed Drs. Price and Judson as his mediums in the conclusion of peace at Yandabo.

The cruel and inhuman treatment shown to Ann, the beloved wife of Dr. Judson, who had but lately become a mother, so undermined her health that she died shortly afterwards, just after leaving Moulmein on her voyage home. Her grave, marked by a humble tombstone, is on Amherst Point, at the entrance to the Salween River, thirty miles from Moulmein.

LAĆKA-MARA-ZEIN, OR KŰTHŌDAU *(Royal Work of Merit).*—This remarkable shrine is situated to the north-east of Fort Dufferin, to the south-east of the foot of Mandalay Hill, and is reached from town by driving right through the East Gate and along the East Moat Road to the foot of the hill. It was erected in 1859 by Mindòn Min, father of Thibaw, the last King of Burma, and consists of a central gilded pagoda,

KU'THO-DAU, OR 729 TABLETS, MANDALAY.

(Photo by Signor Beato, Mandalay.)

surrounded by three quadrangular brick walls, about sixty yards apart. Between these parallel walls were built masonry pedestals, which support the slabs of Sagyin marble, on both sides of which are engraved in the round Pali character, with commentaries in Burmese, the whole of the Buddhist Law. There are in all 729 slabs, each from five to six and a half feet in height, with a breadth across the widest part of three feet, and a thickness of four inches.

The inscriptions are as follow :—

> 111 Stones contain five Vini or Canon Law.
> 208 Stones contain Ab-bhi-Dhamma-pitaka.
> 410 Stones contain Sûtta-law or Nikè.

Over each slab a small pagoda has been built with arched entrances opposite the two faces of the slab, by which means the light is cast on the surfaces, and facility is given for the study of the text.

These small pagodas are each about twenty feet in height, and run in parallel lines round the central larger pagoda. This is of the usual shape, and has a flight of steps extending half way to the summit, on each of the four sides, similar to those of the Shwè-zi-gòn pagoda at Pagan.

On the western side of the large pagoda is a small structure of masonry, which contains the dedication stone, erected by Mindòn Min on the completion of the work.

The outer wall is flanked by a number of rest houses of masonry, all of which are now more or less in a ruinous condition.

The entrance is from the south side, the huge gates on the other side being usually kept closed.

From the top of Mandalay Hill the appearance of these lines of white pagodas reminds one most forcibly of a camp of bell-shaped tents.

MAHA MYAT MÙNI : OR, ARAKAN TEMPLE.—This famous shrine is situated at the extreme end of eighty-fourth street, which crosses a road about 100 yards north of the Queen's kyaung.

It is distant about two-and-a-quarter miles from the west gate of Fort Dufferin. A metalled road leads right up to the western entrance, and a gharry will take you there in about a quarter of an hour from the West Gate.

The shrine has four entrances, one facing each of the cardinal points, consisting of covered ways of corrugated iron, guarded at the extreme ends by two colossal leogryphs, one on either hand. At intervals, huge porches with massive gates are placed, the interiors being adorned with mural frescos, by modern artists, depicting the imaginary horrors of the seven Buddhist hells, exceeding in fearful intensity the scenes described in Dante's "Inferno."

Others, on the other hand, depict scenes from the popular *Nami-zat*, in which an account is given of Buddha's visit not only to the different hells, but to the bright and pleasant country of the *Nats*. Squatting about, in various nooks and corners, are the *Bè-din-Sayas*, or fortune tellers, who, for a few annas, gull the credulous pilgrim, with peeps into futurity. The standard work on astrology is the *Dhet-tûn*, a copy of which is found in front of every saya.

Tradition says that this volume was rescued from the flames by Dèwadat, the cousin of Gaudama Buddha, who had ordered all such works to be destroyed. From this it will be gathered that the science was prescribed by Buddha, and is not at the present day openly countenanced by the priesthood.

In spite of this, however, the *sayas* appear to drive a thriving business, and their numbers do not seem to diminish. On a feast day a clever man will net as much as forty or fifty rupees at a sitting. They are highly flattered when a *Thakin* or European gentleman patronizes their art. On two occasions, when friends of the writer had their fortunes told, once at the Shwè Dagòn pagoda, and once at this shrine, the prognostications proved correct in each case, in several particulars. One (an Assistant Superintendent of Police) was told he was to be transferred to another country whereby he would be benefitted, both pecuniarily and otherwise. Within a month the said officer *was* transferred to

PLAN OF
ARAKAN TEMPLE
MANDALAY

Scale of Feet

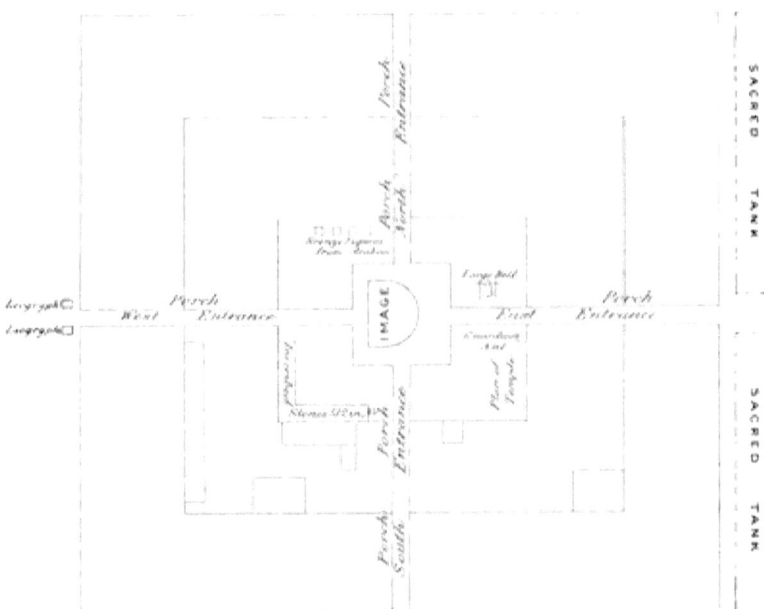

the North-west Provinces, and is now a District Superintendent of Police there !! *(This is a fact.—G.W.B.)*

The stalls under the covered ways contain a most miscellaneous variety of wares, many of them strangely out of place within the precincts of a shrine of such sanctity.

At the western entrance, several stalls expose for sale small marble figures of elephants, horses, turtles, dogs, and images of Buddha of the three orthodox shapes. Most absurd prices are asked by the vendors, but the usual price paid is from Rs. 3/- to Rs. 4/- a dozen.

They are made in close proximity to the pagoda, of the chips from the larger images there manufactured.

Gongs, both triangular and round, are also offered in large quantities, as well as dolls and puppets worked by strings.

Booksellers also drive a roaring trade, the " yellow-back " of the Burman being four anna books of songs, some of which would hardly bear translation, and cheap dramas, such as are acted in every way-side village by strolling players.

On the eastern side may be seen vendors of live fish and small birds, confined in jars and cages. The former are caught by the vendor in the nearest tank or *nulla*, and are eagerly bought by pious worshippers at a pice each, to be conveyed to the sacred tanks near by, there to be released, gaining great merit to the purchaser. In a similar way the birds (common brown reed-sparrows) are purchased, to be set at liberty, and thus saved from death. It is said that these sparrows are so accustomed to their enforced incarceration, that they return to their cages voluntarily after being released, to be resold to others, probably the same day, or the next morning. This system of supply and demand suits the casual Burmese to a nicety.

Close to the sacred tanks on the eastern side are a number of cake and sweetmeat sellers, who vend the offerings made to the fish and turtles in the square tanks close by.

The presence of these stall-holders on all sides of the temple and the adjacent corridors, with hosts of itinerant vendors interspersed, and the noise and din of barter and purchase, suggest to the mind the scene depicted in the New Testament at the purging of the Temple at Jerusalem.

In close proximity to the shrine itself, the gold and silver leaf sellers have their stalls. This leaf is of Chinese manufacture, and is sold in small square bundles containing 100 leaves, separated by small squares of Chinese paper. The packets of gold leaf sell at from Rs. 3/- to Rs. 4/- a packet (*saing*), and the silver at Rs. 2/- a packet.

On one side will be seen men employed in covering the ordinary bricks used in the construction of the new temple with gold and silver leaf. For a gilt brick eight annas is charged, and for a silver one four annas.

It is only quite lately that silver leaf has been obtainable, and its use is very much restricted ; gold, the emblem of royalty, wealth, and honour being universally used, even for the exterior and floors of sacred buildings.

The stamped tin plates exhibited on the walls in various parts of the new building are prepared on the spot, and record how " Moung Gyi and his wife Ma Ngë visited the holy shrine, and presented 100 bricks or a cartload of lime, or erected a pinnacle pagoda or *hti*, thereby storing up for themselves great merit."

The shrine itself, which contains the image, is a square masonry structure, having strong lattice work doors on the north, south, and east sides. The image itself faces the east. The original temple was destroyed by fire in 1884, and the holy image was much damaged. A stream of molten gold 700 ticals in weight, which had melted and run off the surface of the image, was found in the ashes. The present cramped and unsightly building was run up hurriedly to save the figure from spoilation, and will be replaced by a new receptacle of fitting design and ornamentation. The image is of brass, the burnished face itself only exhibiting that metal, the rest of the figure being covered with gold leaf, in some parts several inches in thickness.

MAHA-MYAT-MŪNI IMAGE, ARAKAN TEMPLE.
(Photo by Signor Beato, Mandalay.)

The figure is the usual *tinbingè*, or sitting form, the legs being crossed, with the left hand open on the lap, and the right hand resting on the right knee and pointing downwards. This was the attitude assumed by Buddha sitting in meditation under the famous *Maha-Baudi* tree, after the attainment of supreme wisdom.

The image, which is about twelve feet in height, all the limbs being suitably proportioned, is placed upon a *palin*, or throne, similar in shape to the "Lion Throne" in the Royal Palace, the height of it being about ten feet. This figure is, to the Upper Burman at least, an object of almost greater sanctity than the Shwè Dagòn or Shwè Hmau-dau pagodas of Rangoon and Pegu. The history given below will explain the causes which account for its special sanctity.

HISTORY OF IMAGE.—It was cast in the year 146 A.D. by Chanda Surya, King of Dhammavatti in Arakan, and owing to miraculous powers it exhibited, soon became very famous. It was originally enshrined in the Maha Mûni Temple, situated on the Thi-la-gyè-ri (Kyauktau) Hill, about twenty miles to the N.N.E. of Old Arakan.

The old chronicles state that at the request of Chanda-Surya, the Buddha consented to the construction of a colossal metal figure of himself, on which he breathed seven times, saying : "My younger brother, Maha-mûni, you remain here to be worshipped by human beings, Nat and Brahma." *(Yule's Mission to the Court of Ava*, page 166.)

The image was cast in three pieces, and according to one chronicle the fitting together of the several parts was facilitated by Divine intervention, when the incident above took place.

So highly venerated was this image, that from the earliest times pious pilgrims from most distant Buddhist countries have been in the habit of coming to the shrine to pay their devotions.

Owing to this celebrity, it was most earnestly coveted by the Kings of Pagan, Ava, Prome, and Pegu, and many invasions of Arakan were undertaken for the sole purpose of obtaining possession of the sacred image.

This honour was reserved for Bo-dau-pya, King of Burma, who reigned from 1781 to 1819 A.D.

In 1784 A.D. an invasion of Arakan was contemplated and carried out under the command of Ain-shè-min, the Crown Prince. The invading army was composed of four divisions. One dropped down to Minbû, and proceeded across the Yomas by the Talak Pass. Two other divisions dropped down to Padaung, just below Prome, and crossed the Yomas by the Taungûp Pass. The fourth division proceeded to Bassein, and after collecting a flotilla of serviceable boats and boatmen, proceeded by way of Cape Negrais, hugging the sea-shore to Sandoway, where it arrived about the middle of December. Advancing with the other columns, the city was invested and captured, after a feeble resistance, the King Maha Thamada, together with his wives, taking to flight. They were, however, overtaken and carried prisoners to Amarapura. The image was taken down and dragged by the victorious army over the Taungûp Pass to Padaung, whence it was conveyed in triumph by boat, or raft, to the capital. In addition to the image, several bronze figures of Rakkhas, or Hindu demons and elephants— one with three heads—were also brought away, as they were supposed to be the guardians to the sanctuary. An enormous cannon, twenty-nine feet in length, was sent by water to Amarapura, where it now lies, buried in jungle, amid the ruins of the old city.

As already noticed, the magnificent shrine, which formerly protected the image, was burnt down in 1884, and the building of the new masonry edifice to replace the former one is now proceeding.

The elevation of the proposed structure, which has been approved by Mr. Hoyne Fox, of the Public Works Department, and the architect of the handsome public buildings in Rangoon, is hung up in a shed to the south-east of the central shrine.

The work is progressing rapidly, and already the immensely thick walls on which the whole enormous superstructure will rest have been finished. According to the proposed plan, and the part already completed, the lower or ground floor consists of open arched colonnades surrounding the relic chamber. The arches and cornices are highly ornamented with elaborate carved tracery of wood, which has been covered with whitewash and paint to make it resemble stucco-work, to be in keeping with the rest of the structure. The stucco appearance is so real, that it is only by observing the nails at the back that the deception is discovered. The affairs of the temple and its management are vested in a Committee of Lay Trustees, about fifteen in number, nominated and appointed by the Chief Commissioner.

The regular income is about Rs. 500/- per mensum, Rs. 300/- of this amount is received as rent from the numerous stall-holders in and around the temple. The balance Rs. 200/- is obtained by the collection daily of the droppings from the image of gold-leaf, which had imperfectly adhered, or had been mislaid by devotees.

The average amount of gold applied monthly to the image is 180 packets, which at Rs. 4/- a packet gives a total value of Rs. 720/- per mensum. This amount is, of course, considerably exceeded on the occasion of great feast days, at the beginning and end of the Buddhist Lent, when the number of worshippers exceeds many thousands.

The huge collection boxes also contribute to the income derived, the amount received from this source being from Rs. 80/- to Rs. 120/- per mensum. In the vicinity of the temple are several objects of interest to the visitor.

On the north-east side will be seen the huge bell presented to the temple by Einshè-min, the eldest son of Bo-dau-pya, in 1785, the year after the image was removed from Arakan. Its dimensions from actual measurements are as follows :—

Exterior circumference at lip	21 feet.
Height up to shackle	6½ ,,
Thickness at lip	4½ inches.
Weight (from inscription)	40 tons.

As is usually the case, it has an inscription in Pali and Burmese on the exterior, recording the donor's name, the weight, dimensions, etc., and invoking blessings on the pious giver.

Behind the bell, to the north, is a large zayat, constructed from the material of the old temple, which had to be removed before building operations could be properly commenced. It is throughout covered with mosaic panels of glass of different colours, similar to that seen in the royal chambers of the palace.

On the inner side of the eastern porch is a marble figure representing the guardian *Nat* of the shrine.

In the far corner of the south-east inner court are some temporary sheds which contain the offices of the trustees, and the chests for the reception of cash offerings. In front of these sit the clerks employed, who grant to each donor a printed receipt for the amount received.

Hanging on the wall are two plans of the proposed temple now in course of construction. One of these it will be observed, bears the signature of Mr. Hovne Fox, of the Department of Public Works, and has been accepted by the trustees, as the approved plan. It is a pity, though, as pointed out by Mr. Oertel, of the North-West Provinces, that the design is such a crude mixture of Italian and Burmese art. How much better would it have been if the Burmese architects had proceeded to Pagan, and there studied *in situ* the magnificient details of the Ananda, the That-pin-ñ or the Gaûda-palin, and then worked out their design in keeping with these incomparable fanes.

A magnificent structure in the national style of architecture would have been the result, a fitting receptacle for the most sacred and precious image in the whole of Burma.

In the inner courtyard on the south and west sides, are two oblong sheds which contain a number of inscribed stones.

The originals in the shed on the south side are arranged in rows, and were collected from various parts of the country, viz : Ava, Shwêbo, Panya, Salin, Pagan, Sagaing, Talôkmyo and other

places, by order of Bo-dau-pya, and placed within the precincts
of the temple for safe custody.

There are in all 512 of these stones. The majority are of soft
sand-stone, such as is seen lying on the surface of the ground in
the neighbourhood of Pagan and Salin. The inscriptions are in
Pali and Burmese, and record a complete history of the building
of the principal shrines in the country, with the number of slaves
attached to each, and the grants of land made by different rulers
for their up-keep.

As the original stones were fast crumbling to pieces, and the
inscriptions were becoming obliterated, Mindôn Min had a
complete copy made of all the stones, on slabs of white marble,
procured from the royal quarries in the Sagyin hills, about
sixteen miles north of Mandalay. These are all methodically
arranged and numbered, and are kept under lock and key in the
shed on the west side, and may be inspected on application to the
elder in charge, who keeps the key.

These stones have not as yet been fully examined, but steps
are now being taken to obtain a complete copy of their contents
with a view to publication, when much valuable light will be
thrown on the early history of the country.

To the archæologist a vast mine of literary wealth is stored
in this damp and noisome chamber.

On the eastern side, beyond the limits of the courtyards
surrounding the temple, are the sacred tanks, which are well
stocked with all kinds of fish and fresh water turtle, the gifts of
pious worshippers, who gain merit or *kutho*, in saving the lives
of these creatures, by purchasing them and liberating them in
these sacred tanks.

An anna's worth of biscuits or gum-rice will soon collect specimens of all kinds round the spectators, many being of large size.

In the hot weather of May and June, when the tanks
dry up, much merit is gained by emptying chatties of water
into them, large numbers of pots being kept filled for the
purchaser near by.

MAHATHEKYA MARAZEIN KYAUK-DAU GYI PAYA.—This enormous marble image of Buddha is enshrined in an unsightly and unfinished building, situated behind some *zayats* or resthouses at the corner where the North and East Moat Roads meet. The dimensions of the image from actual measurements are as follows :—

1.—Height	24 feet 9 inches.	
2.—Width across knees	20 ,,	
3.—Width across shoulders	13½ ,,	
4.—Width of hand across the back of it	3½ ,,	
5.—Length of first finger	4 ,,	
6.—Length of thumb	3 ,,	
Circumference of thumb	3 ,,	

The piece of stone from which this image was carved, was procured after years of search from the Sagyin hills near Madaya, a few miles north of Mandalay, and was brought thence to the shore at Mandalay on a raft of boats, towed by the *Maya-Man Sekkya* steamer, and thence conveyed on rollers to the present site. The carving of the image was finished in 1865, when it was dedicated amidst great rejoicing, the King himself being present at the festivities. The square courtyard of the pagoda is surrounded by eighty smaller pagodas, twenty on each side, enshrined in each of which is a sitting figure of Buddha.

The foundations of the temple, intended to have been built by Mindòn Min to enshrine the image, are seen around, but it seems very improbable that the building of it will now be completed.

The row of zayats or rest-houses which skirt the road at this corner, were built by Mindòn Min for the use and occupation of candidates presenting themselves for the *Patama-byan* examinations in the Pali language. These were held yearly in Mindòn Min's reign, and candidates who passed by the four different standards received certificates and robes of honour.

Since the annexation of Upper Burma no examinations have been held, but with the sanction and approval of the Local

Government, they are to be revived under the supervision of the Education Department.

The standards are as follows :—

PATAMA-NGÉ.

(*a*) Kaccayana's Grammar (text, translation and parsing).
(*b*) Abhidhammatha Sangaha (text and translation).
(*c*) Matica (text and translation).
(*d*) Dhatûkatha (text and translation).

PATAMA-LAT.

(*a*) Kaccayana's Grammar (text, translation and parsing).
(*b*) Abhi Dhammatha Sangaha (text and translation).
(*c*) Matica (text and translation).
(*d*) Dhatûkatha (text and translation).
(*e*) Yamaka Books, 1-5 (text and translation).

PATAMA-GYI.

(*a*) Kaccayana's Grammar (text, translation and parsing).
(*b*) Abhi Dhammatha Sangaha (text and translation).
(*c*) Matica (text and translation).
(*d*) Dhatûkatha (text and translation).
(*e*) Yanaka, Books 1-10 (text and translation).
(*f*) Abhidhanappadipika (text and translation).
(*g*) Chanda (text and translation).
(*h*) Alankara (text and translation.

PATAMA-GYAW.

(*a*) Kaccayana's Grammar (text, translation and parsing).
(*b*) Abhidhammatha Sangaha (text and translation).
(*c*) Matica (text and translation).
(*d*) Dhatûkatha (text and translation).
(*e*) Yamaka, Books 1-10 (text and translation).
(*f*) Patthana Kusalatika (text and translation).
(*g*) Abhidhamaappadipika (text and translation).
(*h*) Chanda (text and translation).
(*i*) Alankara (text and translation).

Awards will be given as below to successful candidates :—

Patamagyaw	Rs. 150.
Patamagyi	Rs. 100.
Patamalat	Rs. 75.
Patama-ngè	Rs. 50.

A suitable robe will also be given, together with a certificate signed by the President of the Examination Committee (The Director of Public Instruction). In the case of Patamagyaw, the certificate will be signed by the Chief Commissioner.

It is hoped by these means, the study of Pali, the sacred language of Buddhists, may be fostered and encouraged.

THE QUEEN'S KYAUNG.—This truly magnificent structure, which was erected between 1881-85 by Sûpyah, the chief queen of King Thibaw, is situated in A Road, the most southern of the roads leading from the city to the bank of the river, and along which—at one side—runs the shore branch of the Burma State Railway Line.

To reach it from the hotel or Palace, the best route to take will be along the West-Moat Road, continuing straight on through the Chinese quarter (72nd street) until you cross the railway branch line in A Road. Proceeding down this road for about 150 yards, a large collection of *Kyaungs* will be seen on the left, conspicuous amongst which, for the golden leaf with which it is covered, is the Queen's Kyaung. It is said that a good deal of the money spent on the erection of this building by Sûpyah Lat was obtained from the proceeds of the State Lotteries which were held in the grounds on the other side of the road. The structure was commenced in 1881, but was barely finished when the builder of it was deported in 1885. The ceremony of "pouring out water" was only performed by the Queen when passing along this road with the King on their way to the steamer, when the procession consisted of two regiments of Native Infantry leading ; then a Mule Battery, followed by the King and Queen in a Bè-yo, or bullock-gharry, the rear being brought up by a European regiment.

SHRINE, A-HTU-MA-SHI MONASTERY.

(Photo by Signor Beato, Mandalay.)

Although this Kyaung is the residence of a Sadaù, or Buddhist Bishop, and his followers, no objection is taken to European visitors.

The wood-carving is excellent, but its effect is spoilt by the lavish expenditure of gold leaf with which the whole building, both exterior and interior, is covered.

The panels of the walls are ornamented with carved figures of different animals, conspicuous amongst which, from their frequent occurrence, are the hare, the peacock, and the tortoise.

A-HTÚ-MA-SHI KYAUNG.—This remarkable building, which certainly deserved its title (" The Incomparable,") was unfortunately destroyed by fire, together with the Hman-kyaung, in close proximity to it, in 1892.

Its ruins are to be seen immediately to the south of the *Kutho-daw*, and a cursory inspection of them will give the spectator some idea of the magnitude of the undertaking. It was erected by that pious monarch Mindòn Min, and was of peculiar construction.

From an inspection of the ruins, it will be noticed that it was built in the shape of a parallelogram, with opposite sides of 200 and 150 feet respectively. In design the building consisted of five walled terraces of diminishing size, one above the other, and rose to a height of nearly 100 feet.

The posts which supported the top-most terrace were said to be sixty-six cubits in length. The structure throughout was of massive teak timber, to which bricks of large size were nailed, and the whole neatly covered with stucco-work. The girth of the pillars was considerably added to in this way, as can be distinctly seen by looking at the remains still standing.

The interior contained two large images of Buddha, made of wood from the sacred Maha-Baudi tree of Bodha Gya. The interior decoration was most superb. The door-posts, doors, cornices round the posts, mouldings in the panelling of the walls, were all most magnificently carved, and the whole interior, even to the floor, was covered with gold leaf.

Attached to the large central hall, and forming part of
the general structure, was the *Bedegat-taik*, or library, which
contained a valuable collection of Pali manuscripts on palm
leaf.

The amount expended by the King on this kyaung was never
known, but has been roughly estimated at from seven to ten
lakhs of rupees.

EIN-DAU-YA PAGODA.—This handsome shrine is situated to
the left of B road, about 400 yards beyond the bridge which
crosses the Shwè-Da-Chaung.

It was erected in 1847, by Pagan Min, on the site formerly
occupied by the house or palace he occupied when Crown
Prince.   Hence the name *Ein*, house ; *Dau*, royal ; *Ya*, place.

In shape it resembles the pagodas commonly seen in Lower
Burma. The base or plinth is a square, each side measuring
about 250 feet, and is succeeded by three successive receding
terraces, from the top-most one of which the bell-shaped stupa
rises.   This part is much ornamented with stucco figures in relief,
the lower representing heads and arms of *Belûs*, the arms being
joined to one another by a pattern of semi-circular bead-work.
The upper consists of buds of the sacred lotus.   The pagoda is
about 90 feet high, the *hti* on the top being both handsome and
massive.   Flights of steps lead up on each of the four sides
to the top-most terrace, and the shrine is enclosed by a neat
iron fence.

In the vicinity of the pagoda is a chalcedony image of
Buddha, which was brought from Ceylon in Pagan Min's time.

SET-KYAT-THI-HA TEMPLE.—This temple is so named from
the enormous brass image which is enshrined in it.

This image was cast by Bodau-Pya in 1826, A.D., and was
enshrined in the Gauda-gû-ti temple.

Its dimensions and weight are as follows :—

Height	16½ feet.
Width across knees	13½ ,,

Weight, 26,723 viss, or nearly forty-four tons.

EIN-DAU-YA PAGODA, MANDALAY.

(Photo by Signor Beato, Mandalay.)

During the reign of Pagan Min, the image was removed from Ava to his capital Amarapura, and erected in a spacious compound immediately to the south-west of the city, on the banks of the Taung-tha-man Lake. At the instigation of his Queen, Sûpya-Lat, King Thibaw gave orders for it to be removed to its present site, and certain ministers, including the Kin Wûn Mingyi, the Wet-ma-sût Wundauk, and others, were told off to superintend its removal.

It was removed from its pedestal and placed on a sledge specially constructed, and surmounted by a seven-roofed pyathat ; 3,500 men in the King's service were told off to drag the sledge, four strong ropes being used, and after nineteen days hard pulling, the present site was reached.   Throughout the progress of the image, the streets were decorated, refreshments provided, bands of music played, and the immense concourse of people shouted. The arrival of the sacred image was announced by firing cannon. After every arrangement had been made, the image was successfully hoisted up by means of ropes and pulleys, to the *palin* on which it now rests.

On the completion of the work, the King and Queen rewarded the engineers and smiths by giving them rings, precious stones, and golden cups. On the 8th, of the waxing moon of *Nayôn* (June) 1885, the removal of the image was completed. Five months later, King Thibaw and his Queen were deported to India.

The best way to reach the pagoda is to go south, past the King's bazaar, when the gilt spire of the pagoda will be seen to the right.

ROMAN CATHOLIC CATHEDRAL.—This beautiful building is situated at the south-west corner of the city walls, and its graceful spire, surmounted by a huge gilded cross, renders it a conspicuous object from all parts of the city.

The building was erected in 1890 at a total cost of Rs. 60,000, the whole of which was defrayed by Kyaung-taga Paul Oûpho, a wealthy Burman Roman Catholic.

L

The principal dimensions are :—

Nave—Length, 150ft. ; breadth, 80ft. ; height, 40ft.

Tower—Height, 150ft.

The tower contains four bells of the following dimensions :—

No. 1.   Diameter at mouth, 3ft. 6in.

No. 2.   „   „   „   2ft. 6in.

No. 3.   „   „   „   2ft.

No. 4.   „   „   „   1ft. 6in.

PAINTINGS.—Executed by an artist from Rome, and copied from the original masterpieces in the Vatican galleries. They represent :—

1. The Nativity at Bethlehem.

2. The Institution of the Eucharist, or Last Supper.

3. The Resurrection of Our Lord.

4. The Ascension of Our Lord.

ALTARS.—There are three altars in carved teak wood. The workmanship is Burmese, but the designs are taken from a French work and executed by a European master.

1. The High Altar, in pure Gothic style, entirely gilt, and adoring angels on either side, the gift of Kyaungtaga Paul Oûpho. This altar is dedicated to the Sacred Heart.

2. The altar on the Gospel side, dedicated to the Blessed Virgin Mary, is the gift of the late Bishop Simon.

3. The altar on the Epistle side, dedicated to St. Joseph, and entirely gilt, is the gift of Magdalena, wife of Kyaungtaga Oûpho.

The interior of the Church is illuminated by candles on lustres and branches, to the number of 364 lights, on grand occasions. The lamp before the High Altar is in gilded bronze. The lustre in front of it, holding thirty-six candles, is of crystal, and was presented to Mr. John Paul.

The hours of service are :—

Sundays and Holy Days, Low Mass, 6.15 a.m.

High Mass, with Sermon, 8 a.m.

Rosary, with Benediction, 5.30 p.m.

On Week-days Mass is celebrated at 6 a.m.

The choir consists of native voices, chiefly Burmese men and boys, and is conducted by the Reverend Father Paul.

SIGNOR BEATO'S STUDIO.—Visitors to Upper Burma should not fail to pay a visit to Signor Beato's Studio in C road, Mandalay.

He arrived in Mandalay in 1886, at the time of the annexation of Upper Burma, and has succeeded in establishing an excellent business as a dealer in Burmese curios.

Originally a photographer, he was present throughout the Crimean war, the Indian Mutiny, General Sir Hope Grant's Expedition to China in 1860, Admiral Hooper's Naval Campaign in Japan in 1864, the United States Expedition to Corea in 1870, the Soudan Campaigns, including the Nile and Suakim Expeditions, and the Expedition to Upper Burma in 1885-86.

Soon after his arrival in Mandalay, he established his present flourishing business. His long residence in Japan of 24 years, gave him the experience necessary for successfully conducting such an undertaking.

Here can be obtained, besides photographs of all places and peoples of Upper Burma, and the countries adjacent to it ; works of art in wood, metal (especially old and modern Shan silver work), ivory, silk goods (both printed and embroidered), images of Buddha, costumes and arms of indigenous races, and quantities of other curios and objects suitable as mementos of a visit to this interesting country.

Signor Beato undertakes the packing and despatch of all articles purchased from his studio, and has for a number of years carried on a large export trade with Europe, America, and other parts of the world.

Employing as he does a large number of workers (over 800 in number) in the different art industries, he is able to command the best specimens, and hence those who patronize his studio, may rest assured that they will get the real article, at a reasonable price, and of the very best workmanship.

Most of the articles hawked about the streets, and offered for sale at the doors of hotels and private bungalows, are articles

L 2

rejected by him as being of inferior workmanship, or having flaws or blemishes.

As Signor Beato has been connected with Mandalay for a number of years, he is naturally in a position to render willing help to the tourist. A visit to the studio, therefore, and an interesting chat with its genial and courteous proprietor, will put the traveller on the right road to obtaining all he wants in the way of curios, and getting information and "tips" as to the sights of the city.

LEPER ASYLUMS.—These are situated at some distance to the south of the civil lines, and are two in number. One, called the St. John's Leper Asylum, occupies an advantageous site in the Manaw-Yaman Royal Garden and is connected with the Roman Catholic Mission. This Asylum was started by Father Wehinger about four years ago, and at the present time contains about 150 patients. It has received liberal support from the charitably disposed, both in Lower and Upper Burma, and the zealous superintendent is now on a mission to Europe to collect funds for the extension of the work of the Asylum.

The other asylum is situated a few hundred yards nearer the town on the same road, and is ably superintended by the Reverend W. Winston, of the English Wesleyan Mission.

Both institutions deserve the earnest support of all charitable people. One of the most grievous sights at a pagoda feast or other assemblage, is the spectacle of these poor victims exposing their sores and diseased limbs to excite the pity and receive the alms of passing strangers. Until legislation steps in and demands the compulsory segregation of those suffering from this awful disease, the next best thing to do is to support the noble efforts of these missionary bodies, to induce the victims voluntarily to seek the shelter of the asylums, where their sufferings will be mitigated, and their lives rendered more comfortable than they otherwise would be, if left as formerly, to roam the streets.

The superintendents of both institutions are very pleased to receive visitors and conduct them over the buildings.

ROUTE XIII.

TO SAGAING.

SAGAING, the classical name of which was Jeyapura, is situated on the right bank of the Irrawaddi, immediately below the old capital Amarapura, and opposite to an older capital still, In-wa or Ratanapura, as it was called. It is now the head-quarters of the Commissioner of the Central Division, and also of a Deputy Commissioner and the courts and offices subordinate to him, and has besides the Bazaar, a Telegraph and Post-office, Police lines and Civil and Military Police Hospitals. The population in 1891, was 9,934. The town is one of the most picturesquely situated as well as the most salubrious of any in Upper Burma, and enjoys a climate unequalled by any other station. Before the annexation it consisted of a number of small villages or hamlets, nestling amid the shady groves for which the place is famous. On all sides were (and still are) orchards and flower gardens frequented by the King's Ministers and Court Officials, who came here either to escape the cares of affairs of State, or to hold a quiet retreat at one of the numerous shrines for which the place is celebrated. Since the occupation and the inauguration of Local Self-government and the opening of the Mû Valley Railway, a large accession of population, chiefly natives of India, has obtained, and in consequence trade has improved, and with it the general appearance and up-keep of the town.

COMMUNICATIONS.—The town is served both by the Mû Valley State Railway, and the steamers of the Irrawaddy Flotilla Company.

Local trains to Mandalay and *vice versa*, run every three or four hours. Two trains a day run from Sagaing to Shwèbo and the stations beyond, and *vice versa*.

The Mandalay-Myingyan and Mandalay-Myinmû Ferry Steamers stop daily, both on the down and up journeys. The cargo steamers stop when cargo is offered. The principal trade is in fruit, chillies, wheat, paddy, cotton, sessimum, gram, salt and onions.

To the north of the town and parallel to the bank of the river runs a range of hills, the summits of which, in almost every instance, being crowned with pagodas, and in some cases flights of brick and stone steps lead up to them from the bank of the river. In the sequestered valleys and ravines amidst these hills are the homes of the hermit *phongyis* some 700 in number. A description of these will be found elsewhere.

HISTORY.—The name Sagaing is said to be a corruption of two Burmese words, *sit*, a kind of tree ; and *kaing*, a branch. The origin of the name is given in the *Maha Yazawin*, or royal history of the Kings of Burma as follows :—

Two blind sons of a king of Old Pagan were placed upon a raft, and drifted down the river. At Sagaing the raft was caught in the branches of an over-hanging *sit* tree, and detained for some time. Hence the name *Sit-Kaing*, or as it is now rendered, Sagaing. The legend further states that these princes floated on down the river till they came to the neighbourhood of Prome, and that from them came the race of kings who ruled in Therakettra from 483 B.C. to 95 A.D.

On the breaking up of the Pagan monarchy in A.D. 1291, owing to its conquest by three Shan brothers, Sagaing was a dependency of Panya.

Thiha-thû, one of the three brothers, had a son named Athin-khara by his Shan wife. This son was made governor of the province of Sagaing, and in 1312 A.D. he declared himself independent of his father, and established his rule over the country extending up to the borders of Manipur. This line of

Shan kings ruled at Sagaing for forty-nine years, when the country was conquered by an incursion of Shans from Môhnyin and Mogaung.

The Sagaing Sovereigns were :—

1.	Athin-khara	1315 to 1322 A.D.
2.	Tara-Bya-Gyi	1322 „ 1336 „
3.	Shwè-daung-det	1336 „ 1339 „
4.	Kya-bwa	1339 „ 1349 „
5.	Nau-rhata Min Bè	1349 „ (7 Mos)
6.	Tara-bya-Ngè	1350 „ 1352 „
7.	Min-bauk Thi-ha-pati	1352 „ 1354 „

After the break-up of this dynasty it remained under Shan rule (the capital being at Ava) till A.D. 1554, when Ava was captured by Bayin-Naung, the Talaing King of Pegu. It remained under Talaing rule till A.D. 1599, when the united Talaing Burman Empire became dismembered.

In 1733 the Rajah of Manipur invaded the Chindwin Valley, and pushed his armies as far as Sagaing. A fight took place at the Kaung-hmû-dau pagoda, about five miles from the town, and to this day *dah* cuts are seen on one of the pagoda gates, said to have been made during the fight.

Sagaing became the capital again in 1760, when Naung-dau-Gyi, the eldest son of Alaungpya, succeeded to the throne. On his death Sin-byû-shin re-transferred the capital to Mòt-sò-bò (the modern Shwèbo).

The ruins of the old city walls show that they were very strong and substantial, and the plateau to the north-west of the present town, behind the hills, is thickly strewn with ruins of pagodas and other buildings.

The principal objects of interest at Sagaing are :—

1. The Pagodas in and around the town.
2. The Fort.
3. The *Gyaungs* in the Sagaing Hills.
4. The *Ohn Min Thonzè*, or Thirty Caves.

A short description of each will now be given.

PAGODAS.—To attempt to describe *all*, or even a small number, of the hundreds of pagodas in and around Sagaing would be an unnecessary and in many cases an uninteresting task. The principal are :—

1, The Kaung-Hmû-dau ; 2, the Nga-dat-gyi (Wetûn-Wûn); 3, Abaya Zèdi (Ratana-muni) ; 4, Paya-pyù ; 5, Uriama-Kaung-hmû ; 6, Htopayòn (Htôparima) ; 7, Zèdi-dau (Aung-Myèlauka) ; 8, Yan-aung-myin ; 9, Pôn-nya-Shin ; 10, Pû-damya Zèdi ; 11, Sin-mya Shin (Ratana Zèdi).

KAUNG-HMÛDAU PAGODA, OR RAJA-CHÛLA-MANI.—This remarkable and unique structure is situated on a slight eminence to the south-west of the town, from which it is distant about five miles, and is a conspicuous object for many miles both from the the river and the railway. The peculiarity of the pagoda is its remarkable shape, which is unlike that of any other to be found in the whole of Burma. It consists of three low receding terraces, on which is built an enormous dome-shaped structure without cavity or ornament, except a massive umbrella which crowns it.

It was built by King Thado-dhamma Raja in the year 1636 A.D., as recorded in the *Maha Razawin*, and on the stone inscription set up on the pagoda platform.

In the relic-chamber is said to be an image of Buddha, of gold, the weight being that of the King's body.

The following events in the stages of its erection are taken from the dedication stone :—

Cleared jungle at site of pagoda, Tuesday, 5th, waxing moon of *Pyatho*, 997 B.E. (January, 1635).

Levelled site, Friday, 8th, of waning moon of *Kasòn*, 998 B.E. (May, 1636).

Construction commenced 1st of waning moon of *Nadau* (December, 1636).

Completed and fixed Umbrella, Saturday, 8th of waning moon of *Kasòn*, 1011 B.E. (May, 1645 A.D.)

STATISTICS OF MATERIAL USED.—No. of bricks used, 10,126,552. Baskets of red-earth for mortar 650,505. Iron

KAUNG-HMÛ-DAW PAGODA, SAGAING.

(Photo by Seymour Beatte, Mandalay.)

work for umbrella, 3,480 viss. (1 viss=3·65 lbs). Gold for umbrella, 1,011 ticals.

DIMENSIONS.

Circumference	900	feet.
Height	151½	,,
Diameter	286	,,

Stone gutters 60 in number. Stone posts encircling pagoda, each 4½ feet high, 812.

Number of shrines for Guardian nats, 120.

The lower terrace of the pagoda, is surrounded by 240 niches, containing images of Buddha. From a close inspection of the exterior, it appears that at one time, the whole surface must have been gilded, although at the present time plain white-wash, and that in sparse quantities, has been used.

The stone posts which surround the base, need more than passing notice. As before stated, they are 812 in number, each being four-and-a-half feet high, with a diameter of about eight inches. The tops are moulded, and on the inner side of each cavities have been chiselled out for the reception of lamps, most probably the open earth-oil lamps formerly in universal use. When the light from these was thrown on the gilded surface of the pagoda, the effect must have been very grand.

A number of *tagundaing* surrounded the shrine, but these are now in a ruinous state, as are also the " caves " or shrines, in which the 120 figures of the guardian *nat* are enshrined. These figures are represented as a man with a crown on his head, sitting with his right elbow resting on his right knee, the left arm being doubled and free. In the right hand a lotus bud is held, and in the left a javelin.

Many Arakanese and Siamese captives taken in war, were assigned as slaves by different Kings, as is recorded on the stone inscription at the pagoda.

ITINERARY.—The pagoda is about two-and-half miles from the Ywataung Railway Station, the first station after leaving Sagaing. As however, it will probably be found that trains are inconvenient, the best way to visit it will be either to ride or to walk. A jungle cart-road runs from Sagaing, passing through the village of Ma-gyi-sin, where most of the inhabitants are makers of white marble images of Gaudama, the marble being procured from the Sagyin Hills, north of Mandalay. Passing through this village, and the next, Ywataung, where brass-work is the trade, the huge mass of the pagoda will be seen before you.

NGA-TAT-GYI TEMPLE.—The written notice hanging in a *zayat* near the image, gives the following authentic information concerning the construction of this huge image, and the *tazaung* in which it is enshrined.

It was erected by Min-yè-nanda-meit, son of Thalûn Mintaragyi, between the years 1648 and 1658 A.D.

Extensive repairs both to the image itself, and the *tazaung* in which it is placed, were carried out by public subscription in 1890.

The image is built of brick, covered with cement or plaster, and represents Buddha in the ordinary *tin-byin-gwè* or sitting posture. The principal dimensions of this colossus are :—

Height	42	feet.
Breadth across knees	$28\frac{1}{2}$	,,
Waist	27	,,
Circumference of head	21	,,
Diameter of eye	3	,,
Length of ear	6	,, 4 inches.

The image is placed on a plinth about thirty feet in height, from which rises the five-roofed *pyathat*, from which the shrine gets its name.

ITINERARY.—The shrine is situated on the outskirts of the town. The best way to visit it will be to take a gharry at the railway station and drive right through the town, along Browning Road past the police lines and court-house. The road ends abruptly at the entrance to the pagoda.

ABAYA ZEDI (or Ratana Mûni).—This pagoda is situated about 200 yards south-west of the image, and is a well-built structure in a good state of preservation.

ZAYATS AT KAUNG HMŪ DAU PAGODA.

(*Photo by T. O. Ochil, Esq., N.W.P.*)

In shape it consists of five square receding terraces, surmounted by an ordinary bell-shaped pagoda with a gilt top crowned by a *hti*.

This pagoda was built in 1543 A.D. by Dùtiya-Min Gaung, King of Ava.

Its erection was due to the fact that the King had a son born mute (*Bur. a-thi*). The Brahmins asserted that in order to remove this affliction the King should erect a pagoda. The pagoda was erected, and "the dumb spoke." So says the tradition.

PYA-PYÈ was built by King Sin-byû-shin, son of Alaungpya. It is situated to the north of Nga-tat-gyi, and is of no special sanctity.

NYI-AMA KAUNG-HMÙ.—These two pagodas, now in ruins, were built by two sisters (*nyi-ama*), the Pagan and Sagain princesses, daughters of Narapadigyi, King of Ava, who ruled from 1649 to 1674 A.D. They are now surrounded by dense thorny jungle, and are difficult of approach.

HTÙ-PAYÒN (HTÙPARIMA).—This unsightly and unfinished shrine was built by Narapadigyi, King of Ava, in 1651, but was never finished. The ruins consist of three concentric tiers of brick-work, with niches for the reception of images. The surface was not plastered. The flat top is now covered with grass and other jungle growth.

It is situated between the back of the police lines and the river, and is plainly visible from the deck of passing steamers.

ZÉDI-DAU.—This handsome structure is situated to the north of the American Baptist Mission Compound, and presents a good view from the river.

It was built in the year 1782 A.D. by Bo-daw-pya, the founder of the city of Amarapura, and stone only was used in its construction. It is of the usual shape, about eighty feet in height, and the base is surrounded by a fence of white marble pillars, with niches cut in the tops for the reception of lamps. This idea was evidently borrowed from the Kaung-hmù-daw.

Two large-sized bells, with inscriptions, hang in the court-yard, and in one corner, in a small masonry structure, is the dedication-stone, which records the building of the pagoda, the lands set apart for its endowment, and the slaves provided for its superintendence.

SIX-MYA-SHIN PAGODA.—This pagoda, which is now in ruins, was built in 1530 A.D. by Môhnyin Mintaragyi, King of Ava. It is situated near the burial ground, which is called after the pagoda.

PADAMYA-ZÊDI.—This pagoda is situated on one of the prominent peaks of the Sagaing Hills, to the north of the present town, and is best reached from the village of Wachet, on the river bank, north of Sagaing. The name Pada-mya means jewels. The ascent is made either from the east or south sides. That from the east is steep and rugged, while from the south the ascent is more gradual and less trying.

A magnificent view of the surrounding country is obtained from the summit. On the sides of the hills grow many valuable plants of medicinal qualities.

PONYA-SHIN ZÊDI.—This shrine is situated on the summit of Nga-pa-daung, one of the highest peaks of the Sagaing hills. It was built by Pônya-Shin, the Chief Minister of Thi-hatha, King of Panya, who reigned from 1412 to 1422 A.D. A zig-zag flight of steps leads up to the pagoda from the eastern side, and a less sloping ascent can be made from the south-east.

THE FORT is situated on the bank of the river at the western end of the town. It was built, together with the two others, on the opposite bank of the river at Ava during Mindôn Min's reign, and was constructed by French or Italian engineers in his employ.

These forts occupied a highly strategical position command-ing one of the most difficult pieces of navigation in the Irrawaddi River, the channel at this place being much blocked by rocks and shoals.

On the approach of the fleet of steamers in 1885, the Burmese scuttled several steamers and flats in the fair-way, thinking thereby to block the channel. These wrecks can still be seen at low water. The fleet, however, passed safely through, but the result has been that the channel has been vastly improved and the shoals cut away.

No guns were mounted on this fort, nor was it occupied, as all opposition ceased at Ava opposite, and the fleet passed on unopposed to its moorings off Mandalay.

GYAUNGS IN THE HILLS AT SAGAING.—A *Gyaung* in the vernacular means a valley, or ravine ; but in Sagaing the name is applied to the monasteries and religious buildings built in the valleys, in which live, surrounded on all sides by the bare and rugged hill-sides, communities of very religious and austere monks and nuns.

From the river these establishments are not visible, but on ascending to the top of any of the hills at the back of the village of Wachet the eye is enchanted by the view of these vales, in which nestle, amidst groves of graceful trees, and surrounded by pretty flowering shrubs, the monasteries of this austere sect of hermits.

When the writer visited them in 1894 he was shown a list, or register, carefully kept by the hermit, in which the name of every resident was entered. These at the time numbered 657. There were originally only nine, but there are now twenty-four of such establishments. Paved, zig-zag paths lead from one to the other, and to the pagoda platforms on the summits, and some are supplied with tanks and wells cut out of the rock.

In the hill-sides, at the back of the monasteries, a series of caves have been cut out of the solid rock by the hermits themselves, the aperture being closed in each instance by a massive teak door, and in these dark, unwholesome cells, with the doors shut, excluding both light and air, these recluses spend from five to eight hours a day in silent meditation. As a lesson on the hold which Buddhism has on the minds of its followers, this is a most remarkable and at the same time a most convincing argument.

Attached to each *gyaung* are several lay-pupils, whose duty it is to bring in supplies of wood and water, and to collect the offerings of the pious supporters in the villages and town below.

They are so celebrated amongst Buddhists that no pilgrim from the lower province would think of returning to his home without paying them a visit.

Caves of similar construction and use were numerous in Pagan and its neighbourhood, and also in the hills near Kyauksè and in those immediately opposite Mónywa in the Lower Chindwin District.

OHN-MIN-THONZÈ (THIRTY CAVES).—This name is misleading, for no caves, such as we understand the term, exist. The shrine referred to consists of a gallery containing forty-nine figures of Buddha, said to have been cut out of the solid rock. They are in the usual sitting position, and in front a colonnade has been built on a terrace twenty feet wide, which is supported by masonry buttresses. An archway faces each image.

The shrine is situated on the land side of the hills, and can be seen very plainly from the train, and from the Myótha uplands on the opposite side of the river.

Sagaing is provided with a good dâk bungalow, where visitors can get all they want.

Those visiting the station for one day only will find it more convenient, probably, to get what refreshment they require on the ferry steamer which runs between Sagaing and the shore at Amarapura.

PLAN OF
AMARAPURA

Scale ⊢——|——|——|——|——⊣ 1 Mile

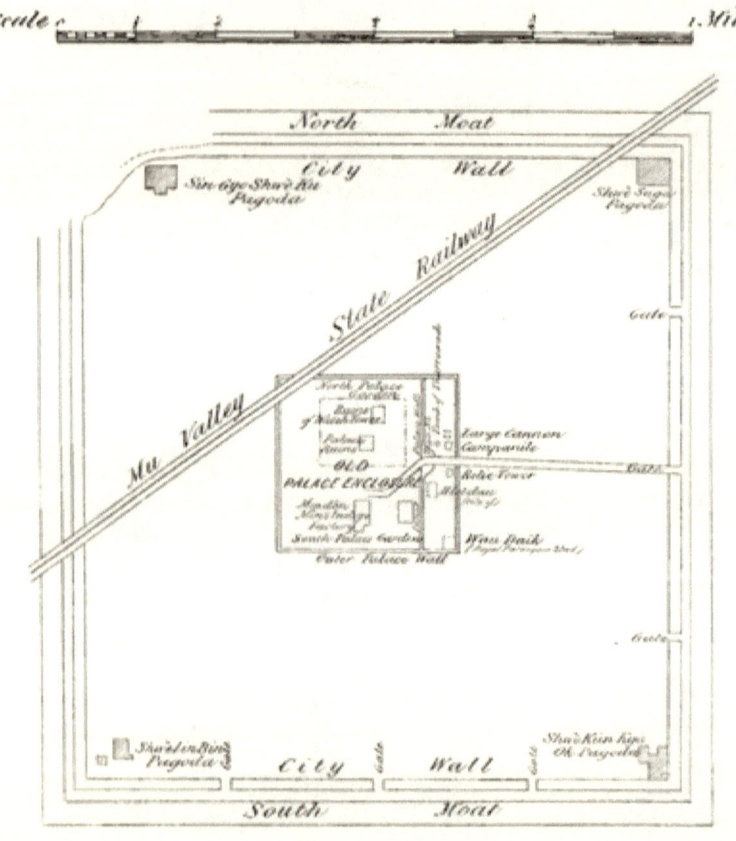

ROUTE XIV.

AMARAPURA.

ROUTE.—The best way to get to Amarapura is to take the train from Mandalay to the Amarapura Station on the Mu Valley Railway. A good metalled road runs out to the populous villages on the site of the old extra-mural city, so that if trains are not suitable the distance can be covered in a gharry.

Amarapura, or the "Immortal City," was built on the peninsula situated between the Irrawaddi River and the Taung-Tha-man Lake. It is distant about eight miles to the south of Mandalay, and about five miles north-east of Ava.

Its founder, Bo-dau-pya, who ruled from 1781 to 1819 A.D., having gained the throne by the murder of his nephew, Maung-Maung, and all his adherents, thought that he might escape the evil influence clinging to the palace at Ava by removing to a more salubrious site.

After search had been made, it was decided to fix upon the peninsula already referred to. The new city was laid out in the form of a square at the widest part of the peninsula. A brick wall surrounded it, twelve or thirteen feet high, with a battlemented parapet similar to the one at Mandalay. The wall was supported on the inner side by an earthen rampart, which however, in some places, was not completed. The four walls were each about 2,500 yards in length, but in the north-west, where the river ran close by, the corner was cut off obliquely.

Each face had three gates, protected by masonry traverses, and at regular intervals bastions were placed. About 100 feet from the wall a moat nearly eighty-one feet wide extended along the whole of the east and west sides, the greater part of the north, and part of the south. This moat, unlike the one at Mandalay, had both escarp and counter-scarp of brick.

At the gates these converge to a width of about twelve feet, across which wooden bridges were placed. Along the escarp ran a low battlemented wall about four feet high. The walls were built of bricks, with mud mortar, except at the gates, where lime mortar was used.

The streets, as at Mandalay, ran at right angles to the walls, from gate to gate, dividing the city into rectangular blocks.

The palace occupied the centre, its walls running symetrically with those of the city, and was enclosed by three successive walls. Outside of all was a stockade of teak posts, and within this, at a distance of about forty feet, a brick wall. The chief entrance was to the east. At a distance of about 400 feet from this gateway a second brick wall extended right across the palace enclosure, from the northern to the southern walls.

Most of the palace buildings, being wooden structures, were removed from Ava, and on the 10th of May, 1783, the King, with his wives and his whole Court, including the sacred white elephant, entered the new city in grand procession.

Amarapura remained the capital from 1783 to 1823, when Ba-Gyidau, the King, transferred his capital to Ava. It again became the capital in 1837, during the reign of Pagan-Min, but was finally deserted in 1860, when the present city of Mandalay was built. As on the transfer from Ava, most of the present buildings in the palace at Mandalay were removed from Amarapura. At the present time little remains of its former greatness but the ruins of the city and palace walls and a number of delapidated pagodas and other religious buildings. Straight avenues of tamarind trees, surrounded on all sides by fields of maize, now mark the alignment of the once busy thoroughfares.

The limits of the city walls can easily be judged from viewing the large pagodas standing at each of the four corners.

HUGE CANNON, AMARAPURA.

(Photo by Skinner Ksettle, Mandalay.)

They are called :—

Sin-Gyo-Shwè-Kû Pagoda	N.W. Corner.
Shwè-Daga Pagoda	N.E. ,,
Shwè-Lin-Bin Pagoda	S.W. ,,
Shwè-Kûn-Gya-Ôk Pagoda	S.E. ,,

They were built by Bo-dau-Pya soon after the foundation of the city, and are of no special sanctity or importance.

All four are in a more or less ruinous condition. Within the city walls are now thriving fields of Indian corn, sessemum, and other cereals. Threading your way through these by the rough foot-paths which lead from field to field, towards the centre of the city you come to the remains of the palace walls. Entering through the eastern gate, on the left will be seen the ruins of the Swè-dau-zin, or relic tower, in which a tooth of Buddha *(Swè-dau)* was said to have been enshrined. Immediately opposite this, to the north of the road, are the ruins of the *Bahòt-zin*. or Campanile, where the *Bahòt*, or immense drum, marked the time to Palace and City. Nothing now remains of these buildings but a heap of bricks and rubbish. Up to a year or two ago, however, they were more or less perfect.

Lying alongside of, and half buried by the ruins and the surrounding jungle, lies the enormous cannon captured from the Arakanese in 1784, at the same time as the sacred Maha-Myat Muni image in the Arakan temple and transported to Amarapura by sea and river.

The principal dimensions taken by the writer from actual measurements are :—

Exterior length	28 feet 10 inches.		
Circumference below breech	9	,, 4	,,
Circumference at mouth	8	,, 2	,,
Calibre		11½	,,

The cannon is at the present time (1895) so buried in ruins and thorny jungle that a careful inspection is rather difficult. It is constructed of bars of iron, about an inch and a half square, which run longitudinally throughout the entire length. Round

these bars lateral hoops or rings of similar bars are shrunk on,
and the whole has been welded together. From the
imperfect welding of the bars of the barrel, it would appear that
the monster was rifled, but this of course was not so. The vent
for such an " infant " is absurdly small. Five pairs of enormous
rings are welded on to the upper surface, apparently for the
purposes of transport by means of long poles carried on men's
shoulders. In appearance and construction it reminds one of
" Mons Meg " on the terrace at Edinburgh Castle.

Lying in close proximity is another of lesser size of the same
peculiarity of construction, and a few yards to the east, buried in
rubbish and jungle is a third, about seven or eight feet in length,
with a calibre of about sixteen inches, which from its chubby
appearance was probably a mortar for throwing shells or bombs.

The low heap of rubbish immediately to the west of these
cannon marks the site of Shwè-bo Min's grave. He was better
known as Tharrawaddi Min.

We now pass on through the *Tiga-ni* or Red Postern to the
Inner Palace enclosure. To the right will be seen the ruins of
two buildings ; the one to the north was the *Nan-Myin* or Palace
Watch Tower, from which the King viewed the city without
going forth from the Palace precincts.

The larger building to the south is all that remains of the
Palace proper, and this is fast falling into hideous ruin.

As already stated, the wooden buildings were removed
in toto by Mindôn Min on the transfer of his capital to
Mandalay.

To the south of the Palace buildings are the ruins of the
Indigo works constructed for Mindôn Min by a Frenchman in
his employ. These consist of a series of masonry tanks or vats
24 in number, each 18 feet square, connected by drains and
pipes to the furnace at the southern end of the building. Water
was supplied from the deep, square, bricked tank close by, which
formed an ornamental piece of water in the south Palace
garden.

BAHOZIN AND SWĒ-DAU ZIN, AMARAPURA.

(Photo by Nizwar Beato, Mandalay.)

These works, like the Cotton factories at Sagaing were one of the many white elephants (not the sacred variety) of this enlightened but credulous monarch.

The railway line to the shore now cuts off the north-west corner of the palace walls, which contain no other remains or ruins which need describing.

To the north-east of the city walls are the remains of the old elephant keddah where the King and Court formerly witnessed the final capture and taming of the elephants. The operations were carried on in the valleys between the Shan hills to the west of the city. The elephants were driven along these valleys to the open plains beyond, being guided by decoy females into the *cul-de-sac* of teak posts, at the further end of which was the keddah. By these means the royal stables were stocked.

THE EXTRA-MURAL CITY.—As was the case at Mandalay, the city proper or *Shwè-Myo-daw*, contained only the palace of the king, the houses of the ministers and their followers, and the dwellings of the *ahmudan* or soldiers.

The wealthy mercantile community lived to the west of the city, where the long avenues of tamarind trees mark to this day the once busy streets. When Mindòn Min removed to Mandalay in 1857, he caused all the inhabitants to follow him, and land was given to each householder in the new capital.

The present inhabitants of Amarapura settled here after the transfer, and are now engaged in the silk-weaving industry. The noise of the looms commences from the early morning, and work is carried on by busy house-wives late into the night.

Here the most beautiful silk pu-tsos or waist cloths are manufactured, so prized throughout the length and breadth of the country. To those interested in silk manufactures, a very instructive morning might be spent in strolling through the village, and as the looms stand, as a rule, under the shade of the trees or houses, every facility exists for a close inspection.

Before returning to Mandalay, the tourist should, if possible, visit the immense Chinese temple, the enormous sitting figure of Buddha, and the Maha-Thet-kya-yan-thi temple. A short description of each will now be given.

MAHA-THET-KYA-YAN-THI TEMPLE.—The best way to reach this temple, which is situated to the south of the village of Taung-tha-man, on the southern bank of the lake of the same name, is to take a boat or canoe from the village of Amarapura, the distance across the lake being about a mile and a half. It can also be reached by the lengthy wooden bridge which, a little to the west, spans the lake. As however, the bridge is old and shaky, and the planks incomplete, the boat journey will be preferable. The temple itself is an inferior and rude copy of the Ananda temple at Pagan, hence it is frequently called by that name.

It was built in the year 1211 B.E., or in 1849 A.D., by Pagan-Min—the immediate predecessor of Mindon Min—to enshrine the marble image of Guadama which he caused to be carved from the huge block of stone brought to Ava from the Sagyin Hills by order of King Ba-gyi-dau.

This immense stone was conveyed from the foot of the hills on a double boat raft, along a canal specially dug for it, and deposited at Ava.

From Ava it was brought via the Taung-tha-man lake to the neighbourhood of its present site, canals being specially constructed from the lake to the place where it now stands.

After being carved it was placed in position on the palin or pedestal by means of an inclined plane of earth, which was afterwards removed.

Some idea of the size of the original block of stone can be formed from the fact that the smaller images of Guadama which are enshrined in the colonnade which surrounds the pagoda platform were carved from the chips of the colossus. The images are about two feet high, and number about forty.

The following are the principal dimensions of the image as it now stands :—

MAHA THET KYA YAN THI TEMPLE, AMARAPURA.

(Photo by Seguor Beato, Mandalay.)

Height	16 feet, 9 inches.	
Width across knees	12 ,, 0 ,	
Length of thigh	6 ,, 4 ,,	
Circumference of head	12 ,, 6 ,,	
Circumference of arm	4 ,, 9 ,,	

The temple covers a base of 133 feet square and rises to a height of 115 feet, the *hti* or umbrella is 11 feet high with a circumference at the base of 9 feet, 6 inches. Enshrined in the pagoda are twelve gold and 358 silver images.

The above information was obtained from the dedication stone, a noble slab of marble 5 feet in height, 3½ feet in width, with a thickness of 13 inches, standing in the north-east angle of the colonnade which runs right round the limits of the pagoda platform.

In external appearance the Temple somewhat resembles the Ananda at Pagan.

The three porches or vestibules on the north, south and east sides are elaborately covered with carved stucco work, and each is provided with a lofty arched doorway with smaller ones on either side. The body of the building rises by two successive receding platforms to a height of 50 feet. From this four successive terraces rise to a height of 22 feet, succeeded by the mitre-shaped "sikra" 16 feet in height. This is crowned by an ordinary bell shaped pagoda 18 feet in height on the summit of which is the *hti*.

The corners of the lower terraces are ornamented with smaller pagodas with square bases, and those of the upper with imitation vases. At the top corners of the "Sikra" are crowned figures of the *manhù-seeha* or "lion men." The whole surface is whitewashed, so that the temple is a prominent object for a distance of several miles.

THE RESIDENCY.—In the grove of mango trees between this temple and the banks of the lake, is the site of the Residency in which Major Phayre, and the other members of the Embassy were entertained by the king in 1855. Nothing now remains of the buildings in which the Embassy and its followers were located for several months.

The following account of the buildings is taken *in extenso* from the description given by Captain Henry Yule, the secretary to the mission. " . . . . After the Myit-ngè was passed, the course lay through a curious zig-zag channel, until the lake on the south of the town was reached. About noon a bridge over the lake was reached, to which the vessels were moored. The further progress to the Residency, an abode specially fitted up for the Mission, was made on foot, although elephants which were in attendance, may have been employed. The distance did not exceed three-quarters of a mile, but the day was hot and oppressive, and the roads heavy with recent rain. The road was lined throughout, on both sides, with the Burmese militia, rough and shabby looking fellows, but all armed with muskets and *dhas*. The regulars or quasi-regulars, who continue on duty in the neighbourhood of the capital, were clad in red jerkins of coarse cloth, having tin bandoliers belted round the waist, and hard heavy broad-brimmed bell shaped hats of gilt or green lacquer on a bamboo sub-structure. The irregulars were armed in the same way, but clad more at discretion.

"The cavalry were ranged at wider intervals behind ; mean enough and unformidable they looked, poor fellows, on their shabby ponies armed with short spears and *dhas*. Some of the officers, however, were magnificent, if not military in display, with their gold-mounted, high pommelled saddles, having on each side, beneath the stirrup, a huge dependent flap of buffalo leather, brilliantly gilt or picked out with rampant dragons.

"Two *Wúngyis* and an *Atwin Wún* gave Major Phayre and his party a hearty welcome to the Residency, and tried to impress upon them the great solicitude His Majesty, Mindòn Min, felt for their comfort and happiness during their stay in Amarapura. The Mission Residency was enclosed in a matted bamboo paling some seventy to eighty feet square, with a gate on the east and west sides.

PAGODA, OLD AMARAPURA.

(*Photo by Signor Beato, Mandalay.*)

"Round the outside were sheds for some 600 Burmese soldiers who continued to be posted there during our stay; nominally for our protection, partly doubtless to watch our proceedings. Similar sheds, for our own escort and followers ran round the interior of the enclosure. The house itself was a very large bungalow with many roof-ridges and gables, between which, as we soon learned, copious discharges of rain descended on the rooms below. The skeleton was of substantial teak timber, walled and floored with bamboo. There were two very large public rooms, one of which was upwards of eighty feet long; but our party was rather unreasonably large, and the individual accommodations were somewhat scanty, even including two small cottages at each gate.

"The long front room, which we used as a dining-room, was adorned with large Chinese tubs, containing artificial trees covered with flowers and fruit. These represented jacks, loquots, mangoes, custard apples, peaches, etc., and the fruit was edible, or meant to be so, consisting of little rolls of sweets-meats suspended by loops of wire, intended (as we were informed) to be consumed and replaced daily. The trees, as models, were not badly done, and formed rather pretty decorations.

"The room was carpeted with stamped rugs of Chinese felt, was furnished with chairs, tables and a punka, and was hung with large Chinese lanterns and Anglo-Indian wall-shades. These were filled every evening with little yellow indigenous wax candles, not much superior to rush lights.

"Outside the saloon was a wide verandah looking down upon a spacious portico, and this portico was a theatre for our recreation. It was a great circular shed, with a conical roof supported by a central post, like that of a single poled tent. On the further side was a proscenium of blue cloth with gilt valance, and orthodox stage doors, adorned with gilt pilasters and pediment in the Burmese style. . . . In the theatre portico and in the verandahs stood immense silver water jars, each of the largest capable of holding a couple of men without difficulty.

" Huge silver ladles lay across the mouths for public use.
These jars had a truly royal appearance."

Such is the account given by Yule of the Residency,
prepared for the reception of the Embassy on the banks of the
Taung-tha-man Lake.

COLOSSAL FIGURE OF BUDDHA.—This enormous brick image
is situated near the Amarapura end of the wooden bridge which
spans the Taung-tha-man Lake, south of the old town.

It was erected by the Taung Mingyi, one of the chief
ministers of Pagan-Min, in the year 1214 B.E. or A.D. 1852.

It stands on an oblong pedestal nine feet high, and its
principal dimensions from actual measurements, are as follows :—

Total height	45 feet
Width at thighs	33 ,,
Width at shoulders	24 ,,
Diameter of head	12 ,,
Length of ears	9 ,,

The image is in a good state of preservation, and has been
lately cleared of jungle-growth and white-washed. The face has
a somewhat pleasing expression for such a monster. As is
usually the case, it faces the east.

In the next enclosure to the north, and not more than fifty
or sixty yards from the image, is a small pagoda built after the
shape of the Kaung-hmu-dau at Sagaing.

THAT-TA-TANA PAGODA.—This remarkable and unique
structure is situated in the grove to the north-east of the big
image, among a number of other pagodas and monastic buildings,
the majority of which are in ruins.

In design it is circular with four extended niches, in each of
which is a marble Gaudama.

Although only thirty feet in height, it consists of fifteen
receding tiers of niches containing small marble images of
Buddha. In the lowest row are forty-three images, and in the
highest sixteen. The summit is crowned by a *hti* of the usual
shape and construction.

It was erected in Pagan Min's reign by public subscription.

CHINESE TEMPLE.—This remarkable and curious building was erected about sixty years ago (1835 A.D.) during the reign of Tharrawaddi Min. It is situated in one of the shady streets of the old extra-mural city, close to the Amarapura railway station, and is surrounded by a massive brick wall about thirty-five feet high. The entrance is guarded by two quaint marble lions, one on either side. The chief doorway is circular in shape having a diameter of about twelve feet. The temple consists of three separate courtyards, one behind the other. At the northern end of each courtyard is a temple with a series of shrines, the principal one being the innermost. The large central image of white marble is the Buddhist rahanda Shin-û-pa-gôk, the ruler of the oceans and seas. Above this is the small image representing the principal deity Buddha. On either side of the principal shrine are rows of grotesque figures representing celebrated disciples of the great Teacher.

The two smaller chapels on either side and in separate courts, contain figures of demons, one of most ferocious aspect having three heads and six arms.

On either side of the shrines are racks containing curious brass and iron spears, clubs, pikes and halberts, while in front are brazen vessels of peculiar construction in which incense is burnt. The courtyards are open to the sky, are paved with flags and shaded by graceful trees which have apparently been planted for that purpose. The temple is superintended by a resident priest, who is most solicitous in his attentions to visitors. He has a few pupils, who come to the temple daily to receive instruction in the Chinese language.

PA-HTO-DAU-GYI PAGODA.—This lofty fane which is seen in close proximity to the railway line, was erected in the year 1829 A.D. by king Bo-dau-pya.

In a small shrine at the north-east corner of the platform is the dedication stone, which gives the history of the pagoda. From this we learn that its classical name is Maha-We-zeya-yan-thi pagoda, that its cost was 185,200 viss of silver, and its dimensions were as follows :—Base, 256 feet square. Height, 256 feet. Diameter of hti, 18½ feet.

Within it were enshrined relics of Buddha and 10,000 vessels of gold, silver, precious stones, and pearls.

It is without exception the most shapely pagoda in Upper Burma, and resembles much the Shwè-Dagôn or Shwè-Hmau-Dau of Lower Burma. The base consists of four successive receding terraces, at the corners of the lowest terrace are massive leogryphs, while the second and third terraces have gourd-shaped ornaments.

The fourth, or highest terrace, from which the stupa rises, is flanked at the corners by pagodas, about thirty feet in height, with square bases or plinths. On each of the four sides a flight of stone steps runs up to the topmost terrace, from which a commanding view is to be obtained of the surrounding country. The pagoda platform has a massive wall round it, with four porched gates, one facing each of the flights of steps already referred to. The whole exterior surface is white-washed and the precincts are kept scrupulously clean and free from rubbish and jungle growth.

The enormous crowds of worshippers at its annual festival are evidences of its sanctity.

ITINERARY.—Starting from the Amarapura station, cross the line at the level crossing east of the station, and proceed into the village towards the bank of the lake. While a boat is being prepared, turn up the village street to the left and have a look at the Chinese Temple or " Talôk Kyaung " as the Burmans call it. After an interesting ten minutes here, your boat will probably be ready, in which cross the lake to the opposite bank and make straight for the white Temple surrounded by a massive wall.

This is the Maha-Thet-kya-Yan-thi Temple, in which is enshrined the huge marble image. After an inspection of this temple and its surroundings, either return by boat to the Amarapura end of the lengthy wooden bridge, or proceed

PA-HTO-DAU-GYI, AMARAPURA.
(Photo by Signor Beato, Mandalay.)

towards the west to the southern end of the bridge and cross the lake by means of it. The colossal image will be seen close by on the Amarapura shore. The road to the village from the image runs past the That-ta-Tana Pagoda. Continue along the shady streets till you come to the Shwè-Lin-Bin Pagoda at the south-west corner of the old city walls, looking in *en route* at the Pa-to-dau Pagoda. Proceed along the cart-track outside the south wall, and enter the walled city by the south gate, making your way across the fields to the palace walls. After inspecting the cannon, etc., and palace buildings, make your way to the level crossing to the west of the palace walls. From here the return journey can be made along the line to the station.

If time permits, instead of returning to Amarapura, walk along the line towards Myohaung, and to the east of the railway line, which runs parallel to the eastern wall, you will come to the elephant keddah. A walk of about a mile and a half will bring you to the station at Myohaung, and thence you can return by train to Mandalay.

ROUTE XV.

TO MINGÛN.

Mingûn is a picturesque village, situated on the right bank of the Irrawaddi river, about nine miles above Mandalay.

It is celebrated for the ruins of an enormous unfinished brick pagoda, and a huge bell, both of which are within a few minutes walk of the bank of the river.

The name Mingûn signifies the "rustic or temporary palace," and was given because here Bo-dau-pya who reigned from 1781 to 1819, A.D., spent—on and off—more than twenty years in putting together the enormous pile of bricks, which is now called the

MINGÛN PAGODA.—As stated above, this pagoda was erected by King Bo-dau-pya, who himself laid the foundations, and superintended the work. It was intended to have been the biggest Buddhist pagoda in the world, and on it the king is said to have spent 10,000 viss of silver, notwithstanding that the workmen employed were all impressed by a system of covée, as was usual under the rule of these despotic kings. Captain Hiram Cox, who was a special envoy sent by the Governor-General of India in 1797 A.D., to the court of Bo-dau-pya, and resided for some months at Mingûn during the progress of this great work, has left a very lucid description of what he saw.

The lower storey was provided with several chambers for containing the sacred offerings and relics presented by the royal founder. The principal chamber had an area of 15 feet square, and a height of 10½ feet. The interior was lined with sheet-lead,

HUGE PAGODA, MINGÚN.

(*Photo by Native Photo., Mandalay.*)

and the top was composed of beams of lead five inches square. This device is said to have been the king's own. It is no wonder then that what was finished of the pagoda collapsed with such disastrous results when the great earthquake of 1839 took place.

The Burmese represent that endless and priceless treasures were deposited in the chambers, but Cox, who was an eye-witness, tells us that most of the gifts were very inferior— images, said to have been of gold and silver, but which on closer inspection proved to be a less valuable metal, marble images, plated models of pagodas and kyaungs, sheets of coloured glass, white umbrellas, and a soda-water machine !

After many years had been spent on its construction, and it had reached one-third of the proposed height, the work was suddenly abandoned in consequence it is said of a prediction of the pònnas or Brahmins of the court, who foretold that when the pagoda was finished the king would die. In this unfinished state it lies to the present day, a hideous mass of unsightly ruin. It covers an area of about 450 feet square, and its total height is 162 feet, or one-third of the total height proposed.

The plinth consists of five successive low terraces, from the upper one of which, with sides of 230 feet, the cubical pile rises. Towards the top it contracts in successive terraces, and here the work ends.

The effects of the earthquake are plainly visible. The north-east corner has entirely collapsed, and masses of masonry like huge boulders lie about in endless confusion.

A somewhat slippery and dangerous footpath leads up this rent to the top of the ruin.

On each of the four sides are niches of enormous size, ornamented similarly to the throne, in which gigantic images would have been placed.

In a grove of trees near the ruin is a miniature of the structure, from which the intentions of the founder can be clearly seen.

THE MINGÛN BELL.—In close proximity to the pagoda is the immense bell cast by Bo-dau-pya to match the pagoda. It is said to be the second biggest bell in the world. The principal dimensions are :—

			Ft.	In.
External diameter at lip	...	...	16	3
Internal „ 4ft. 8in. above	...		10	0
Interior height	...	...	11	6
Exterior „	...	...	12	0
Internal diameter at top	...	...	8	1

Thickness of metal, from 6 to 12 inches.
Weight, 55,500 Viss, or nearly 80 tons.

It was cast on the opposite side of the river, on an island called Nan-dau-kyûn, and was brought over on two boats to the Mingûn side. Canals were cut for the passage of the boats to the present site, the mouths of which, after the entrance of the boats, were dammed up. The level of the water in the canals was then raised by partially filling them in, and the bell brought into position between the immense posts and beams which were erected for its support.

After the huge beams had been passed through the shackles the dams were removed, the boats subsided, and the bell remained suspended. Owing, doubtless, to the severe earthquakes mentioned above, the bell was thrown down, and now lies resting on its lip, at a slight angle, leaving between it and the ground a narrow passage, through which a tolerably thin individual can with some discomfort squeeze.

Burmese bells have no clappers, but are struck with a deer's horn or billet of wood on the exterior of the lip. As Yule says, it would require a battering ram to elicit the music and tone of this monster.

Peculiarities of construction are noticed by closely scrutinizing it. The upper part appears to have been strengthened by running the metal through coils of chain. This is observable from the interior. Patches of white and yellow

IMMENSE BELL AT MINGÛN.

(Photo by Square Bros. Mandalay.)

metal seen in different parts of the surface are evidently
unmolten lumps of gold or silver, thrown in at the time of
casting. The same custom prevails at the present day, when
images or bells are cast.

In front of the big pagoda are the ruins of the two
immense leogryphs on either side of the steps leading from
the river. These were originally 95 feet high, and the marble
eyes, Cox tells us, were 13 feet in circumference.

Since the above description was written, steps have been
taken by the district magistrate to obtain funds for raising
the bell. The appeal having been generously responded to
by all classes of the community, and sufficient funds having
been raised, the committee appointed to superintend the work
entered into a contract with the Irrawaddy Flotilla Company
to raise the bell, and rehang it on iron pillars. The work of
raising it by means of powerful screw-jacks and levers was
successfully accomplished in March, 1896, and the massive iron
columns and beams from which the bell will depend are now
being cast at the Flotilla Company's works at Dalla, opposite
Rangoon. The beams and pillars have been made of a strength
sufficient to support a hanging weight of 100 tons—a weight
exceeding by 20 tons the estimated weight of the bell.

As it has no clapper it will perhaps be necessary to
provide some mechanical contrivance to elicit sound from its
huge lips.

In connection with the raising of the bell, a feast was
held at Mingûn in the month of March, 1896, which was
attended by crowds of Burmans, and also by the European
residents of Mandalay. During the continuance of the feast,
the Irrawaddy Flotilla Company, with their usual foresight, ran
hourly steamers, day and night, between Mandalay and Mingûn,
and *vice versâ*.

Behind the pagoda rise two parallel ranges of picturesque
hills, crowned in most instances with pagodas. The highest
point is about 1,373 feet, and from this summit a magnificent view

of the surrounding country, with the Ruby Mines Hills, the Set-kya-daung in Myingyan, and the Kyauksè Hills are plainly visible.   The principal pagodas in the neighbourhood are :—

1.   Ain-dauya-Paya, 75 feet high, built in 1662 A.D. by King Maha Dhama Raja.

2.   Set-dauya-Paya, 75 feet high, built by Bo-dau-pya in 1790 A.D.

3.   Sinbyu-mè Pagoda, 105 feet high, also built by Bo-dau-pya in 1790 A.D.

4.   Shwè-Myindin Pagoda, 38 feet high, built in 1056 A.D.

5.   Sûdaung-pyi Pagoda, also 38 feet high, and built at the same time by the same king.

ITINERARY.—There are two ways of making the trip to Mingûn and back.   The most expeditious is to hire a launch from the Marine Transport Officer at the shore, or from the Irrawaddy Flotilla Company, whose office is close to the shore.   Failing to obtain a launch, take a gharry to Obo village, at the extreme north of the bund, and from here cross the river to Mingûn on the opposite bank.   The charge for a boat there and back would not be more than a couple of rupees.

MODEL OF MINGÛN PAGODA.

(Photo by Signor Beato, Mandalay.)

ROUTE XVI.

AVA.

Ava, or In-wa, is situated on the left bank of the Irrawaddi, and is at present included in the Sagaing district, opposite which town the ruins of the old city lie.

The historical name is Ratana-pura, or "City of Gems," and in poetical language it is called Shwè-wa, or the "Golden Entrance."

HISTORY.—The city of Ava was founded in A.D. 1364 by Thado-min-bya, a prince descended from the ancient Tagaung dynasty. He conquered the Shan kingdoms of Panya and Sagaing, into which the country was then divided.

It continued to be the chief residence of the kings who ruled in Upper Burma, with various intervals up to the end of the last century, and became so celebrated that the kingdom, of which it was the capital, was generally designated the kingdom of Ava. Lord Dufferin, during whose Vice-Royalty the ancient kingdom was annexed, took his title as Marquess of Ava.

Nicolo de Conte, a Venetian traveller, was the first European who visited the city. He was there in A.D. 1440. In 1526 the capital was taken by the Shans of Mohnyin and Mogaung, who held it till 1554, in which year Sin-Byu-Mya-Shin ("Owner of many white elephants") King of Taungù, took possession of the city and thoroughly destroyed it. On the breaking up and dismemberment of the kingdom of Pegu in 1601, Nyaung-Min, a natural son of Sin-Byu-Mya-Shin, re-established the city and kingdom.

M

In 1751 Ava was again captured by the Peguans, or Talaings, when the Burman King, Maha-Dhamma-Raza-Tibati, was taken prisoner, conveyed in triumph to Pegu, and subsequently murdered. The Talaings held the city only for a few months, when they were expelled by Alaungpya, who occupied it with his forces in December 1753.

Alaungpya, however, fixed on his native place, Môksobo, as his capital, and when Ava was visited by Captain Baker, a British Envoy, in 1755, he found it to contain only about a thousand families, and no buildings of any importance.

On the accession of Sin-byû-shin, the third son of Alaungpya, in 1763, Ava again became the seat of Government, and remained so till 1783, when Bo-dau-Pya removed to his new capital, Amarapura. In 1822, however, a disastrous fire devastated the city and destroyed many of the public buildings. A vulture also alighted on the "*Shwè-Pyathat,*" which incident was declared by the Brahmin astrologers to be a bad omen. Consequently the king was advised to rebuild Ava. In 1823 Ava was therefore re-occupied, and remained the capital till 1837, when Tharrawaddi removed to Amarapura.

Since that time the city has gradually deteriorated, and its once beautiful temples and other buildings have been allowed to fall into ruin. The city was in reality built on an island at the mouth of the Myit-ngè or Dota-watti river. An artificial channel called the Myit-tha Chaung was dug from the Myit-ngè to the Irrawaddi river, cutting off the corner, on which the city was built. Two walls, the outer and the inner, inclose the city.

On the north or river face, the outer wall ran regularly along the bank of the Irrawaddi, and was a mile and a half in length. The south-east and west walls were each about a mile in length, but, unlike the walls of Amarapura or Mandalay ran irregularly, the east and west walls converging in irregular alignments towards the south. The inner city wall was oblong in shape and its northern and eastern sides were those of the outer city. These walls were about half a mile square.

The palace occupied the centre of the inner city, and was enclosed by its own special brick wall, surrounded by a moat, the water being supplied from the Myit-ngè river.

Of the palace buildings the "*Nan-Myin*" or palace watch tower is the only one remaining. It suffered much from the great earthquake of 1839 and is now considerably out of the perpendicular.

The outer city walls abutting the Irrawaddi are still in a fair state of preservation, but the inner wall, and that surrounding the palace, are in ruins. The space between the two walls is now occupied by smiling fields of maize and other crops, interspersed amongst which are scattered hamlets, many still bearing Talaing names—ruined monasteries, temples, and pagodas, amid avenues and groves of magnificent tamarind trees.

The scene on entering the deserted city is exceedingly pretty. Level spaces of green sward are intermingled with patches of cultivation, while on all sides avenues and clumps of shady trees are to be seen.

The principal temples in and around the old city are :—

Laûka-thara-pu, Thin-ban Paya, Laûka-Manaung, Yatana-Manaung, Zina-Manaung, Nga-Manaung, Shwe-zi-Gòn Pagoda.

LAÛKA-THARA-PU is situated to the west of the inner city, and forms a prominent landmark for a distance of many miles, both from the river and the interior. This pagoda was never finished, the founder having died before its completion.

During the troublous times of 1886-87 it was used as a watch-tower and signal-station by the British troops, and to gain access to the flat summit a flight of steps was cut in the solid mass of the pagoda.

The pagoda is surrounded by a massive brick wall enclosing the courtyard of quadrangular shape, each of the four walls having in its centre a porched entrance surmounted by a *pyathat* of stucco work.

The other pagodas mentioned are situated to the south of the old city, and are all more or less in a state of ruin.

M 2

A long wooden bridge with massive causeways and retaining walls of brick runs from the south gate to the important suburb of Tada-û, which is the head-quarters of the township, and enjoys considerable trade.

THE FORTS.

There are two of these—one situated on raised ground east of the old city near the right bank of the Myit-ngè, which here enters the Irrawaddi ; the other to the west of the city walls, in close proximity to the main river. These forts were constructed by French or Italian engineers in the service of Mindôn Min.

The one to the west is in a good state of preservation, and has masonry walls and fosse of considerable strength, supported by earthen ramparts.

The fort is quadrangular in shape, each side measuring 165 yards. Underground chambers beneath the gun platforms were constructed for the protection and storage of ammunition. The guns, forming the armament of the fort, now lie unmounted and broken on the glacis. They are of cast iron, having a calibre of about $2\frac{1}{2}$ inches. All of these guns have one or both trunnions missing. They were thus treated on the surrender of the fort to the British on the 27th November, 1885. The gun carriages are now lying beneath an old kyaung in the eastern part of the city.

During the progress of the British expedition up the Irrawaddi in November, 1885, it was fully anticipated that severe opposition would be offered at this formidable redoubt.

The failure on the part of the Burmese troops to stop the advance of the British steamers beyond Myingyan, where earthworks nearly a mile in length had been constructed along the bank of the river, had been telegraphed to the king.

On the afternoon of the 26th November, 1885, the Pangyet Wûn, with several other officials, arrived from Mandalay with despatches from the Kin-Wûn-mingyi treating for peace, but without success.

The next morning the flotilla advanced to Ava, where from the activity displayed at the fort, a big fight was anticipated ; however, just as all preparations had been made, a flag of truce was hoisted, and the General was informed that a telegram had been received from the capital that no opposition was to be offered. British troops were subsequently landed, the fort was occupied, and the garrison, consisting of over one thousand men, disarmed.

SIN-BYU-MA-SEIN'S KYAUNG.—This handsome and massive masonry kyaung is situated within the outer walls of the city at the north-east corner, and is a conspicuous object from the deck of passing steamers. As its name implies it was erected by Sin-Byu-Ma-Sein, one of Mindôn Min's queens,—the mother of Sûpyalat, the chief queen of King Thibaw. The site was formerly that of the *Thathana-baing's* monastery, and hence was of special sanctity.

In shape the building is oblong, and consists of three successive receding floors or terraces, from the uppermost one of which the various apartments rise. A lofty corridor runs right round the building, communicating with the open terrace or verandah by many arched doorways. The roofs are five in number, and each is surrounded by a cornice of stucco work with the usual horn-shaped tips or corners.

The Kyaung was formerly occupied by from forty to fifty resident monks, but has for some years been abandoned, owing, it is said, to its being haunted. During the "*wa*" or season of Lent, the kyaung is, however, still used by the people of the neighbourhood as a quiet resort in which to pass the day and to fast.

SET-KYA-THI-HA SITE.—This is situated close to the Sandamûni Pagoda in the south-east corner of the outer city. It contained the huge marble image of Buddha similar to the one removed in 1885 from Amarapura to Mandalay.

ROUTE XVII.

SHWÈBO.

The town of Shwèbo is situated in the centre of the district of the same name, and is 16½ miles west of Kyauk-myaung on the Irrawaddi.

The Mû Valley railway runs right through the town, the distance by rail from Mandalay being about sixty-five miles inclusive of the ferry journey from Amarapura to Sagaing.

The modern town of Shwèbo is situated in the south-west corner of the old city walls, the civil station being to the east of the old city, and the cantonments on the high ground about two miles to the north-east.

It forms the head-quarters of the Shwèbo district, and contains the Court and Offices of the Deputy Commissioner and the Courts and Offices subordinate to him, a District Jail, Dispensary, Civil and Military police lines, Mission stations of the Church of England and Roman Catholic communities, and a good sized Railway station. For the convenience of travellers a Dâk Bungalow in close proximity to the Railway station is maintained by Government. The population of the town in 1891 was 9,368.

In 1888 Shwèbo was constituted a municipality, the committee consisting of six *ex-officio* members, and eight members appointed by the Local government.

The Cantonment, as stated above, is at some distance from the town, its affairs being managed by the military authorities.

Of the old city but little remains besides the ruined walls, and the moat surrounding it on all sides. Like other ancient

PLAN OF
SHWEBO

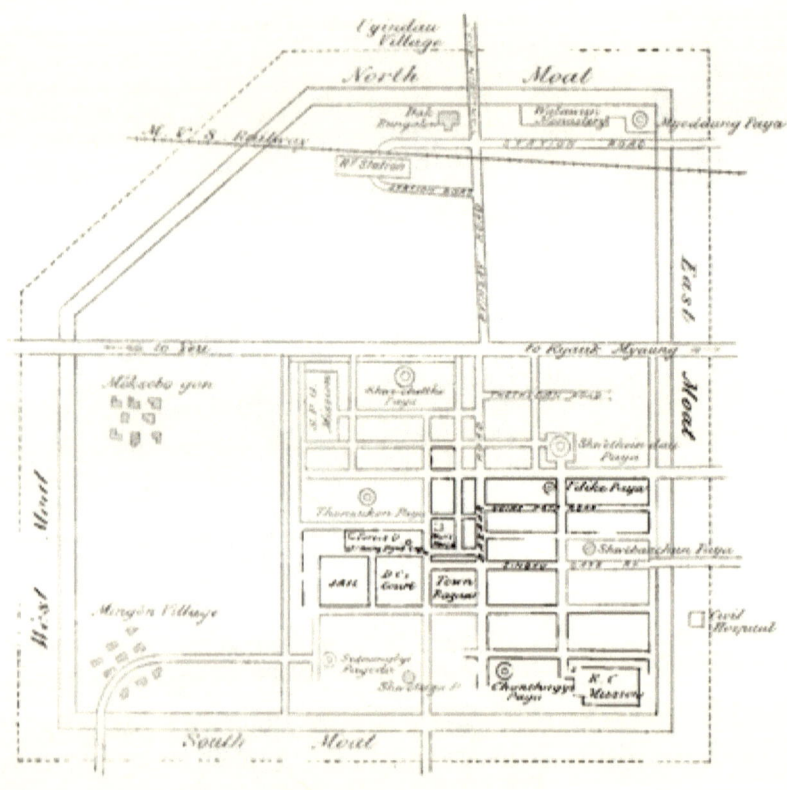

capitals in Burma the city was built in the form of a square, the north-west corner, however, was cut off. The whole was surrounded by a wall, outside of which was a broad and deep moat. The walls on the east and south sides were each 2¼ miles in length, each having three gates. The northern and western walls were not so long, owing, as already stated, to the fact that the north-west corner was cut off. In the centre of the city stood the Palace, surrounded by a brick wall, the remains of which, especially on the west and north sides, are still to be seen. The palace site is where the Jail now stands. Near the west wall and within the old city is the village of Môksobo-gôn, where Alaungpya, the "Napoleon of Burma," and the founder of the city was born.

Between the present Court-house and the office of the Public Works Department stands a modest shrine of wood, similar to the *pyathat* erected in monasteries. Beneath this lie the remains of the mighty conqueror.

HISTORY OF SHWÈBO.

The rise of Shwèbo and the building of the city commence with the history of its founder, Alaungpya.

In 1751 A.D., during the reign of the Talaing King Pyinya-Dalla, the Kingdom of Ava was invaded. An army of 60,000 Talaings, with a large flotilla, ascended the Irrawaddi, the land forces marching along the western bank of that river. The army was commanded by Yûva Raja, the younger brother of the King, with Talaban, a celebrated Talaing general, as second in command.

Having assembled at Sagaing, the army crossed over to the investment of Ava. After burning the outer city, the gates of the inner city were forced, and the King and his queens taken prisoners.

The city was looted and thoroughly destroyed, the bulk of the army returned to the lower province, carrying with them the captive King, and a garrison under Talaban was left, with orders to consolidate the Talaing power in the upper province. Previous to the departure of Yûva Raja a proclamation had been issued announcing the establishment of Talaing rule, and calling upon all officers of the late Government to repair to the capital (Ava) to take the oath of allegiance to the King of Pegu. To more distant places special messengers were sent to administer the oath on the spot.

The principal officer of Môksobo-gôn at the time was one Aung-zè-ya. He was exceedingly ambitious and patriotic, so, when the Talaings arrived to administer the oath, he entertained them favourably; but at night, when they were all asleep in his house, he had them killed.

Having committed himself in this way, Aung-zè-ya gathered a few adherents around him to resist the 300 Talaings who had been sent by Talaban to avenge the murder of his ambassadors. These were ambushed by Aung-zè-ya near the old city of Halin, a few miles south-east of Môksobo-gôn, and a great many were killed. This success brought large numbers to his standard when he took the offensive, and, as history relates, drove the Talaings out of the upper province, and finally subjugated the whole of what is now called Burma. He then assumed the kingly title, and was crowned as Alaungpya *(the Embryo Buddha)*. It is the Burmese rendering of the Pali title *Bodisativa*, or Buddha elect. As was to have been expected, Môksobo was made the capital of Alaungpya's empire, and the surrounding district was most favoured by him and his successors.

The city now called Shwèbo had five titles conferred on it.

1. Yathana-theinga, *i.e.*, the place where the ten precious things are collected.

2. Kôn-Baung, so called from a ridge of elevated ground in the neighbourhood, running north and south.

3. Môksobo, the hunter's village.

4. Yan-gyi-aung, in memory of the victory over, and subjugation of the Talaings.

5. Shwèbo.

The current report that Aung-zéya was by profession a hunter, and in consequence his village—which afterwards became his capital—was called Môksobo, is not founded on fact. The village of Môksobo existed long before his time.

The city established by Alaungpya flourished as long as its founder lived. On his death in May, 1760, Naung-dau-gyi, his eldest son, who succeeded to the throne, made Sagaing his capital; but Sin-byu-shin, who succeeded in 1763, re-transferred the capital to Môksobo Myo. After his death, Ava, and then Amarapura, were successively the capitals, and it was not till Tharrawaddi seized the throne, with the help of men from Shwèbo, that a new interest was taken in the place. In commemoration of the help he had received from the Shwèbo people, he took the title of Kôn-baung-min.

Shwèbo again came to the front, when in 1853 Mindôn Min, with the aid of men from this district, raised a rebellion, and succeeded in ousting his half-brother Pugan-min from the throne.

In 1867, the Padaing Prince, son of the Crown Prince, who had been assassinated in the Summer Palace, escaped being massacred and fled to Shwèbo, where he raised the standard of rebellion against the King. He ultimately surrendered himself, and was executed within the Royal city.

Acting on precedent, it is stated that Sùpya-lat used all her persuasive power on Thibaw to induce him to flee to Shwèbo on the approach of the English army in 1885.

The districts of Hladau, Tabayin, Tazè, Yeù, and Shwèbo itself furnished the best fighting men in the whole country, and it took several years after the annexation for the British Government to disperse and break up the numerous parties of gang-robbers and rebels, which infested the country. This part of the country is now the most peaceful and orderly in the whole of Upper Burma.

In the king's time the city and district were governed by a W'ùn, appointed by the king himself.

At the time of the annexation, the *Wûn* in power was Boh Byin. He at once tendered his submission, as did also his subordinates, to the British General, and was of great assistance in the settlement of the country.

He was awarded a pension by Government, and two of his sons are now in Government service, one being Maung Tûn, K.S.M., the present town-ship officer of Shwèbo.

Boh Byin died in the early part of the current year (1895).

Of objects of interest Shwèbo has but few. The ruined walls of city and palace can still be traced.

The old "Hlûtdaw" or Supreme Court, which stood near the bazaar, collapsed last year. The shabby lop-sided *pyathat* near the Court-house, marks the last resting-place of the ashes of the great Alaungpya.

The large house and compound surrounded by a bamboo fence in the centre of the town was the residence of the Governor Boh Byin.

Of pagodas the following are the principal :—Shwè-taya, Sû-taung-Byi, Shwè-Chet-tho, Thôn-Sûkôn, Walû-wûn, Myo-daung, Shwè-thein-dan and Shwè-bau-kyûn. A short description of the principal of these will now be given :—

SHWÈ-TAZA PAGODA.—This shrine is situated close to the south wall, within the old city. It was erected by Alaungsithu, the grandson of Kyanvit-tha, in the year A.D. 1091. During the reign of Bo-dau-pya it was renovated and embellished by the Alôn Wûn, Û-Set-Po, who was known in Shwèbo as Nè-Win-Bayin (" Lord of the setting sun.")

An annual festival is held at the full moon of *Waso* (July).

SÛTAUNG-PYI PAGODA.—Situated opposite to the south-west gate of the city, within the walls.

It has no particular history. An annual festival is held in the month of *Wagaung* (August).

SHWÈ CHET-THO PAGODA.—This pagoda was built by Alaungpya, after he rose to power. It is situated nearly in the centre of the city, and is covered with white-wash.

ALAUNGPYA'S BIRTHPLACE, SHWEBO.

(Photo by Seymour Bence. Mandalay.)

A festival is held annually in the month of September.

THÔN-SÔ-KÔN PAGODA.—This pagoda is situated between the jail and the Society for the Propagation of the Gospel Mission grounds.

Originally three small pagodas were erected in close proximity to one another on a rising piece of ground.

During the reign of Mindôn Min, he ordered the present pagoda to be erected, enclosing the three original ones, and enshrined within the later erection was an image carved from one of the original posts of Alaungpya's palace. The pagoda is now covered with white-wash, and a festival is held in its honour in the month of October.

WALAWÛN MONASTERY.—This monastery is situated in the extreme north-east corner of the city walls, and in close proximity to the Myo-daung pagoda. It was founded many years ago, and is mentioned on the stone inscription at the Maha-Nanda Lake, as having received certain benefits.

MYO-DAUNG PAGODA.—As the name implies, is situated at the north-east corner of the city walls. It is said to enshrine an emerald alms-bowl of Gaudama, which was brought from Pegu by Alaungpya, and is now shabby and neglected.

SHWÈ-BAU-CHÛN PAGODA is situated close to the east wall within the city.

It was built by Naung-dau-gyi, eldest son of Alaungpya, in the year 1790, is covered with white-wash, and has an annual festival held in the month of *Wagaung* (August).

SHWÈ-THEIN-DAN PAGODA is situated to the north of Shwè-bau-chûn, and has no special history. The annual festival takes place in the month of *Tawthalin* (September).

MISSION STATIONS.—The Church of England Mission was established by the Society for the Propagation of the Gospel in Foreign Parts, in the year 1887.

The Roman Catholic Mission was established many years ago, and a new church and mission house have lately been erected.

MAHA NANDA LAKE.—This large lake is situated about a mile to the north of Shwèbo town, and has a length of about two miles, with a breadth of one mile.

According to the inscription erected by Mindòn Min, which is set up on the bank of the lake, it was originally dug by order of Narapiti, whose son Anaurhata (not the Pagan monarch) ruled in Ratana-singa. This was in the year 572 A.D. Alaung-tsithu, king of Pagan, in 1151 A.D., extended and repaired the lake, and adapted it for irrigation purposes.

He also caused to be dug the Gyogya, Singut, and Kadu tanks. The Palaing tank was dug by Patama-Min-Khaung and the Yimba tank by Dûtiya-Min-Khaung who reigned in 1480 A.D.

By repairing all these tanks, providing sluices and irrigation channels, Mindòn Min, in a manner, compensated the Shwèbo people for the help they had given him in seizing the throne from his half-brother Pagan Min, in 1853 A.D.

Steps are now being taken by the Officers of the Irrigation branch of the Public Works Department, to put these tanks in a state of repair. Dûtiya-Min-Khaung caused a canal to be dug from the Mû River to convey water into the Palaing tank.

The Mû however has twice changed its channel since this work was carried out, and where the river formerly flowed is now a dense jungle, known as the Mû-dain-tau (Shallow Mû Jungle).

When Mindòn Min resided at Shwèbo, prior to his accession to the throne, he inspected these works, and in 1857 repaired the embankment of the canal, but the force of the waters seeking entrance into the Mûdain jungles in the floods was so great that the bunds gave way, and no efforts were afterwards made to repair them.

HALIN-MYO.—The site of this ancient city, the classical name of which was *Hanlha-nagara*, is a little to the south of the modern village of Halin, about twelve miles south-east of Shwèbo.

Tradition says that 799 kings reigned in this city. It was founded soon after the death of Guadama Buddha by In-za-thè-na (commonly called Kûla-pan-min) who came from Benares.

The remains of the city wall are still to be traced. The modern village contains 2,276 inhabitants who are chiefly engaged in the manufacture of salt.

Brine springs are numerous, and the remarkable phenomena of hot and cold springs of water issuing from the ground in close proximity to one another are seen. The earth around the brine springs is like jelly, and shakes like a blanc-mange if pressed with the foot.

ROUTE XVIII.

PAGAN.

The ruined city of Pagan is situated on the left bank of the Irrawaddi, about eighteen miles below the modern town of Pakôkkû.

The remains of an endless number of pagodas, temples, monasteries, and other religious buildings, extend along the river bank from the cliffs above Nyaungû on the north, for a distance of eight miles, with a breadth of nearly four miles.

The City of Pagan itself was surrounded by a wall and rampart on all sides. The remains of this wall, with the gates (twelve in all), are still to be traced on the north, east, and south sides. The wall on the west side abutted immediately on the river bank, the channel at that time skirting the hills to the west ; of late years the channel has shifted to the Pagan side, and in consequence of the erosion of the bank, the wall on the river face has long since disappeared into the river, the bank being strewn for a long distance with its remains.

Before attempting to describe the former glories of this ancient city, it will be necessary to give a historical summary of its foundation and growth, as far as it has been possible to ascertain from the records of the Maha Razawin or Royal Chronicles, the translation of stone inscriptions which are very numerous around and within the ruined shrines, and the traditions gleaned from the present inhabitants of the locality.

History.—The ancient and powerful monarchy of Tharet-khettara (near the modern town of Prome), came to an end about

PLAN OF
PAGAN

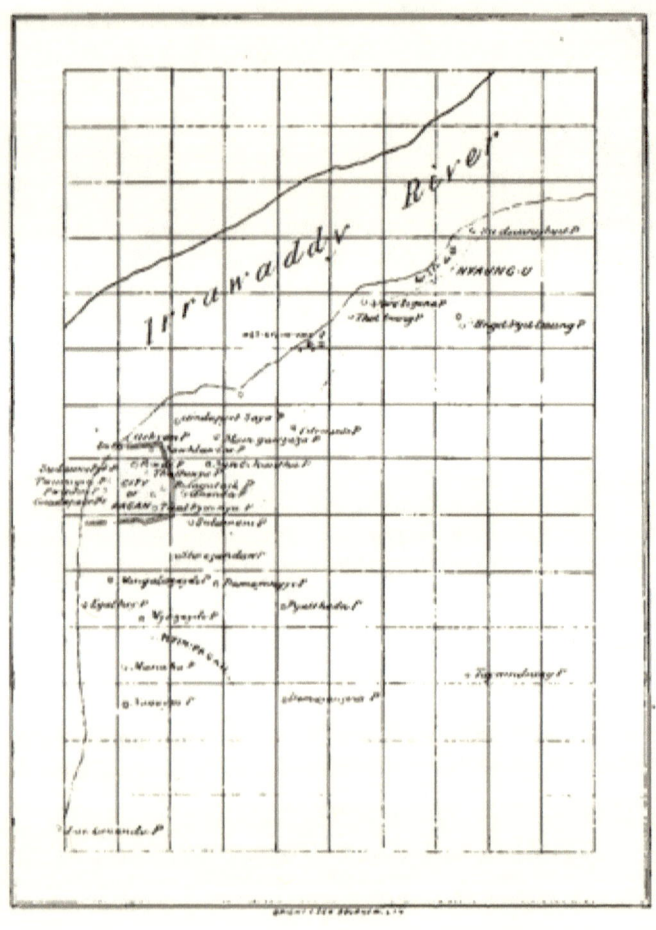

95 A.D. The kingdom at that time was composed of three powerful tribes, the Pyû, Kanran, and Mramma. It is conjectured, either that civil war led to their dispersion, or, what is more probable, that the kingdom was invaded and conquered by the Talaings from Pegu or Suvanna Bhumi, of which the capital was Thatòn (see Route VIII).

From whatever cause the dissolution took place, the tribes separated. The Pyû, under their leader Thamûd-darit, a nephew of Thû-pinya, the last King of Tharetkhettara, fled to the north and established themselves in the neighbourhood of the modern Pagan.

The capital was fixed at Paukaya-Myo, near the present village of Taungvè, between Nyaungû and Taung-Yin. Nineteen villages united to form the capital.

The country at this time was said to be over-run with fabulous monsters and other terrors, which are called to this day by the superstitious natives the *Yan-thû-Nga-û*, *i.e.*, the five enemies. These were a fierce tiger, an enormous boar, a flying dragon, a prodigious man-eating bird, and a huge creeping pumpkin, which threatened to entangle the whole country.

The five "enemies" were destroyed by Pyû-saw-di, a prince of the old Tagaung dynasty, who had lain hidden in the village of Malè after the destruction of Tagaung by the invaders from the east. He came down the Irrawaddi accompanied by his tutor, Yathè-gyaung, and, as stated above, slew and destroyed the "enemies" of the people, and married the daughter of Thamûd-darit.

On the death of the latter, however, Yathè-gyaung was permitted to assume the kingly power, but on his death, Pyû-saw-di ascended the throne, and is said to have reigned for 75 years. The fabulous beasts already referred to were no doubt different powerful tribes of aborigines successively overcome by Pyû-saw-di, in the consolidation of his kingdom.

During the reign of Thin-lè-gyaung, the seventh king of the dynasty, the capital was removed to Kyauksaya, the new city then founded being named Tha-yi-pittasa (a village of this name still exists three miles south of Myin-Pagan). This city remained the capital till Theik-daing-min's reign, the eleventh king of the dynasty, when it was removed to Thamadi and named Tampawadi. The present village of Pwa-Zaw stands on this site, and a pagoda in the neighbourhood is still called the Thamadi pagoda.

On the death of Htûn-kyet, the eighteenth king of the dynasty, one of his chief Queens married a priest, who ascended the throne under the title of Thingayaza. It was he who established the Burmese era in use at the present day, which commenced in the month of March, 639 A.D. Shwe Ôn, the son of Htûn-kyet had fled to the village of Palin, four miles up the river, and was subsequently recalled to the capital, when he married Thingayaza's daughter and succeeded to the throne.

For the next 200 years few events of importance happened. Pyin-bya, the thirty-third king, who ascended the throne in A.D. 839, founded the city of Pagan, which remained the capital till the extinction of the dynasty by the Shans in 1298 A.D., a period of 450 years. The classic name of this city was *Pâgama*, and of the kingdom *Ari-mad-dana*, *Tampadipa*, and *Puga-rama*.

Pyin-bya was succeeded in A.D. 871 by his son, Tan-net, who was assassinated by a groom, in his stables, named Nga Kwè, a descendant of Thingayaza's, who had been brought up in obscurity at Salè. After the murder of the king he ascended the throne under the title of Salè-min-kwè. One of Tannet's queens, however, who at the time was pregnant, fled to the village of Kyaung-bya, on the opposite side of the river, where she gave birth to a son, who afterwards ascended the throne under the title of Kyaung-Byû. He seized the throne by treachery, putting Taung-thû-gyi, the king to death, and marrying his three chief queens. Two of these were *enceinte*, and subsequently gave birth to Kyi-so and Sok-katè. The third queen bore a son, Anaurhata-zaw, who became so famous in the history of Pagan. Kyi-so and Sok-katè attaining to manhood, forced Kyaung-Byû to abdicate, when they both successively occupied the throne.

Anaurhata had fled to Popa, where he raised an army, and marched against Pagan, defeating and killing Sok-katè in a pitched battle fought near the village of Pwa-Zaw. He then ascended the throne as the 40th King of the Pagan dynasty (A.D. 1010.)

During a period of 269 years, from the time Anaurhata ascended the throne to the Shan invasion in 1279 A.D., twelve kings reigned in Pagan, and as it was at this time that the monarchy was in the zenith of its glory, and most of the religious buildings, now for the most part in ruins were constructed, a short summary of each reign will be given :—

ANAURHATA ZAW, 1010 to 1052 A.D.—It was during the reign of this king that the Kingdom of Pagan was consolidated and the Buddhist religion was firmly established.

The country, on the accession of Anaurhata, was filled with dragon worshippers, whose priests were called "Ari." This corrupt worship Anaurhata determined to extirpate. His religious zeal was excited by the preachings of a celebrated Buddhist priest, named Arahan, who arrived at the capital from Thatôn. The King was converted, and in his zeal expelled the false priests of Ari, and invited learned Rahans from Thatôn to settle in his dominions. He then sent Ambassadors of high status to Manûha, the King of Thatôn, begging for a copy of the *Tripitika*, or Buddhist Canon. His messengers were haughtily received by Manûha, who refused to comply with Anaurhata's request. On this, Anaurhata's anger being aroused, an expedition was fitted out and despatched for the conquest of Thatôn, and the acquisition of the coveted scriptures. After a siege, lasting several months, the city was taken and utterly destroyed. King Manûha, his wives and children, his nobles, priests, and artificers, were carried away in triumph to Pagan, together with five elephant loads of the sacred books, and an innumerable following, designed by the king to erect similar temples to those he had seen at Thatôn in his capital.

As many of the inhabitants of Thatôn were either of pure Hindoo or mixed origin, these were included in those brought into captivity. This fact accounts for the distinctive Hindoo type of architecture to be met with in many of the principal shrines erected during this period.

This king spread his dominion from Bengal to Yûnnan, and died in 1052 A.D., after a remarkable and eventful reign of forty-two years. He is said to have been gored to death by a wild buffalo.

TSAW-LU, 1052 to 1057 A.D.—This king was killed by his foster-brother, Nga-Ra-man, Governor of Pegu, who revolted and captured Pagan. Nga-Ra-man was, however, defeated and killed by Kyan-yit-tha, the brother of Tsaw-Lu.

KYAN-YIT-THA, 1057 to 1058 A.D.—This king is generally accepted as a legitimate son of Anaurhata, by a daughter of the King of Vaisali in Tirhoot, but common report states that he was the son of Yazataman, the Ambassador sent by the king, who had courted and married the princess on the journey from India. Anaurhata however did not know of this, and the princess was received into the palace, and after a time gave birth to Kyan-yit-tha.

During this king's reign of twenty-eight years, the kingdom of Pagan reached the zenith of its prosperity, and many of the largest and most beautiful of the Pagan pagodas and temples were erected by him. Of these the most celebrated are the Ananda and the Shwè-Zi-Gôn.

ALAUNG-TSI-THU, 1085 to 1160 A.D.—He was the grandson of Kyan-yit-tha and is credited with having reigned for seventy-five years. He invaded Arakan and placed Let-ya-min-nan on the throne. A stone inscription in Burmese at the Maha-Baudi Temple of Buddha-Gaya near Patna, records the pledge of homage made by Letya-min-nan to Alaung-tsi-thu.

During this king's reign the Shwe-gû and That-pin-yû Temples were erected at Pagan. He is said to have been brought to the Shwè-gû Temple when very old and feeble, and there smothered in a heap of clothes by his younger son Nara-thû.

NARA-THÛ OR KULA-KYA-MIN, 1160 to 1164 A.D.—Narathû was the younger son of Alaung-tsi-thû, the elder, Min-shin-zaw having left Pagan and settled in the neighbourhood of the modern Amarapura. On his father's death he came down to Pagan, was graciously received by Nara-thû, but the same night was poisoned. Nara-thû was the builder of the huge unfinished Dhama-yan-gyi Temple.

He cruelly murdered with his own hand one of his father's queens, the daughter of the Raja of Palik-hara in Hindostan.

The Raja, on hearing of the murder of his daughter, revenged her death by despatching to Pagan eight trusty men disguised as Brahmins. These without difficulty, gained access to the palace, killed the king with a sword when in the act of blessing him, and then killed one another, so that *all* died in the palace. In consequence of this Narathû is known to this day in history as *Kula-kya-min*—the king dethroned by foreigners.

MIN-GYIN-NARA-THEIN-GA, 1164 to 1167 A.D.—This king was the son of Kula-kya-min, and was killed by one Aungzwa by order of Narapadi-tsi-thu, who then became king.

NARAPADI-TSI-THU, 1167 to 1204 A.D.—During this king's reign many learned rahans flocked to the capital from Ceylon, and the Buddhist religion flourished. This king built eight of the great temples of Pagan, the most celebrated of which were the Sûlamani, Gaûdapalin, and Dammaya-zika.

ZEYA-THINGA, 1204 to 1227 A.D.—This king was the youngest of the five sons of Narapadi-tsi-thû. He is chiefly famous for having built the Baûdi Pagoda, a poor imitation of the original at Buddha-Gya in Bengal.

KYA-ZWA, 1227 to 1243 A.D.—This king had an uneventful reign of sixteen years. He built the Pya-tha-da Temple. He was succeeded by his son Uzana.

UZANA, 1243 to 1248 A.D.—He was killed while elephant hunting, and was succeeded by his son Nara-thi-ha-pati.

NARA-THI-HA-PATI, 1248 to 1240 A.D.—One of the first acts of his reign was to build the Min-gala Pagoda, the ruins of which exist to this day.

In his reign the Chinese invaded the country and occupied Pagan. The King fled precipitately to Bassein. After looting the city and destroying many of its temples, the Chinese retired. On account of his flight this king is known in history as *Talôk-pyè-min*, *i.e.*, "the king who fled from the Chinese. On his return from Bassein he was killed by his son The-ha-thû, Governor of Prome, who forced his father to swallow poison.

The Pagan dynasty may be said to have come to an end with the flight of Nara-thi-hapati.

On the departure of the Chinese the Shans rose to power, and established powerful kingdoms at Panya, a few miles below the site of Ava, Myinzaing (in the Kyauksè district), and Sagaing.

LIST OF PRINCIPAL TEMPLES BUILT BY PAGAN KINGS AT PAGAN.

ANAURHATA (1010 to 1052 A.D.)

Tan-Gyi Pagoda (on the hill-top west at Pagan).
Tuyûin-dan Pagoda.
Lauka-nanda Pagoda.
Shwè-Zigôn (1st Pagoda).
Shwè-San-daw Pagoda.
Bôt-talin Pagoda.
Tapet-kayût Pagoda.
Ko-thein-na-yôn Pagoda.
Mau-tin Pagoda.
Sat-thwa Pagoda.
Ma-Shet Pagoda.
Kan-Myo Pagoda.
Tamôk Pagoda.
Kyauk-Saga Pagoda.
Kû-Byauk Pagoda.
Nyaung-dau Pagoda.

SAW-LU-MIN (1052 to 1057 A.D.)

Ka-ka-lanpa Pagoda.

KYAN-YIT-THA (1057 to 1085 A.D.)

Ananda Temple.
Small Ananda Temple.

Min-Bo Chantha Pagoda.

Pè-yatana Pagoda.

Naga-yòn Temple.

Thet-dau-ya Temple.

Thet-dau-shè Temple.

Myin-mi Temple.

Myin-hmyau-raza Temple.

Yin-ma-than Temple.

Yin-ma-na Temple.

Kaung-Dan Temple

Pa-khet-lwè Temple.

Kû-Kôk Temple.

Pa-sit-tôk Temple.

Kû-byat Temple.

Kû-bè-zat Temple.

Kû-byauk (Small) Temple.

Kû-byauk (Large) Temple.

Kû-ni Temple.

Pyan Kyi Temple.

Sau-la-wûn Temple.

Kyin-wût Temple.

ALAUNG-TSI-THU (1085 to 1160 A.D.)

Shwe-kû Temple.

That-pin-nyû Temple.

NARA-THU (Kula-kya-min, 1160 to 1164 A.D.)

That-pin-nyù Temple (Completion of)

NARAPADI-TSI-THU (1167 to 1204 A.D.)

Sûla Muni Temple.

Damaya-zika Temple.

Gaûda-palin Temple.

Myè-bòn-tha Temple.

Ka-zùn-oh Temple.

Sa-Gyo Temple.

Thi-kya-taung Temple.

Kyauk-paya-hla Temple.

ZAYA-THINGA (1204 to 1227 A.D.)
  Baû-di Temple.
  Sit-tana Temple.
  Ti-lo-min-lo Temple.
  Gaûda-palin Temple (Completion of)
KYA-ZWA (1227 to 1243 A.D.)
  Pya-tha-da Temple.
TALOK-PYE-MIN (1248 to 1279 A.D.)
  Mingala Pagoda.

Many of these temples are now known only by name, their sites having long since been forgotten. On the other hand, others have been carefully tended and repaired, and at the present time are visited by crowds of worshippers on fast days, and at the annual feasts held in their honour. Of these, the Ananda, That-pin-yû, Gaûdapalin, Nagayòn, Pumpkin, and Manûha's Temples are the best examples. With the exception of the Mingala Pagoda built by Talòk-pyè-Min, and a few others of a like shape, resembling the Shwè Dagôn at Rangoon, the type of temple most common at Pagan is what the Burmese call the "*Ku*" or cave.

It consists generally of a massive image chamber, with arched doorways and corridors surrounding it, on which are built successive receding terraces, from the uppermost of which rises the mitre-shaped bulging spire, or *sikra*, probably adopted from similar shrines in Buddhist India. The four corners of this spire are elongated and curved inwards, and on this rests the small ringed pagoda, the whole being crowned by the *hti*, or umbrella.

The chief shrine is sometimes on the ground floor, and sometimes at a considerable height from the ground.

We will now proceed to describe more particularly the most celebrated of these shrines.

TEMPLES IN AND AROUND THE MODERN PAGAN.

ANANDA TEMPLE.—This is one of the most beautiful and at the same time most conspicuous of the Pagan temples. It was

DISTANT VIEW OF ANANDA TEMPLE, PAGAN.

(Photo by P. O. Oertel, Rang., N.W. Ry.)

built in A.D. 1058 by King Kyan-yittha, one of the sons of Anaurhata, the conqueror of Thatôn.

The name Ananda is a corruption of *Nanda-si-kû*, or Caves of Nanta, and was probably given by the common people, who were accustomed to hear and read of Ananda, the cousin and favourite disciple of Gaudama.

The *thamaing* states that five rahandas of high estate came to Pagan from the Himalaya region. They told the King that they lived in caves on the Nanda-mula Hill (probably Nanda Divi Peak, near Simla). The King thereupon desired them to describe fully their home to him. The result was the erection of this temple.

In shape it is a square of 200 feet to the side, from the middle of each of which projects a gabled porch, or vestibule, thus converting the plan into a perfect Greek cross.

The account written by Colonel Yule in his " Mission to the Court of Ava," published in 1858, is so perfect that it is reproduced here *in extenso* :—

"The vestibules are somewhat lower than the square mass of the building, which elevates itself to a height of 25 feet in two tiers of windows. Above this rise six successively diminishing terraces, connecting by curved converging roofs, the last terrace just affording sufficient breadth for the spire which crowns and completes the edifice. The lower half of this spire is the bulging mitre-like pyramid adapted from the temples of India ; the upper half is the same moulded taper pinnacle that terminates the common bell-shaped pagodas of Pegu. The gilded *hti* caps the whole at a height of 168 feet from the ground.

" The building internally consists of two concentric and lofty corridors, communicating by passages for light opposite the windows, and by larger openings to the four porches.

" Opposite each of these latter, and receding from the inner corridor towards the centre of the building, is a cell or chamber for an idol. In each, this idol is a colossal standing figure, upwards of 30 feet in height. They vary slightly in size and

gesture, but all are in attitudes of prayer, preaching, or benediction. Each stands facing the porch and entrance on a great
carved lotus pedestal, within rails, like the chancel rails of an
Anglican Church. There are gates to each of these chambers,
noble frames of timber rising to a height of 24 feet.

"The frame bars are nearly a foot in thickness, and richly
carved on the surface in under-cut foliage ; the panels are of lattice-
work, each intersection of the lattice marked with a gilt rosette.

"The lighting of these image chambers is, perhaps, the
most singular feature of the whole. The lofty vault, nearly
50 feet high, in which stands the idol canopied by a valance
of gilt metal, curiously wrought, reaches up into the second
terrace, and a window pierced in this sends a light from far
above the spectator's head, and from an unseen source, upon
the head and shoulders of the great gilded image. This
unexpected and partial illumination in the dim recesses of
these vaulted corridors produces a very powerful and strange
effect, especially on the north side where the front light
through the great doorway is entirely subdued by the roofs
of the covered approach from the monastic establishment."

The figures represent the four Buddhas of the present
" kalpa " or cycle, viz. :

Kakasanpa	Burmese—	Kañka-than.
Kona-gamana	,,	Gaûna-gôn.
Kasyapa	,,	Kathappa.
Gaudama	,,	Gaudama.

The temple is surrounded by a massive wall of masonry
pierced on each side with a porched gate.

On the north side the entrance was formerly flanked by
two immense leogryphs, only the haunches of which now
remain. At the entrance of the vestibule or chapel on the
western side in a separate enclosure is a representation of the
" kyi-dau-ya," or footprint of Buddha.

The corridors round the building contain niches at regular
intervals, in which are placed stone images of Gaudama, and

NEAR VIEW OF ANANDA TEMPLE, PAGAN.

(Photo by Nicholas Bros., Mandalay.)

other figures representing scenes from the Jatakas describing the previous existences of Gaudama Buddha. These figures, from certain peculiarities of the arrangement, and ornamentation of the hair of the female figures, bespeak their Indian origin.

The architecture of these great temples, to use the words of Yule, "excites wonder, almost awe." There is no actual and authoritative record as to what class of people built this, and the other great temples, but history tells us that when Anaurhata captured Thatôn he brought away with him all the artificers in the city. As Thatôn was in close communication with India for many hundreds of years before Anaurhata's advent, it is probable, nay, almost certain, that the city contained many Hindu colonists, who were carried away to captivity by the victorious king. To this day in Pagan the people call these peculiar shaped temples *Kula-kyaung* — the temples built by foreigners. The chief architectural feature in all is the pointed arch, not only for the doorways, but for the roofings of the passages.

Mr. James Fergusson, the archæologist, states that "in no other country of Asia, from the Euphrates to the Ganges, is the existence of such form in buildings of the period to which they belong, to be met with."

On the exterior, about four feet from the ground, a dado of glazed terra-cotta tiles, with figures in relief, surrounds the temple. These figures represent warriors, ogres, birds, beasts, fishes and reptiles. The camel, or Indian dromedary, is conspicuous among the animals; a stranger to Burma, but common enough in India.

Flights of steps lead up from the ground floor to the highest terrace, but the ascent is somewhat hazardous, owing to the absence of railings in parts where one has to walk along the projecting cornice of the corridor.

The whole of the exterior and interior is white-washed, rendering it a conspicuous object for a distance of many miles.

ITINERARY.—The Ananda temple is situated about a quarter of a mile to the east of the old city wall, in close proximity to the modern village of Pagan. It is distinguishable both by its size and shape, and by the copious coverings of white-wash applied by pious *Kutho* seekers.

THATPINYÛ TEMPLE.—This gigantic pile is situated within the old city walls, about 500 yards to the south-west of the Ananda.

Its height is 201 feet, the loftiest of the larger temples.

It was built about the year 1100 A.D. by Alaung-tsi-thû, King of Pagan, the grandson of Kyan-yit-tha.

The name signifies "The Omnicient."

The body of the building is a square, with sides measuring 185 feet each. Outside this runs a lofty corridor containing numerous arched openings into the courtyard of the temple. The principal entrance is from the east, the porches at the other entrances being small and incomplete. The peculiar characteristic of this temple is the immense height of the square body of the structure before diminution of size.

This is to allow ample space for the central image chamber, for, unlike the Ananda and other shrines, the principal image chamber is nearly fifty feet from the level of the ground.

Facing the eastern entrance is the flight of steps which leads up to the image chamber. This chamber has three arched openings facing the south, east and north, and on the western side the huge image is placed directly under the apex of the pagoda.

The basement corridor runs right round the central building, and is adorned with numerous repulsive-looking figures of Gaudama, one on the north side, representing the Buddha in a sitting attitude, with his legs dangling from the *palin*, *à la* school-boy.

A peculiarity of the Thatpinyû is the presence of a second corridor at the height of the first terrace.

Steps lead up through the walls to the upper terraces, and from the topmost one a magnificent view of the surrounding country and its ruined shrines is to be obtained.

THAT-PIN-YÙ TEMPLE, PAGAN.

(Photo by Signor Beato, Mandalay.)

The diminutive modern-shaped pagoda to the east of the Thatpinyû was erected by King Thibaw, but the dedication stone has unaccountably disappeared, having most probably bee destroyed by some of those whose names were inscribed thereon as pagoda slaves.

ITINERARY.—The Thatpinyû temple is situated within the ruined walls of the ancient city, close to the modern village of Pagan, and from its great height is easily seen from a distance of some miles.

GAÛDAPALIN TEMPLE.—This temple was commenced by Nara-pati-tsi-thû about the year 1200 A.D., but the king died before it was completed, the work of finishing it being carried out by his son Zaya-thinga.

The name *Gaudapalin* was given to the shrine, because it was built on the mound formerly occupied by the *Gauda* dragon.

The temple is within the walls of the old city, and is situated to the west of the Thatpinyû. The height is 180 feet.

In plan the body of the temple is square with four porches, one on each face, the principal entrance being from the west. The mass of the temple is surrounded by an arched corridor, with openings to the exterior.

The principal image chamber, as in the Thatpinyû, is at some height from the ground, and from this a gradation of receding terraces leads up to the bulging spire, which is succeeded by the ordinary ringed pagoda. The "*Hti*," alas, came down in 1892, and has not since been replaced.

THE BAUDI TEMPLE.—This was built about the year 1219 A.D. by Zaya-thinga, the son of Narapaditsithû, King of Pagan, and stands in the centre of the modern village of Pagan. As its name implies, it is a copy of the Maha-Baudi Temple at Buddha-Gya, although much smaller than the original.

The base is quadrangular, from which rises the tapering spire, similar in shape and construction to the Sikra of the Jain Temples of India. Both the base and the spire are covered with niches, which contain seated figures of Buddha, the interstices being filled in with mouldings and panels of stucco work. The workmanship is rude and unfinished when viewed from near by, but from a distance the appearance is unique and pleasing. In the small court-yard in front of the shrine are placed about 33 stone slabs, containing inscriptions relating to this and other shrines in the neighbourhood. These have been collected from various places to save them from destruction.

DHAMMA-YAN-GYI TEMPLE.—This huge temple covers a larger area than any other at Pagan. It, however, was never completed, its founder, Nara-pati (*Kula-kya-min*), having been killed in 1164 A.D. by Indians.

In shape and general arrangement it resembles the Ananda. In the centre are two caves, or image chambers, one above the other, and on each of the four sides is a vestibule or chapel, containing sitting figures of Buddha.

The court-yard of the temple is surrounded by a most perfectly constructed brick wall, the bricks of which are so evenly laid and so perfectly squared that it would be difficult to insert an ordinary table knife between the interstices.

SULAMÚNI TEMPLE.—This is situated to the north-east of the Dhamma-yangyi, and from its height and solidity ranks as one of the "giants" of Pagan, although the upper part has long since fallen down. The name is said to mean the "treasure shrine."

It was built by Narapaditsithû in the early part of the 13th Century A.D. In shape and general appearance it resembles the Thatpinyû, but the upper part, as already stated, is dilapidated and in ruins.

As, however, it has never been plastered or renovated in modern times, a close inspection gives one a very good idea of the general construction and decoration of these "cave" temples.

The orginal mouldings round the doors and windows remain intact in many parts. The exterior appears to have been beautified and embellished with large coloured glazed tiles.

DHAMMA-YAN-GYI TEMPLE, PAGAN.

(Photo by Skeen Pusto, Mandalay.)

The battlemented parapets surrounding the different terraces were similarly decorated, many of the tiles remaining in position to the present day. The tips of the horn-like flamboyant rays surmounting the pediments of the arches of doors and windows were composed of white glazed tiles, so that when new this shrine must have presented a magnificent spectacle, in the full blaze of an eastern sun.

The ground plan consists of a single corridor running round the building. Remains of mural paintings of an ancient design are still visible in places, but most of the interior has at some time or other been whitewashed.

The upper story consists of a large image chamber, surrounded by a corridor, but this chamber, unlike that of the Thatpinyû, has not been placed directly under the shaft of the pagoda.

Like the Dhammayangyi, a well-built wall surrounds the temple. This is pierced on each of its four sides by massive porched gateways.

To the east of the Sulamûni a separate inclosure contains ninety-nine brick caves. These were built for the accommodation of hermit monks, a sect very numerous in ancient times, and still to be found in large numbers in the *"gyaungs"* of the Sagaing hills (vide Route XIII.)

DHAMMAYAN-ZIKA TEMPLE.—Situated south-east of Dhammayangyi. Was built by Narapaditsithû at the end of the 12th Century A.D., but is now in ruins.

SHWÈ-SAN-DAU TEMPLE, *i.e.*, "The temple of the sacred hair," stands to the south of Thatpinyû. It was built by Anaurhata at the beginning of the 11th Century, and is of the Shwè-Dagòn type. In a long, badly lighted brick chamber, to the west of the pagoda, is an enormous recumbent figure of Gaudama, 68 feet in length. The ceiling is covered with rude paintings of palm trees.

A curious *palin* or altar for the reception of offerings is seen on the east side, consisting of a flat paving stone, similar to those with which the court-yard is paved, mounted on four stone pillars—a miniature cromlech.

PAHTO-THA-HMYA TEMPLE.—About 250 yards to the south-west of Thatpinyû. The image chamber is on the ground, and not at some distance above it as in the other larger temples.

Between this ruin and the Thatpinyû is a ruined shapeless building which was apparently a Hindu shrine. The doorway is supported by a stone lintel, which, however, is fractured and tottering to its fall.

Lying in the door-way is an almost life-sized figure of a Hindu god. It has four arms and hands, in which are held dagger, sword, mace, and javelin. The face is obliterated, and the image has evidently been cast down from its throne to allow the shrine-robber to search for buried treasure. Similar figures, though smaller, are seen in niches on the exterior walls.

SHWÈ-KÛ (i.e., Golden Cave) TEMPLE.—This was built by Alaung-tsi-thû towards the end of the eleventh century A.D., and is situated within the old city between the Gaudapalin and Ananda temples. It stands on an elevated terrace, and the principal shrine faces the north. In construction it consists of a central image chamber with a well lighted corridor running all round it.

Let into the walls on either side of the entrance to the shrine are two inscribed stones. These have been covered with thitsi or wood varnish, and are in a good state of preservation.

In one of the windows on the west side of the shrine is a peculiar tombstone-shaped mass of brickwork, supported by a wooden beam running through it. Here, it is stated, an immense pair of betel-nut cutters were kept, used in trials by ordeal.

The legend is that a priest was accused of theft of gold from a woman. Resorting at once to the temple he placed his hands between the knives and called upon the nat or spirit to vindicate his innocence. The cutters refused to work and the priest was set at liberty. After this manifestation the hnyat-gyi miraculously disappeared.

SULA-MÛNI TEMPLE, PAGAN.

(Photo by Messrs Watts, Mandalay.)

It was to this temple that the aged king its founder was brought, and there smothered under a heap of linen by order of his son Min-shin-saw.

BIDIGAT TAIK.—This building is situated a few yards to the north-east of the Shwè-Kû temple, and although not strictly speaking a temple, has interesting associations.

It is said to be the original building erected by Anaurhata, on his return from the conquest of Thatôn, in which he deposited the five elephant loads of the sacred books, for the possession of which he had undertaken the investment and capture of the city. That this wretched, ill-lighted, ill-ventilated structure was used for the purpose is highly improbable.

Another site is pointed out by intelligent villagers as being that of the original Bidigat-Taik, or library in which the sacred books were deposited. The present building is apparently used as a cow-shed.

TI-LO-MIN-LO TEMPLE.—This temple is a conspicuous object from the summit of the Gaudapalin, and is seen to the north-east at some distance beyond the city walls. It was built by Zaya-thinga in the beginning of the thirteenth century, and has a curious legend in connection with its construction which is as follows :— Narapaditsithû was healed of a malignant sore on his thumb by one of the minor queens who bore a son named Zeya-thinga. This queen begged the king to appoint her son as successor to the throne, to the exclusion of the four elder princes, his half-brothers. The king from feelings of gratitude secretly desired to do so, but was afraid of the dissatisfaction it would cause to the other princes. The matter was referred to the court Brahmins, who decided that five white umbrellas should be placed with their handles in the ground, one to represent each of the princes. This was done, and it was found that four of the umbrellas inclined towards that of the youngest prince, Zaya-thinga. He thus became the successor of Narapaditsithû, and ascended the throne under the title of " Nan-taung-mya," i.e., " the king who begged many times for the crown."

On his coming to the throne, he commemorated the circumstances connected with his accession by building this temple, calling it " Ti-lo-min-lo," *i.e.*, " desired by umbrellas and also by the king." It is situated close to the cart-road leading from Pagan to Nyaung-û.

We have now finished the most important of the Pagan pagodas and temples, and will proceed by the road passing in front of the Gaudapalin to Myin-Pagan.

TEMPLES IN AND AROUND MYIN-PAGAN.

MINGALA ZÈDI.—This pagoda, which in shape resembles those ordinarily met with in the lower province, was built by Talôk-pyè-min, a short time before he fled from his capital on the approach of the Chinese forces.

It is said in the Maha Yazawin that this king pulled down 1,000 large temples, 10,000 smaller ones, and 3,000 of those built by *Kulas* (foreigners) to erect stockades at Palin, north of Ngaung-û, for the defence of his capital. In the relic chambers of one of these temples, an inscription on a sheet of copper was found, foretelling the invasion and destruction of the capital, during the reign of a king whose wife would bear twins. As one of Nara-thihapati's queens had given birth to twins, the king submitted to the inevitable, and ceased further defensive preparations. On the near approach of the Chinese he took refuge within the precincts of the Mingala Zèdi, which he had partly erected, and was dragged thence by his ministers, and despatched by water to Bassein.

The pagoda is situated to the west of the road connecting Pagan with Myin-Pagan, and is about a mile south of the Gaudapalin.

SIN-MYAT-KU and NWA-MYAT-KU are the names of two ruined temples to the east of the road, just at the descent into Myin-Pagan. No particular history is attached to them, nor are they specially conspicuous.

GAUDA-PALIN TEMPLE, PAGAN.

(*Photo by Seigner Route, Mandalay.*)

MANUHA'S TEMPLE.—Crossing the dry bed of the stream which runs through Myin-Pagan, and ascending the slope on the opposite side, this temple will be seen to the east of the cart-track. In front of it stands an enormous stone, "*thabeik*," or alms-bowl, nearly ten feet in height. Facing the east are three massive brick and plaster figures of Gaudama, the centre one, which is the largest, having the following dimensions :—

Width across thighs	...	...	46 feet.
Height ...	...	...	54 ,,
Diameter of Head	...	...	12 ,,
Width of mouth ...	...	...	5 ,,
Length of thumb ...	...	...	7 ,,

On either side of this monster the smaller ones of similar shape are placed. At the back of these, within the same shrine, is the enormous "*Shin-bin-tha-yaung*," the principal dimensions of which are as follows :—

Length ...	..	...	... 90 feet.
,, of Ear ...	...	...	11 feet 4 inches.
,, ,, Nose ...	...	...	5 feet.
,, ,, Mouth ...	...	...	6 ,,
,, ,, Little Finger	...	...	13 ,,

The shrine or image chamber is surmounted by a spire and "*hti*" similar to that of other pagodas.

This was built by Manûha, the king of Thatôn, who was brought prisoner to Pagan by Anaurhata in the early part of the eleventh century A.D.

He obtained funds for this, and other works, by the sale of a magnificent ring which he possessed.

MANÛHA'S NAN-PYA.—This small temple is of particular interest, because, like the Kyauk-kû-ohn-min temple two miles to the north-east of Nyaungû, it is built (externally at least) of stone. This stone is hard and of a dark green colour, of a kind not known or procurable in the neighbourhood, and was probably brought from distant Popa.

N

The roof of the temple is supported by four massive stone pillars, each of the sides of which measures five feet in breadth. They are about twelve feet high, the capitals being moulded and adorned with foliage.

Each side of the different pillars is decorated with panels containing carved figures of three-faced "*nat*," holding in the hand an offering of the sacred lotus flower. The windows are of perforated stone, similar to those in the Kyauk-kû-ohn-min. The exterior wall is faced with stone, to a depth of about ten inches, the interior, with the exception of the pillars, being of brick. The exterior corners and the sides of the windows are carved with delicate tracery of a unique kind.

The building is now in ruins, and is at present used as a sort of lumber-room by the priests of the monastery hard by. It was erected by Manûha in the eleventh century.

NAGA-YÔN TEMPLE.—This shrine stands on an eminence immediately to the south of Manûha's temple, from which it is distant about 500 yards. It was built by Kyan-yittha in the early part of his reign. Tradition says that he at one time was shielded from his enemies by a "*Naga*" or dragon, whose abode was on this hill. It is more probable that the idea was drawn from the fact that Buddha was thus shielded. The temple consists of a central shrine, over which the arched roof meets. This chamber contains a wooden gilded standing image of Gaudama, about 28 feet in height, with the right hand extended with the palm upwards, and the left arm reversed with the hand hanging down, standing on a throne of lotus leaves. The image faces the north, and the porch or chief entrance is from that side. On either side of the central figure on separate pedestals are smaller figures.

The central figure is surrounded by a halo of *Naga's* heads, the one immediately over the head of Buddha being much larger, and with the hood extended, forming a canopy over the figure.

Round the shrine runs a corridor, the walls of which are adorned with paintings of a rude kind.

NAGA-YÒN TEMPLE, PAGAN.

(Photo by Seymour Rustow, Mandalay.)

From the body of the temple rise a number of diminishing terraces, from the uppermost of which rises the mitre-shaped stem, succeeded by the ringed pagoda and "*Hti*." The building is surrounded by a brick wall, with a porched gate on each of the four sides. The pagoda-shaped upper portion is white-washed, rendering it conspicuous for some distance.

Kû-byauk Temple.—This was built by Anaurhata, and is situated about one mile to the south-west of the Naga-yon.

Laṅka-nanda.—This is the white-washed temple immediately to the west of the Kû-Byauk, and was also built by Anaurhata. It stands on the bank of the river.

Thit-sana.—This is situated about three miles south of Kû-Byauk, and is the largest of the ruined temples seen to the south.

TEMPLES IN AND AROUND NYAUNGÛ.

Shwè-zi-gôn Pagoda.—This important and well-kept shrine is situated on the rising ground north of Wet-gyi-in, between West Ngaung-û and Pagan.

The name is derived from the fact that the pagoda was built on a bluff (Bur. : *gôn*) abutting the river at a place where the current is very strong (Bur. : *yè-si-hti*).

The first shrine was erected by Anaurhata, but over this Kyan-yit-tha built the present structure.

In shape it is somewhat similar to the ordinary pagodas of Lower Burma, but lacks the graceful contour of the Shwè-Dagôn or Shwè-Hmau-dau. Its height is barely 150 feet. Flights of steps lead up on each of the four sides of the square plinth to the terraces above, from which an excellent view of the surrounding country is to be obtained.

Some very interesting glazed brick tiles, with figures in bas-relief, run round the plinth. These depict scenes from the Jatakas. At the foot of each is inscribed a few words in some language, apparently Pali. The whole surface of the pagoda is richly gilded, shewing thereby that it is a shrine of great sanctity.

N 2

In the north-west corner, within a small arched masonry chamber, are a number of inscribed stones recording gifts of land and slaves to the pagoda by successive sovereigns.

At the south side, in a raised wooden zayat, are two hideous figures representing the guardian " *nat* " of the shrine.

There are four entrances, one facing each of the cardinal points. That from the north, or Nyaungû side is flanked on either side by a gigantic leogryph, and the passages leading up to the pagoda, are paved and walled on either side for some hundreds of feet.

HNET-PYIT-DAUNG.—This name is given to the cluster of white pagodas situated about a mile to the east of Nyaungû. There are four principal pagodas named as follows :—

1. Lè-puin Paya.   2. Hmya-tha Paya.
3. Thami-pwet Paya.   4. Hnet-Daung-Pyit Paya.

These pagodas were erected many hundreds of years ago, and their history is mixed up with the early traditions and legends of the place.

During the time of Pyû-sau-di, one of the " five enemies "—an immense bird named Ti-laing-ka—lived in the neighbourhood, making his abode on a lofty " *Leppan* " tree on the top of a hill.

His attendant, Nga Kau, supplied him daily with seven girls for his meal. Pyû-sau-di, on one occasion, met this man on his way to the bird with his morning meal. He had previously been supplied with a bow and five arrows by Tha-Gya-min, king of the Nats. He approached the bird, in company with the others, and killed it with an arrow from his bow. At the place where the bow and arrows were presented " Lè-Hnin " pagoda was afterwards built. At the place where Pyû-sau-di tried the bow the " Hmya-Tha " pagoda was built. At the place where the seven girls were hidden by Pyû-sau-di the " Thami-Pwet " pagoda, and on the hill where the bird was pierced by the arrow the " Hnet-Daung-Pyit " pagoda.

So much for the legend. The pagodas remain to this day, and are known by names given above.

ANCIENT PAGODA AT PAGAN.

(Photo by F. O. Oertel, Esq., N.W.P.)

In the neighbourhood of these pagodas are several small caves cut out of the soft sand-stone rock. They are not now utilised as monastic retreats, but are the home of swarms of bats. In the vicinity are several wooden monasteries of recent construction. Near one of these, a beam of fossilized wood, suspended from a tree, or beam, does duty for a bell, and the sound emitted from this, when struck with a billet of wood, is most metallic and resonant.

KYAUK-KÛ-ÔHN-MIN TEMPLE.—This is the most northerly of the temples of Pagan, and is situated in a gorge, about a mile and a half to the north-east of the town of Nyaung-û.

It was built by King Narapaditsithû in the twelfth century, and remained inhabited and in a good state of repair till the middle of the seventeenth century, when it was finally abandoned and allowed to fall into ruin. The caves (Ôhn Min) were excavated by Thi-ha-thû, King of Ava, in the fifteenth century.

The name Kyauk-kû means "the crossing of the rock, or stone," and the following legend accounts for it :—

A priest named Shin-Gauda-wara, of Hnet-Pyit-Daung, was accused of adultery by a woman, and in order to vindicate himself, stated that if he were innocent of the offence, a *damma* and a huge piece of rock would float, the one up stream against the current, and the other *across* the river to the other bank. Both these events took place, the priest returned to his *kyaung* triumphant, and his honour was vindicated.

On hearing of this, the King decided to commemorate the event by erecting two temples. One was called Kyauk-kû (stone-crossing) temple, and the other was called the Damma-ba temple. The latter was situated at the entrance to the gorge, close to the river, but its remains are not now to be identified.

The Kyauk-kû temple is built on the southern side of the gorge, about a mile from the Irrawaddi.

The structure consists of three storeys, or terraces, built against the south bank of the gorge. The lowest storey, or cave,

is built of green sand-stone, of a kind known only in the neighbourhood of Popa.

The blocks are well squared and fit very closely together ;
the chisel-marks are still distinctly traceable. The image-
chamber, which is on the ground floor, is 42 feet in length from
east to west, and 25 feet broad from north to south. The groined
ceiling is supported by two stone pillars, on each side of the
image. The image itself is of brick, covered with plaster, and is
of the usual "sitting" type.

The walls on the inner side contain a number of niches at
regular intervals apart, for the reception of images and figures.
These, for the most part, are cast down, and lie in hideous ruin
on the floor of the chamber.

The entrance to the chamber is by a porch, succeeded by an
arched aperture. This arch is now in a ruinous state, and only
half of it remains.

The lintel of the doorway is a massive squared piece of
timber, probably teak. The jambs are carved, representing
scenes and figures from the Jatakas.

The interior walls appear to have originally been plastered,
and on this faint traces of mural paintings of a rude kind, in
umber and yellow ochre, are still discernable.

To the left of the image, a small doorway leads to the passage
from which the caves are reached. These, as already stated, are
of later construction. They originally extended right through the
soft sand-stone hill to a gorge to the south, but have fallen
in towards the middle, and are now dark, unventilated, and
untenable. By the aid of a torch, some portion of the interior
may be explored, but it is infested with bats, the smell from
which is over-powering and offensive.

The upper storeys of the temple were in all probability later
additions, as they are constructed entirely of brick, and rest in
part on the upper edge of the gorge. The stone-work of the
lowest storey is much split and rent, probably by earthquakes in
early times. The rents, however, have been patched up and

repaired with bricks, the red streaks of which, in the interstices, are plainly visible. The upper storeys contain several empty chambers and passages, on a level with the plateau stretching to the south.

ITINERARY.—From the village of Nyaungû the footpath leads past the Infantry Barracks to the gorge beyond. By following the footpath up the gorge for about a mile the ruined temple will be seen on the south side.

PYAN - DAU - KYI TEMPLE. — This temple was built by Narapaditsithu, the founder of Kyauk-kû, immediately to the north of it, on the edge of the gorge. As its name implies, it was built at the place from which the king *looked back* on the Kyauk-kû temple, when returning from his visits to that shrine and its monastic establishments.

PAUNG-DAU-Û PAGODA.—This temple is situated on the high cliff to the north of Nyaung-û, at the entrance to the gorge in which the Kyauk-kû temple is situated. The name means "the temple of the bow of the royal barge," and was so called, because here the royal barge was moored, while the king proceeded by land to the temple up the gorge. In the sand-stone cliff on which this pagoda stands, several caves have been excavated by the priests living in the neighbouring *kyaungs*, and here the more austere of the fraternity spend fixed periods in silent meditation.

ITINERARY.—The best way to "do" Pagan is to leave Mandalay by the express steamer on Wednesday or Saturday morning, arriving at Nyaung-û about eight o'clock the following morning.

A well furnished rest-house provided by Government will be found here on the hill-top, in close proximity to the steamer *ghat*. The first day could be spent in visiting the Paung-dau-û, Kyauk-kû-ôhn-mm, Hnet-pyit-daung, and Shwe-zi-gôn shrines. The next day could be spent in visiting the lacquer-ware factories in Nyaung-û, and in shifting camp to Pagan village, about two-and-a-half miles south of Nyaung-û. Accommodation of a rough kind can be had, either in the police lines, or in zayats in the village. From this centre, the principal shrines and the remains of the city are within easy walking distance, and could all be visited in one day. To attempt to visit and examine *all* the ruins, *three months* could easily be spent.

The visitor must understand, though, that if he shifts camp to Pagan from Nyaung-û, he must provide himself with every necessary, both for sleeping and feeding.

Were ponies procurable, the best way of course would be to make the Circuit-house at Nyaung-û the centre, returning there for meals and rest. It might be possible to hire a pony or two in the village, but arrangements would have to be made beforehand to prevent disappointment, and the traveller would require to provide his own saddle and stirrups, as the native saddle and stirrups are unsuited to Europeans.

Should the visitor, however, be pressed for time, and the steamer waits for him only one hour off Pagan, as has been suggested to the Irrawaddy Flotilla Company, his best plan will be to make tracks for the Gaudapalin temple, the nearest to the river of the three " giants." Safe and well lighted flights of steps lead up to the topmost terrace of this temple, from which a very fine view of the miles of ruins is visible.

ANCIENT PAGODAS, PAGAN.

(Photo by A. A. Girod, Esq., M.R.P.)

TABLE OF APPROXIMATE DISTANCES BY RIVER BETWEEN BHAMO AND MANDALAY.

	Bhamo	Sawaddy	Shwegu	Moda	Katha	Paya	Tagaung	Kyanyat	Male	Thabeikkyin	Kabwet	Kyaukmyaung	Nga Singu	Shenmaga
Bhamo														
Sawaddy	30													
Shwegu	55	25												
Moda	80	50	25											
Katha	110	80	55	30										
Paya	130	100	75	50	20									
Tagaung	160	130	105	80	50	30								
Kyanyat	180	150	125	100	70	50	20							
Male	193	163	138	113	83	63	33	13						
Thabeikkyin	205	175	150	125	95	75	45	25	12					
Kabwet	237	207	182	157	127	107	77	57	44	32				
Kyaukmyaung	247	217	192	167	137	117	87	67	54	42	10			
Nga Singu	250	220	195	170	140	120	90	70	57	45	13	3		
Shenmaga	296	266	241	216	186	166	136	116	103	91	59	49	46	
Mandalay	320	290	265	240	210	190	160	140	127	115	83	73	70	24

ROUTE XIX.

MANDALAY TO BHAMO BY STEAMER.

Two services of steamers between Mandalay and Bhamo and *vice versa* are maintained by the Irrawaddy Flotilla Company, *viz* : the Express, and the Cargo.

The steamers of the Express service leave Mandalay every Monday morning, arriving at Bhamo on Thursday morning. The Cargo steamers leave Mandalay every Thursday morning, arriving in Bhamo on the following Tuesday morning.

The steamers of the Express service are specially fitted for the convenience of first class passengers, whereas the Cargo steamers tow a flat alongside, in which are accommodated the stalls of bazaar sellers, who do a roaring trade with the villagers at each halting place. The people of the riverside villages depend entirely on the bazaar boat for their weekly supply. It is most amusing to watch the arrival of purchasers, who rush on board, often before the steamer is moored. It is a novel experience to the Burman, to have to settle on the merits and price of the article he wants, in the short space of a quarter of an hour. In the big bazaar at Mandalay, he will spend half a day, and consume several betel-nuts, before the purchase of a Rs. 1/8 cotton *loungyi* has been negociated. As may be conjectured, the first sound of the steamer's whistle puts everyone in a state of fervid excitement. The second blast, sees the transfer of various articles to the purchaser's basket ; while the third blast, and the ominous squeaking of the ropes, as the steamer is being released from her moorings, sends the villagers scuttling ashore, full of laughter and merriment, and apparently well satisfied with their bargains.

MAP OF
IRRAWADI RIVER
from
BHAMAW to MANDALAY

A small Burmese girl, about twelve years of age, in the presence of the writer, sold in the short space of a quarter of an hour, goods to the value of Rs. 55/, chiefly tobacco, salt, onions, chillies, turmeric, and other dry goods. Her stall was at times surrounded by a crowd three or four deep, and yet she was able to detect a Punjabi policeman walking off quietly with a bundle of tobacco leaves. Her remarks, concerning the policeman's female relations in the distant Punjaub were unkind, but they assisted considerably in the restoration of the pilfered tobacco.

ROUTE.—Leaving the *Ghat* at 8 a.m., the steamer proceeds on its voyage, passing numerous islands and sand-banks. The hills to the west of the river are the Sagaing Hills, which attain their greatest altitude in the neighbourhood of Min-gûn.

Long before reaching this village, the huge mass of bricks forming the remains of Bodaupaya's abortive attempt at pagoda building, is seen. A full account of this pagoda, and the massive bell alongside it, are given in Route XV. The island in the river opposite Min-gûn is called Nan-daw-kyûn, or Palace Island," because here, Bodaupya erected a temporary palace, where he spent, on and off, some twenty years of his reign in superintending the construction of the pagoda and its accompanying bell. The bell was, in fact, cast on this island.

Proceeding onwards through sand-banks and islands, to the east will be seen the fruitful country irrigated by the waters of the Madaya canal.

Sixteen miles above Mingûn, and on the same bank of the river, Shein-ma-gà is reached. The village is prettily situated on a bight in the river, but the approach of steamers is obstructed by a large sand-bank which had formed opposite the village. The three low hills to the east are the famous Sagyin Hills, from which, for generations past, the white marble, of which images of Guadama are made, has been procured. The vicinity of these hills has lately been declared a ruby-bearing tract, and the right to search for stones is sold by Government. A run of twenty-four miles brings us to Kyauk-Myaung, passing *en route* several large

islands, and on the left bank Singû, the head-quarters of the
northern sub-division of the Mandalay district.

Kyauk-Myaung, on the right bank, about three miles above
Singû, is in the Shwêbo district.   It is connected with Shwêbo
by a metalled road.   For some years after the annexation, this
part of the country was much disturbed by roving bands of
dacoits and river pirates.   The walled bazaar at Kyauk-Myaung
was converted into a fort, and occupied by troops.   Under a
large Banyan tree just outside the fort is a small cemetery,
containing several graves of European soldiers and blue-jackets,
who lost their lives during the early years of the occupation.

Here lie the remains of Lieutenant McDonald, the Paymaster
of H.M.S. " Ranger," who was killed in action.   His burly figure,
deep voice, and kindly manner will long be remembered by
those who knew him in Rangoon, Bassein, and Moulmein,
previous to the outbreak of the war.

About ten miles above Kyauk-Myaung on the right bank, at
the bend of the river, we come to Kabwet.   This is the head-
quarters of the Burma Coal Mines Company.   Coal has been
worked for a number of years in these parts and the fields were
visited in 1855 by Mr. Oldham, the geological expert who
accompanied Colonel Phayre's mission to Mindôn Min.

Coal of good quality is found here, but the concession has
not yet been fully developed.   The company has lately acquired
a prospecting license over a large area of coal-bearing land in the
neighbourhood, and there is some talk of a line of rails being run
to the coal fields, from Kinû station on the Mû Valley Railway.

Kabwet is at the entrance to the third defile, and the river
for some miles contracts considerably, flowing through hilly
country, the hills on either side rising up from the banks and
being clothed to their summits with profuse tropical vegetation.
Towards evening Thabeikgyin is reached, twelve miles north of
Kabwet.

Two miles below Thabeikgyin, the small island of Thi-ha-dau
is passed, close to the right bank.   It is crowned by a gilded

pagoda, and has besides, several monasteries in a ruined condition. Prior to the annexation, the monasteries were inhabited, and the pools below the islands were the home of a species of carp, which were held sacred. Many of them were gilded about the head and fins, and a royal order made fishing within three miles of the island a penal offence. The kyaungs are now deserted and the fish dispersed. Û-Hmat the "Ruby King" of Mogok, has lately repaired the pagoda, which has an annual festival attended by vast crowds, from all parts of Upper Burma.

The village of Thabeik-gyin is prettily situated on the sloping banks of the river. This place is the port for the Ruby Mines District, and a metalled road, sixty-one miles in length, runs from the river bank to Mogôk. At the following places on the road, dâk bungalows have been provided for the convenience of travellers.

Wa-Byû Daung	11	miles.
Kyauk-Lè-Bein	6	,,
Shwè-Nyaung-Bin	15	,,
Kabaing	9	,,
Kyat-Pyin	11	,,
Mogôk	9	,,
Total	61	miles.

About twelve miles to the north west of Mogôk is the hill station of Bernard Myo, so called from Sir Charles Bernard. The station is 7,555 feet above sea level, and is garrisoned by troops from the Shwèbo cantonments.

THE RUBY MINES OF BURMA.

Sixty-one miles from the river Irrawaddi, in a north-easterly direction from Mandalay, the former capital of ex-King Thibaw's dominions, amid ranges of mountains separating Burma proper from the Shan States, the famous ruby bearing tracts are found.

It is from these Mines that the greater quantity of the world's supplies of rubies have been secured.

Under the rule of the Kings of Burma these tracts were held as a State reserve, and were jealously guarded from the eyes or presence of suspicious foreigners. King Mindon Min, the father of ex-King Thibaw, most persistently refused to allow Dr. Oldham, the geological expert who accompanied Colonel Phayre's mission to the Court of Ava in 1867, to visit these tracts. The only European who had visited the mines in the days of the native rule was a French priest, named Père Guiseppe D'Amato, who found his way there some fifty years ago, and reported his experiences to the Royal Asiatic Society. Under native rule all stones above a certain size were by law declared the property of the king, and were made over, or supposed to be made over, to the king's officer in charge of the mines.

The tracts were parcelled out into small allotments, which were let to licensed miners, called in Burmese "*twin-tsas*," or "eaters of the mine." Each party consisted of from four to eight men, and their mining was carried on in the most primitive fashion.

A shaft, about three feet square, was sunk until the ruby bearing earth or "*byûn*" was tapped. The sides of the shafts were lined with green twigs and brushwood, kept in position by pegs driven into the sides of the excavation. This was done to prevent the sides from falling in. As soon as the "*byûn*" was reached, it was conveyed to the surface, and carried to the nearest stream or pond to be washed and sifted, and the rubies were then extracted. As most of the mines were situated in the valleys, of which Mogòk was the centre, these "*twins*," or shafts, rarely reached a greater depth than thirty feet, and when this was exceeded, the incoming waters drove the miners from the workings, and compelled them to repeat the process on a fresh site. In the rainy season, mining operations were entirely suspended.

Soon after the taking of Mandalay by the British in 1885, a flying column was despatched to these outlying tracts, to secure possession of the mines, on behalf of the British Government.

In 1887 a company, called the Burma Ruby Mining Company, was formed in London, and by the payment of four lacs of rupees yearly to the Indian Government, acquired the exclusive rights over all ruby bearing tracts in the neighbourhood. Directors were appointed, and an efficient staff of experts and trained miners were sent out to Burma. For the first few years of their lease the company confined its main efforts to tunnelling into the matrix of a hill close to Kyat-pyin, ten miles from Mogôk, in the hopes of finding valuable "pockets" of gems. Their efforts in this direction were unattended with any great measure of success, and the extensive blasting operations that had to be carried out, told seriously on the funds at the disposal of the Company. Under the advice, therefore, of the Engineer-in-Chief of the Company, the scene of operations was removed to the Mogôk valley, and the extensive works erected at Kyat-pyin are now but little used.

At Mogôk, rubies have been extracted for many hundreds of years, in the primitive way described above. It therefore occurred to those responsible, to improve upon the native system of extraction, by the aid of steam power and efficient mining appliances.

The works of the company at Mogôk cover an area of about 100 acres, the whole of which is enclosed within a barbed wire fence. When visited by the writer a few months ago, an area of about 200 yards square had been excavated to a depth of about fifty feet; the byûn or ruby bearing gravel was then reached. To prevent the mine from becoming flooded, powerful steam pumps, working night and day, were employed, and the water thus raised was conducted in pipes to the surface, and utilized in the washing process. From the lowest depths of the mine, a light tramway was laid, up an inclined plane to the mills on the surface, the byûn as quarried being placed in trollies, and hauled up by a stationary engine with a steel hawser. The output was, at the time of his visit, four hundred trollies a day.

On reaching the mills, the first operation consists of separating the soil from the stones. This is done in a series of mills somewhat resembling a pug-mill used in brickmaking. The larger stones escape through the lower interstices, and the residue is passed through others of finer guage, until nothing remains but a collection of small stones and pebbles. These are conveyed to the sorting sheds, and the rubies are picked out by experts under the close supervision of European Inspectors.

To an amateur, the rubbish heap is a mine in itself, and appears to be a mass of gems, but the red stones seen are not rubies, but spinels, of various colors and sizes. Besides rubies, sapphires and garnets are found in abundance. The writer was shewn a finger bowl filled with rubies, as the result of a week's washing, but none of them were of great size or value.

In another part of the concession the native workings are carried on. Licences are granted by the company, and a royalty of sixty rupees a month is paid by each party, generally consisting of from four to six workers. Although the ground has been previously mined in bygone years, the efforts of the native workers are frequently rewarded by the finding of valuable stones.

The labourers employed by the Company are mostly Meinthas or Chinese Shans, of fine physique and endurance. Many people say that these labourers discover and secrete the best stones when mining, but one has only to see the mines and the stuff that is brought out of them in the trollies, to prove how fallacious such a statement is.

The Company employs from twenty to twenty-five Europeans on its staff, and some hundreds of Meintha coolies, and now that an efficient method of extraction is carried out, it may be expected that more prosperous days are in store for the Company, and that its shares will rise in value. Under the new lease lately sanctioned by the Government of India, the yearly tribute has been considerably reduced.

The next place of importance touched at is Kyan-hnyat, twenty-two miles north of Thabeik-kyin. It is the head-quarters of the Tagaung Sub-Division of the district, and carries on a good trade with the interior.

The course continues due north, past the villages of Hintha, Yè-yin and Magyidaung, till Tagaung is reached. The third defile may be said to end here, as the hills recede from the immediate neighbourhood of the river banks, and the river itself spreads out into a broad channel, in which are many sand-banks and islands.

TAGAUNG, according to the Maha Razawin, was established in the sixth century before Christ, by Abhi Raja, a Tshatriya prince of Kapila-vastu in Bengal. He crossed the country, via Munipur and established himself on the upper Irrawaddi, calling his city New Hastinapura. Thirty-one kings are said to have reigned in Tagaung. This monarchy is said to have been destroyed by an invasion of the Tarôk and Taret. These are the Chinese and the Manchûs. This invasion took place about the commencement of the Christian era.

Very extensive and valuable ruins exist in the neighbourhood of the present village, which fully substantiate and corroborate the Burmese historians. Terra-cotta tiles bearing Sanscrit legends in Gupta character, are dug up in large numbers, and a large stone slab, with a Sanscrit inscription in the Gupta alphabet of Samvat 108, or A.D. 416, has been unearthed, which conclusively proves that Tagaung had close intercourse with Bengal, via Munipur and Assam, in very early times.

It is a pity that no systematic exploration of these ruins has been made by orders of Government, the results, when such an undertaking has been completed, will no doubt help considerably in the elucidation of many problems connected with the introduction of the Buddhist religion into Burma, and the connection in the early ages between that country and India.

The principal pagodas in the neighbourhood of the old city are the Shwè-zigòn, Shwè-Zedi and Paungdau-Kya. These are in a fair state of preservation and were very extensively repaired by order of Alaungpya in the last century.

TIGYAING, on the right bank, is the next halting place. The village is pleasantly situated on the slope of a rocky hill, which rises from the water's edge. The name was given by the Burmese conqueror in olden times from the fact that the first governor was presented by the king with a *Ti* (umbrella) and a *Gyaing* or sceptre. The hill is covered with pagodas, monasteries and other religious buildings, and the summit is surrounded by a rude fort or stockade composed of loose stones. This is stated to have been constructed by the Chinese during their invasion of Burma, in the latter part of the last century. In the hills behind the village are some caves of recent construction, hollowed out of the lime-stone rock, of which the hills are composed. Immediately opposite Tigyaing on the left bank is Myadaung. This was the seat of government of the *Wûn* or governor, when under Burmese rule. For some time after the annexation, a garrison was maintained at Tigyaing for the suppression of the numerous dacoit bands that infested the district.

Soon after leaving Tigyaing the mouth of the Shwèli river is passed on the left bank. This river flows through the Shan States, and taps some of the most extensive teak forests in Upper Burma. These were formerly leased to the great Moulmein forester Maung Mûn Taw, and latterly to Messrs. McGreggor & Co., of Rangoon.

It was these forests that supplied the magnificent timber used in the construction of the palace and other buildings in Mandalay. Above the confluence of the Shwèli with the Irrawaddi, the channel widens considerably, and numerous islands and sand-banks occur.

KATHA, on the right bank, is the head-quarters of the district of the same name, and has lately been connected by rail with Sagaing and Mandalay. Both town and district are notorious for the poisonous climate they possess; the cemeteries, it is said, are large and well filled. About 16 miles above Katha, and on the same bank of the river, is Moda.

It was here that several employés of the Irrawaddy Flotilla Company were treacherously taken prisoners in 1885, and conveyed to Tigyaing for execution.

After leaving Moda, the river's course for several miles is due east, the steamer threading its way through numerous small islands, passing the villages of Wûnbaigon and Kyauk-talòn till Shwegû is reached on the left bank. This village is the head-quarters of the Shwegû sub-division of the Bhamo district.

Just above Shwegû, the large island of Kyûn-dau-gyi is passed. This is celebrated for the immense number of pagodas and other Buddhist buildings it contains.

One of the principal of these is the Shwè-ban-gau pagoda, said to enshrine part of the forehead bone of Buddha.

In the month of *Tabaung* (March) a feast is held on the island which is attended by large crowds of people from the neighbouring districts.

We now enter the second defile, the scenery in the neighbourhood of which is very fine. The river here contracts to a width of about 200 yards, and flows through rocky banks. On the right bank a cliff, nearly 800 feet in height, rises straight out of the water. The depth of the water in the defile varies from six to eight fathoms above Kyûndaw, to from 20 to 27 fathoms in the narrowest part. The small pagoda on the rocks, near the big cliff, is called Let-saung-gan pagoda. From the deck of a passing steamer, it looks barely six or seven feet in height, but the misapprehension is removed when a man is seen alongside of it.

At the upper end of the second defile, on the left bank, is the village of Sin-kan, and a few miles above this on the same bank Sawadi. After passing Sin-kan the mountains retire from the bank of the river, and the country consists of fertile cultivated plains. Below Sawadi the river channel gradually broadens to a width of nearly three miles. Below Bhamo itself, it is intercepted by the large island on which the village of Úbyaw is situated.

BHAMO or *Ba-máu* as it is called by the Burmese, is situated on the left bank of the Irrawaddi a few miles below the confluence of the Taping with that river. The town is so called from two Shan words, *Man* a village, and *Mau* a potter. By the Chinese it is called *Tsin-gai*.

The native portion extends along the left bank of the river for a distance of about a mile and a half, terminating to the north in the old fort. It was here that the British residency was situated, prior to the annexation. The fort or stockade now contains the jail and the military police lines. In the low water season from November to May, the steamers moor near the steep bank to the south of the town. Behind this is a deep depression forming a plain or *maidan* in the cold weather, but covered with from fifteen to twenty feet of water in the rains. This forms, when free of water, the parade and recreation ground for the garrison. The Fort is situated to the east of the town, and was built after the occupation. It is rectangular in shape and is surrounded by a broad dry ditch, beyond which barbed wire entanglements are laid down to prevent a rush. It contains barracks for the accommodation of the garrison, which consists of two companies of Europeans, a full native regiment, and a mule mountain battery.

The population of Bhamo was 9,000 in 1891, when the last census was taken. It consists principally of Chinese, Shans, Kachins, Palaungs and a few Burmans. The Chinese inhabitants though similar in dress, differ considerably in outward appearance and habits, according to the province or district from which they have come. The principal are those from Momein, Talifu, Kaung Taung and the Panthays. The latter are Mahomedans by religion, and were nearly annihilated in 1868, when they rebelled against the Pekin Government.

All classes of Chinamen wear the characteristic baggy blue trousers, with loose white coats and round felt skull-caps.

STEAMER GHÂT, BHAMO.

(Photo by Signor Festa, Mandalay.)

Panthays are distinguished by their white clothes, shaven heads, and turbans in place of hats or caps.

The bulk of the trade with Western China is carried on by the Chinese, who form the wealthiest class of the community. The principal article of trade is raw cotton. This is grown extensively in several districts of Upper Burma, and when prices are favourable at Bhamo, almost the whole crop from Upper Burma is brought up, mostly in flats, and exported to Yünnan by caravans of mules. When the Bhamo market is closed, the cotton is sent to Rangoon, and thence shipped to China.

Next to the Chinese, the Shans form the most numerous section of the community. There are many branches of this sect, the principal being Shan-Gyi or pure Shans, Shan-Palaung, Kampti-Shan from the upper waters of the Irrawaddi, and Palaungs. The latter are distinguished by their clothing of blue cloth and by the enormous black turbans worn by the women. These in shape resemble somewhat the tall hats worn by the Parsis.

The Kachins seen in Bhamo, are not permanent residents of the town, but temporary sojourners from the hills to the east. There are numerous tribes of them. The Kachins themselves recognise two great divisions :—Kakûs, or Kachins from the river sources ; and Zin-pyau or Eastern Kachins. These tribes differ both in dress and speech. The Kakû men wear a twisted turban of cotton cloth, a sleeved coat, dyed with indigo, and a loin cloth oblong in shape, about the size of a bath towel. The women wear a striped turban of twisted cloth, an inner jacket or jersey with short sleeves, a coat with long sleeves, the shoulders and cuffs being ornamented with patches of red cloth, on which cowries are sewn. To cover the loins they have an oblong piece of cloth, slightly longer than the men's, with a fringe of embroidery at the end and a girdle of cowries.

Among the Zinpyaws, the women wear turbans of folded cloth, and girdles of twisted rattan round the waist, sometimes to the number of twenty-five or thirty. They also wear garters of black rattan just below the knee, as a sort of set off to the leg.

Prior to the annexation, the Kachins had it pretty well their own way in the hills separating China from Burma, and levied blackmail on all caravans passing through their country. Under British rule, order and peace have been restored amongst these savage people, and the chief caravan routes are held by a chain of police posts, extending up to the Chinese frontier.

The American Baptist Mission have a prosperous boarding school and mission for Kachins in Bhamo, which was established some years before the British occupation. Here, these children of the hills may be seen at their best, and under the civilizing care and influence of the missionaries, they are scarcely to be distinguished from the more civilized Burman of the plains.

Bhamo contains few buildings of interest to the traveller. The pagoda in the civil lines is of Shan construction, and is of unusual shape, the shaft being much longer than is usually the case. It is, however of no special sanctity, and is of recent construction. The Chinese temple in the native town is worth a visit, to those who have never seen similar shrines. No objection is made to European visitors.

About a mile beyond the jail the Taiping river joins the Irrawadddi from the east, and in the angle between the two rivers, the remains of the ancient Shan city of Tsampanago are situated. From an inspection of the ruins of the walls, it appears to have been built in the form of a square, each side measuring a little over a mile. A broad moat surrounded it, the remains of which are still plainly visible. Tradition states that the city was founded in the time of Gaudama Buddha, and that in the year of religion 218 the Shwè-Kyina pagoda was erected. This pagoda is still in a good state of preservation, and is situated north of the old city between it and the Taping.

On the destruction of Tsampanago, a new city of the same name was erected on the right bank of the Taping, a few miles east of the original city. The ruins of this are also visible. A third city, called old Bhamo, due east of the modern town, at the foot of the Kachin hills, was also a former capital. Beyond the

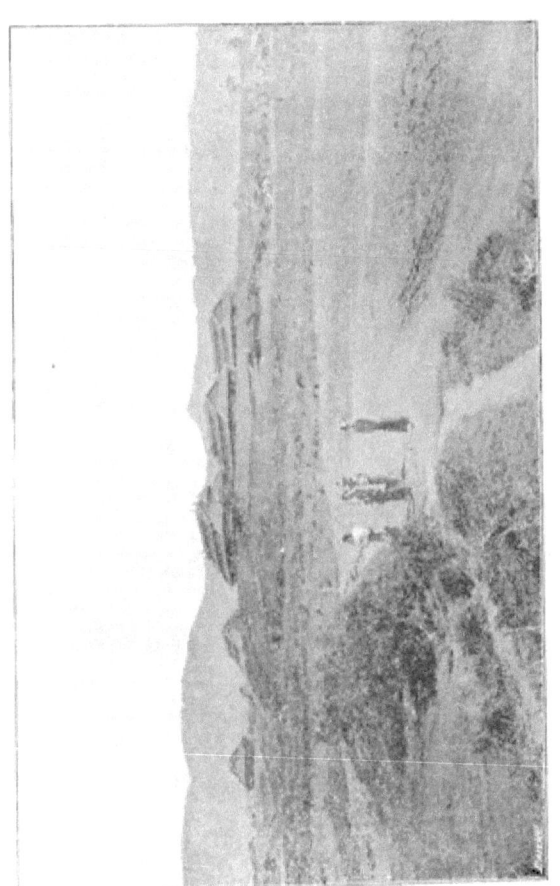

THE FORT, BHAMO.

(Photo by Signor Reale, Mandalay.)

city walls, and a few ruined pagodas, nothing remains to attest the former greatness of these ancient cities.

The village between the jail and Tsampanago is inhabited by Assamese, the descendants of prisoners of war, captured in the last century by the Burmese, when Assam and Eastern Bengal were invaded by them.

ROUTE XX.

BHAMO TO MYITKYINA.

A small paddle-steamer of the Irrawaddy Flotilla Company runs between Bhamo and Myitkyina, a distance of about 140 miles, during the low water season from November to April. The journey up and down takes five days, and the scenery for the greater part of the distance is grand and striking.

Leaving Bhamo at 9 a.m., the course is N.E. past the mouth of the Taiping River, which joins the Irrawaddi from the east, just above the old Shan city of Tsampanago. The large island to the left is Kyûn-Khûn, which in the rains is covered with water. For some distance the river flows through a level plain, and its channel is split up by several low islands, covered with grass and thorny bamboo.

After passing the village of Phaten on the right bank, the channel becomes blocked by huge isolated boulders of black rock. The small pagoda near the right bank, called Kyitau-thein pagoda, marks the entrance to the first defile. Opposite to Pulan village, on the right bank, the river is from 700 to 800 yards broad. The village opposite is Thamangyi, and, like many others in the defile, is inhabited by Phwons. These people are supposed to be an aboriginal race who were expelled from China, and who ultimately settled, on, or near, the banks of the Irrawaddi. The village is situated on the summit of a cliff from eighty to ninety feet above the water.

Just above Thamangyi, the channel of the river, which is here 600 yards broad, narrows to 200 yards, flowing for some short distance through dark and jagged rocks. Above these

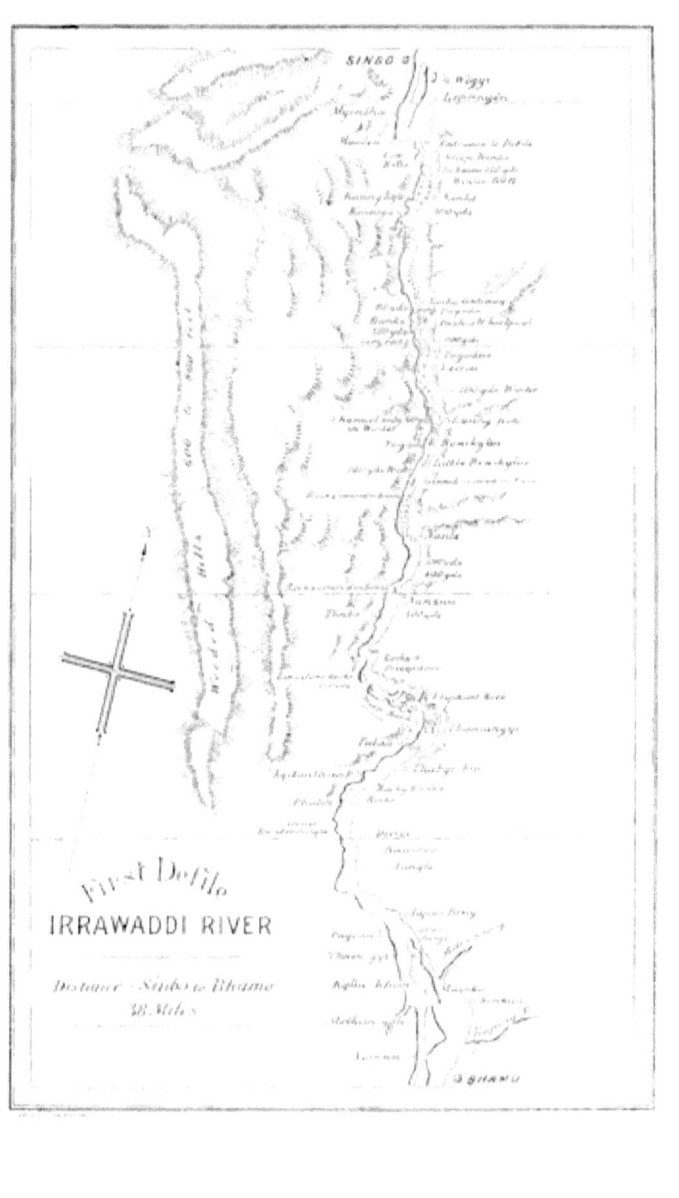

First Defile
IRRAWADDI RIVER

Distance - Sinbo to Bhamo
81 Miles

narrows the breadth is 800 yards. The general direction is now
to the N.W. between rocky and precipitous banks, till the
Elephant Rock is seen in mid-stream. The Eastern passage is
100 yards wide and the Western 150 yards. This rock rises
40 feet from the water in the dry season, but is entirely covered
in the rains. In rising water, whirl-pools form in either channel,
and as the course suddenly swerves at right angles, navigation,
even in the low water season, is both difficult and hazardous. A
clear reach of a mile and a half, with an average breadth of
800 yards, is succeeded by a rocky gorge 150 yards wide, through
which the waters rush with violent impetuosity. The scenery in
this bend of the river from the Elephant Rock to the narrows
mentioned, is very wild and romantic, and from the deck of the
small paddle-steamer, the passage appears to be blocked in every
direction, by pile upon pile of frowning rock, heaped along the
banks in hideous confusion, through which the waters of the river
glide with extraordinary velocity. The general direction is now
north for three miles past the village of Tònbo on the right bank.
From this point the north-easterly direction is maintained for
three miles, passing on the left bank the village of Nansan,
perched 100 feet above the river at low water.

Through this part of its course, the river flows between
sloping banks, unimpeded by rocks. On the right, hills rise
gradually from the river bank, to a height of about 800 feet.

After passing Nantè village, rocks re-appear near the left
bank, and the channel is blocked by two rocky islands
separated by about half a mile from one another. The width
here, and for some distance, is about 400 yards. We now
approach in mid-stream Little Bowikyûn Island, which is
succeeded by the larger island of the same name, on the southern
point of which is a small white pagoda. This is situated about
45 feet above low water mark. From Bowikyûn the northerly
course is maintained, and a little above the island, the channel
narrows to 60 yards only in the dry season. Above these
narrows, the channel broadens out to an average breadth of

100 yards till the village of Laung Pòk on the left bank is passed. Above this village the rocks re-appear, hugging the left bank till the channel contracts to a width of 100 yards only, through which the whole waters of the river rush with increasing velocity. Just above this rapid, on the left bank, is the village of Lema, to the north of which are four small pagodas occupying a prominent position on the cliffs overhanging the river. A stretch of two miles, with an average breadth of 800 yards, is succeeded by a contracted channel, the breadth of which is 150 yards only. From this point the course is to the north-east, between rock-bound banks. We now approach the dreaded Pashio whirl-pools, the passage through which in the rains is impossible for a steamer. Just above the whirl-pools the channel contracts to 80 yards only. Above this rocky gateway the river flows through hilly country, past the villages of Koungkyi and Nantè, the channel gradually contracting from 500 to 250 yards, until the bend to the north-east is reached, where it is only 150 yards wide in the rains, and 80 feet during low water. Two miles beyond, the channel opens out, the rocks disappear, and the northern entrance to the defile is passed. The breadth at this gateway is 250 yards. From this point till Sinbo is reached the river spreads itself out to a width of from 1,200 to 1,500 yards, having on the left bank the villages of Leppangòn and We-gyi.

Some idea of the strength of the current can be imagined from the fact that it takes a powerful little paddle steamer seven and a half hours to perform the journey up, a distance of thirty-eight miles only.

The first defile differs from either of the others both in length and grandeur. The chief characteristic, is the number and variety of the irregular masses of broken rock, which line either bank of the river, many rising abruptly from the stream, and others piled up in a series of rocky and precipitous headlands.

The flood gauge at Sinbo registers from 80 to 90 feet, and in the height of the rains, the waters sometimes rise to the height of the old shed behind it.

VIEW-IN FIRST DEFILE, IRRAWADDI.

(Photo by C. O. (abld, E.q., N.H.P.)

The distance from Sinbo to the confluence is 106 miles, and from Sinbo to Myitkyina eighty miles, so that the confluence of the N'Maika with the Malika is twenty-six miles above Myitkyina.

In the rains a small steamer of the Irrawaddy Flotilla Company plies between Sinbo and Myitkyina, the up journey taking twenty-five hours steaming, and the down twelve hours.

For some miles above Sinbo, the width of the river is never less than 800 yards. Sixteen miles north of Sinbo, the Mo-goung River joins the Irrawaddi from the west. Immediately opposite the mouth is the village of Shwè-m. A run of four miles brings us to *Hatha* rapid, the navigation of which is somewhat dangerous. Numerous reefs and shoals of large shingle abound, and the water is so clear, that the bottom can be distinctly seen, although the depth is considerable.

After passing Halew on the right bank, the river bends to the west, flowing through thickly wooded banks as far as the village of Talaw-gyi. Just above this, the Nantapet River joins the Irrawaddi from the east. From this confluence the general direction is due north for about four miles, when the stream sweeps round to the south-west, the banks being lined with dense growth of kaing grass and wild plantains. After passing the Netsè Rocks the general direction is north-east, passing on the left bank the village of Û-lauk, above which are the two large fertile islands of Kaing-taung, the soil of which is peculiarly suited for the cultivation of the poppy. Above these islands is the large village of Maing-maw, called after the large walled Shan town which formerly existed three miles from the river.

After passing on the right the villages of Palaw and Akyè, and on the left Sanka, the course shifts to the west and even the south-west as far as Katkyo, which is the largest village met with north of Bhamo. The village contains a good number of Chinese, who control the trade with the neighbouring Kachin tribes.

Above Katkyo the direction is due north, passing on the left bank the large villages of Waing-maw and Ywa-dau. Three miles above the latter, and on the opposite bank, is Myitkyina, immediately facing which is the large island of Naung-talaw. Above this island is Maingna, which in the King's time was the last and most northerly village on the Irrawaddi acknowledging his rule. In 1895 Myitkyina was made the head-quarters of a new district, and since that time much has been done to introduce a regular system of government, into these distant and outlying regions.

The Mû Valley State Railway is being extended from Mogoung to Myitkyina, a distance of forty miles, and when this is opened a great impetus will be given to the trade of the Upper Irrawaddi.

The Chinese border runs parallel to the river at a distance of from thirty to fifty miles to the east, and several good caravan routes are known to exist between the Irrawaddi and the western confines of Yûnnan. There is, therefore, every reason to expect that Myitkyina will in time become a great centre of trade. At present, beyond the Barracks and usual Government Offices, it contains few houses, and no large native community.

As already stated, the confluence of the two rivers, Malika and N'Maika, is twenty-six miles north of Myitkyina. Just below is the Tang-pè rapid. The fork at the confluence is a mountain 1,200 feet high, running sheer to the water's edge.

The Malika and the N'Maika are not navigable for launches or boats for more than six miles above the confluence, on account of impassable rapids. That on the western branch is called Law-naw, which means "to say one's prayers"—a name very suggestive. The natives say that both rivers rise in the months of March and April, such rises being due both to rainfall and melting snow. The name N'Maika means in Kachin "bad river," or "bad water," and is given because of the difficulties of navigation.

In the western or Malika river, rafts are employed by the Kachins to descend the stream from three points. These are Santa, Sawwan, and Nkum-naga. Boats are seldom used. The natives say that both branches flow for a long distance through

VIEW IN FIRST DEFILE, IRRAWADDI.

(Photo by Signor E. 189, Mandalay)

rocky defiles. Colonel Woodthorpe, of the Survey of India, crossed the Malika 120 miles above the confluence and found it 85 yards wide and five feet in depth; this was in the month of May.

Major Hobday, of the Intelligence Department, crossed the N'Maika twenty miles above the confluence, in the month of January, and found the stream to be 93 feet deep.

The exact sources of the Irrawaddi have never been properly ascertained, but it is nearly certain that both branches take their rise in the lofty mountains of Eastern Thibet.

Two miles from the confluence, on the Malika, is the Kwitao Ferry, where caravans from China cross the Irrawaddi *en route* for the Ruby Mines at Nanyazeik, and the Jade Mines near Kamaing.

A strong police post is maintained here, where all Chinese immigrants deposit their arms and ammunition. These are returned to the owners on their return journey to China.

ROUTE XXI.

RANGOON TO MANDALAY BY RAIL.

The mail train for Mandalay leaves the Phayre Street Station at 6 p.m. daily. Three classes of accommodation exist, the rates being as below :—

First Class, Rs. 30/- ; Second Class, Rs. 12/- ; Third Class, Rs. 6/-.

As already stated, the difference between the first and second class rates is so great, that many travellers elect to travel second class. The latter accommodation is very good indeed, the only apparent difference being, that the first class carriages have cushioned seats, whereas the second class have cane only ; but this is a small matter, when nearly every traveller is provided with his own bedding and rugs.

Emerging from the ill-lighted and cramped central station, which is a disgrace to such a centre of trade as Rangoon, the train passes through the eastern suburbs of the city, and after a run of six minutes pulls up at Pazûndaung, an important suburb, and the business quarter of Rangoon, where the rice mills are situated.

This is the old "*Push-'im-down*" quarter of Tommy Atkins of half a century ago.

The Pazûndaung creek is here spanned by an iron bridge, in the construction of which, many engineering difficulties had to be overcome, owing to tidal influences and faulty foundations.

After leaving Pazûndaung, on the right will be seen the numerous rice mills, on which the greater part of the trade of the port depends. The paddy is brought to the go-downs of the

VIEW IN FIRST DEFILE, IRRAWADDI.

(*Photo by Nepaar Kutter, Mandalay.*)

mills and the depôts in the Rangoon River by the cultivators, and after being milled, is conveyed in lighters to the Rangoon River for shipment.

The view to the left of the great Shwè-Dagòn, glittering in the light of the setting sun, is most pleasing. The general character of the country from Pazûndaung to Pegu is the same throughout. Dabein, Tòngyi, Kyauktan, Tawa, are all large centres of paddy cultivation, and these flat, uninteresting areas extend almost uninterruptedly as far as Taungû. After a run of 46¼ miles, Pegu is reached at about 8.10 p.m., where passengers are allowed half an hour for dinner.

The refreshment-rooms are let out to contractors, under the general supervision of the officials of the railway. Passengers are warned not to leave their carriages without a servant in charge, as this line, in common with those of India, swarms with light-fingered gentry, in spite of the stalwart Punjabi policemen, who come to the salute at every wayside station.

After satisfying the inner-man (a task, by the way, anything but possible at some refreshment-rooms), the train proceeds onwards through the darkness, crossing the Pegu River by a massive iron bridge of considerable length; and passing and stopping at several smaller stations, where the guard seems to have most protracted discussions with the station-master, Pyûntaza is reached, eighty-eight miles from Rangoon. This is the end of the first section of the railway, and is a depôt for spare engines, carriages, and trucks. The town has sprung up since the opening of the railway, to the detriment of Shwè-Gyin, the former head-quarters of the district, situated on the Sittaung River, about fourteen miles due west of the railway station.

Pyûntaza, and the next station, Nyaung-lè-Bin, are situated in the middle of an immense area of rice cultivation, which brings in a large revenue to Government.

Leaving Pyûntaza at a little after 11 p.m., the traveller will probably "turn in" for the night. Before doing so, he should carefully bolt the door, and securely fasten the windows with the

leather catches provided, otherwise he will probably awake in
the morning at Pyinmana, to find he has been relieved of all
his belongings, even to his watch and keys, from beneath his
pillows !! (It is not so long ago, that a gentleman arrived in
Rangoon in his sleeping suit, having been relieved of all his
effects while in an uneasy sleep.) Taungû is reached at the
unearthly hour of 3 a.m., but as the traveller may wish to break
his journey here, a short description of the place is given.

The town, which contains 17,517 inhabitants, is situated on
the right bank of the Sittaung River, which rises in the hilly
country north-east of Yamèthin, and after a circuitous course of
350 miles, enters the sea at the head of the Gulf of Martaban.

From 1852 to 1885, when the upper province was annexed,
it was a very strong military station, and had a large garrison,
both of infantry and artillery ; but of late years the military
station has been abolished, and the prosperity of the town has in
consequence suffered. It is pleasantly situated at some distance
from the Karen Hills to the east, and is a very healthy station.

A small square redoubt was constructed by the military
authorities, about thirty years ago, on the angles of which, light
guns were formerly mounted.

Most of the military buildings have been removed to more
important posts in Upper Burma.

In the Karen hills to the east, most excellent coffee is grown,
supplies of which have driven all other kinds from the market, at
least in Burma. On the higher ranges, potatoes are found to do
well, and English fruit trees have also been tried with some
success.

HISTORY.—Taungû was for many centuries the capital of an
independent kingdom. The ancient capital was called Dwa-ya-
wadi, and was built on the site of the present suburb of Myo-gyi.
In 1510 A.D. Taungû was founded, its classic name being Kè-tù-
ma-ti. The ruins of the walls are still visible, as well as those of
the palace of Min-gyo-nyo, the founder of the dynasty. In 1610
A.D. Taungû was captured by the King of Burma, and from that

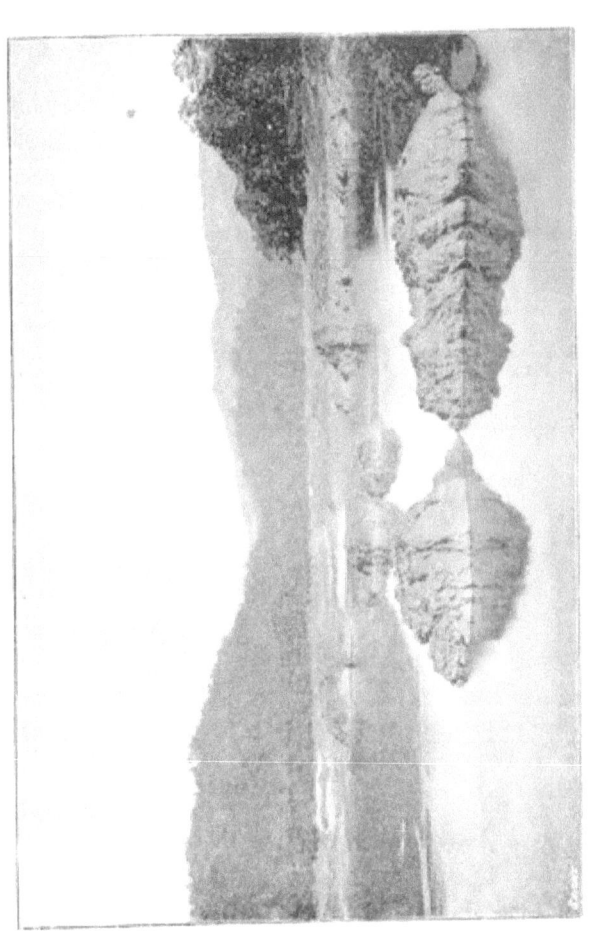

VIEW IN FIRST DEFILE, IRRAWADDI.

(Photo by Nizam Bros., Mandalay.)

time up to the outbreak of the Second Anglo-Burmese war, remained part of that kingdom.

Six miles west of Taungû are the ruins of Dha-nya-wadi, an ancient capital, and thirty-one miles south are the ruins of Ze-ya-wadi, which was founded in 1550 A.D. by Bû-yin-naung of Pegu.

The town has considerable trade with the Karen Hills, and the Shan States beyond.

Leaving Taungû at 3.15 a.m., passing several small stations *en route*, the old frontier is passed after leaving Myohla, and the rest of the journey is through the recently acquired province of Upper Burma.

Pyinmana is reached at 6.20 a.m., and the train stops sufficiently long to enable the passengers to make a hasty *chota hazari* of coffee and toast. This town was formerly called "Ningyan," and is still known as such to the Burmans of the district. The name was changed, to prevent endless confusion with "Myingyan" on the Irrawaddi. In the neighbourhood are extensive forests of teak, which in the king's time were leased to Messrs. Darwood & Co., of Rangoon. The most valuable and marketable timber has nearly all been extracted, but extensive areas still exist, which are carefully conserved by the officers of the Forest Department.

After leaving Pyinmana, the whole aspect of the country passed through changes. From Rangoon upwards, the country consists of vast plains of low-lying land adapted for paddy growing.

This is maintained for some distance north of Taungû, when it is replaced by tree forest, bamboo and elephant-grass jungle. Beyond Pyinmana, and thence to Mandalay, the dry zone is entered, and the country consists of open plain, covered with sparse growth of thorny bushes and vast quantities of mimosa and cactus, interspersed with arid patches of cultivation. The flat plains give place to gentle undulating ground, which extends from the banks of the Irrawaddi on the west, to the foot of the Shan Hills on the east.

O

Just after leaving Pyinmana Station, the railway crosses a broad tributary of the Sittaung by a handsome iron bridge, and at 9 a.m. Yèmèthin is reached.

This is the head-quarters of the third section of the railway, and is also the head-quarters of the district which takes its name from the town. A short halt is made here for breakfast, Yèmèthin enjoying the reputation of supplying a good " square " meal, well served. From Yèmèthin, a run of half an hour brings us to Pyaw-bwè, where a large depôt for military police is kept. The climate of Pyaw-bwè seems particularly suited to ponies, large numbers of which are kept here.

At the 299th mile Nyaung-yan is reached, in the neighbourhood of which is a large lake formed for irrigation purposes. At 11 a.m. Thazi junction is reached, and passengers for Meiktila alight here. The cantonment and town of Meiktila are situated at the terminus of the branch line, thirteen miles in length, on the banks of a large and beautiful lake. This lake has a circumference of several miles, and is fed principally by streams from Popa Mountain, which rears its lofty summit forty miles to the east.

In the small brick building on the big bund at Meiktila, a stone inscription records the history of the lake, from the earliest period. From this it appears that King Anaurhata passed by it with his armies, on his way to Kyauksè in 1014 A.D.

He ordered the banks to be cleared of jungle and brushwood, and in doing this, four brick chambers were discovered containing images of the guardian *nat*.

A mounted officer was deputed to ride round the lake. He started at six o'clock in the morning and returned at sunset ! having ridden right round it. (He must have had a very slow pony.) He reported that the water in the channel from Popa was flowing into the lake without touching the ground !

In consequence of this, Anaurhata ordered one of his noblemen to build a town on the banks, which was called Ma-ti-la, from the Burmese *Ma* not, *ti* touching, and *la* to come, i.e., *Coming without touching.* This name in the course of ages has been corrupted into " Meik-tila," the ancient name of a country in Bahar, not far from Patna, which is mentioned in Maha-Zaneka, one of the famous " Zats."

The cantonments are to the west of the lake, and here are kept a wing of a British regiment and a full regiment of Sepoys. Meiktila is considered the healthiest place in Upper Burma. The houses of the British officers are picturesquely situated on the banks of the lake, which is admirably suited for sailing.

The Burmese have a saying, that when the plant at present growing on the pagoda, in the precincts of the monastery at Thazi, shall be as thick as the stock of a Burmese plough, the village will become a large town. Whether the tree is growing or not, the village is, at alarming bounds, and the saving is at least in part likely to prove true. This is no doubt owing to its favourable situation on the railway line, and further to the fact, that the Government road from Myingyan on the Irrawaddi, to Fort Stedman and Taungyi in the Southern Shan States, here meets, and crosses the railway. The total distance from Meiktila cantonment to Fort Stedman is a little short of 132 miles.

Bungalows are provided at convenient distances where everything in the shape of furniture, cooking utensils, and table crockery is provided by Government.

In consequence of these excellent communications, Thazi is fast becoming a great entrepot of trade, both with the Southern Shan States, and the country to the west of the railway line.

Leaving Thazi at 11.7 A.M., Thèdau is reached shortly before noon. Two miles to the west is Wûndwin, the head-quarters of the sub-division, and which, in the king's time, was the residence of the *Wûn,* or governor. A good deal of fighting took place in the neighbourhood, in the troublous times succeeding the annexation, as the numerous graves of European soldiers bear witness.

Myittha is a great halting-place for traders from the neighbouring Shan States. A good deal of trade is carried on in paddy.

O 2

It is the head-quarters of the southern sub-division of the Kyauksè district.

A marked difference in the features of the country is observed, some few miles before reaching Kyauksè. The scrub jungle and clumps of cactus give place to smiling fields of paddy and plantations of sugar-cane and plantains.

This change is due entirely to the system of irrigation carried out in the Kyauksè district. By means of it, two crops are secured in the year, and the unusual sight (to a resident from the deltaic districts) of one field being planted out while the next to it is being reaped is often witnessed.

Kyauksè, as its name implies (*Kyauk*, stone, and *se*, a weir) is the base from which the system starts. A small river, called the Zau-gyi, emerges from the Shan Hills immediately to the east of the town, and across this several stone dams (nine in number) have been constructed, which hold the water back. From these sources, canals lead off to the surrounding thirsty plains, and by means of smaller channels, the water is distributed over the fields as required.

This most perfect system of irrigation was planned and carried out, many years ago, by the Burmese government, and although now under control of irrigation officers of the Public Works Department, beyond deepening existing channels, cutting new ones, and straightening others, little improvement was needed. The fertility of this district proves, in a most positive manner, the benefits accruing to a country by such works, where the rainfall is both scanty and uncertain. The revenue of this district is nearly seven lacs, while that of the Meiktila and Yèmèthin districts is barely one and a half and two lacs respectively.

The railway station of Kyauksè is situated at the foot of a rocky hill 735 feet in height, the summit of which is crowned by the Shwè-Tha-Yaung pagoda, erected by Shin-Mwè-lôn, the Shan wife of Anaurhata, king of Pagan, by whom she was expelled from the capital. An annual feast is held in her honour in March, when thousands of pleasure-seekers from Mandalay and the neighbourhood visit the pagoda, and special trains are run from Mandalay, to meet the wants of the worshippers.

From the summit of the hill—up which a flight of stone steps has been built—a splendid view of the surrounding country is to be obtained, well repaying the fatigue of the journey up. From Kyauksè onwards, the line runs at a considerable distance from the Shan Hills, which as Mandalay is approached, present a comparatively level contour for many miles. At Singaing—one of the stations passed—excellent snipe-shooting is to be got in the months of December, January, February, and March, and it was here that the late Prince Albert Victor was taken to shoot, on the occasion of his visit to Mandalay in 1890.

After passing Paleik, where no stoppage is made, the last of the large iron bridges, which spans the Myitynge (*"Little River"*) is crossed. This river rises in the Shan States, and falls into the Irrawaddi just north of the old city of Ava.

Soon after passing the Myitgnè station, the high embankment across the lagoon, south of the old capital, Amarapura is crossed, and the line runs parallel and close to the old city wall, with its now empty moat intervening. The line approaching on the left is the branch line running from the shore, just opposite the town of Sagaing, which joins the main line at Myohaung (*old city*) station. After a short stay here, the last three miles is run into Mandalay station, the line passing through, for the most part, the *"Kathè"* or " Manipuri" quarter of the town. On the left, near the large flat-topped, red brick ruins of a pagoda, is the famous Arakan Temple, or shrine containing the huge brass image brought from Arakan in the last century, a full description of which will be found in Route XII.

Representatives from the different hotels meet the train on arrival, and hackney carriages are procurable just outside the station yard.

ROUTE XXII.

MANDALAY TO MOGAUNG BY RAIL.

THE Mû Valley Railway is so called, because from Sagaing northwards, as far as Kawlin, it runs more or less parallel to that river, at a distance from it, to the east, of not more than twenty miles. Just below Kawlin, several ranges of mountains intervene between the Mû and the railway, which, for the remainder of the distance, runs through fertile valleys, with outlying spurs intervening, across which latter, some very steep gradients are encountered. From Mawkûn northwards the line runs parallel and in close proximity to the Namyin River, which joins the Namkong, draining the lower portion of the fertile Hûkong valley at Mogaung.

The Secretary of State for India has lately sanctioned the extension of the line from Mogaung to Myitkyina on the right bank of the Irrawaddi, some 200 miles north of Bhamo.

Reconnaissance parties are also at the present time (1895) making surveys through Assam, across the Patkoi range of mountains, which separate north-east Burma from Assam, with a view to the linking up of the Burma with the Bengal system of railways.

ROUTE.—From Myohaung on the main line, three miles from Mandalay, a branch line runs to the river bank, at Amarapura shore station, passing through the old city, which has been described in Route XIV.

Leaving the train here, the river is crossed in a comfortable ferry steamer provided by the railway, passengers being landed at Sagaing.

The terminus is in close proximity to the river bank. Loaded trucks and spare carriages are brought over on specially arranged barges, and are hauled up or down the banks by stationary engines, with the aid of pontoons and wire ropes.

Sagaing having been fully discussed in Route XIII., it will be unnecessary to further describe the town. Ywataung $2\frac{1}{2}$ miles out, was the depôt for the new railway, and originally had a large staff of engineers and other officials. It also had carriage factories and fitter's shops, similar to those at Insein, on the Irrawaddi Valley State Railway. Under recent orders received from the Government of India, the separate establishment has been broken up, and the entire work is carried out at Insein. Consequently, Ywataung is at the present time a station of deserted offices and bungalows, and the "glory has departed from Israel."

To the west of the station will be seen the huge dome-shaped mass of the Kaung-hmù-dau Pagoda, described in Route XIII.

The next station is Sayè nine miles on, in the centre of a good wheat growing country. Between this station and Padù, a large lake or tank exists, which in the rainy season covers an area of many square miles. In the neighbourhood of Padù Railway Station, attempts have been made to introduce Indian settlers.

As an inducement to military policemen to settle in the country on the conclusion of their term of service, Government has agreed to grant tracts of land to these men on favourable terms.

The present village contains about 200 persons, and is known as *Kula-Ywa*, " the foreigner's village."

Fifty-three miles from Sagaing is Shwèbo, fully described in Route XVII.

Kinù, fifteen miles north of Shwèbo, is fourteen miles from Yeù on the Mù River, till quite recently the head-quarters of a separate district, but now a sub-division of the Shwèbo district.

There is some talk of connecting Kinù with the Thingadau Coal Mines to the east by a light railway line. Should this be done, impetus would be given to the coal-mining industry.

At present, the produce of the mines is conveyed by a light tram to Kabwet, and thence in flats to Mandalay.

Tantabin, in the king's time, was a very important place, being the head-quarters of the Pyinsala-nga-wûn-myo, and has at the present time a population of 1,584, the majority of whom are engaged in mat-making.

At Tungôn, the line approaches to within four miles of the Mû. This station draws a good deal of traffic from the northern townships of the Yeû sub-division.

KAMBALÛ is the head-quarters of the northern sub-division of the Shwèbo district, and will probably grow, as it is in the centre of a good grain producing district, through which the railway runs.

After leaving Kambalû, cultivation becomes scantier, and the country is more sparsely populated.

Pintha, Kyaikthin and Ko-daung-bo are already benefitting by the new railway, and in time will grow.

KAWLIN has the reputation of being one of the most unhealthy stations for Europeans in the whole of Upper Burma. It is situated in the centre of a fertile rice plain, surrounded almost entirely by ranges of forest-clad hills. Prior to the Wûntho rebellion in 1890-91 the town-ship was greatly harassed by the Sawbwa's men, and on the outbreak of hostilities was attacked and burnt by them.

Since the absorption of the Wûntho State into the Katha district, Kawlin has enjoyed comparative immunity from violent crime. The town is forty miles due west of Tigyaing on the Irrawaddi. A Public Works Department Road connects the two places, passing through the Mau-gûn-daing Pass, at an elevation in its highest part of 1,500 feet. The scenery in parts is very beautiful.

From Kawlin, a run of eight miles brings us to Wûntho. This, in the king's time, was formerly under a Wûn appointed from the capital, and he was subordinate to the Shwèbo Wûn. Owing to the great help given by the Wûn in the suppression of the rebellion of the Padaing Prince in 1867, he was made a Sawbwa with almost independent powers. During the reign of King Thibaw he acquired greater power, and in the lawless times succeeding the British occupation, he succeeded in extending his rule to several of the adjoining town-ships. After the advent of the British, he removed his court from Wûntho to Pinlebû, as being more out of the way, and consequently more secure from interference. His independence was recognized by Government, and he was allowed to retain possession of a good deal of the country he had acquired by his former raids. It soon, however, became evident to the civil officers of the neighbouring districts, that he would prove " a thorn in the flesh " to our rule. Raids into British territory became the order of the day; criminals from our side sought and obtained a welcome refuge in the Wûntho State, and their surrender was refused. This unsatisfactory state of affairs was brought to a climax in 1891 when the Sawbwa's men attacked and burnt Kawlin. An expedition under General Wolseley was despatched, and Wûntho was occupied. The Sawbwa fled the country and sought refuge in China, where he is still said to be.

The town is pleasantly situated in a fertile valley, surrounded on all sides by tree-covered hills, those to the north-west being the Maugin Range, the highest summit of which is Maing-thòn, 5,450 feet. Mau-kin hill close to the town is 1,500 feet in height.

After leaving Mau-kan (twelve miles from which are the gold-bearing tracts), the line crosses the range of hills by the Kyauktalòn Pass. The construction of this section of the line was a work of considerable engineering difficulty, some of the gradients being very steep.

The line runs along the scarped edge of the precipice, at the foot of which flows the Meza Chaung, the scenery reminding one forcibly of snatches of the Highlands of Scotland.

After a slow but steady descent Meza is reached. Thence onwards to the junction, the line passes through comparatively level country with patches of cultivation. Indaw (royal lake) as the name suggests, is in the neighbourhood of a large fishery, about which the people of the place have some curious stories. It is said to be bottomless, and yet people are never drowned in its waters. The Sawbwas of Mohnyin, on receipt of their appointment, cast gold into its waters to propitiate the *nats*. Naha-kaung is the junction where the branch line from Katha joins the main line. This line, 13 miles in length, crosses the barrier of hills between the main line and Katha by the Pa-sût Pass. It is of considerable elevation, and the gradients are in parts one in fifty.

After an hour's run from the junction, the train draws up at the terminus on the river bank, close to the steamer ghât.

Katha is so called from the fact that in former times a Kachin feast was held here yearly in honour of the *nats*. It was by them known as the *Ka-sa*, which has been corrupted by the Burmese into Katha.

The town at the census in 1891 contained a population of 1,464, but since the opening of the railway has slightly increased. It is the head-quarters of the district and of the military police battalion. A dâk bungalow is provided for the convenience of travellers, and is at some little distance from the railway terminus.

From Naha-kaung north, the line runs through the fertile valleys of Mawlû and Mawkún to Mohnyin, the present terminus, about 60 miles from Mogaung. Mohnyin is frequently mentioned in the *Maha Yazawin* as being the capital of a very powerful Shan Kingdom. In 1426 A.D., the Sawbwa invested and took possession of Ava and established a Shan dynasty in that capital.

The ancient city of Mohnyin was some three miles to the south-east of the modern village of that name. The remains of the walls, and of the moats which encompassed it, are still to be found. From an inspection of these remains, the city appears to have been built in the form of a parallelogram, the longer sides each five-and-a-half miles in length, and the shorter sides about half-a-mile each.

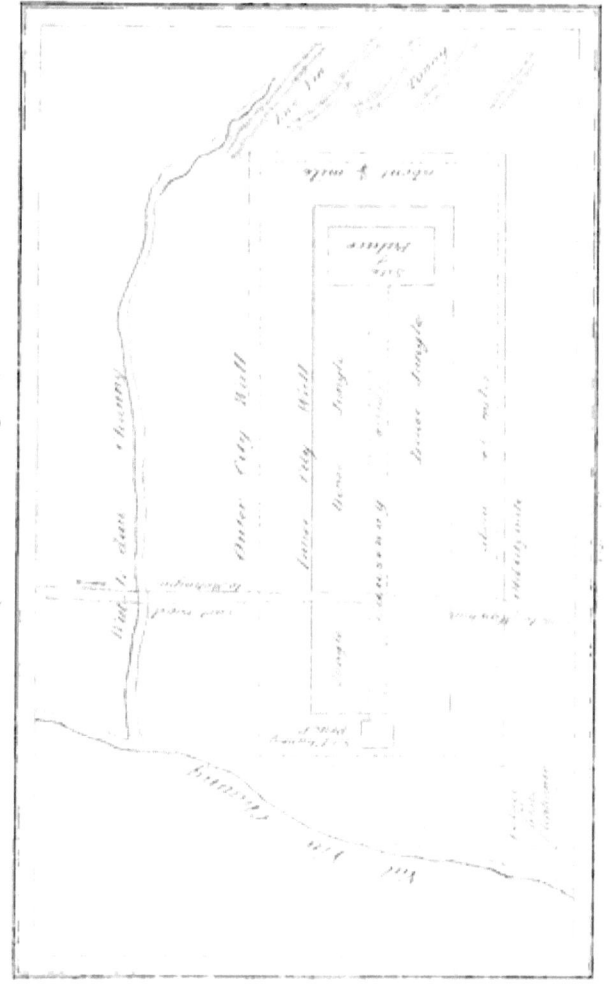

PLAN of ANCIENT
CITY OF SAMPÔN
(near Mohnyin)

The Eastern outer wall of the city was close under the Lwè-Yin Mountains.

The northern wall ran parallel to the Wùt-lè-dau stream, which rises in the Lwè-Yin Mountains, and joins the Nat-Yin stream not far from the site of the north-west corner of the old city wall. The only superficial brick remains are those of an exceedingly old Buddhist temple or pagoda, situated at the eastern end of the old city, between the outer and inner walls. From this a *saung-dan* or raised cause-way ran through the inner city to the palace at the eastern end.

The pagoda was surrounded by a platform and a retaining wall—parts of the latter being in a fair state of preservation. The bricks are of enormous size.

The shrine itself is so overgrown with dense jungle and vegetation, that its existence would not be noticed by a casual observer. A path has to be cut, with the help of Kachin dahs, before a near approach can be made.

In shape it resembles one of the many brick shrines so common in Pagan. A " Cave " or chamber existed on the ground floor, but this has fallen in. On the west side, a tunnel into the relic chamber has been made by shrine robbers.

The relic chamber has been broken into, and its contents appropriated. It consisted of a small square sandstone vault, covered by a slab of the same kind of stone, now lying on the east side of the pagoda.

HISTORY.—By the inhabitants of the district, the city is called Sa-lòn, but this name is not used in the *Maha Yazawin.* Local traditions state that it was established by the Shans, some time succeeding the destruction of Tagaung and the founding of Pagan.

The whole site is now covered with thick forest trees, and unless closely looked for, no remains can be detected. From the fact that trees, with a girth of from four to six feet, are found growing from the mounds of both walls and cause-way, it would appear that the city is very ancient. Authentic records formerly existed in one of the village monasteries, but were destroyed during the Kachin raids of King Thibaw's reign.

At the south-west corner of the outer walls is the site of the ancient elephant palace, where the *Sin-byu-dan* or white elephants were kept. Tradition states that, in the height of its prosperity, the city boasted of seven white, and 10,000 of the common variety, used in war-fare.

The linking up of twenty-six miles of line to the north of Mohnyin has been completed, and the whole section to Mogaung is now approaching completion.

	Pakôkkû	Pakan-gyi	Yesa-gyo	Amyin	Sadôn	Mônywa	Alôn	Lemyé	Shwe Za Ye	Kan-ni	Thin-dau	Man-ka-dau	Mingin	Ú-yin-ma	Chaung-wa	Sha-dau	Kywé-ywa	Kale-wa	Budet	Ma-sein	Kindat	Pantha	Yu-river	Sit-taung	Paung-byin	Hsawng-hsup	Uru-River
Pakôkkû	:																										
Pakangyi	27	:																									
Yesa-gyo	34	7	:																								
Amyin	64	37	30	:																							
Sadôn	69	39	32	12	:																						
Mônywa	76	49	42	20	10	:																					
Alôn	84	57	50	31	18	18	:																				
Lemyé	95	61	61	34	29	20	11	:																			
Shwe Za Ye	98	71	64	44	31	22	14	3	:																		
Kan-ni	112	85	78	58	45	36	28	17	14	:																	
Thin-dau	152	125	118	98	85	76	68	57	54	40	:																
Man-ka-dau	162	135	128	108	95	86	78	67	64	50	10	:															
Min-gin	180	153	146	116	111	104	96	85	82	68	28	18	:														
Ú-yin-ma	197	170	163	133	131	121	113	94	99	77	37	27	17	:													
Chaung-wa	205	178	171	141	139	130	121	110	107	93	53	43	39	8	:												
Sha-dau	216	189	182	152	150	140	132	121	118	104	64	54	46	21	11	:											
Kywé-ywa	226	199	192	162	160	150	142	131	128	114	74	64	54	37	30	21	:										
Kale-wa	235	208	201	171	169	159	151	140	137	123	83	73	55	46	38	30	10	:									
Budet	244	217	210	180	178	168	160	149	146	132	92	82	94	85	77	39	58	62	:								
Ma-sein	274	247	240	210	208	198	190	179	176	162	123	112	108	93	100	53	72	71	30	:							
Kindat	288	261	254	224	222	212	204	193	190	176	136	126	117	108	91	62	81	102	44	14	:						
Pantha	297	270	263	233	231	221	213	202	199	185	145	135	127	107	123	93	112	109	93	40	:						
Yu-River	328	301	294	264	262	252	244	233	230	216	176	166	158	131	130	120	109	101	129	68	63	:					
Sit-taung	373	346	339	308	307	297	289	278	257	241	220	210	175	166	155	181	138	136	174	172	84	57	30	:			
Paung-bwin	389	362	355	325	323	313	271	261	316	304	264	254	167	183	167	120	159	164	185	172	98	88	88	17	:		
Hsawng-hsup	416	389	382	352	350	340	332	321	318	304	264	254	214	227	210	181	200	201	181	175	128	120	124	93	60	:	
Uru-River	421	394	387	357	355	345	337	326	323	309	269	259	251	231	224	186	205	205	186	171	147	133	124	93		44 45	5
Homalin																											

ROUTE XXIII.

PAKÔKKÛ TO KINDAT AND HOMALIN UP THE CHINDWIN RIVER.

Weekly communication between Pakôkkû and the stations on the Chindwin river is maintained by the steamers of the Irrawaddy Flotilla Company, Limited. In the rains, when the river is in flood, the ordinary twin-screw steamers are employed, but in the low water season from November to May, stern-wheeled steamers of light draft are found more suitable.

The steamers start from Pakôkkû, a station on the right bank of the Irrawaddi, a little below the confluence of the Chindwin and Irrawaddi rivers.

The first halt is made at Pakan-gyi, on the right bank of the Chindwin, twenty-seven miles from Pakôkkû. The channel lies between the banks on the Pakôkkû side, and the large island of Kaing, which forms part of the Myingyan district. Seven miles above Pangangyi we come to Yèsagyo, which is the head-quarters of the northern sub-division of the Pakôkkû district, and is a place of considerable trade.

The course is now to the north-west, through numerous islands and sand banks, similar to those encountered in the Irrawaddi, until the large and important village of Amyin is reached, on the left bank, thirty miles above Yèsagyo. Amyin was an important place in the king's time. It was one of the five *Myo*, ruled by a special *Wün*, the others being Kyaukyit, Nabek, Alagappa, and Payeinma.

MAP OF
CHINDWIN RIVER
from
PAKOKKÚ to KINDAT

Scale of Miles

The village is laid out with much neatness, and is sheltered by numerous shady trees. That Buddhism flourishes here is evident, from the numbers of well built monasteries and substantial pagodas seen on every side.

Below Amyin, the channel is much obstructed by rocks which impede navigation when the water is low.

Two miles above Amyin, on the right bank, Sadôn is reached. It is a large and important village and is connected with Salingyi by a metalled road. As these names imply, the chief manufacture and export is salt. The soil in this neighbourhood is highly impregnated with that mineral, and a considerable revenue is realised from its manufacture.

Ten miles above Sadôn, on the left bank of the river, Mônywa is situated. It is one of the nicest and most picturesque stations in Upper Burma, and is the head-quarters of the Lower Chindwin district.

Besides the Deputy Commissioner's court and offices, it forms the head-quarters of the Lower Chindwin Military Police Battalion, and is an important station for forest revenue. The population in 1891 was 6,316. The hills immediately opposite to the town are called the Mônywa Hills, and are visible from a great distance. The western side of these hills contain artificial caves, hewn out of the limestone rocks, of which the hills are composed, and are inhabited by a sect of austere monks, similar to those found in the " gyaungs " of the Sagaing Hills.

Eight miles above Mônywa, and on the same bank of the river, is Alôn, a place of great importance in the king's time, and the residence of a *Wûn*.

It was the seat of government for some years after the annexation, when Mônywa was finally decided on as the future head-quarters, and the town was laid out, and the courts and offices built.

A metalled road runs from Mônywa on the Chindwin, to Myinmû on the Irrawaddi, thirty-seven miles in length, passing through the large village of Chaungû, twenty-two miles from

Myinmû. A good deal of the Mandalay-Chindwin trade is carried on by this route, and the Irrawaddy Flotilla Company propose to put down a light tramway alongside the present road, if Government will give the necessary guarantees. As an extension of the Mù Valley Line from Sagaing has been on the tapis for some time, it is probable that the tramway will not be constructed.

Opposite to Alôn some picturesque hills, topped by pagodas, are seen. These formed the stronghold of the dacoit bands which molested the garrisons at Alôn, during the early years of the occupation. The channel here is much impeded by rocks and shoals. Fourteen miles above Alôn we come to the Shwe-Zè-ye Rapids, where the river narrows considerably, and passes through a short but rocky defile, rendering navigation in the floods difficult, and even impossible for small craft. When the river is low, the dangers of course are merely nominal. A few miles above this defile, Kanni on the right bank is situated. The place is so called from the precipitous red-clay cliffs which here line the right bank of the river.

Kanni was formerly the head-quarters of a W'ûn, and was in former times the rendezvous for expeditionary forces proceeding to Manipur and Assam.

So far, from Pakôkkû upwards, the country on either bank of the river has been flat, and uninteresting, consisting of fields of cultivation and groves of palm trees. From Kanni northwards, the river flows through hilly country, the hills, especially on the right bank, rising straight from the water, and attaining a height of several hundred feet, clothed throughout with forests of trees, many of great girth and height.

From Kanni, the general north-easterly direction is maintained as far as the village of Mau-ka-tau, passing on the left bank the villages of Waya, Ôn-ma, Taung-dan and Singalè. A good deal of trade is carried on between Maukatau and the Yeû and Shwèbo districts, in the dry weather.

Above this village the river sweeps suddenly round to the south-west, and after a run of eighteen miles Mingin is reached.

This is the head-quarters of the southern sub-division of the Upper Chindwin District, and in the Burmese king's time was an important military post. The town is picturesquely situated on the hill-sides, which here rise straight up from the water.

It is an important station of the Bombay Burma Trading Corporation, Limited, and just below the town, in 1885, four European assistants were treacherously murdered, by order of a *Thandau-zin* specially despatched in a launch from Mandalay for the purpose, by Sûpya-Lat, the Queen, and the Taing-da-Mingyi.

On one of the highest points overlooking the river is the *kin* or outpost, now occupied by the military police.

The Circuit house is pleasantly situated on an eminence, close to the bank of the river.

After leaving Mingin, the north-westerly direction is resumed as far as Chaung-wa, seventeen miles from Mingin, when the direction is to the north-east, as far as the village of Kyaw-ywa, ten miles from Chaung-wa. From this village, a run of nineteen miles brings us to Kalè-wa, 226 miles from Pakôkkû.

Just below Kalèwa, the river takes a sudden bend to the westward, sweeping round precipitous cliffs on the right bank, several hundreds of feet in height. The approach from below by steamer is very grand, the river at the bend being studded with small rocky islands covered with pagodas. During the floods, the navigation of this bend is exceedingly risky.

Kalèwa, as the name implies, is at the entrance (*wa*) of the Kalè Valley. Just below the village, the Myittha River joins the Chindwin. This river rises in the Yaw and Baungshè country, and after a northerly course of about 200 miles, turns suddenly to the westward at Kalè-myo, and enters the Chindwin at Kalèwa. It has a most tortuous course, receiving from the west many smaller streams from the Chin Hills, and is only navigable for country boats during the rainy season.

Kalèwa is the nearest port on the Chindwin to the Chin Hills, and is distant about 40 miles from Fort White. The

officer commanding the Chin Hill troops lives here, as do also
several officials connected with the Commissariat Department.

Nine miles above Kalèwa, on the left bank, is the village of
Balet. In the neighbourhood are the ruins of an old city. Balet
itself contains many inhabitants of Portuguese and French
extraction, the descendents of prisoners of war taken by the kings of
Burma from Syriam, Rangoon and Bassein during the last century.
Nine miles above Balet, and on the same bank of the river, we
come to Massein, a large village with considerable trade. A run
of thirty miles brings us to Kindat, the head-quarters of the Upper
Chindwin district. The Government Offices and Jail are
protected from floods by bunds. To the east of the town is an
immense swamp, which is filled in the rains, and dries up in the
hot weather. It is owing to this swamp, that Kindat is so
proverbially unhealthy.

In the Burmese times the place was a strong military post,
as the name implies (*Kin*, a look-out, *Dat*, or *Tat*, a fort or
stockade).

At the outbreak of hostilities in 1885, several employés of
the Bombay Burma Trading Corporation were seized and kept
in irons here, on orders received from the capital. The *Wûn*
also, who was favourable to the British cause, was also kept under
arrest, together with his wife and family. They were relieved
by a force under Colonel Johnson, the resident of Manipur.

In the dry weather, when the water is low, and navigation
difficult, the steamers of the Irrawaddy Flotilla Company,
Limited, do not proceed further north than Kindat, but in the
rains, when the river is in flood, they proceed as far as
Homalin, 147 miles north of Kindat.

This part of the Chindwin valley is very sparsely populated,
and villages are few and far between. The first halting place is
at Pantha, on the left bank, fourteen miles from Kindat.

After a run of nine miles, the mouth of the Yû river is passed.
This river drains the Kubo valley, and receives from the north
the Tamû Chaung. It was by this route that Lieutenant Grant

proceeded to the relief of the Manipur garrison in 1891, when the Chief Commissioner of Assam, and several military officers were massacred by orders of the Sonaputti.

The next important place is Sittaung, thirty-one miles north of the mouth of the Yû. It was here that General Graham landed with his forces, and proceeded to the relief of Manipur after the massacres. Paungbyin on the left bank, twenty-seven miles above Sittaung, is the head-quarters of the Legayaing Sub-division of the Upper Chindwin District.

We now come to the small independent Shan state of Hsawng-hsup, seventeen miles to the north of Paung-byin. After a run of forty-four miles the mouth of the Uyû is reached.

This river is one of the most important tributaries of the Chindwin, and rises in the region of the Jade Mines, west of the Indaugyi lake. It is navigable for 150 miles from its mouth for steamers of light draft, during flood time. A good deal of the jade is despatched to the Chindwin by this river.

Homalin, the terminus of the steamer's run, is situated five miles north of the mouth of the Uyû. It is the head-quarters of a township, but has very little trade.

Exploring steamers of the Irrawaddy Flotilla Company have steamed for six days north of Homalin, as far as the falls in 26° 30′ North Latitude. The stream for a greater part of this distance was strong and deep, and the width similar to that below Homalin.

The inhabitants of this part of the country are Shans, Shan-Kadû, Chins, and Kachins of various clans, many being savage and almost unapproachable.

The sources of the Chindwin have not been properly ascertained, but are supposed to be in the hilly country between 95° and 96° west longitude and 26° and 27° north latitude. As however, a considerable rise in its waters takes place *before* the annual rains set in in June, it is thought that its sources must be in the snowy mountains further to the north, which form the north-eastern off-shoots of the Himalayas.

Time taken by Steamer in high flood.

Up	Pakòkkû to Mònywa	1	Day.
	Mònywa to Maukatau	1	,,
	Maukatau to Kalèwa	1	,,
	Kalèwa to Kindat	1	,,
	Kindat to Paungbyin	1	,,
	Paung Byin to Homalin	1	,,
Down	Homalin to Kindat	1	,,
	Kindat to Mingin	1	,,
	Mingin to Mònywa	1	,,
	Mònywa to Pakòkkû	1	,,

ROUTE XXIV.

MANDALAY TO MAY-MYO.

May-Myo is so called from Colonel May, one of the pioneer officers of the field-force during the expedition of 1885-86. He was one of the earliest to discover the salubrity of its climate, and its adaptation as a hill station or sanatorium.

By the Burmese the town is called Pyinûlwin. It is situated on a plateau to the east of Mandalay, at an elevation of nearly 4,000 feet.

A road, 178 miles in length, has been constructed, and is maintained by the Public Works Department, from Mandalay to Lashio, the head-quarters of the Superintendent of the Northern Shan States.

This road is bridged throughout, and is metalled for the greater part of its length from Mandalay to May-Myo, a distance of forty-three miles.

For the first seventeen miles to Kywet-na-pa, at the foot of the hills, the road is in excellent condition for wheeled traffic.

The rest of the road is merely a cart track, in some places rocky and hilly, in others level and clayey.

Starting from the Deputy Commissioner's Court-house at Mandalay, it runs due east, past the king's gardens, in which the St. John's Leper Asylum is situated. It joins the western bund of the Aungpinlè lake, and skirts along the margin of the lake for several miles, passing the village of Aungpinlè on the right, where the European prisoners were confined in the First Anglo-Burmese war. The general direction is then south-east, towards the jagged and precipitous rock at the foot of which lies the village of Kywetnapa, on the banks of the Myitngè or Doktawaddi river.

At the thirteenth mile Htôn-bo is reached. A convenient Public Works Department rest bungalow is provided, where a halt can be made for breakfast.

After leaving Htônbo, the road proceeds in a south-east direction into the *tarai*, or low ground, at the foot of the hills. Crossing this valley, you arrive at the village of Kywetnapa, at the seventeenth mile, from which the entrance to the pass is made. The road ascends steadily, by easy gradients, till Nyaung Bau is reached at the twenty-third mile. Soon after passing the twenty-first mile post, the road runs along the western face of the summit of the hills, and a most magnificent view of the plains below, and the country beyond, opens out. On a clear day, the conical peak of Popa, 105 miles distant, is plainly visible to the south-west.

The Sagaing hills, the Mandalay hill, and the Myotha uplands appear in the far distance as mere mole-hills, while the Irrawaddi flows uninterruptedly through the plain, its course being plainly discernible from the glitter of its waters.

The smaller stream meandering through the plain, on its way to join the parent stream, is the Myit Ngè or Doktawaddi, which rises in the Northern Shan States, and after a circuitous course enters the Irrawaddi to the north of the old city of Ava. At Nyaung Bau, which has an elevation of 1,600 feet above the plains below, the temperature is appreciably reduced. Another Public Works Department bungalow is found here, where a comfortable night's rest can be obtained, especially if the trip is made in the hot weather. Leaving Nyaungbau at daylight, the road for two miles descends slightly, and then the upward course is resumed till Thôn-daung is reached, eleven miles from Nyaungbau. From thence onwards to May-Myo, a distance of eight miles, it runs along comparatively level country, on the plateau of which May-Myo is the centre.

May-Myo is the head-quarters of the Pyin-û-lwin Sub-
Division of the Mandalay district. It is a military cantonment,
and a civil and military police-station.

The principal public buildings are the barracks and
officers' quarters, the court-house, military and civil police
posts, the Public Works Department and Forest Department
rest-house bungalows, and the postal and telegraph offices. There
is also an inland trade customs station, where returns are kept
of the traffic from and to the Shan States.

The following table shows the total traffic through the
station for the year 1894-95 :—

Trade.		No. of Passes Issued	Elephants.	Ponies and Mules.		Pack Bullocks		Porters.	Carts.
				Loaded	Un-loaded	Loaded	Un-loaded		
With trade	Imports	3,593		981	95	32,766	2,068	8,517	6,247
	Exports	3,177		1,131	113	31,107	2,501	7,209	5,200
Empty	Imports	256		18		96		233	465
	Exports	291		8		499		764	546
Government Account	Imports	43		123		16		26	175
	Exports	63		14		72		17	336

CLIMATE.—The following statement shows the particulars
of temperature and rainfall for an average year :—

MONTH.	AVERAGE TEMPERATURE.		RAINFALL.
	Maximum.	Minimum.	
January	71.1	44.4	0.88 Inches.
February	74.3	47.5	0.63 ,,
March	84.6	56.0	0.62 ,,
April	87.0	62.3	0.69 ,,
May	85.7	66.0	3.51 ,,

Month.	Average Temperature.		Rainfall.
	Maximum.	Minimum.	
June	78·5	66·9	9·46 Inches.
July	77·0	66·0	8·09 ,,
August	76·0	65·7	10·98 ,,
September	74·5	65·0	9·32 ,,
October	73·9	57·2	1·30 ,,
November	71·6	47·4	4·79 ,,
December	67·3	37·8	Nil

Total　50·30 Inches.

To the Burmans of the plains, the climate is unsuited, but natives of Northern India, Gourkhas, and Europeans, who pay adequate attention to dress and dwelling-houses, enjoy excellent health.

HISTORY.—Of the history of the place little is known. It appears to have been alternately subject, either to the King of Ava, or the Sawbwa of Thonzè.

Alaung-pya settled some thousands of his Siamese and Shan captives in the neighbourhood of Pyinûlwin.

The captives were originally kept in and around Ava, and many were allotted as slaves to the King's Ministers. These were styled *Letyadaung;* they carried spears, and wore *kamauks* of cowhide.

The remainder of the captives were found to suffer in health from the heat of the plains, so they were settled in the neighbourhood of Pyinûlwin in the following six villages :—Nachcik, Pagin, Pyinûlwin, Singaung, Thabyeik, and Wetwin. These villages were known as the *Letya Chaukywa* (the "six villages of the captives"), and their descendants still occupy them. In the neighbourhood of the town are the remains of an old fort, said to have been built by the Chinese, during one of their incursions into Burma.

Mindôn Min started works here for the formation of a large lake, to supply his capital with water, but it was never completed.

Now that the Shan Hills Railway has been sanctioned, which will pass through May-Myo, it will no doubt, in the near future, become the hill resort of large numbers of people from Mandalay, and even from Rangoon and other parts of Burma. Although the site has neither the elevation nor the scenery of many of the Indian hill stations, it is the nearest approach to be got at present, and as such will doubtless be a popular resort.

ITINERARY.—The best way to get expeditiously to May-Myo from Mandalay is to ride. With two ponies, and a bullock-cart for servants and kit, the journey up can be comfortably made in two days.

Starting your cart off to Htônbo (thirteen miles) the previous evening, and leaving yourself at 6 a.m. next morning, a couple of hours' riding brings you to Htônbo, where your breakfast awaits you. After breakfast, send off cart and spare pony to Nyaung Bau (ten miles), proceeding yourself in the cool of the afternoon. Send your cart on at night or early morning to Thôndaung (eight miles). Sleep yourself at Nyaung-bau, leaving at daylight, and breakfast at Thôndaung. After breakfast, despatch cart to May-Myo, and ride on yourself in the cool of the afternoon.

The return journey can be made in one day, by sending off your cart and servants to Nyaungbau the day before, with your spare pony. Leaving at 6 a.m. you reach Nyaungbau (nineteen miles) about 9 a.m. in time for breakfast. Continuing on, with the fresh pony, you arrive at Htônbo (ten miles) in $1\frac{1}{2}$ hours, whence the remaining thirteen miles can be done in a hired gharry previously arranged for.

The charges are Gharry, (with two ponies) to Htonbo Rs. 12/-. Bullock cart to May-Myo, and back, including halt of three or four days Rs. 15/-.

From May-Myo the road passes over undulating country till about the 80th mile. Here is met a deep gorge which runs right across the country. The old path across it is called the Goteik

Pass, from the name of the village on the far side of the gorge. It is roughly about 1,000 feet below the general level of the plateau, and at some points only a few hundred wide at the tops of the precipices. The river at the bottom of the gorge is crossed by an iron bridge, near it is a natural bridge, the top of which is 400 feet above the river, over which it is proposed to take the railway. At mile 126 the Numsein River is crossed by means of an iron bridge, and Thibaw, the chief town of the Shan State of that name is reached at mile 133. This is the residence of the Tsaw-bwa, whose palace is built of teak-wood, in the ordinary Burmese style, while all other buildings in the town are of bamboo. A European officer called the "Adviser" is stationed here. The river, the Myit-ngè (the same which joins the Irrawaddi ten miles below Mandalay) is crossed here by a ferry.

Lashio is at mile 178. It is the head-quarters of the Superintendent, Northern Shan States. The station is well situated on a hill, the height of which is 3,000 feet above the sea-level. There is a very fine view over the Lashio valley and beyond to the surrounding hills.

Beyond Lashio to the north, at a distance of about thirty miles, is Theinni, and Kun-lòn ferry on the Salween is about eighty miles to the north-east.

MANDALAY LASHIO ROAD.

STAGES.

Htònbo	at	13 miles	Nyaung Pyne	at	96 miles	
Nyaung Bau	,,	23 ,,	Pyoungoung	,,	105 ,,	
Thòndaung	,,	31 ,,	Laikaw	,,	116 ,,	
May-Myo	,,	43 ,,	Kinthi	,,	127 ,,	
Wet Win	,,	54 ,,	Thibaw	,,	134 ,,	
Omathi	,,	66 ,,	Konsa	,,	143 ,,	
Myaung Kyaw	,,	79 ,,	Se-en	,,	153 ,,	
Chaung Zòn	,,	87 ,,	Noung-mòn	,,	163 ,,	

Lashio at 178 miles.

INDEX.

INDEX.

INDEX.

THE END.

www.ingramcontent.com/pod-product-compliance
Lightning Source LLC
Chambersburg PA
CBHW021934110726
47901CB00003B/833